Praise for FALSE HEARTS

'*False Hearts* is that rarest of things – a fast-paced thriller with tons of heart and soul. Set in a chillingly believable future, it's bursting with original concepts and unforgettable characters. I defy anyone to put it down' SARAH LOTZ

'I thoroughly enjoyed it, from its explosive beginning right through to a very satisfying end . . . the highlight of my year's reading' JAMES OSWALD

'A strong debut from someone who's clearly got what it takes' PETER F. HAMILTON

'Just fantastic. Rarely have I torn through a book so quickly. Dark, smart, fast-paced and sexy' SAMANTHA SHANNON

'Gorgeous prose, vividly rendered characters, and a story that moves like a ballistic missile . . . the mysteries are deep and the tension stays high' WESLEY CHU

'An intriguing and fast-paced tale' *Heat*

'Its vision of the future is seductively terrifying' *SFX*

'Fast-paced murder mystery . . . expertly explores themes of identity, totalitarian governments, cults, mind control, and familial love' *Publishers Weekly*

'A chilling read that will have you gripped from page one . . . a must-read' *Woman's Own*

'Will leave a lasting impression on many readers. A thought provoking, fast-paced tale which uses characterization to capture reader's imaginations. A truly great read from a great writer' *Starburst*

FALSE HEARTS

Laura Lam was raised near San Francisco, California, by two former Haight-Ashbury hippies. Both of them encouraged her to finger-paint to her heart's desire, colour outside the lines, and consider the library a second home. This led to an overabundance of daydreams. She relocated to Scotland to be with her husband, whom she met on the internet when he insulted her taste in books. She almost blocked him but is glad she didn't. At times she misses the sunshine.

Lauralam.co.uk

@LR_Lam

By Laura Lam

The Micah Grey Trilogy

Pantomime

Shadowplay

Masquerade

False Hearts

FALSE HEARTS

LAURA LAM

PAN BOOKS

First published 2016 by Macmillan

This edition published in paperback 2017 by Pan Books
an imprint of Pan Macmillan
20 New Wharf Road, London N1 9RR
Associated companies throughout the world
www.panmacmillan.com

ISBN 978-1-4472-8644-8

9 8 7 6 5 4 3 2 1

A CIP catalogue record for this book is available from the British Library.

Printed and bound by CPI Group (UK) Ltd, Croydon, CR0 4YY

In memory of my father,

Gary Lyle Richardson (1945–2015).

You were weird and wonderful, and I'm glad you were able to read an early draft of this before you rejoined the Cycle.

ACKNOWLEDGEMENTS

As with any book, there are a great many people to thank. This was a fun book to write, but it was a departure from my previous fantasy, so I was nervous. Many people helped me find the confidence to keep going.

Thank you to my agent, Juliet Mushens, for invaluable early feedback, always being in my corner, and being fabulous and amazing. Many thanks also to her incredible assistant, Sarah Manning (not the *Orphan Black* character). To my original acquiring editor, Julie Crisp, and to editor extraordinaire Bella Pagan, as well as Louise Buckley and Lauren Welch. Everyone at Tor, both UK and US (thank you, Marco Palmieri), has been amazing to work with and so enthusiastic about my work – it's been a blast.

I sent this book to so many people over many drafts, and received so much great feedback that truly transformed *False Hearts*. Thank you to my husband Craig and two of my closest friends, Erica Bretall and Shawn DeMille, who always read my really, really ugly first drafts before I send them out to anyone else. Thank you to my mom and staunch cheerleader, Sally Baxter. Much gratitude to Kim Curran, Amy Alward, Katharine Stubbs, Cassandra Rose Clarke, Wesley Chu, Lorna McKay, Hannah Beresford, Mike Kalar, Jonathan Butcher,

Nazia Khatun, Colin Sinclair, Vonny McKay, Lisa McCurrach, Katie Kemp (for neuroscience help specifically), Leah Woods, Justina Ireland, Tristina Wright and Ann Godridge. Whether you saw the very early drafts or the nearly finished one, I appreciate you taking the time to read and tell me what you thought. Thank you to several sex workers who read scenes about Tila's work and made sure I hadn't unintentionally fallen into any stereotypes. Thank you to Nick Harkaway for the name of Sudice for the company when I asked for suggestions on Twitter. I think that's everyone, but if I forgot someone because my inbox is too disorganized, I'm super sorry and I'll buy you a coffee.

I did a lot of research for this book. The initial idea came from reading an article about Daisy and Violet Hilton and wondering what it would be like to be connected to someone every minute of every day, and how strange it would be if you found out your literal other half had kept something from you. Alice Domurat Dreger's book, *One of Us: Conjoined Twins and the Future of Normal*, really impacted the twins' view of being conjoined, their relationship to each other, and how they were perceived by the outside world, both within the Hearth and San Francisco. I was also inspired by Lori Lansens' work of fiction *The Girls*. I watched a lot of documentaries and interviews with conjoined twins: *The Twins Who Share a Body*, *Abby & Brittany*, *Two Hearts*, *Bound by Flesh*, *The Twins Who Share a Brain*, and more. I asked a few twins about their relationships and also observed my twin nephews, Ruben and Kade. For cults, *Last Days* by Adam Nevill and *Whit* by Iain Banks were some fictional influences, as was the film *Martha Marcy May Marlene*, and documentaries such as *Jonestown: The Life and Death of Peoples Temple*, *Jesus Camp* and *Cults: Dangerous Devotion* gave me some invaluable insights. I also read numerous articles on various cults. I read *Mapping the Mind* by Rita Carter as a good resource on neuroscience, and I looked at the History Channel's City of the Future's entries for San Francisco, which inspired some aspects of my near-future city. I have a fuller list of resources on my website, if you'd like to learn more.

As ever, thank you to the readers who picked up the book and spent some time with Taema and Tila. You're the reason I can keep doing this.

False face must hide what the false heart doth know.

William Shakespeare, *Macbeth*

FALSE HEARTS

PROLOGUE

TAEMA

San Francisco, California

This is the first time I have ever been alone.

The first time that I have ever woken up to silence and emptiness next to me. The only sounds in the room are the beeping of the heart monitor and my own laboured breathing.

It isn't supposed to be like this.

Groggy from the medicine, I raise my hand to hover over the hot wound, throbbing even through the pain of the IV. It is the first time my hand has been able to linger three inches above my own chest. Below my shaking fingers is the deep cut that will heal into a thin seam from just below my collarbone to right above my navel. Beneath the newly grafted skin and reconstructed breasts is a titanium sternum – bulletproof, so they say – and half of my ribs are made of the same substance. Below that metal sternum is my new, false heart. The old heart is gone, cut out and replaced with an upgraded model that will never tire. I can almost imagine I can hear its mechanical ticking.

This is the first time I've ever been lonely.

The doorknob to the recovery room turns. My automated heartbeat doesn't quicken, though the old, fleshy one would have. I still feel the thrum of adrenalin. The door opens, and for the first time, I see my own, moving reflection. My full mirror image. The same brown skin, the mane of curly hair. The same long nose and dark eyes, features hollowed in fear and pain. My twin, Tila.

Are my knees that knobby? I ask myself, almost laughing from the ridiculousness of the thought. The drugs still rush through my system, and everything is dreamily gold-tinged.

She's trailing her IV with her. I can barely move, so she shouldn't be up, but Tila doesn't let a small thing like pain stop her. I'm surprised she hasn't triggered the alarms. She probably disabled them – she's always been clever with her hands.

We're not supposed to see each other for a few days, so we grow used to being separate. As usual, she's ignored all the rules and advice and followed her own heart. It is really her *own* heart now. She creeps closer, her bare feet swishing along the floor.

'T?' she whispers.

'T,' I answer. We always call each other T when we are alone. I close my eyes, a tear falling down my cheek. *What have we done?*

Painfully, I move over on the bed as best I can. We haven't just come out of surgery, if the date on the wallscreen is correct. They put us in a medical coma for a few days to speed up healing. I find the fact they can do something like that more than a little frightening. Neither of us has ever been to a hospital before this. There aren't any in Mana-ma's Hearth.

Tila slides into the bed. On her chest, in mirror image of mine, is the same wound that will one day become a scar. Beneath her false sternum is another new, false heart. I wonder if they are set to the same rhythm and even now beat together.

Gently, we turn onto our sides, pressing our foreheads together. Then and only then can we fall back asleep, in the position we have fallen asleep in for the last sixteen years. Now three inches of emptiness separate us, when before there had been nothing, and our heart had beat as one.

ONE

TAEMA

Ten years later

I'm starting where it all falls apart.

Tila is late for dinner.

We meet twice a week, once at her place and once at mine, though lately it's always been at my apartment in Inner Sunset. She says she's staying late at work, but I never know if that's true. I hate it when she keeps secrets. It used to be that we couldn't.

Outside, fat drops of rain drum against the glass window. The sunset has faded to darkness, a few stars just bright enough to shine through the San Francisco fog. I pace across the living room, peering at the blurred view of the city skyline, the green shimmer of the algae farms in the bay, the lights of the hovercars flying past. I paid a lot extra to have the penthouse for this view, but at the moment it does nothing for me. All I can do is be irritated at my sister.

Back in the kitchen, I push the curls from my face. I use my auditory implants to ping Tila, but there's no response. I turn on the wallscreen, but the moving images and sounds irritate me, and I shut them off. The scar on my chest twinges. It's psychosomatic. There's no way it could actually hurt, not after so many years. I rest my fingertip on the top of the rough line of healed skin. It's been almost a decade to the day since the surgery.

I sigh and set out the food, the time flashing in the corner of my ocular implants until I send it away. Her shift at Zenith supposedly ended over an hour ago. She works at the hostess club at the top of the TransAm Pyramid. Not a bad gig, but not for me. I don't think I'd be as good at pretending.

I've made Tila her favourite curry, adapted from a recipe from the Hearth. I could have ordered it from the replicator in the corner of the kitchen, but I needed the distraction of doing something with my hands. It's time to tell her I quit my job this afternoon, and I accepted a new job offer I couldn't refuse – in China. I don't know if Tila will want to come with me.

Or if she should.

The doorknob turns. I stand and rub my palms along my skirt. Tila flies in, dishevelled and wild-eyed. Her short, teal hair is wet and plastered to her skull, contrasting with my brown curls. Her clothes are flashy where mine are plain. Her face is different than mine now too, from trips to the flesh parlours. They're not drastic changes, but we no longer look identical.

It isn't until she rushes to me and clutches the front of my shirt, on either side of my scar, that I realize she's covered in blood. She's wearing a man's coat I don't recognize, and it gapes open, dripping onto the floor. Her light blue dress is splattered red, the rain smearing it into a garish watercolour.

My mind takes a beat to process it. 'Are – are you hurt?' I ask, trying to pull back to go for the first aid kit. But if it's that much blood, she might need more than bandages. Fear rushes through me, and I can't seem to catch my breath.

She doesn't answer right away. Her mouth flaps open, and

then shuts. She lets go of me, backing away from the door. 'Not my blood. You have to help me, T. Oh God, you *have* to help me.'

I tense. *Not my blood.* 'If it's not your blood, whose is it?' My breath comes faster, hitching on the inhale. My sister feeds off my fear, grabbing my shirt so hard the fabric rips. 'What the hell is going on, Tila?' I ask.

Expressions of fear and guilt flit across her face like shadows. 'Please, Taema. Please. I have to get out of the city right now. Both of us do. Hide out somewhere. The Sierras? If only Mana's Hearth would let us claim sanctuary.'

Mana's Hearth is exempt from Pacifica jurisdiction. That she would mention *going back*, despite everything that happened ten years ago, and that she wants to bring me too, is what tells me just how serious this is. 'Tila, slow down. What have you done?'

'I haven't done anything, Taema. It didn't happen the way they'll say.' I can see the whites of her eyes, the tension lines around her mouth. Despite her surgery, her face reminds me too much of that last day in Mana's Hearth when we thought we would die in that redwood forest.

The tips of my hands tingle and my vision swims. 'OK. OK.' I force myself to try and calm down. 'What *haven't* you done?'

Sirens sound outside the high-rise apartment. I startle – you hardly *ever* hear them in San Francisco any more. They're growing louder.

Tila presses against me. 'Oh God, they've found me. Must have tracked my VeriChip. I knew I should have torn it out. Can I hide? There must be somewhere I can hide!'

Her panic is infectious, but I have to be the pragmatic twin she expects. The twin she needs. 'No point. All the police will have infrared sensors. If you didn't do this, then it'll be fine, right? They'll take you in for questioning and then let you go.' I don't want to be the calm twin. I want to grab her, shake her, demand she tell me what has happened and whose blood she's wearing.

Tila only sobs, resting her hand just below my collarbone, right on my scar. I rest my hand on hers. I can feel the mechanical beating of her heart. Despite our obvious terror, our hearts beat at their same, steady pace.

'It'll be all right, T,' I say. 'I promise.'

She looks at me, dangerous and untamed. I barely recognize her. 'You can't promise that, T. You can't promise that at all.'

Red and blue lights flash outside the window. A police hovercar floats outside the balcony, rain falling off its sides. The search light illuminates the room, paralyzing us in the bright beams. Three police jump down onto the tiny balcony, their boots splashing in the puddles on the concrete. Tila's shaking, burrowing close to my side. I wrap my arm around her, but I'm shivering just as badly.

They open the sliding glass door, but too hard. The glass shatters. Fragments spill into my living room, as if the rain outside has crystallized.

'SFPD!'

'Really, now,' I say, looking at the glass and rain scattered across the living room. Fear shifts to anger. 'Was that necessary?'

The police look between us. They are all wearing bulletproof Kalar vests over their sleek, dark blue uniforms. Cops almost never wear Kalars, not in this city that prides itself on its lack of crime. The whites of their eyes shimmer in the light with their extra implants.

An Indian-American woman with curly hair tamed in a knot at the nape of her neck clutches her gun, shifting her stance. The other man, white and brown-haired with a face so generically good-looking I'll forget what he looks like as soon as he leaves the room, begins to make a perimeter of my apartment. Perhaps he thinks extra back-up is hiding behind the couch. The last man, their leader, is black with a gold tattoo I can't make out peeking over the collar of his uniform. He narrows his eyes at us, focusing on Tila and her teal hair: 'Tila Collins?'

She doesn't answer, keeping her head bowed.

He steps forward and grabs her upper arms. For a second, I fear she's going to resist and try to run for it, but then she goes limp.

'What's going on here?' I ask. 'She says she hasn't done it, whatever you're after her for.'

They ignore me. Gold Tattoo says, 'Tila Collins, you are under arrest for murder in the first degree. You have the right to remain silent. Anything you say can and will be used against you.'

When was the last time he had to read anyone their Miranda rights?

Gold Tattoo pulls Tila from my grasp. My hands fall useless at my sides. Tila tilts her head up at him and spits in his face.

Gold Tattoo wipes the spittle away, expressionless.

The wind leaves my lungs as the full implications sink in. Murder. There hasn't been a murder by a civilian in San Francisco in years. Not since Pacifica was formed after the United States fractured forty years ago. Not since VeriChips and implants and cameras on every corner.

'Tila?' I ask as Gold Tattoo marches her back to the hovercar, handing her over to Curly Hair. I sound forlorn, lost.

She throws a pleading glance over her shoulder as they push her inside. 'Taema!'

Within moments, they are all gone save Gold Tattoo. He towers over me, but he looks so young. He might not be, with flesh parlours everywhere, but it's hard to find him terrifying when it looks like he only learned how to shave yesterday.

A sob lodges in my throat. It's all I can do not to break into pieces in front of this man. One moment, I was annoyed that dinner was growing cold, and now my apartment is a mess and my sister is accused of murder. I can't wrap my head around the word. *Murder*. It's Tila. My sister. I know her better than I know myself.

Don't I?

'Miss Collins?' There might be a hint of concern behind the brusque tone. He's close enough that I can make out his tattoo: a California grizzly bear.

I find my voice. 'My sister's just been taken for murder. How do you think I feel?'

He has no answer to that. Within moments, the sirens blaze again as they take my sister away from me.

'Who's she meant to have murdered?' I ask, my voice tight. That word again. It's ugly.

'A body of a man was found at Zenith under suspicious circumstances. I can't say anything more.'

My hands ball into fists. Gold Tattoo notices the movement, his hand resting on his gun. My lungs burn from holding in the sobs.

He pauses. I realize why he's stayed behind.

'I'm to go in for questioning too? Why didn't you take me with Tila?'

He shifts slightly. 'Yes, Miss Collins. We're to take you in as a precaution. You'll be going to the station. Your sister is being taken elsewhere.'

'Where?'

'I'm not at liberty to say.'

I fold over, trying to take in deep breaths but still hyperventilating.

'Miss Collins.'

I hold up a hand. I think of the Hearth, how Mana-ma taught us to control our emotions. *Let the darkness float away. Let in only the light.* I imagine the chapel on the hill at the centre of the town, the five-pointed symbol carved on its side, the bird calls that floated through the open windows on a spring day. Despite my hatred of her, her techniques work.

I stand up, smoothing my features, shaking my head a little from side to side. 'Yes. We have the same DNA. You'll want to make sure *I* didn't do it.'

He says nothing.

'Am I under arrest?'

'No. You're being detained for questioning. Please grab your things, Miss Collins.'

I look around at my apartment. The wet footprints all over the carpet. The shining bits of glass. The food cold on the table, the plates laid out for a meal we will never eat.

I grab my coat and purse.

As he leads me down the stairs, curiosity seems to get the better of him. 'I shouldn't ask, but do you really think she didn't do it?'

I pause. I still think he's been waxworked – he's too highly ranked to be any younger than late thirties – but his eyes aren't quite as jaded as a lot of older people masquerading in younger bodies.

My hand snakes towards my sternum again, pressing

against the faint seam where they unzipped me and Tila and took us apart a decade ago. Underneath, my mechanical heart beats, beats, beats.

'I know my twin better than anyone else. If she says she didn't do it, then she didn't.'

I'm sure I believe it.

Ninety-nine per cent sure.

TWO

TAEMA

Officer Oloyu, or Gold Tattoo, is all business when we reach the San Francisco Police Headquarters. He has become hard – perhaps on the silent hovercar trip he's changed his mind and decided I must be as guilty as my sister. Or the question in the hallway was an act, and he decided he wouldn't catch the fly with honey. He gazes down at the blank tablet, little more than a white piece of plastic to focus the eyes as he accesses his ocular implant for my file.

He hovers close, almost touching, knowing that it will make me defensive and on edge. Then he strolls to his side of the table, perching on the chair, legs spread wide.

He's offered me a coffee, but it sits in front of me, an oily sheen on top from the artificial creamer, untouched and growing cold. My mouth is dry. All I can think of is Tila. Where have they taken her? What's going through her mind?

Oloyu is the only one in the room. Aren't there usually two, a good cop and a bad one? Granted, all I have to go on is old cop shows they play late at night on the wallscreen.

Oloyu stares at me, unblinking. I can't decide whether or not to be intimidated by him. His splayed body language is aggressive, and it's working – I feel like prey being stalked. Yet his features are still so young, honest and symmetrical. If he really wants to be more frightening in situations like these, perhaps he should make another visit to the flesh parlour.

'When's the last time you saw your sister?' Oloyu asks.

'Almost a week ago,' I answer, keeping my voice flat to stop it quivering. I'm also embarrassed to realize it's been that long. I'd invited her over for dinner twice, but she'd claimed she was working both times. I don't have anything to hide, yet I still feel like this is a test I could pass or fail, depending on my answers. Or that I could accidentally incriminate my sister.

How could you incriminate her? I ask myself. *She couldn't have done anything. Right?*

'And where do you work?'

I swallow. This is all in my file from when he scanned the VeriChip in my wrist. 'Silvercloud Solutions.'

Officer Oloyu makes a show of perusing my file on his blank, white tablet. 'That's a subset of Sudice, right?'

'Yes.' I don't know why he's pretending he doesn't know. Sudice is the biggest company in Pacifica, with offices in San Francisco, Los Angeles, Portland and Honolulu. They supply the drug Zeal to all Pacifica states, and have most tech in the city patented.

'It says here you helped design the VivaFog.' Those machines have been my life's work for the past five years: the machines that take energy from the ever-present fog around the bay and relay it to the coastal apartments. We're going to try and expand to the maritime district this year.

'I was one of the team that did, yes,' I respond. Why isn't he asking the questions he really wants the answer to? Beneath the table, I press my knees hard to stop them knocking together.

Officer Oloyu isn't saying anything out of order, but everything in his body language screams: *I suspect you, either of murder or accessory to it.* I wish I still had that microexpression overlay downloaded to my ocular implants, but I deleted it months ago. I didn't like what it told me about people.

'That's impressive,' Officer Oloyu says. I'm not sure whether or not I sense the underlying subtext I often do from people who know my past: *for someone who grew up in the cult of Mana's Hearth.*

'Thank you,' I tell him, meeting his eyes.

'We contacted your employer, but it seems you quit your job today and have plans to leave the country.'

'Yes, that's correct. That's been in the works for months. It's not a sudden decision.' I feel a flutter of nerves, deep in my stomach. It's a coincidence, but it doesn't look good.

'We're unclear if this is premeditated or a crime of passion.'

'I had nothing to do with *this*. Whatever *this* is. And I'm sure my sister didn't, either.'

He pauses, considering me. The overhead lighting leaves half his face in shadow. I look down at my stone-cold coffee. I want water, but I don't ask him for it.

'Did your sister seem different at all, the last time you saw her? Distressed in any way?'

'No. She seemed the same as usual. Laughing, joking. We went to an Ethiopian restaurant in the Mission.'

His gaze goes distant as he makes a mental note with his implants.

This is my first lie to the police. She seemed thinner, she didn't laugh. She picked at her food, when usually Tila has a voracious appetite. I kept asking her what was wrong, but she said she'd just been working too many late nights at the club. The lie fell from my mouth before I thought about it, and I can't take it back.

They've mapped my brain to see if I'm lying. A model floats above our heads, delicate and transparent, dotted with neuron clusters like stars. Oloyu glances up to check. Between my mechanical heart not growing as excited as a flesh one and my Hearth training, nothing happens. I could lie with impunity. If they map Tila, she can too.

'So nothing unusual over the last few weeks? No signs she was keeping anything from you? You two must be close.' Again, I can hear from his tone what he really means: *close enough that if one of you did it, the other would know about it.*

'Closer than you can ever imagine,' I say, my voice sharpening with fear. I don't want him to see he's struck a nerve, but by the flint of his eyes, he knows he has. I decide I'm not going to let him scare me, even if terror still rolls in my stomach. Even though I hate the Hearth and all it stands for, another one of Mana-ma's sayings come to me: *They only have power over you if you let them.*

'Does your sister have any enemies?' Oloyu leans forward. I can't stand anyone that close to me unless it's Tila or someone I know extremely well. But I lean forward on my elbows, right in his face, ignoring the mirrored window behind him and whoever watches me through it. I'm still scared, but I haven't let it paralyze me.

'Everyone *loves* Tila. She can go buy food and make a new friend.' That's true. If we take a shuttle somewhere for a holiday, I read, ignoring those around me. Tila will become fast friends with whoever is sitting next to her: an old man with a white beard, a new mother and her squalling baby, and once a Buddhist monk in his saffron robes.

She can make enemies as well: people who don't like her because of her blithe way of speaking, her easy enthusiasm. I'm sure there are probably a few other hostesses at the club who are jealous of her. She can charm clients with a half-lidded glance and she often crows to me about how she receives the lion's share of the tips. Tila seems to know what it is each person wants and reflects that back to them, flirting by acting like one of the ribald men as easily as playing the coquettish minx. Heaven knows where she's learned all that. I sure haven't.

'Nobody at all?' Officer Oloyu presses.

I shake my head. 'None that come to mind, no. Sorry I can't be more helpful.' I'm not sorry I haven't given them anything to incriminate my sister. Or at least I hope I haven't.

He presses his lips together. 'Now then. The question you must be expecting: where were you at 1700 hours this evening?'

'On the way home from work on the MUNI.' My voice has stopped shaking, and I feel as though I'm no longer attached to my body. That I'm just a floating head. I have taken full control of my emotions, like Mana-ma always taught us to do in the Hearth.

'Which line do you take?'

'Clement Lot.'

'You do understand we'll be checking the cameras.'

'I'd expect nothing less.'

Officer Oloyu narrows his eyes. At first, he thought he had me. Now, he thinks I'm being secretive, and he's right. But there's not much more he can do without concrete proof, and I'm not giving him anything. Even if there was anything to give.

'Can I have any details of the case, or is it all confidential?' I ask. 'Maybe if I understand what's happened I can think of someone who might wish to harm my sister. Whose body did they find? Was it a guest of the club?' I'm desperate for more information. Anything to help piece together what happened tonight. Murder. The word keeps pulsing through my mind, until it doesn't even seem like a word any more.

'We can't name the victim,' Officer Oloyu says. The unspoken: *not to you.*

Thanks for nothing. 'Right. Well, if you can't tell me anything, and I have nothing to tell you, is there anything else you need? Or can I go home and clean up the mess you made of my apartment?'

'I don't appreciate your tone, Miss Collins,' Oloyu says. 'You don't seem overly upset by tonight's events.'

Fuck you, I want to say. *You don't have the first clue how I'm feeling.* Instead, I look at him calmly. 'Am I free to go?'

'For now.'

'Good.' I stand and clutch my purse, and then I bend down and look him in the eye. I'm pleased to see him move back slightly. 'I'm not upset because I'm sure she's as much of a victim in this as whoever died tonight.' I lean back and pull my collar down. It's a good way to unnerve others. In San Francisco, where everyone has made such an effort to appear flawless, nobody likes to see such obvious signs of imperfection. Tila taught me the trick. For all she changed her face and hair to not look like me, she kept the scar.

Oloyu looks at the scar with a mixture of fascination and embarrassment.

'You can't spend sixteen years with someone, *every* minute of *every* day, and not know if they're capable of murder or not. I'll do *whatever* it takes to clear her name.' I push my collar up and walk out. His eyes on my back make the hairs on my neck prickle.

•

Officer Oloyu follows me from the interrogation room to the hovercar, and we rise and fly along the coast of the bay towards my apartment in Inner Sunset. The last thing I want to do is see more of him, and I wonder why a senior policeman is taking the time to chauffeur me back instead of some rookie. I haven't seen any other police officers except for the two who took Tila away – it's almost as if they don't want anyone else to see me.

I ignore Oloyu and stare out the window. It's full night by now, and San Francisco glitters below us. The sight of it helps me forget my anxiety and terror, at least for a moment.

I love this city. It's the complete opposite of Mana's Hearth. In the Hearth, the lake is ink-black at night. In San Francisco, the algae farms make the bay glow green. To my right is Angel Island, and the ruined Alcatraz, the building too decayed by the salt and wind to visit, and the man-made islands where the rich live in their sumptuous houses. The Golden Gate and the Bay Bridge lead towards the city skyline. Billboards advertising Sudice products flash their garish colours: implant upgrades, a new Zeal lounge downtown, the virtual reality centre next to Union Square Mall. The car passes between buildings: greenhouse skyscrapers with their lush, forest-like interiors, multi-level apartment towers, most of the windows lit, small silhouettes staring out the windows towards the bay.

Scattered throughout the city are revenants risen from the Earth after the Great Quake of 2055 – antiquates of architecture preserved and joined with their modern counterparts in a hybrid of old and new: Coit Tower, the skyscrapers on California Street and near the Embarcadero, the old iconic Ferry Building at the base of the newly built air hangars above and the piers jutting out into the gentle waves of the bay. And there, just coming into sight, the TransAm Pyramid, twice as large as the old Transamerica Pyramid. I can't look away from the glowing top floor, home to Club Zenith.

San Francisco.

Our new home after we'd left the Hearth. At first, we'd hated it. It was too different, too new, and we'd had to learn about its ways while struggling with our newly separated status. Eventually, we'd grown to love it. The freedom it gave us. The opportunities. Now, I fear I'll grow to hate it again.

Officer Oloyu clears his throat. I turn to him, trying to bring something approximating a smile to my face, but it fails.

'I'll tell you a little about the case,' he says, grudgingly. 'I've been given the go-ahead by my superior.'

Why the change? 'All right,' I say, slowly. The flashing lights of the city play across his face, catching in his eyes.

'You are not permitted to share this information with anyone. Understood?'

'Yes.'

'The victim has not been formally identified yet, but another hostess says they called him Vuk. He was tall, muscular, wore a sharp suit. Tipped very well. Spent a lot of time in the Zeal lounge. Tila was one of his favourites.'

'Vuk,' I say, tasting the name on my lips. The retinal display of my implants tells me the name means 'wolf' in Serbo-Croatian. I send the text away. 'Why are you telling me this?'

'We want you to come back in tomorrow,' he says. The hardness has left him again. I prefer him without it – it doesn't suit him. Too forced.

'Why?'

'You'll see. Please come to the station tomorrow at 0900. Take the MUNI. Come through the back entrance.'

'This is not a request?'

'No.' We've reached my apartment. He sets the hovercar down on the balcony. I sigh at the sight of my broken sliding glass door. At least the worst of the rain has stopped.

I get out without saying goodbye, stepping into my damp living room. I turn around, watching Oloyu lift the police car away.

'Vuk,' I say again. 'Who were you?' A rich man, if he frequented the club, who liked to plug into the Zeal virtual world fantasies. I can just see a Sudice billboard for Zeal, flashing through the fog. A woman in a Chair, wires hooked up to her arms and temples, eyes closed, a smile on her face. Above her head, her dreams come to life – she's clad in armour, and fighting a sinuous monster. The billboard blinks again. She's flipping head over feet, wearing a skintight star-spangled uniform, an Olympic athlete. One last blink, and the tagline: *Find your Zeal for life. What will you dream today?*

What were Vuk's dreams when he was plugged into that Chair, and did Tila join him in them?

I look down over the city again, wondering how I'll find out who he was and how he entangled Tila in this mess.

THREE

TILA

They've given me an old-fashioned paper notebook to write my last will and testament, with a pencil blunt enough I can't kill myself with it. I'm sure I still could, if I wanted to.

I refused a tablet. I don't want them sneaking and reading this as I write. So here I am, with my paper and pencil. I'm more used to this than most people in the city – out in the Hearth, there are no fancy gadgets and very little technology.

I'm not going to write my last will and testament. What's the point? I don't have much to leave and my only next of kin is Taema, so everything goes to her. I couldn't send any of my stuff to my parents at the Hearth even if I wanted to, since we're apostate and all that.

So I'm just sort of scribbling, seeing what will come out. It passes the time, I guess. There's nothing else to do. The cell is cold and boring, with everything grey and beige, though I do have a window that shows a tiny patch of blue sky. Maybe writing this will distract me, at least a little, from the fact they're going to kill me soon.

There's no point sugar-coating it – it'll happen. My lawyer is half-heartedly trying to put up a defence, buy me more time, but I don't know why he bothers. The trial's in a few weeks. Though can you really call it a trial if there's no jury, just some judge deciding your fate? The government is keeping it all hush-hush. The media aren't meant to know – most of the people here don't even know who I am or what I'm meant to have done. I overheard the guards talking about it. I'm not in a normal prison. They don't even have prisons in San Francisco any more, there's so little crime. I'm locked away somewhere else, but we didn't travel long so I think I'm still in Northern California. Maybe they took me to the Sierras? The air seems colder and crisper.

If it ever does get out, I wonder if they'll let me read the news feeds. They'll call me all sorts of names. Some will be true. Some won't.

The judge will say I'm a criminal, and then they'll put me in stasis. Freeze me like a popsicle, and then I might as well be dead. That sounds flippant, I know, but that seems to be the only way I can write about it without crying.

Shit, never mind. There's tear stains on the paper now.

Putting people in stasis is Pacifica's answer to capital punishment. They're not killing them, but cryogenically freezing criminals. It happened a lot more in the early days of Pacifica, after the United States split up. Now, maybe only a dozen people, tops, are put into stasis every year. It's only for the really hopeless cases, those who don't respond to Zeal therapy and will never be redeemed. I guess they think I'm unredeemable.

Hardly anyone who goes into stasis comes back out. It does happen – some tireless lawyer will discover someone frozen was actually innocent. They come out of it, disoriented, to find years have passed them by. One woman was taken out after thirty years. Her husband and mother were gone, most of her friends had moved away. She ended up committing suicide, because she felt the rest of her life she got back wasn't worth living.

How would I react if I was frozen and woke up in fifty years to discover Taema was old and frail, or gone entirely?

I don't really have to worry about it, though. People coming out of stasis has only happened a handful of times in forty years. Not good odds.

Then there are the outages. Whole wings of people in stasis losing power, and they die before anyone can fix it. So convenient, right? The government always claims it's an accident. They promise to install a back-up server. Then they never do. One day, I'm pretty sure they'll be an outage on everyone in stasis. Whoops. Away they go.

Thinking about living without Taema has weirded me out. I can't get it out of my head. I'm alone in this cell, and my sister's miles away. I'm still not used to being alone, even ten years after we separated. Tomorrow is our surgery anniversary. Whoo. The first sixteen years of my life were spent looking over my sister's shoulder, or resting cheek-to-cheek with her to look at someone together.

I wonder sometimes if I started on this road as soon as they took the knife to us. She's my better half, Taema. She's the one with the sensible head on her shoulders, who would talk me out of doing stupid shit as kids because she didn't want to be drawn into my trouble. She was usually drawn in anyway, though. It's not like she had much of a choice.

If the news does get out, she'll have to dodge paparazzi drones left and right – how many alleged murderers have an identical twin they were once conjoined with? *And* grew up in that crazy cult in the redwoods across the bay? They'll have a field day. At least she's not here in the cell with me, and she's not going into stasis ~~when~~ if I do, so that's something.

Ugh. I'm almost tempted to crumple this whole thing up and flush it down the toilet. I'm not stupid. Even though this is paper, they can read whatever I write on here and they're going to rake through it with a fine-tooth comb to see what I'm trying to hide. When I'm in the shower or something, they'll sneak in here and read it.

WON'T YOU, ASSHOLES?

It's a waste of time. I might as well tell you now. There's not going to be any confession in here. Don't hold your breath.

The guards just dropped off my food. Boring meals of algae and vat-grown meat. The guards seem to like the look of me. Men always do. Plenty of women as well. But then their eyes drop to my chest, to the white scar against my brown skin, peeking over the collar of my prison uniform. They can't hide their fear at what it represents: that I am only half of who I used to be.

•

I've just been sitting here the last few hours, trying to think of what to write next. It's dusk outside now, and the stars are coming out one by one in that little patch of sky by the window. It reminds me of the fireflies Taema and I used to chase in Mana's Hearth when we were little. We were good at catching them. We walked sideways then, like the lake crabs, but we never slowed each other down. One of us would reach out and sweep the fireflies into jars, take them back to the house to light our bedroom, and let them out a few hours later. I miss those days.

It was after I left the Hearth I learned the fireflies had only recently come to California, introduced to the area a few years after the Great Upheaval. How strange, that if that hadn't happened, those memories wouldn't have existed.

Out there, I think Taema has been trying to help. The lawyer's dropped a couple of hints. Plus, I know her. Obviously.

She's not going to sit around, playing with her VivaFog machines, waiting for me to die. Or basically die.

She'll be trying to follow a trail, to piece together what happened. I hope she doesn't, and that the trail goes cold. I don't want her to find out what I did that I shouldn't have, and what I didn't do that I should have. How I lost my innocence while she still has hers – but she might have to lose it, if she wants to save me.

Yep, that's cryptic as hell. But remember: no confessions. Not from me.

Since I'm not going to write my last will and testament, and I'm not going to confess, I figure maybe I'll write a different sort of testament, or a different kind of confession. It won't be a beautiful story. Taema has a way with words, not me. She's the thinker, following the rules, lost in her machines and books. I'm the unpredictable artist, always wanting to do things on the spur of the moment. Guess that's why I'm here now.

I don't even know who I'm writing to. The general masses, maybe, if this somehow leaks to the press. Or maybe I'm writing to my sister.

So this is the story of Taema and me, the life we had. Maybe, while writing it, I'll figure out where it all went wrong.

FOUR

TAEMA

The first thing I do when I'm home is turn on the bots to clear up all the broken glass and to dry the carpets. I order a new door from the replicator, which will be ready by the morning, and draw the curtains against the breeze.

Everything's been searched. They haven't trashed the place, but so many things are not quite where they should be, and the whole apartment has the aura of being manhandled.

I turn music up loud in my auditory implants and try to set it to rights. I help the bots clean. I throw out the meal I spent all afternoon making, my appetite gone. I order a NutriPaste from the replicator and force the tasteless goop down my throat to keep my blood sugar even. I focus on cleaning with every fibre of my being, the pulse of the beats of scrubbing driving out all thought.

When everything is perfect again, I can no longer deceive myself.

I stand in the middle of my silent, spotless kitchen. My eyes snag on the cookie jar on the counter.

Tila and I have keys to each other's places, of course. Our schedules have always been different – I work the standard nine to three, whereas Tila works nights. When we meet for dinner, it's actually closer to her breakfast. When she first moved out eight months ago, I found it really difficult, and I wasn't good at hiding it. I felt betrayed. When we fight, we know the perfect way to wound the other, but it's like hitting a mirror – the glass cuts us just as deeply.

After that first, terrible fight, she left me an apology note in the cookie jar. Problem is, she eats more cookies than I do, so it took me three or four days to find the note. It worked, and I forgave her, not that I can ever stay mad at her for long. Over the next few weeks, she kept leaving notes in the cookie jar, dropping them off on the way to work for me to find on the way home. They were silly, full of in-jokes and puzzles. Then when she started acting more distant, working more hours at the club, they stopped. I haven't even checked the cookie jar in days.

I open it. There are no cookies, only a few scattered crumbs, but there is a note. I unfold it with trembling fingers.

T,
I'm doing something possibly dangerous tonight.
If everything goes well, I'll come here and take this note away before you find it. If you do find this, and you don't know where I am, then everything has gone belly up.
And I'm sorry. I'm really sorry.
T

I blink, my eyes unfocused. She has kept something from me. For days? For weeks? For months? Lying to me, doing . . . whatever it is she's been doing, and leaving me in the dark.

I crumple the paper in my hands. I have to get rid of it. If they come back and find it, it'd look beyond incriminating for both of us. I glance around nervously. What's to say they aren't already monitoring me through the wallscreens or my implants? I've heard the rumours that Sudice monitors all implant feeds, and reports crimes to the government.

I incinerate the note over the stove. After it's nothing but ashes, I take ten deep breaths, forcing the fear and pain away. I can almost hear Mana-ma's voice in my ear:

The world is around you. You can change it. Be the change you want.

I shake my head, as if her voice is a buzzing fly. I don't want to hear her in my head just now. I had enough of Mana-ma in my head as a child. The woman at the head of the Hearth, pulling her strings, weaving her web, ensnaring us all.

The breaths calm me enough that I can push the hurt, the terror and the panic deep into the back of my mind. I shut down my conscious thoughts, focusing only on the physical. I hold the heels of my hands to my eyes until dark spots dance behind my eyelids. Everything's so jumbled. I've always hated being alone. My thoughts are too loud.

I go to the spare room. It was Tila's before she moved out. It's been searched, but there wasn't much for them to go through. A plain bed, an empty dresser, the closet filled with spare linen. I remember how it used to look when she was here: a rainbow of clothes littering the floor, leaving a trail from the bed to the closet. High-heeled shoes kicked off in a corner. Empty coffee mugs left on bedside drawers caked with dried make-up powder. The police would have been lucky to find anything at all under all the chaos.

I stand there for a moment, looking at the perfectly made bed. The searchers took the time to put it back to rights. I suppose that's polite. Tears prick the corners of my eyes, but I take more deep breaths until they go away. I reach forward and muss it a bit. Tila never made her bed. 'What's the point?' she'd say. 'You're just going to get right back into it at the end of the day.' I used to be the one to make the bed, back in the Hearth, with Tila sighing and occasionally patting down a pillow to keep me happy. I pull the covers back again. Tila's not here.

I go back to the kitchen. I bring up my contacts list on my ocular implants, scrolling through the names. I want to speak to someone, though I don't think I can share anything about what's happened. My gaze pauses on a few exes – David, Simone, Amrit. I used to be so close to them. I almost married David, but then I realized he didn't know how to love and could only keep people at arm's length. Now I have no idea what they are doing. There are no friends I want to tell – most are colleagues. Tila's the one with all the friends. I'm slower to trust and, perhaps like David, I never truly let anyone in. Normally it's Tila I'd turn to, and I can't turn to her now.

I send the names away. I still want to believe this has been some big misunderstanding. I can't pretend, now that I've found that note.

'Tila, what have you done?' I ask the empty room. There, alone in the dark, I realize another lie I told myself.

I'm far less than ninety-nine per cent sure she didn't do it.

•

I lie awake all night, trying to piece together everything Tila has told me in the last few weeks; but if she's given me any hints, they don't jump out at me. After I finally stumble from my bed, I'm too tired to even yawn. I project the news from my implants directly onto the white table as I drink coffee, and then I set the coffee down.

There's no headline.

How is there no headline? I scroll through the pages, open other news sources, then another, until several are sprawled out over the white table. Nothing. Nothing about the first violent, brutal homicide in almost eighteen years, committed by a civilian, who also happens to be a former member of a well-known cult? If that's not headline news, I don't know what is.

I can't help but be a little relieved, too. It's taken a long time to make that cup of coffee, to sit down in that seat, to steel myself to look. And there's nothing.

I blink and send the news away.

When the coffee – if it can even be called that, for it's almost caffeine-free and from the replicator – is gone, I have no idea what to do with myself.

I pop a few Rejuvs and curl up on the sofa, a second cup of coffee beside me. I don't read. I don't watch the wallscreen. I stare at the ceiling and clear my mind.

It's no use. The anger still creeps in. My thoughts can only turn to Tila. I imagine her, with her blue, spiky hair, that teasing grin she always wears. It's like she's darting through my cerebrum, laughing. *You can't find me,* she seems to call. *You don't know what I've been up to, do you?*

I fling one of the couch throw pillows across the room. It's an empty, childish gesture.

'Why didn't you tell me?' I yell at the empty room. My voice drops to a whisper. 'How can I help you if I don't know what you've done?'

The tears come again, and this time, I let them. They trickle down my cheeks, warm and salty. I don't wipe them away. Memories of us in the Hearth flash through my mind. Going to our secret spot in the woods, whispering to each other for hours. Playing cards with our parents, Tila and I on the same team. Our voices lifted in harmony during sermon. The first time I saw her in that hospital room. She came back to me as soon as she woke up. Those first years after surgery, when we always walked holding hands because we still had to be connected in one way or another. And then the look on her face last night. The stark fear, the whites of her eyes showing. It was as if I didn't know her at all.

This is not a dream. It's too real. And there's no going back.

'Why did you lie to *me*, of all people? What do I do?' I ask the empty room again.

There's no answer.

Until there is: the implant in my ear beeps.

I have a message.

•

I'm back in the SFPD interrogation room. I came in by a back entrance, with my hood up to partly obscure my face.

Officer Oloyu stares at me from across the table. His eyes look tired, though his face doesn't show it. I doubt he's slept, but he's popped a few Rejuvs to keep him going, just like I have.

'Why am I back here?' I ask, ignoring the pleasantries. I have water this time instead of coffee, but I still don't touch it.

'Have you read the news this morning?' Officer Oloyu asks.

'I've noticed what's not in it.'

An eyebrow quirks, along with the corner of his mouth. 'Quite.'

'How did you keep this quiet?'

'Who controls the media bots?' he counters.

Decent point.

'Your sister is out of the news because this is part of something larger. If we're to find out what's really going on, we have to get to the bottom of it before they peg we're onto them.'

'Them? Who's them? What does this have to do with me?'

'This has everything to do with you.' He takes a breath. 'The SFPD have a proposition.'

His body language has changed again – palms out, brown eyes calm but firm. He still looks heartbreakingly young.

My hand goes to my chest. I shake my head. 'I don't understand. Why do you need me?'

'What do you know about the Ratel?'

'The Ratel?' I echo faintly. They're the main remaining source of crime within the city. The government has been trying to eradicate them for years, but they're tenacious. They intimidate businesses; they have a hand in the property market, and some say within certain branches of the government or Sudice. Like everyone, I've heard the whispers that the Ratel have grown more powerful in recent years, morphing from an annoyance into something more significant and dangerous. I always figured it was just rumour, but looking at Officer Oloyu's face, I'm no longer so sure. What else have they been keeping from the media bots?

Something stirs in my memory. Tila joked about the Ratel a couple of weeks ago. Or I thought it was a joke. I'd reprimanded her for being late to one of our dinners yet again.

'Just ping me if you're going to be late. Obviously I'm not your mother, but you never used to do this,' I'd said, turning away from her.

'Oh, relax, T,' she responded, with that infuriating tilt of her head and flash of white teeth. 'It's not like I'm hanging out with the Ratel. I'm just late.'

I remember wondering at the time why she'd even joke about such a thing. I feel sick.

Officer Oloyu is still waiting for a response. 'A little,' I manage.

'Do you know what they traffic in more than anything else?'

My breath hitches. 'Not really.' I've never had any dealings with them. I go to work. I come home. I live my life as a law-abiding citizen of San Francisco.

'They traffic in dreams. More specifically, the information from dreams.'

'Zeal?' I ask, confused. Sudice own that. I've only plugged into Zeal a few times. It did nothing for me.

'No. Something new. Something different. The next step beyond Zeal. Have you heard of Verve?' He watches me.

I look at him blankly. 'Never.' What would the next step beyond Zeal be? Zeal enacts fantasies, becoming catharsis for pent-up emotions. People start doing it in their early teens, and it's often a lifelong habit. After they let off steam and come out from their fantasies, the after-effects are soporific. Any anger or violent urges are suppressed, and if they build up again, the craving for another visit to a Zeal lounge kicks in. Tila and I arrived in San Francisco several years after those our age were hooked, and we never fell into it as much as the others. It's integrated into therapy, into brainloading information. Most people use Zeal every day, in one form or another.

He hesitates, searching my face for signs of falsehood. I fight the urge to squirm.

'There are two reasons Verve is bad news. First, unlike Zeal, there is no comedown. If you enact a violent fantasy, then when you come out, you don't feel sated. If anything, a desire for violence is heightened. If it were widespread, we'd see a very clear upswing in crime. Second, Verve is a way for the Ratel to mine dreams for information. It's like a virus. Once you take it, it locks into your implants. Until the half-life leaves their system, the Ratel can watch what they see, hear what they hear, and even spy on their dreams.'

I don't respond right away. This doesn't sound possible. That's advanced technology, and if Sudice or the government haven't already done this, then how have the Ratel? Unless . . . perhaps they stole it from them? It's not like Officer Oloyu would ever admit something like that happened, not to me.

He's still waiting for me to say something. 'OK. That's fascinating, but what does it have to do with me?'

'You and your sister are from Mana's Hearth.'

My stomach tightens, and my knees start shaking again. I clench them together, digging my fingertips into my thighs. 'Yes. So?'

'Well.' He leans back in his chair, considering me again. 'Lucid dreamers are immune to being influenced by Verve. They could pump you full of the stuff, and not be able to look through your eyes or listen through your ears.'

My breath stops. How could he know about that? 'What makes you think I'm a lucid dreamer?'

'Because anyone who leaves Mana's Hearth is.'

'Not enough people leave the Hearth for you to confidently make that hypothesis.' My science is showing.

'There's enough. And let me guess – you rarely go to Zeal lounges.'

'So? Plenty of people don't.'

'The drug does nothing for you. Never has. You don't wake up feeling your anger has bled from you, or elated by whatever fantasy you had. Why take the drug when you can lucid dream each night?'

I shrug noncommittally.

'Your skills can help us.'

He pauses again. My tongue feels glued to the roof of my mouth.

'You really didn't know what your sister was doing, did you?' Officer Oloyu asks. He sounds almost sorry for me. My anger flares again, but I clamp it down. I want to understand, and yelling at a police officer won't help me. I hate that he's seen how in the dark I am.

'This murder at Zenith isn't a crime of passion,' Officer Oloyu says.

'My sister didn't *murder* anyone.' Although if they're right, and Tila's been keeping secrets from me, how would I even know?

'Maybe she murdered this Vuk, maybe she didn't.'

I say nothing.

'I am cleared to tell you a little more about him, if you're curious?' He smiles, not waiting for an answer. 'He was a representative for an anonymous philanthropist. Or that's who he claimed to be. But we've exposed that for a pack of lies. The cover allowed him entrance to many places he wouldn't otherwise have been permitted. Fundraisers. Exclusive parties. The Zeal room at Zenith.'

I look up, searching his face, but I can't read him.

'Vuk wasn't an innocent client, just another regular of the club. He was part of something darker. He was a member of the Ratel. We think perhaps he was trying to replace the Zeal in the back room with Verve. Lots of important people come to that club. If the Ratel could get into their heads . . . think of the secrets they could find, and how lucrative that could be for them.'

I can't suppress a shudder. My mind is spinning with this information. 'So, what, you think Tila caught him and killed him for it? If so, didn't she do you a service?'

Officer Oloyu shakes his head. 'From what we can gather, your sister had an existing relationship with him. Last night was not the first time they'd been seen together. She might even have been working with him.'

I can't help it. I laugh, though it's high and nervous. Inside, I'm frozen with terror. I can imagine some things of Tila – but this? Never. 'The Ratel. You think Tila – my sister – has somehow become involved with the biggest criminal organization in Pacifica?'

Officer Oloyu shakes his head. 'We don't *think* . . . we *know* she is involved with them. There's more than enough evidence to prove it. What we don't know is *why*. Your sister is clever. Whatever she's been up to, she's left very little trace.'

'My sister *is* clever. Clever enough to know to stay far away from the Ratel.' It doesn't make any sense. Tila, my Tila, involved with the underground crime syndicate? There has to be some mistake.

'What makes you think she has anything to do with this? What's she said?' I ask.

'She's not saying much.'

I bet she's driving the police up the walls. She knows how to toy with people.

'Can I speak with her?'

He shrugs a little. 'She doesn't want to speak with anyone. Even you. Specifically demanded it, actually.'

I feel like I've been punched in the stomach. Why the hell wouldn't she want to see me? It's all I've been thinking about since her arrest. If I could just see her, talk to her, clear these doubts – I know I could help her. If she'd let me.

'The man she killed—' Officer Oloyu begins.

'Is accused of killing,' I interrupt, my voice razor-sharp.

With a sardonic smile, he tilts his head. 'Vuk was a hitman for the Ratel.'

My stomach plummets. I take a few sips of the tepid water to give me time to untangle my thoughts. 'Was he . . . after Tila?' She could have died yesterday. I hadn't really considered that before now. I swallow, hoping my thoughts aren't flitting across my face. Why would she be a target?

'We don't know if he was actually out for your sister. Our sources say he wasn't on assignment last night, but our sources could be wrong.'

'Seems like there's a lot you don't know.' I'm testy, but he's still dangling what he really wants from me out of reach, and I'm impatient and frightened.

Officer Oloyu ignores the comment. 'Your sister wasn't meant to be working last night. Another hostess, a woman named Leylani, was meant to be manning the Zeal lounge, but she never showed up for work.'

I sag a little with relief. 'See? Tila could have come into the wrong room at the wrong time, had to defend herself against this Vuk. But do you even know if that could have happened? Is there a murder weapon, and if so, can you link it to her? What about the cameras in the Zeal lounge? You couldn't have found a murder weapon, or she'd be charged rather than just accused. How do you know she has anything to do with this?' The questions fall from my lips, faster and faster, until I'm breathless.

'Funny,' Oloyu says. 'When we interviewed your sister, she posed the same scenario. Almost verbatim.'

I glare at him, but he only stares at me calmly, and then makes a gesture with his fingers. The wallscreen to my left turns on. It's a recording from my interrogation yesterday, my eyes blazing at Officer Oloyu. That angry, I look more like my sister than the woman I see in the mirror every morning. I watch myself snarling at him: *'You can't spend sixteen years with someone, every minute of every day, and not know if they're capable of murder or not. I'll do whatever it takes to clear her name.'*

He flicks it off. 'Do you still mean that?'

My nostrils flare in anger. 'Of course I mean it.'

Officer Oloyu leans forward. He's smiling, that open, sweet smile, and it makes me want to hit him. He's glad he's slipped under my skin. '*This* is why we need you, Taema. You understand how she thinks, what she'd do. But there's more than that, isn't there?'

I say nothing.

'She's stumped you. She's managed to keep part of her life secret, and it's burning you up. You want to believe that she hasn't done anything, that she's just as innocent as you want her to be – but she's lied to you, no matter what. That hurts. So. You can help us, and you can find out the truth once and for all. Whatever it is.' He leans even closer. 'There's not much time. We may have kept the case out of the papers, but she'll still go to trial. And if she's convicted . . .' he trails off.

'They'll put her in stasis,' I say. 'But then if exculpatory evidence comes to light, she'll be set free?'

'If it's brought to light, yes.' He gives an expectant pause.

'What do you want from me?' I whisper.

He sighs and rubs his forehead. 'Personally, I don't think your sister killed Vuk. Or if she did, it was an accident or self-defence. She's been working on her own in the Ratel, I'd gamble. And she's grown close.'

He's changed his tune since yesterday. 'What if she grew *too* close, and they already know she was an infiltrator?'

'No sign of that. What we figure is that the Ratel were after someone else that night in the club, and that assignment was interrupted. They don't know your sister's been taken. We've moved fast and we have kept this a small, tight operation. Only a handful of police officers and higher-ups know who your sister really is. We're keeping her out of the city. This situation gives us a unique opportunity to get close to the Ratel. They haven't infiltrated many people with Verve, but if we don't stop them, it's only a matter of time. The Ratel are a threat against San Francisco and all of Pacifica. They have to be stopped. So far, your sister has given us some information to work with, but not enough. We need more.'

He looks at me, and I begin to suspect what he's about to ask of me. He's read me to the bone. I do want – need – to find out what's going on with my sister. What she hid from me and why. More than that, I need to get her out of prison, as much for me as for her. The thought of going through life separated from her, alone forever . . . I don't think I can face that.

'We can't let your sister out to go back undercover.' The corners of his mouth tighten. I think he's holding something back.

'No. You asked her and she refused, didn't she?'

A rueful hint of a smile. 'She did. But it would have been a tough sell to my superior, even if she did agree. She was found by the owner of the club, sitting in a pool of blood. That doesn't exactly make her seem like someone who would be easy to work with. She's too much of a liability.'

I flinch at that mental image.

'Then there's you.'

I swallow, my eyes glued to his face.

'You're intelligent, but you also play by the rules, unlike your sister. You could do this. Infiltrate the Ratel. We believe your sister has already been recruited as one of their lucid dreamers, delving into Verve dreamscapes, monitoring their implant feeds.'

'But she hasn't told you that.'

'No, but from another source we know her exact position within the Ratel.'

'What source?'

He holds up a finger. 'We obviously can't tell you that, unless you sign on.'

'Sign on, and . . . pretend to be my sister?'

'Yes. You'd go undercover into the deepest, darkest underbelly of San Francisco. You'll need to *become* your sister in order to go into the inner circle of the Ratel. This is much bigger than the first civilian murder in years, whether the victim was a hired killer or not. This is a chance for us to learn more about the inner workings of the Ratel, what their plans are, and to stop them from using Verve to access people's secrets. We can learn more about Verve, about who's actually in charge of the Ratel – and then bring them down, once and for all.'

I blink at him. Surely the Ratel can't be *that* much of a threat?

'If you do this, then I've been authorized to let you know that even if your sister did kill Vuk, all charges against her will be dropped. Any crimes you might need to commit as part of the investigation will also be pardoned, within reason. Is that a deal?'

I fight the urge to grab at the opportunity, even as traitorous hope rises within me. I feel sick. Not only at what it is they've suggested Tila has managed to do – for reasons I simply can't comprehend – but also that they now expect me to do the same thing. That I *can* do the same thing.

I am *not* Tila.

'If I was going to do this – how am I supposed to know what to do, or how to infiltrate the Ratel?' I ask.

Oloyu doesn't hesitate. 'We can train you and give you the information you need. The skills that will keep you alive. And we'll have a partner for you.'

My breath catches. Somehow, the idea of working with a stranger seems even more frightening than working alone.

'I don't even look much like my sister any more,' I say, my voice weak with protest.

'That can be changed.'

I raise a hand to my cheek, thinking of scalpels and flesh parlours.

Officer Oloyu interlinks his fingers together, leaning forward, his face starkly earnest. 'So, Miss Taema Collins – are you going to join us and save your sister?'

My mouth opens, but I have no idea how to answer.

FIVE

TAEMA

They give me one hour to make up my mind. They can't give me any longer. If I'm going to do it, they have to start prepping me right away, so that 'Tila' isn't out of circulation too long.

I go to Golden Gate Park, taking the MUNI. No unmarked hovercars any more – nothing to make me stand out. For this one hour, I am not alone. The SFPD are tracking my VeriChip, watching me through camera drones. I fight the urge to hunch my shoulders, to somehow disappear from their sight. I can't.

I go through the entrance to the glass dome that covers Golden Gate Park. Though evening is lengthening, it's still as bright as early afternoon from the artificial light within. It's always open, even in the dead of night. Tila and I used to come here at midnight for picnics sometimes, watching mothers with day shifts walk their babies in prams, or joggers flitting along the paths, their toned bodies covered in bright neon logos, moving adverts for sports tech. Most people have nano muscle inserts to keep them in shape these days, including me and my sister, though we also take pride in doing it the old-fashioned way, or at least making the odd attempt. I want to take off down the paths, running at full speed until my lungs burn, but I run to stop myself from thinking, and I can't run away from my own mind, not now.

I sit under a willow tree, taking off my shoes and dipping my toes into the water of the lake. It's quiet here, with its false eternal daylight, the wafting scent of flowers and cut grass. I search the news with my ocular implant again for a moment, closing my eyes and letting the words scroll past my darkened eyelids. Still no headline about my sister. There's an article about the mayor of San Francisco and her bid for re-election. She smiles with white teeth from the feed. Sudice says they will announce a new product next week at the tech expo. The city is building more housing and orchard towers to meet rising demand. Nothing in the news about crimes, or the Ratel. I wonder how often they cover up what really happens in this city. If the public doesn't find out about it, has it happened at all?

Endless adverts flash from the corners of my vision. Go on holiday to Dubai, or New Tokyo. Order this mealpack from your replicator tonight. Another Zeal advert flashes and I bring it forward. This one shows a man sleeping calmly, but over his head he's screaming at his boss and walking out, slamming the door behind him. He wakes up, stretching, smiling at the camera. '*I've let it all out,*' he says, his voice tinny in my auditory implants. '*I'm ready to face the day.*' A blink and he's in a suit. The same tagline twines above his head: *Find your Zeal for life. What will you dream today?* I send it away, a headache blooming in my temples.

My sister and I surprised people in San Francisco by taking to the implants with ease, considering we were about eleven years behind almost everyone else. The doctors and such never realized how many hours we had already spent learning to control our minds, so that implants were only a small side step.

I sigh and lie down in the grass. I try to pretend I'm sixteen again, in Mana's Hearth, before we ever found that other tablet and learned that everything we thought we knew had been a lie. But it's no use. That daydream won't come. How can it? Tila isn't by my side.

I open my eyes.

I've made up my mind, though it was never really in question. Officer Oloyu knew I'd say yes before he even asked me.

•

I'm to meet my new partner immediately. I don't even go back to SFPD headquarters to give Oloyu my answer; I ping him through my implants.

I'm back on the MUNI. I swipe my VeriChip at the entrance, the fare deducting from my account, and take the elevator underground. I only wait a minute for the train heading towards downtown, and find a seat in the corner. The train pulls away. I cross my legs as the green glow from the underground algae plants passes by. Everyone looks sickly in this light, and my eyes dart to and fro. I keep rubbing my palms over my knees. Who am I meeting? What have I signed up for?

I get off at the Mcallister and Pierce stop and walk the few blocks to the address I've been given. It looks like a residential house – one of those sweepingly beautiful, reconstructed Victorian houses, painted in pastel colours. I've always admired them, and when I came into a shocking amount of money for my role in the VivaFog, I debated buying one. But Tila scoffed, thought they looked like gingerbread houses, and so I held off. I wonder now why I let her talk me out of it. It didn't seem important. How many times have I let her decide for me what I really want? Even now, I'm not making my own decisions, not really. This was all started by my sister, without her telling me anything.

I shake my head of the cobwebs of thoughts and climb the

stairs, knocking on the door. It swings open on its own. I step in cautiously, a shiver running down my spine. The door closes behind me. Inside, the hallway is empty. No picture frames on the walls, no flowers, no tables strewn with personal items.

'In the kitchen,' a male voice calls.

I walk through, trying to keep my tread firm rather than hesitant. A man leans against the table, arms crossed over his chest. He's muscled, with strong eyebrows, a slightly hooked nose, and scars on his knuckles and forearms that, in this city of image perfectionists, draw my eyes.

'Hello,' he says, pleasantly enough.

'Hi,' I say hesitantly. It seems very informal after all the interrogation rooms at the police station. The kitchen looks as stark and un-lived-in as the hallway.

'I'm Detective Nazarin,' he says, moving towards me and holding out his hand. I take it. His handshake is warm and firm.

'The undercover agent,' I say, feeling stupid.

'Yes.' He doesn't elaborate. I wonder what he's done as part of the Ratel. What I might have to do, now that I'm joining him. He sees me eye the door nervously. 'We're the only ones here.'

'I thought there'd be others.' A whole team, determined to keep me safe.

'There will be. But not until they're needed. Do you want a drink?'

I do, but I shake my head, clasping my hands into fists. I'm shaking again, and it irritates me, but being here means it's real. It's happening. I'm about to start training with this scarred stranger who could probably snap my neck without breaking a sweat.

'Do you want to go to a room and settle in, or have a tour and get started?'

'I'll get started.' It's not like I'd be able to relax here.

He walks ahead of me, his stride sure and powerful.

One room is filled with dozens of wallscreen monitors, showing the street outside and other locations through the city. Others show long streams of code, blinking in the dim light. Empty chairs and desks line up in front of them.

'The rest of the team will mostly be watching us from the SFPD headquarters, but they can be based here occasionally, once we're undercover.'

So many screens. There's the outside of the TransAm Pyramid. There's the outside of my apartment building, and Tila's. The police station. Warehouses. Stark skyscrapers.

'Right,' I say, for lack of anything better.

He shows me the other rooms. Many of them are empty. There are a few bedrooms, stark as hotels. I throw my bag into one that has a good view of the park. He doesn't show me his room.

The last area of the house is the training room. It's large, with that gym smell of rubber, metal, old sweat and cleaning solution.

To the right is a practice mat, weights and staffs along one wall. My eyes are drawn instead to the brainloading Chair on the right.

He sees the hesitation, his brow drawing down in confusion. 'You knew brainloading would be the main component of the training, correct?' he asks. 'We don't have time to do it another way. Your file says you used a Chair frequently when you came to San Francisco, to catch up on all you and your sister hadn't learned while at the Hearth.'

At the mention of my sister, I suppress a flinch. I'm here

because of her. This is all happening because of my twin, but I still miss her with a pain deeper than my scar. I stand unnaturally still, every muscle tense. I force myself to appear unconcerned. I'm annoyed my fear is so obvious. 'It's fine,' I say, keeping my voice smooth. 'I just haven't used one for years, is all.'

That machine was one of my first introductions to modern technology after the actual surgery. Upon realizing just how damn ignorant we were, Tila and I had jumped into Chairs willingly enough, brainloading information on history, politics, math, science and anything else that captured our interest. Tila had been more interested in art history and other cultures, whereas I'd been drawn to science.

People were surprised by how easily and quickly we integrated the information. Most people had a fifty per cent retention rate. Good, obviously, for hours of information pooled into a brain, and people often finished degrees by age sixteen or seventeen, so we were grossly behind. It didn't take long for us to catch up. From our training with Mana-ma, we had a ninety-five per cent retention rate.

It wasn't long before others expressed interest in our abilities, though our background was kept largely under wraps. Tila found a tutor for her art, and I found a mentor to further my education in engineering. Tila grew sick of it all a lot sooner than I did, leaving her mentor in order to do her own art without plugging into the Zealscape. I stayed, and I did well.

After I finished my education, I never touched a Chair again. I hate the feeling of information trickling into my brain. It's like it fills my skull with noise and pushes out who I am. I always woke up after a night of downloading information as tired as when I'd gone to bed, muttering facts to myself as I made coffee. Perhaps it was harder for us because of our high retention rate, or the fact that Zeal is not as pleasurable for us as for others. In any case, I prefer to learn things the way the brain was meant to absorb it.

The Chair by itself is fairly antiquated. As of a few years ago, most people can download information directly into their brain, with extra implants in the hippocampus and frontal cortex. They don't have that in Zeal lounges, but it's the inevitable next step. Neither Tila nor I have those extra implants, and I'm glad they haven't asked me to get them. I'd rather have the Chair.

'You have your room to store your things, but I'm afraid you'll be sleeping here, most of the time,' Nazarin says. 'Come on, let's go have some coffee. I'll help fill you in on what you can expect over the next few weeks.'

Finally. Oloyu hadn't gone into a lot of detail about the day-in day-out plans of being undercover. He didn't know.

He makes the coffee – well, orders it from the replicator – and sets the makings on the table. I've been in his presence over half an hour and I still have no idea what to think of him.

'So. We don't have long to train you,' he begins. 'Tila works at the Verve lounge a few times a week. We know where she goes and what her shifts are, and we do know how she communicates with them. We can tell them you're ill, which means you can miss one, maybe two shifts, but after that they'll expect you back. I can't have the luxury, so I'll still be working my usual night-shifts while you brainload.'

'Verve . . . lounge?' I ask.

'That's what she does for them and how she rose so fast through their ranks.' He seems frustrated that I'm confused. 'Surely Oloyu told you about Verve?'

'Some. That it's different from Zeal, and they need lucid

dreamers to mine it. I didn't realize that I'd have to do it so soon. Or that there were lounges for it.'

'By the time that happens, you'll be trained and know what to do.' His words are so confident I allow myself to believe them, at least a little.

'OK,' he continues. 'Today, you'll be contacting people with your cover story, and we're going to switch your VeriChip to your sister's. Once that happens, you'll contact your friends to tell them her cover story, and then you'll be able to contact the Ratel. We'll also start your training. It'll be physical, hand-to-hand combat, and weapons, and as much information as you can retain. I'm here every step of the way, and any questions you have, you can ask me.'

Despite his harsh features and his scars, his eyes are warm. It steadies me a little more.

'How long have you been undercover?' I ask.

'A little over two years.'

That's a long time. If he's deep undercover, that means he might not have been able to contact his close friends and family, and even if he could, he'd have to lie to them day in and day out about what he was really doing with his time.

Like Tila lied to me. And how long will I be doing this? A few days, weeks, months? Years?

I push the thought away, but a worse one follows in its place. 'Have you . . . met my sister?'

'I have. Not often, but we were at some of the same parties, and I saw her in passing if I dropped off deliveries at the Verve warehouse.'

A strange thought. I feel strangely exposed. 'What about . . . the fact we don't look alike?'

'Visiting a flesh parlour will be one of the last steps.'

I touch my face. Like everyone else, I've been to flesh parlours and erased a line here, a dimple there. I've never done anything drastic, but I'll have to change my hair, my nose and my cheekbones. Not much, but enough I won't recognize myself so easily in the mirror. Enough that I'll look like Tila again. 'Can I change it back . . . after?'

'There's no reason you can't.'

I'm not reassured. I stare at the dregs of my coffee, counting my steady heartbeats.

'Do you feel ready for the first step?' he asks gently.

I look up, pressing my lips together. 'Sooner we start, the sooner it's over with.'

He gives me a smile, and it transforms his face. His eyes light up, and they crinkle around the corners. I can almost forget the scars hiding beneath the buzz cut of his hair, and the smile puts me a bit more at ease, despite the strangeness of this day.

He gives me my script but leaves me alone to make the calls, saying he's only a ping away if I need him. I thank him, glad he won't be hovering.

One by one, I go through my few friends and colleagues. I'm only amending the story of my life a little – or what was going to be the story of my life, before all this happened. I'm to say I'm going to China earlier than I planned, and Tila's coming with me. Once I change my implant, I'll phone Tila's friends. It'll be my first undercover role: to convince them that I am my sister. I shiver at the thought.

After those first calls are done, it's physical training. Detective Nazarin takes me to the room with the Chair and the gym. He faces me, crossing his arms over his chest. 'You have muscle mods, correct?'

I nod. 'Enough to keep me toned without having to exercise much.' Because I'm lazy.

'Good. That'll help with recovery. Fighting techniques will be part of the information you download, but let's see how you are on your own.'

He runs me through a basic diagnostic, figuring out how much weight I can lift or press, how flexible I am, how fast and far I can run. His fingertips rest on the pulse of my neck, taking my resting heart rate. I look up at his dark brows, the scars, the square jawline. He's attractive in a dangerous way.

'Slow resting heart rate,' he says.

'They programmed it that way.'

He smiles a little, and again it lights the harshness of his face.

I think I do a little better than he expected, which is good, but I can tell he wishes I were stronger than I am. I think of my sister – the muscles on her arms. She claimed it was from dancing with customers at the club, plus a few extra implants. I didn't wonder at the time why she felt the need to be so much stronger. How dangerous are the Ratel – has she needed to physically protect herself?

Nazarin teaches me self-defence moves. I've never taken any kind of combat sport, though I've often wanted to. Tila convinced me to go with her to dance classes instead. Some of the moves I learned in capoeira transfer pretty well, at least.

Overall, though, it's a thoroughly humbling experience. Detective Nazarin doesn't hurt me, but after a while his light blows start to ache. My limbs aren't moving as quickly or as seamlessly as I'd like. Nazarin easily dodges my paltry attempts to attack him.

'You're small and quick. Your best hope is to avoid the blows. If you came up against someone like me in a real fight, you wouldn't stand a chance.' He probably weighs about half again what I do, so he has a point. It grates, but I learn.

He's not a bad teacher. He doesn't shout – he tells me what I do wrong, but praises what I do right. As my muscles grow more exhausted, his voice seems to hum near my ear: 'Duck, left, back,' and I move almost without thinking.

Detective Nazarin calls a stop after three hours. I'm panting, but proud of myself that I kept going and didn't ask for breaks except the odd gulp of water. Nazarin is glazed in perspiration, but strangely, he smells good. Musk and cologne and clean sweat.

'Strong start,' he says. 'Soon, you'll be better.'

Once it's wired into my brain.

'Now,' Detective Nazarin says, 'it's time for you to legally become Tila, at least for a little while.'

•

I have enough time to shower and choke down some vat jerky and dried fruit before Detective Nazarin takes me to meet Dr Kim Mata, a biohacker working for Sudice, Inc.

We can't go to the Sudice headquarters: they're the parent company of VivaFog and I've already told my co-workers I'll be on a jet to China imminently, and it would compromise Nazarin's cover. But we can't bring Dr Mata to the safe house. Instead we make our way down to one of her empty properties. She's often hired by the SFPD to do these sorts of jobs, Nazarin says, but she keeps it quiet from Sudice. I'm surprised she's able to.

Time to switch identities.

On the way there I lean against the window, my tired muscles quivering. It feels good, though, like my mind has connected better with my body now that it has that particular buzz of exercise exhaustion. I'll take some Rejuvs when I get back, and between that and my implants, tomorrow my muscles won't even be sore, but I'll be that much stronger.

How much stronger do I have to be? What exactly do they think is going to happen?

We meet Dr Mata in one of her townhouses by SF State. The walls are pure white and there is no furniture. Dr Mata is Japanese-American and tiny, barely coming up to my shoulder, and I'm not the tallest of women. She's also one of the few people in San Francisco who has let herself age, at least a little. There's the barest hint of wrinkles around her eyes and at either side of her mouth. It's refreshing to see a face that looks lived in, evidence of countless smiles reflected on her skin. I estimate she's about forty-five. She has dark hair cut in a bob to the corner of her jaw, and a face that's always on the verge of grinning.

'Can't keep away from me, can you, darling?' she says, dimpling at Detective Nazarin.

'My heart beats only for you, Kim,' he responds, deadpan.

She rolls her eyes. I'm amused by their exchange. Dr Mata is open and friendly, and Detective Nazarin seems more at ease around her. With her easy manner and the way she slouches against the wall, she doesn't strike me as one of the most prominent biohackers in the world and worth a few million credits or more.

'What's it to be this time, sweets?' she asks. Her gaze flicks to me, assessing me from head to toe, before she focuses on the detective again. 'Better not be too trying. I have back-to-back meetings all afternoon and if you tire me out, I'll nap through them.'

'Identity switch,' he says. 'This is a sensitive matter. I saw you returned the confidentiality agreement to HQ.'

'I'm hurt you don't trust me,' she pouts. 'When have I ever let you down?'

'Never. I trust you implicitly.'

In contrast to their earlier banter, he's serious here, and she feeds off it. Dr Mata looks at me again. 'OK. What's up?'

'Kim, this is Taema Collins. Her sister, Tila Collins, has been accused of murder.'

Dr Mata's eyes widen. 'Civilian?'

'Not exactly,' he replies. 'Tila Collins is implicated with the Ratel. Last night she was caught and accused. You know what I've been doing with myself the last few years.'

'Yeah, being an idiot and playing with fire. I've told you time and time again you need to get out of that game.'

'You speak sense as always, but I can't. Anyway, I never would have been able to do what I've done without you.'

She blows him an air kiss. 'Damn right. So you're being taken into protective custody or something?' Dr Mata asks, addressing me for the first time. 'Need a new identity to lie low?'

I shake my head. 'Not exactly. Tila and I – we're identical twins, you see.'

Her eyebrows rise. She looks between us, and her sharp mind fills in the blanks. 'Well. That's a first for me. Switching sisters. You got all the paperwork in order?'

Nazarin nods.

'OK then. Let's get started.'

She motions for me to come closer, and I do. She takes hold of my wrist, turning it over. Her hands are cool and dry. 'Thank you, Dr Mata—' I begin.

She waves her free hand. 'Call me Kim.'

'Kim.' She meets my eyes and grins. There aren't a lot of

people who smile genuinely in San Francisco. She holds nothing back, and I can't help but return the gesture.

She takes a little electrode from a box in her pocket and fastens it right over the tiny mark where the chip lies under my skin. Her eyes unfocus, and on the blank white tablet in her hand is code only she can see. Before long, she has full access to my identity. I shiver, realizing that if she wanted to she could wreak complete havoc with my life. She senses my nervousness.

'Don't worry, buttercup, your identity is safe with me. You don't have anything I don't already have ten times over. Hmm.'

'What?' I ask.

'Your chip wasn't put in at birth. You've only had it for ten years.' Her gaze is piercing. I want to look away, but I don't. 'And no record before that. How'd that happen?'

'I'm from Mana's Hearth.'

'No shit!' she exclaims, her head jerking back. 'Really? Your sister, too?'

'Yes. We came here when we were sixteen.'

She meets my eyes, still holding my wrist. 'Well, before, I thought you were cute and must be at least a bit interesting, to be hanging around with Sugarcube here.' She jerks her head at Nazarin. 'Now, I find you endlessly fascinating.'

I can't help but laugh a little.

'And what's this?' she says, noting the top of my scar.

I pull down the collar of my shirt a few inches. 'My sister and I were conjoined until we left.'

She whoops. 'Now you're officially one of the most interesting people I've ever met. When this is all over, I'm taking you out for a drink. Sound good?'

'All right.' I smile, but it fades. I can't help but wonder if I'll even return to a normal life after this.

'Come on, you charmer,' Nazarin says. 'Can you do the switch?'

She scoffs. 'Can I do the switch? That's just insulting.'

She cocks her head, sending the projection of code onto the wall.

There we are, up on the screen. All those numbers represent our identities. Me and Tila. Side by side. I wonder what she's thinking about, just now, in her cell. I wish she'd speak to me, and I don't understand why she won't. Nazarin says she chose not to, but what if they aren't letting her speak to me? Hope flares within me at the thought. Or perhaps she thinks by keeping quiet she can protect and shield me from all this. Does she realize I'm caught right in the thick of it?

Dr Mata waves her fingers, moving code around so quickly I can barely follow. She clicks her tongue against her teeth. 'There. Done.'

I blink. 'That's it?'

'That's it, buttercup. You're now officially your sister, Tila Collins.' She takes the electrode off my wrist and rubs the skin with her thumb.

'That's scary, how easily you could do it.'

'Don't worry. I'm one of only about three or four people in San Francisco who can do it at all, let alone that quickly. I helped invent VeriChips.'

I rub my thumb over the chip, covered by a thin layer of skin. 'Well, thank you,' I say.

'No prob. But remember, when you're done dipping your toes into danger, come meet me for that drink and I'll reset your own identity.'

'I will.' I'm not sure if it's an invite for an evening of chat or a date. I don't mind either way.

Kim pats me on the shoulder, and then goes over to Nazarin. 'You better not get her hurt, Naz. She's way too innocent for the shit you're about to throw her into.'

My stomach flutters. He looks at me, then away. 'She'll be fine.'

Kim holds out her arms and he gathers her into a bear hug, lifting her off the ground. She whispers something in his ear, but I can't hear it.

'Thanks a million, Kim,' Detective Nazarin says. 'You ready, Tila?' he asks me.

And now I am Tila, for all intents and purposes. At least legally. But for all that I know my sister better than anyone, I'm not her.

'I'm ready,' I say, though I'm not sure I'll ever be.

SIX

TILA

The first cracks between us happened long before the surgery, although Taema would never admit it. When we were little, we were two halves of the same coin. We've gone so far from where we were. So far from that long-ago innocence.

Life was simpler in the Hearth, before we knew for certain it was a prison.

Supply ships came to Mana's Hearth every two weeks, and it was always a big deal for us. A glimpse into a world that wasn't ours.

As soon as we heard the distant roar of engines, we'd find somewhere to watch the ship set down. The men and women, dressed in strange uniforms that clung close to their bodies, looked so different from us as they directed the droids to unload the crates.

It was the droids that fascinated Taema – a lot more than they did me. They weren't something we had on the Hearth, of course, and I thought they were freaky. The blocky machines looked roughly like humans with blank faces, but moved with much less grace as they unloaded the crates onto the lawn and then walked back up into the ship and powered down. Just like that. They moved around, and then they looked dead.

They didn't say anything about droids in the Hearth school,

but Mom and Dad had told us a little bit about them. Kept stressing that they weren't 'sentient'. That they didn't have feelings, and were just machines made to do humans' dirty work.

'Why make them look human, then?' I remember asking. Surely having more than two arms would be better for lifting. Taema and I often found our extra limbs handy.

My parents didn't have an answer to that.

We usually stayed out of sight of the supply ships. Obviously the droids didn't care, but the humans from the city stared something awful when they realized we weren't hugging – that we were connected. Say what you like about Mana's Hearth, but at least they treated everyone equally. When we were younger, this one guy from the supply ship came up to us and actually reached out like he was going to touch the spot where our flesh joined, but I bit him. He jumped back and put his finger in his mouth, sucking the blood. Taema didn't even tell me off for it; she was just as mad. After that, it was just easier to stay hidden and watch secretly.

One day, after the ship took off, we noticed they had left something behind on a rock. We shuffled closer. It was a piece of tech. We'd seen them using things like it – it was called a 'tablet'. It wasn't meant to be left behind. No tech was. The only machines me and Taema had ever seen were the supply ships and the droids, and almost everyone in the village stayed well away when the city folk landed. Sometimes our mom would come and speak to them, relay requests or whatever, but that was it. After the supply ship took off, others would then tiptoe down the hill, performing Purifying rituals with burning sage and whispered prayers, before they could bring themselves to take the supplies back to their homes.

I reached down for the tablet.

'Tila,' my sister said. 'It's forbidden.'

I ignored her, still trying to reach down, but Taema stayed stubbornly straight. I pulled harder, until she grunted in pain, but she didn't budge.

'Come on,' I wheedled. 'We have to turn it in to Mana-ma, don't we? We can't leave it here.' Really, I just wanted to hold it, at least for a moment.

With a reluctant sigh, she leaned forward. I wrapped my hand around the metal and glass.

'You'll get in trouble for touching it with your bare skin,' she warned.

'So will you.'

'Exactly. I'll have to be Purified along with you, and you know burning sage always makes me cough.'

I looked around nervously. How long before people came?

'Let's go to the tree, first,' I said.

'So you can look at it?'

I don't answer.

'It's Impure,' she whispered, her brow furrowed.

I started towards the trees and she followed, her legs stiff and straight.

'We shouldn't do this,' she kept whispering. 'Mana-ma wouldn't like it.'

'Mana-ma doesn't need to know.'

'She knows everything.'

I felt a little bit of guilt, but I squashed it right down.

The tree was our favourite spot in the forest. We went to it whenever we really wanted to hide from everyone else in the Hearth. In the compound it was hard to ever be truly alone, but out in the woods there were only the redwoods and the birds. Our tree was an old, hollowed-out redwood, struck by lightning a long time ago. We shuffled inside, smelling the old smoke and damp greenness of the forest. I loved it there. When we were younger, we'd had tea parties or played cards, whispered secrets, stashed things we didn't want to share. It was our safe space.

I held the tablet in front of me, turning it this way and that. It felt so smooth, hard and cold. It seemed alien.

I found a little button on the side and pressed it, and the screen came to life in vibrant greens, blues and yellows. We both gasped.

How had the people from the city worked it?

I pressed it with my finger.

Words appeared on the screen: *No implants detected. Use manually? Y/N.*

'I'm going to press yes,' I said.

'You know you shouldn't. Mana-ma says it's evil.'

Sometimes she drove me nuts. 'For God's sake. You can't tell me you're not even a little curious.'

Taema set her mouth in that stubborn line we both make when we're not budging.

'If God didn't want us to look at it, it wouldn't have been left there,' I tried.

'It's a test. That's what Mana-ma would say.' She bit her lip. I knew she was curious, almost as curious as me.

'Come on, T,' I said, my voice singsong. 'We'll just take a quick look, then we'll turn it in to Mana-ma. She never needs to know we took a peek. We'll learn just a little more about the world outside.'

We'd spent hours tossing possibilities back and forth about what the rest of the world was like – even if my sister was far more interested in the rules of the Hearth than I was, always quoting the Good Book to me when I broke a rule. When I plucked my eyebrows: *God created us as he wanted us. In his eyes, there are no flaws. To change your body is sacrilege.* When I said I wished we could leave behind the Hearth and go to a city with proper skyscrapers, whatever they were: *God has laid out his plan for us in the glory of nature*. When I complained about going to the meadow with the rest of the Hearth: *One must Meditate to remain Pure and open to God's gifts*. Over and over, even though we both knew it was all an act. Behind closed doors, she wanted to know what the world was like, just as much as I did.

Taema sighed.

I pressed the Y on the tablet.

The screen stayed lit, but neither of us knew how to work it. There was nothing taught about this in the commune. We understood a tiny bit more than others about life outside the Hearth: our parents were (still are?) pretty high up in Mana-ma's inner circle, so they knew plenty and they shared some with us. They weren't meant to and they were sinning by doing so, but they said they wanted us to be prepared, 'just in case'. So we knew that there were things called wallscreens, and flying hovercars that looked like smaller supply ships. That there were buildings made out of smooth stone called concrete. No matter how hard we tried, though, we couldn't imagine it. Not really. So we weren't *totally* ignorant about the big wide world out there – just mostly. And that chafed me.

I rested the tablet against the inside of the tree. I had no idea what to do next. I tapped it again, but nothing happened. I knew that it was a link to the outside world, that I could learn all I wanted to, but I didn't know how to start.

I tapped it once more, grinding my teeth in frustration.

'Maybe you have to speak to it,' Taema said, her voice so small. 'I heard them talking to it before.'

That was right. They'd say 'tablet' first. I kept a finger on the screen. 'Tablet. Search,' I tried, speaking louder.

A new window opened, showing a blinking box. *Enter search parameters* flashed above it.

I looked to Taema for guidance, but she only shrugged, the movement pulling against the skin of my chest. I rested my face against my sister's, our cheekbones touching. My knees were shaking with excitement. Taema's shook too, but more with fear.

'Should I search for conjoined twins?' I whispered. We'd never seen any others. How did they live in the cities? How many were there?

You might wonder if our condition hurt, or if it was awkward, and the answer is no. It never hurt being attached to Taema. Though I could get so mad at her I could spit – and I had before but then she'd spit back and we'd be staring at each other's spit-covered faces and then usually burst into laughter at the stupidity of it all – I couldn't stomp off. There was no way for either of us to have the last word on anything.

Taema looked resolutely away. 'Let's not.'

'Why not?'

'Just don't, OK?'

I was tempted to push her, but then we'd have fought and she'd have been even more pigheaded than before. 'Fine.'

I stared at the tablet again. *Please state your search terms clearly*, the screen reminded us. How did it even do that? Our parents told us about the internet and radio waves, how they floated through the air. Dad said that within the compound, the internet didn't work, but the tech dampeners only worked so far in the forest. If this place was meant to be so Pure, why hadn't Mana-ma stopped service out in the woods, too?

Taema's cheekbone grazed mine. She kept trying to look away but couldn't help herself. Even though we had the whole world at our fingertips, we didn't know what about the world we should learn.

That's it. I'd start with what I did know.

'Tablet. Search for Mana's Hearth,' I said.

Information came up immediately: a list of some kind. I touched the first one with my fingertip, tentatively, and more information loaded. I felt Taema turn closer to the screen. She couldn't resist. We read, side by side.

Mana's Hearth – The Infamous Cult of the San Francisco Bay Area

'What's a cult?' Taema whispered.

I shook my head, confused. 'I don't know, but they seem to think it's bad.' I read through an origin story of the Hearth, written by someone called Tobias Diaz, which fitted mostly with what Mana-ma had told us in sermon:

> Not much is known of the secretive commune set where Muir Woods was once open to the public. The First Mana-ma was Elspeth Foley, a mistress of a prominent politician who was also a member of the Bohemian Grove.

'What's that?' Taema asked. We took a brief break to search for Bohemian Grove. They were a group of rich and powerful politicians who met in the redwoods at Monte Rio once a year to network while pretending they weren't networking. Some of their ceremonies seemed a little similar to what we did in the Hearth, such as the 'Cremation of Care', where they burned a large fire to let go of their worries. We did that every summer equinox down in the meadow, though we didn't wear such stupid outfits. After a few false starts, I managed to bring the screen back to the original page we'd been reading.

As a woman, Elspeth Foley had no chance of ever becoming a full member of the Bohemian Grove, and she was not sure if she wanted to. She began her own commune a few years later, and recruited several prominent relatives of the very same Bohemian Grove members who would not accept her. Over the next few decades, she gradually recruited more members and closed them off from society, until, by her death, it could only be considered a cult.

When one Mana-ma perishes, she will have already chosen and groomed her successor. There have now been eight Mana-mas, with the current one in power for the last thirty-five years. They were settled in the Mojave Desert, by Chimney Rock, but after the Great Upheaval they moved to the redwood grove across the bay from San Francisco.

Mana-mas often have a husband, who is called the Brother, as they are meant to be a Brother to the whole community. They are not actual siblings. The current Mana-ma's Brother died around twenty years ago, though this information is difficult to verify, and she has not taken another.

Many rumours have circulated about day-to-day life in the Hearth. Some say they perform animal or human sacrifice, but that is entirely unsubstantiated. The Hearth does ban any technology invented past 1969, or the Summer of Love. They live the same way that the original Mana-ma lived in the First Hearth. Every Mana-ma has said that the first commune was perfect and it shouldn't change. Their houses have electricity, they play antiquated record players, but there are no computers, and definitely no implants. The Hearth believes that to alter oneself in any way is sacrilege. They avoid modern medicine, relying instead on natural herbs from the

> earth. No make-up, no flashy fashion, no waxworked features at flesh parlours.
>
> What we do know is that in the decades since the Hearth started, barely anyone has ever left. It is rare for a cult to remain stable for so many years. A decade ago, after complaints of curious people trying to sneak onto the grounds, the government constructed a large artificial swamp around the perimeter, making the former site of Muir Woods technically an island. With several thousand members, the commune is largely self-sufficient, but must order in some supplies from outside. Within the grounds, people will occasionally disappear, and no one knows where they have gone. Some claim that Mana-ma kills them herself, though again, is this only sensationalism?

'The swamp is artificial?' Taema asked.

'*That's* the question you ask after reading that?' I said, incredulous. 'This thing accused Mana-ma of being a murderer!'

'That's just another rumour. People don't go missing. They die of natural causes and rejoin the Cycle.' She sounded so matter-of-fact, so certain, and I was jealous of her.

'I don't get it, either. People die out there, too, don't they?' I couldn't help but think: what if they didn't? What if out there people lived forever? Did I want that?

We looked through other links about the Hearth, but none of them seemed as close to the truth as that first one. People writing about us wondered how the Hearth was funded, for our 'tawdry wares' and 'paltry produce' weren't nearly enough to keep us going. Talk about rude. We worked as hard as the others on those stupid quilts and things, and I wouldn't call them tawdry. We helped pick the mushrooms from the greenhouse and send them to the mainland, and it wasn't easy picking for hours on end.

They said that Mana-ma brainwashed us all, twisting our minds to her will, forcing us with drugs until we knew nothing different. I looked at Taema out of the corner of my eye. How nervous she was even being near the tablet, yet unable to look away. I should have believed the Impure technology was evil, too. Why didn't I?

Other sites said that everyone within the Hearth was there because they were twisted and ugly, with missing limbs and scars and other blemishes. I thought of my friends and family, me and my sister. None of us were ugly, were we? Physical beauty was not something we really dwelt on in the Hearth. It wasn't important, as God made us all perfect and we had to only trust in His judgement and continue trying to be the best people we could in this world.

I searched for 'flesh parlour' next. They showed before and after photographs of people who had changed their faces. In the after pictures, it was as if they'd erased what truly made them look like . . . themselves. It was all generic, with no defining characteristics.

I swallowed, feeling Taema stiff and hurt beside me. That seemed . . . wrong. Wicked. Like Mana-ma always said about the outside world.

And what would they think of us, out there? What would they do?

Taema and I didn't speak to each other. We read as fast as our eyes could speed across the text, looking up words we didn't recognize, nudging each other gently when we could scroll down.

We spent hours in that tree. Taema said she'd had enough and closed her eyes, going to sleep. But I kept reading and learning, and appreciated that even if she was afraid of it all, she wouldn't rat on me.

So much of it I didn't understand. At first, I didn't want to believe it. I mean, this was all I'd ever known. I wanted to believe that maybe the outside world was lying, making it all up for some reason. For money, probably. Mana-ma said that was all people out there ever wanted. Money and all the evil they could buy with it.

But deep down, I started thinking about all the ways she treated us and the others. All the things she made us do. Outside wasn't perfect. I'd never expected it to be. I couldn't help but wonder if maybe, just maybe, life didn't have to be like it was in the Hearth.

•

I stuck the tablet in the bottom of our bag and slung it across my shoulder. The movement woke my sister. I knew it was dangerous to take it back to camp, but I also didn't want to leave it out here. I didn't know much about technology, obviously. If it rained in here, would the water break it? I knew that could happen with things like the record player.

Taema was quiet as we slunk back to the town centre with our rocking gait. My arms were around her waist, and hers were around my shoulders. She felt guilty. Both because she'd let herself be close to something Impure and because she knew that we wouldn't be giving it over to Mana-ma. We wouldn't mention it in Confession. I'd get in trouble, and so would she by default. I'd put her in a shitty situation, and I should have felt worse about it than I did.

After reading those articles, I felt like I was seeing everything with fresh eyes. I'd seen a couple of photos of cities as we searched on that tablet deep within the forest, and they seemed so unfamiliar compared to our trees and single-storey houses. But to hear Mana-ma talk about it, San Francisco and the rest of the outside world was a vast cohort (yes, she actually used the word 'cohort' in everyday conversation) of corruption, abomination and filth.

Now I knew what so many people out there thought of our church, our town hall, our little houses all in a row. Our tidy allotments, or the fish smoking over an open flame. Nathaniel, a boy our age who was missing a leg, waving a hand to us as he turned the meat.

I tugged my skirt straight. Simple homespun. Taema and I made the dress ourselves – everyone did, but sometimes they swapped or inherited hand-me-downs. Not us, of course.

I shouldn't care what they thought. They seemed more like aliens than other humans.

Yes, I knew what aliens were. My parents had two pulp science fiction paperbacks, smuggled in when they joined the Hearth as teenagers. My parents loved the Hearth and believed in it, but my dad couldn't bear to leave them behind. He found a logic loophole for himself – they were both editions from the Golden Era of sci-fi and therefore pre-1969, and the far-fetched futuristic tech in them was just fantasy. I'd found them a few years ago: *The Stars My Destination* and *The Voyage of the Space Beagle*. Again, Taema had been annoyed at both me and Dad, convinced we should turn them into Mana-ma. Again, my sister had stayed quiet as I read long into the night, turning the crumbling yellow pages delicately. I'd loved escaping to those other worlds and dreaming about life on other planets.

Our planet was this small: 1,000 acres of redwood forest. I couldn't stop thinking about its past, laid out as it was on the tablet. How it used to be somewhere called Muir Woods. How the swamp was created to keep people out.

Or maybe to keep us in.

After we left, Taema and I hardly ever told people in San Francisco that we grew up in Mana's Hearth. When we did, they usually looked at us the same way the supply ship people did. As if we were unnatural. Aberrant.

I hated that look. It made me feel trapped. Made me want to lash out.

I've written this all down to show what the Hearth was like from the inside. I know you're all as curious as the rest of them. I'll keep telling you about life in the compound, and I won't tell you lies – whether you believe that or not. I can only tell you what it was like ten years ago, since we haven't been back. We're not allowed, even if we wanted to go to that god-forsaken place.

On that walk back, tablet well hidden, a few people were milling around the church, waiting for midweek prayer, dressed in shades of cream and brown. A lot of us had brown skin, brown hair, brown eyes. When we first came to San Francisco, we couldn't believe all the colour.

I remember I looked up at the church. The five-pointed symbol was carved over the door, painted gold and silver. A light was on in Mana-ma's study. As far as I know, she's still the leader out there, as I haven't heard anything about her dying. She'll probably outlive the apocalypse; she's just that stubborn. The supposed wife of God, according to the Good Book. I used to believe that, I really did. But I'd started losing my faith long before I found that tablet, I think. I can't pinpoint what caused that; just a lot of little things adding up. Guess I was proven right.

Mana-ma would probably be pretty interested in a Confessional from me now, a lot more than she was when I told her I'd stolen some cherries from Leila's allotment. Confession was meant to be one-on-one with Mana-ma, but Taema and I were a two-for-one special. A few times, she asked one of us to cover our ears while the other Confessed, but she gave up after a while. We already knew each other's sins, anyway. Obviously.

It's late here in the cell. Earlier today they asked me some questions, some about my sister. I hated every second of it. She's definitely trying to help me, and I don't want her to. What if something happens to her because of me? I thought I was doing the right thing. Now, guilt haunts my every moment. Maybe I fucked everything up beyond repair. Stupid, stupid. So stupid.

I'd rather write about the Hearth. Back then, everything was messed up, but we had each other. We didn't realize how terrible everything was going to become.

Mana-ma would hate that I was writing about all this. She'd be absolutely livid at me for exposing her secrets, but you know what? Fuck her.

I should probably end on some profound note, instead of a swear word. But I told you already: my sister's the one who has a way with words. I have a way of getting things done.

SEVEN

TAEMA

After Dr Mata, we return to the safe house. The sun begins to set. It's been such a long day.

'Meeting Kim for that drink will be fun, if you take her up on it,' Nazarin says, 'though don't be surprised if she busts out a bottle of real tequila and you wake up with the hangover of your life the next day.'

'You speak from experience.'

He winced at the memory. 'Oh, yes.'

I smirk and climb into the hovercar.

I turn to him after we buckle in. 'Did she ask me for an evening out, or a date? I couldn't tell.'

'She'd probably be open to either.' He pauses. 'Do you date women?'

'Sometimes. I'm bi.'

'Is your sister, too?'

'Yep.' I wonder why he asks. It's not as if it's rare in San Francisco.

He looks away and powers up the hovercar, taking off towards the safe house. We don't speak, both gazing at San Francisco and its flashing lights spread out before us, lost in our own thoughts. I lean my head against the window, my eyes fluttering shut as I doze fitfully.

Once we're back in the gingerbread house, it's growing late. I want nothing more than to crawl into bed and pull the covers over me, but Nazarin has to hook me into the Chair for a few hours. Then it'll be time to call Tila's friends – as her – and tell them why I won't be answering their pings for a while.

I sway with exhaustion. All the mental and emotional stress has now compounded with the physical. I pop a few Rejuvs and let Nazarin strap me into the Chair. It brings back memories of my engineering training and waking up with facts and numbers in my head, but not being able to move. I push them away.

I want my sister. I want to hold her close, to tell her everything, to have her tell me it'll be all right. When I'm anxious and my mind moves too quickly, she rubs the back of my neck, easing out the tension, her words soothing in my ear. How many times have I fallen asleep to the sound of her voice?

Tila is not here, and she's the reason I'm doing all this. My whole world has tilted on its axis. Memories of my sister are now tainted by all the lies I know she's told. I didn't see it. How could I not have seen it? How can I ever hope to trust my own judgement again?

'OK,' Nazarin says, drawing me from my thoughts, setting the electrodes on my skull and lowering me down. He even draws the blanket over me, which is an oddly touching gesture. I am shivering, but more from unease than cold. Nazarin takes out the needle, prepping the Zeal and melatonin mixture which will help ease the learning. It's a much lower dosage of Zeal than they use in the lounges – just enough to prep the implants to receive the information.

'We're starting you off with general Ratel info,' he says. 'What we know, so will you. The hierarchy, the main businesses they're involved in, the identities we've managed to scrounge. Some recordings of interrogations, that sort of thing.'

After my nap, I'll be a Ratel expert. I wonder if they're going to have to wipe all this information after this investigation is over, but I decide not to ask now. They can take info out almost as easily as putting it in, these days.

'I have to go out tonight after dark, take up my cover,' Nazarin says. 'But I'll be back by dawn.'

'What do you do for them?' I ask.

'This and that,' he says. 'Mostly I deliver Verve or act as security.'

So he saw my sister when he was picking up or dropping off the wares. He's about to go into the place I'll soon join. I close my eyes and hear the whirr as the machine starts. I can hear the low beating of blood through my mechanical heart in my ears.

'I'll wake you up in two hours. I'll just be in the next room doing paperwork.'

'All right,' I say, already drifting away as the Chair gives off melatonin.

A calm, robotic female voice is the last thing I hear:

Brainload initializing.

•

There are two people in the interrogation room.

A man chained to the table looks haggard, like he hasn't slept in days. He has the same shaved scalp, bisected with scars, as Nazarin. Usually, in these informational dreams in the brainload, the person has no sense of self. But I always remember who I am, and that I'm dreaming. The other man, a detective, I guess, stands tall, but he seems tired. His sandy-coloured suit is wrinkled, as though he's slept in it.

It's almost like I'm an invisible ghost in the room with them. I can imagine what it looks like to walk around. The scientists who examined Tila and me said that was why we retained so much more – because we could visualize and fit things into patterns more easily than those who couldn't control the recordings. Other people can learn to do it, but because of Mana-ma's training we've been doing it since we were small, even if we didn't realize it at the time.

The recording has been doctored, streamlined so the information can reach my brain efficiently. The man looming over the prisoner is yelling at him, and the prisoner glares back. They shout at each other, their staccato movements jerky. There's a jump, as if something has been cut. The view switches from the standing man leaning towards the prisoner, screaming into his face, to him sitting on the other side of the room, appearing calmer. The prisoner now has a red mark on his cheek. I guess that they've fast-forwarded through the intimidation, which I didn't want to see anyway.

The prisoner seems cowed. 'This is how the Ratel works,' he says, his voice and eyes flat. They've drugged him, or broken through some other way. 'The Ratel's hierarchy is set up like a chess game. The Pawn is the lowest level. They run errands, stand guard, collect extortion money from businesses. Deliver drugs or guns. Drive cars. They do what they're told and hope they make a name for themselves. If they do well, they might get promoted to Knight. Some people directly enter the Ratel at this level, but not many. To become a Knight, you have to prove yourself by committing a . . . worse crime than the ones you have already committed.' The man pauses, swallows. He seems haunted.

'What did you do?' the detective asks.

'I had to kill someone,' he rasps, and he shuts his eyes.

'Who?'

'It doesn't matter. They were invisible.'

The detective frowns. 'What–?'

'Do you want to know how the Ratel works or not?' the prisoner interrupts, harsh.

'Go on. Do you want water?'

The prisoner shakes his head. He pauses again, staring down at the table, as if gathering strength. 'After that, you can graduate to a Rook or a Bishop, each with subtly different roles in the organization. They're all under the King, of course, but Pawns and Knights hardly ever see him.'

'Do you know who the King is?'

'I'm a Knight, so what do you think?'

'That's not a yes or a no.'

'It's a no, you dick.' The prisoner leans away from the table, the chains of his handcuffs clinking together. He lifts his head in a defiant tilt. 'That's all I'm telling you.'

The detective opens his mouth to respond, but the scene dissolves.

'Do you know who the King is?'

The question again, asked by a different voice. The faces of the two people in the room are blurred this time, to protect the identities.

'Ensi,' the other person whispers, and the word picks up, echoing around the room: *Ensi, Ensi, Ensi.*

'Who is the Queen?' the voice asks. The Queen is the right hand – and like the chess piece, she goes anywhere. Does anything. Including some of the worst crimes in the Ratel. Most of the time, if you're invited to see the Queen alone, you don't leave the room alive. All this information slots into place.

The other blurred face responds: 'Malka.' It, too, reverberates around the room. That's all they have on the King and

Queen. Whispered names or aliases. How they truly function, who's closest to them – the SFPD hasn't cracked any of that. Even after two years, Nazarin has only seen Malka a few times, and has never seen Ensi.

More snippets of interrogations trickle into my mind. I learn names of prominent members of the Ratel, more details about the relationships between the various pieces on the chess board of San Francisco underground crime. The information changes, and I see tables of the same data, laid out logically, so that my brain will process and store it in a subtly different way. This includes maps of suspected Ratel hideouts, possible combination codes or passwords.

Still later, music floats through my brain, the wavelengths undulating through my mind. Here, my brain finally enters REM, and facts still trickle in through the music, deep into the subconscious. Certain nuggets of information will arise if and when I need them.

So many words, so many sounds, so many pieces of a puzzle that I try to fit together. Throughout it all, I wonder: how much of this does Tila already know?

•

'Wake up,' Nazarin says, his voice low and soothing.

I open my eyes, and his face is the first sight to greet me. His dark brows are knitted together, studying my face. 'How are you feeling?' he asks. He takes off the electrodes and brings the Chair into a seated position.

I press a hand to my temple. 'Like an overly damp sponge.'

He gives me a humourless half-smile. 'I remember that feeling. I made some coffee. Do you want any?'

'Yeah, sounds good.' I rise to my feet, steadier than I expect to be.

I follow him into the kitchen, slumping into a chair. I clamp my teeth together to stop the endless litany of facts streaming through my brain from escaping my lips. Within a few hours, the information will settle, but right now, my brain feels like it's in overdrive.

Nazarin pops a Rejuv and sets the steaming cup in front of me. 'They put a lot more into you than I've ever seen before in two hours. You sure you feel all right?'

'Fine,' I say, trying to sound so. I take a sip of coffee. It's the sanitized San Francisco stuff, nearly caffeine-free, with creamer, but it's warm as it slides down my throat.

'Do you have any questions about what you've learned?' Nazarin asks.

I frown. 'I'm still sorting through it. Maybe later.'

Nazarin glances at the clock above the replicator. Half past six. 'I'll leave you to drink your coffee. But then you should phone Tila's friends. Your first assignment. I have to go.' His eyes are a little puffy, despite the Rejuv.

'Right,' I mutter, staring into the coffee cup. Nazarin stands, and pauses right before he passes me. For a moment, I wonder if he's going to rest a hand on my shoulder. I think I would have appreciated the gesture. In the end, he sighs and leaves me be.

'Hey,' I call after him, and he turns. 'How old are you?'

'Twenty-eight.' Two years older than me. He probably became a cop at eighteen, a rookie recruit around the time I entered San Francisco. 'Why?'

I shrug a shoulder as he leaves. 'Just curious.'

I drink the coffee slowly, laying out all the recently acquired information in my mind. Between this and my already chaotic anxiety about Tila and about what I'm doing, my brain seems too crowded. I want to scream, to let it all out. I clutch the coffee cup tighter, and then force my fingers to relax. I push the chair away from the table and fold my body into a corner of the room, so that both walls press against my shoulder blades. I breathe in, breathe out, and empty my mind of all extraneous thought.

It's time to phone my sister's friends, as my sister, and tell them I'm going away to China.

I can't do it. It's a simple thing, and the easiest job I'm likely to have undercover, and I can't do it. Sweat breaks out along my skin. So much stress and heartache over the last twenty-four hours has been building, and the dam finally breaks. My mechanical heart thumps rhythmically in my chest against my metal sternum – completely immune to the external factors that would speed or slow a biological version.

Tila – why did you do this to me? What were you trying to do? To prove?

My fingertips find the familiar scar as I blink my burning eyes and slow my breathing. I close my eyes, grabbing my emotions and forcing them under control. Even now, I can't escape Mana-ma, but at the moment, I'm glad of her training.

I imagine the fear and the stress as darkness swarming around me to settle on my skin. Then, deep within myself, I kindle a light that starts from my heart and emanates outwards, a pure white to eradicate the darkness. My skin is now clean and glows softly, settling in my mind.

'I'm calm,' I whisper aloud. And I am. I'm almost giddy with it. A last breath, and I'm back to myself.

I meditate for around ten minutes, the tension leaking out from my neck and shoulders. I float in nothingness, in blackness. All anxiety lifts from my skin, in tiny flurries, like soot in the wind. When I open my eyes, I'm almost giddy from the endorphins. I return to the kitchen table, my breath even and steady. The information has ceased overwhelming me. I'm myself again, more or less.

I learned this from Mana-ma, and part of me feels nervous when I do it. As if just by meditating, I'll somehow fall back into her thrall. But I've . . . *we've* been free of her for years.

I set the pings to audio only. Tila has a lot more friends than I do. It never bothered me before, but looking at the list of names downloaded from my implants and projected onto the kitchen table, I feel like she's left more behind in this world than I have. Her artwork. She collects people, and always remembers faces and names. Though I've made some impact with my VivaFog machines, I only have a small circle of friends, and I couldn't say for certain if I'm closer to them than she is to hers or not.

'Here goes,' I mutter, and ping the first name on the list. I have a little thrill of anticipation. I've often wished I could be more like my sister: stronger, braver, so sure of herself, whereas I always questioned myself and my perception of others. I relied on her too much, in many ways. By channelling her, maybe I can start relying on myself.

I start with Diane, the curator of an art gallery nearby. Once, she had an exhibition of Tila's artwork. It was a success and yet after that first and last exhibition, Tila couldn't stand the thought of another gallery opening. She told me they were stealing pieces of her by buying her art. I hadn't understood it: wasn't that the point of making art? You put a little bit of yourself on canvas, or into a sculpture, or onto a page, and then you give or sell it to others so they also enjoy it?

Since then, whatever work she did was never seen by anyone but the two of us. Her paintings are beautiful, and it seems a shame that nobody else shares them, but I respect her decision and the reasons behind it, and so does Diane. They've remained close friends.

'Hey Tils!' Diane says.

'Hey, Di,' I say, folding my face into a smile – even if she can't see it, she'll hear it in my voice. I lean on my right elbow, like Tila does. She pitches her voice different to me, a little lower, but aside from that, our inflections are identical. We can still speak at the same time if we want to. It unnerves people when we do it. Diane's speaking, and I focus on her words.

'. . . You can make it to the gallery this weekend, right? You'll love this new artist. Such dark, fascinating work.'

And here we go. 'Sorry, Di, I'm gonna be out of town for a while.'

'Really? Where?'

'China. Taema's got a job and I'm going with her. Can you believe it?' I strive for Tila's lighter tone.

'Oh, it'll be lovely this time of year. How long are you going?'

'Not sure. I have an open ticket. Might even be a few months.'

'Wish I could come! Are you going to get one of those virtual assistants to help you do everything?'

I laugh and say probably not. We chat for a bit. It's not that difficult at all to be my sister. I was worried it would be, with how much she's changed the last few years. I wasn't sure I'd be able to bridge that final gap. Perhaps it was just different hair, a different face, a different job. I can slip into her personality almost as easily as my own. I thought it'd make me feel braver, but it only makes me all the lonelier.

Diane never asks me what's wrong, or if I'm feeling all right. I've masked everything behind Tila's mannerisms. She's brasher, doesn't self-edit before she speaks. Or at least she doesn't appear to, so it makes it seem she has nothing to hide. Though, obviously, she did.

I say farewell to Diane and make my way through the other names on the list. The only people I don't ping are the friends from Zenith, since Nazarin says we'll be going there soon enough.

When he first proposed that, so soon, I thought he was crazy. But now, as I say goodbye to Tila's last friend on my list, I think it won't be as bad as I fear. Although I have a lot less experience with seeing how the 'hostess Tila' acts at work. Her job is a far cry from anything I'm used to doing – the machines I work with don't speak to me, as I'm not in robotics – and I wonder if they'll see straight through me as soon as I set my foot through the door.

After I finish pinging everyone, I lie down in an actual bed in my room and doze.

Nazarin comes for me a few hours later. When he knocks I tell him to enter, forcing myself to sit up. Though he's only slept four hours, he looks refreshed, whereas I'm sure my hair is frizzy and my make-up has smeared halfway down my face. 'No rest for the wicked, I'm afraid,' he says. 'I'm to plug you back in. I'll be going back out again. I'm needed.'

I get up, pulling my sweater around my shoulders. 'What for?'

'Security for a Verve drop.' He sighs. We go downstairs. My feet drag on every step.

'Who are they selling it to?'

He grimaces. 'They're bribing a Zeal lounge, one of the shitty, off-grid ones, to spike the Zeal with Verve.'

My eyes widen. 'Why?'

'I think they're experimenting with it on a wider scale, and using the Zealots as a testing ground.'

'Fuck.' I say. Zealots are those who become so addicted to Zeal that they spend more of their lives plugged in than out. Sometimes, if their fantasies are too violent or depraved, the government takes an interest, worried that they might pose a threat to society despite Zeal's soporific after-effects. So some go off-grid and take Zeal in unregulated, horrible dumps. Anything for their dreams. Most of them don't live long, spending so much time within the Zealscape they stop eating and waste away. I've always wondered why the government never cracked down on those illegal Zeal lounges. Now, with a sinking feeling, I wonder if it's because letting them starve is easier and cheaper than stasis.

'I know. They have an orderly there, a lucid dreamer, who will be tasked to see how many dreams he can mine and how quickly. There might be more to it as well, but as a Knight, they don't tell me much, and I can't ask questions. I want to stop it, but I can't.'

Because it'd blow his cover. That's another aspect I haven't thought of – how I'll have to see horrible things and let them slide, because to speak up would make me stand out.

I don't want to talk about it any more. 'What are you shoving into my brain this time?' I ask in dread.

'We'll give your brain a rest from Ratel info. Some of the data now will be physical fighting techniques. The rest of it . . .' Unease flickers over his features, and I can feel it mirrored in my own. 'This . . . might not be easy for you.'

'What do you mean?'

'Well, it's to help you with going to Zenith. Help you fit in.'

'You interviewed a hostess?'

His eyes flick away from me.

Oh. Shit. I suddenly understand, and I don't know whether to be hopeful or angry. 'You spoke to Tila.'

He nods. 'Yes. She gave us an interview. For you.'

He's looking for a reaction, but I keep my face blank and still, despite my insides turning to water. 'OK.'

'Are you all right with this?'

What does he expect me to say? Of course I'm not all right with this. I'm not remotely all right with any of this. It'll be the first time I've seen my sister since she was literally dragged from my arms by the police. She's the one who hasn't spoken to me since – for if Detective Nazarin was right, she didn't wish to speak to me. After everything I've discovered about her, everything I've learned she's hidden from me, and everything I know I will learn, will she still look like the same Tila I thought I knew?

'It's what needs doing, right?' I say, with a weak, humourless smile. 'Have to tie off the loose ends before we really go fishing.'

'Yes.' Still, he hesitates. 'If you don't want to do this, nobody is making you.'

'You've changed your tune. What, do you now think I won't be able to do it?' Does he think I'm weak? I don't want him to think me weak.

'No, not at all. I haven't changed my mind in the least. But . . . sometimes, I wish someone had asked me that, the night before I went undercover. Asked me if this was really what I wanted to do, and given me the option to back out, without shame.' His head tilts downward. I can't see his eyes.

'Would you have turned it down?'

'I'm not sure.'

His words frighten me. 'It couldn't be without shame. Not for me,' I say, almost gently. 'I couldn't leave my sister. I might be terrified of what's going to happen. I might be so angry at her for hiding things from me that if she were here right now,

I don't know if I'd hug her or scream at her. But I could never just leave her to freeze. That's not an option.'

He meets my eyes. 'Good.'

Detective Nazarin plugs me into the machine. My eyes grow heavy.

I sleep.

•

Tila's sitting at a table almost identical to the one where I saw all the Ratel people interviewed the last time I was plugged in. It's only been a few days, but I'm shocked at the change in my sister. She seems haggard, and thinner. They've dressed her in a plain, dark blue uniform similar to nursing scrubs. Her short hair is frizzy instead of spiky – prison shampoo, I suppose.

The biggest difference is in her eyes. I've seen it before – she gets the same look when she realizes she has to either start a painting over again or ditch it entirely. The look that screams, *I failed*. It wouldn't matter what I said to her. She couldn't shake that the failure was due to something deep within her. A flaw.

Yet her strength is still there. The bright glint in her eye when she knows she has something the other person wants. I've been on the receiving end of those bright, tormenting eyes before. It could drive me crazy.

Across from her sits Officer Oloyu, the man with the Golden Bear tattoo. I'm half surprised it's not Nazarin for a second; but then, he wouldn't have had time to go see her, wherever she is, interview her, and be back to train me. Oloyu leans forward, but I can tell he's nervous. 'Tell me about the Zenith club, please, Miss Collins.'

Tila plays with a snag of dry skin next to her fingernail, almost as if she's bored. She recites her litany. 'I've worked as a hostess for the last four years. I started in some really shitty clubs, like Gamma Ray. I bounced around a couple of other places, then Sal took me on at Zenith. Right away I knew that was where I wanted to stay.'

She leans back in her chair. She has an audience for the first time in days. After all she's put me through, I find it infuriating that she's still putting on a show.

'That's something I didn't realize going in,' she continues. 'That even though people pay money to go to these clubs, they sometimes still hate you, deep down. Hate that they can't form any genuine connections in real life so they have to pay for you. Or pay for Zeal in the rooms and for you to join in, as they don't have any friends who will link with them. They resent you for it. It can make things plenty awkward, lemme tell you. In Zenith, people are nicer, and really seem to like being around you.'

She'd said something similar to me before, but she'd also shrugged, saying that they loved her too. Love, hate, desire, envy, or simple enjoyment of her company. Sometimes all of it wrapped up together.

'And did Vuk hate you?' Officer Oloyu asks.

That stops her. 'No, I don't think he did.' Her voice is quiet.

'What's the exact specification of your job at Zenith?' Officer Oloyu asks. I can tell he's interested. He's likely never been to a club like Zenith. Not on his salary.

She crosses her arms over her stomach, pulling the fabric tight against her breasts. She knows Oloyu's looking. Her head tilts up, defiant, one corner of her mouth quirked. I know that look, too. 'I suppose – I'll never work there again, will I? I've been called a hooker, a whore, a call girl. All that. Whatever. It's not just sex – sex work rarely is, anyway. I'm their fantasy.' She smiles, and it lights up her wan face. She has reclaimed many of those terms for herself, telling me the words couldn't hurt her if she did. Maybe she's distancing herself from other types of sex work because she's speaking to a police officer. Even if being a hostess is not illegal, she's still nervous. 'These days, so many men and women work all alone, connected to their wallscreens and their small, cramped apartments. They don't seem to understand how to make real friends, or maybe they want some who are a bit less . . . complicated. So they come to clubs like Zenith, where friends, lovers or almost-lovers are all lined up at the ready. There are no expectations, no birthdays to remember or weddings to attend. Connection without attachment. Without strings. Without disappointment.

'So that's what I do. I talk to them. I pour them drinks. I laugh at their jokes. I listen to them. I look them in the eye. Most of the time, that's all they need. They have a nice time, and then they go home to their empty apartments and their wallscreens.'

'And if they need more?'

She shifts in her chair, resting her head on one hand. She's positively chatty, now that she's started. She has a rapt audience in Oloyu, and she wants to entertain. 'It's usually only high-end business people who have enough money to use Zeal in the club. We're exclusive. Best product, best experience, and all the hosts and hostesses are great actors in the Zealscape. For the clients, it's like a mini-holiday in a really expensive virtual reality hotel. The same host or hostess can plug in the whole time, but only if they want to. They get a bonus. Sometimes if they wake up in between fantasies, they'll have physical sex, but that's only if they want to. Same with sex when in the Zealscape. It's not about the sex. Or again, not only about it. It's to feel close to someone, even if it's just for a little while, but still knowing the next day they can get on with their life without any guilt. And the sex is freely given or not at all, and the client can't complain. They all understand the rules.'

And what if they didn't? Would they grow angry? Angry enough to attack Tila?

'And do you stay overnight?' Officer Oloyu asks. He shifts in his chair, probably aroused and uncomfortable with it.

Tila shrugs a shoulder, the movement seamless and elegant. 'Sometimes. Not that often. I have to actually like the person. Want to spend more time with them. Most of the time, I'm happy enough just to stay in the bar and chat and laugh with them. It's a good job. Was a good job.'

She falters, and her mask slips. There's the vulnerable side of my sister. The side that only I see. Then it flits back up, and she's back to figuring out how she can wrap him around her finger. With a dip of my stomach, I realize I've seen her use that expression on me, too.

Here, in the brainload, I finally let myself think what I've avoided thinking for some time now: *has she used me too?* But at the same time, I wonder if it's like back in the Hearth. Where my own mind couldn't be trusted, and Tila had to spend weeks convincing me that we needed to escape. I shy away from that, unable just now to cope with the guilt of how I once believed in Mana-ma unfalteringly.

'And was your night with Vuk an overnight stay?'

She shakes her head. 'No. He liked Leylani for that. I was only a hostess to him.' Her eyes slide to the side, and I know she's keeping something back.

'Right. We need a list of all the people you work with, and what they look like. Your file says you're an artist, so perhaps you can draw them?' Oloyu clears his throat.

My sister narrows her eyes. 'Is this for Taema?'

Oloyu hesitates, as if he's not sure if he should answer. 'This is to help with the investigation.'

She fidgets. 'And I *have* to do it?'

What is she thinking? It used to be I'd always know. She's hesitating, not jumping to help until she knows all sides, works out her advantage. Altruism is not a trait my sister inherited. Not even for me.

When I'm awake, I don't think such nasty thoughts about her. Why am I so cruel when my body is unconscious?

'You agreed you would,' Oloyu continues.

Her mouth twists, but she takes the proffered drawing paper and pencil. She pauses before she draws, tapping the pencil against the table. Why haven't they given her a tablet? Finally, she brings the pencil to paper.

It fast-forwards her drawing, but I stare at her furrowed brow and the way her hair obscures half her face. How many times have I watched her draw?

When she finishes, she holds up the paper. I drift closer, examining the names and the faces. Even sketched in haste, her drawings are beautiful. Dispassionately, Tila gives each name, a short description, and a few key personal details about each person. I feel the information sink into the deep recesses of my brain. As soon as I see these faces in the real world, I'll recognize them.

Officer Oloyu asks her to then sketch and describe the most common clients to frequent the club, especially those she's worked with most often.

At this she finally starts to look concerned. She hides it well enough. But not from me. 'This *is* for Taema. You're putting her undercover, aren't you?'

'I'm not at liberty to say.'

'When you first took me in, you told me you were putting

her in protective custody. You can't do this. Going undercover is too dangerous for her.'

I can't help but bristle. She thinks I'm soft.

Oloyu's mouth twists. 'Why? Because of what you've done as part of the Ratel?'

She scoffs. 'Nice try. No confessions.'

'We already know irrefutably you worked with them. There's no need to be coy. So why isn't your sister allowed to go undercover?'

'So she is undercover.' Her eyes are bright with triumph.

Oloyu's mouth twists as he bites down a curse.

'Gotcha.' Tila smirks and bends over the paper. Again, the strange fast-forwarding as she draws, me unable to turn my 'eyes' away from the quick movements of her fingers holding the pencil. Again, the sketches of men and women appear, their names, their habits, their dreams and desires find a place deep within my mind. I won't forget any of them, even though, if I'd been awake, I'd probably forget about a third of the names.

Officer Oloyu asks my sister more questions, ones that I suspect Nazarin has given him. What is the layout of the club? What sort of food is served? Music played? Cocktail menu? Most popular liquor? A lot of it seems unnecessary. I'm only going to be at the club for an hour or two at most, speaking to the owner, Sal, and to Leylani, the girl who was meant to be entertaining Vuk that night. Still, everything goes into my memory bank.

At the beginning my sister fights back, toying with Oloyu and giving flippant answers. Then she seems to tire of the game and gives him the answers he asks for. By the time the questions end, Tila's visibly wilted, her voice hoarse. Officer

Oloyu thanks her for her time. But before she leaves, she looks at the camera.

It seems like she's looking right at me.

'I don't need saving, Taema,' she says. 'You don't *have* to do this for me. And maybe you shouldn't.'

I can't read her, and it hurts.

She turns and leaves, the door clanging shut behind her. The scene goes dark.

•

When he returns sometime in the night, Nazarin turns off the brainload long enough for me to have a few hours of real sleep. I wake up to the information having settled better within my mind. I still feel tired, as though I've been doing calculus for hours. Brain gymnastics, Tila always called it.

I've had nightmares about my sister. Over and over, I saw her saying that maybe I shouldn't do this. Drawing away from me, her eyes calculating, weighing me up. Maybe she didn't believe I could be her, do whatever she did. Maybe she didn't trust me, that my mind couldn't handle it.

Even despite her manipulations, her games, I couldn't let her go. I could never let her go into stasis without even trying to set her free. She knows that. So why try to warn me away?

Maybe this is even more dangerous than I thought.

I say nothing as I sip my ersatz coffee in the morning. Despite the nightmares, I haven't changed my mind.

The first thing I have to do is send the Ratel a message. Tila is evidently meant to work a shift at the Verve lounge tonight. Nazarin walks me through it. They have untraceable methods of contact. There's a portal on an untracked website where Ratel members can check in. Nazarin knows the code, and he tells me just what to say. I'll miss two shifts: next Tuesday and Thursday.

A message comes back confirming it, and I sign off. The SFPD have changed my VeriChip to show my location as Tila's apartment whenever I'm at the safe house, so if the Ratel do look up my whereabouts, it won't arouse suspicion. Today is Sunday – by next Tuesday, I'll have to go in. It's not nearly enough time to get through all we need to, but it's all the time we'll get.

I go through more brainloading and more physical practice with Nazarin, honing my body and my mind. They give me facial recognition software, to help me recall the faces Tila told me about in last night's session, as well as another program which will help give me instructions if I do get into a physical altercation. I hope I don't have to use it.

Over Chinese takeout ordered from the replicator, Nazarin tells me more about his experiences in the Ratel, though he skitters away from a lot of the explicit details. After two intensive days, I feel more ready than I ever thought I could in such a short span of time.

It's not enough, though.

I still have to change my face.

•

We go to a flesh parlour out of the city entirely.

It was the easiest way to avoid people who might have known me or Tila. The SFPD, the Ratel, Zenith clients, my co-workers – none of them would bother travelling fifteen miles to change their features when there's a flesh parlour on every doorstep.

We take a hovercar over the Golden Gate Bridge flightpath. It's been over a year since I left the city, unless it was for work.

I always mean to explore more, but I've been too busy, usually working on VivaFog machines even at the weekends. When we were younger, Tila and I would take so many day trips from the city. We went up to Monterey, to Santa Cruz, to Berkeley. We'd pack picnics and laze on the beach or in a park, Tila sketching and me reading a book before exploring the shops and the markets. I miss those days.

Nazarin takes us up to Marin, the affluent area where tech workers commute in and out on the underwater high-speed BART. He looks tired. Working for the Ratel by night and training me by day means he's functioning on too little sleep. Rejuvs help, but they're not a substitute for proper sleep. The flesh parlour he's chosen is one of the best in the nation. When the hovercar touches down, my nerves refuse to behave, no matter how much of Mana-ma's training I use.

They're going to change my face.

Not much, but enough. I keep trailing my fingertips along the lines of my brows, my nose, my cheekbones. Nazarin notices but does not say anything. I swallow, putting my hands down. It's not much of a change. And I can always change it back.

We sit in the waiting room. I press my nails so hard into my palms that they leave marks. I'm shaking and I can't seem to stop. Nazarin lifts his hand, pauses as if tempted to take it away, and then rests his hand on top of mine. He gives me a look out of the corner of his eye as if to say: *is this too much? Should I not?* His hand is warm, the palms calloused. I can see the small scars, pale against his skin, which is only a little lighter than mine. I put my other hand over his and squeeze, grateful for the comfort, before taking both hands away.

A nurse pokes his head into the hallway, his scrubs white and crisp, and makes eye contact.

'I'll be right here,' Nazarin says.

I give a sharp nod. I follow the nurse through the bright, white walls and into a room. There's another Chair within. I've had my fill of these things the last few days. They'll knock me out, and through gene therapy and a scalpel, I'll wake up with a different face.

'The doctor will be with you in a moment,' the nurse says, helping me into the Chair and plugging the wires and electrodes into me. I'm still shaking. He gives me something to calm me, until I feel as if I am floating. I listen to the beeps of the monitors and my mechanical heartbeat. It reminds me of that first day I awoke from surgery.

The door opens. In my addled state, for a moment I wonder if it's Tila, coming in to find me, IV trailing behind her.

It's only the doctor, coming to change my face to molten wax and mould me into my sister. The SFPD doctored the files, to make it seem like 'Tila' went back to her original face, and has now changed her mind yet again.

He comes forward and asks if I'm all right. I nod. I'm floating, high above myself. He sends me to sleep, and my last thought is that actually, I don't mind this. My face will change, but I'll look exactly like my sister again.

EIGHT

TAEMA

I'm wearing Tila's clothes.

They're nothing like my usual attire – a coverall for scurrying up a VivaFog antenna, listening to its gentle hum as it draws the fog into its whirring machines, or a dress similar to the ones we wore in the Hearth at weekends, plain, comfortable, unremarkable. All the things this dress is not.

I have never cared much for fashion. We both experimented when we first arrived in the city, excited by the freedom of being able to choose our own clothes; of not having to make everything and alter the torsos; of wearing different clothes from one another. We had fun peacocking ourselves and dyeing our hair, having moving tattoos inked on our skin, playing with materials of strange textures and cuts. I soon grew bored of it, erasing the tattoos, letting my hair return to its brown corkscrew curls, giving the fancy clothes away and buying things that felt more familiar.

Tila erased all the tattoos but one, a stylized broken heart on her thigh in a Polynesian style (we are part Samoan, as well as black and white), the two pieces not quite connecting. Doesn't take a psychologist to figure out the symbolism of that. The waxworker gave the same one to me this afternoon, and it twines from my upper thigh down to my knee.

I swallow, tugging the dress down over my hips. It's a slinky number, the skintight material shimmering purple in one light and midnight blue in another. The boots I wear have thin, faux-leather ribbons that wrap around my legs until they reach where the tattoo begins. I've rubbed lotion with small gold specks all over my legs and arms (the tattoo is already completely healed, along with my face; the marvels of modern medicine), and my limbs glow.

My hair is gone, chopped short, the texture changed from curly to straight and the colour to bright blue. They've mapped the colour to my genes, so I don't have to worry about roots. My nose is shorter and wider, and turns up at the end. My cheekbones are slightly higher, my lips a little fuller, my chin a little pointier. It's subtle, very subtle, but I don't like it. It makes me more conventionally pretty, and more anonymous in this city of perfect faces.

I paint my lips dark purple and outline my eyes in blue. I tip the ends of my eyelashes with silver dust. I have dressed like midnight to go to Zenith. That's me in the mirror, but I can't see myself. Tila looks back at me, but it blurs. Tila. Me. Someone in between. A stranger. I turn away from the reflection.

I slip on a coat and leave the safe house, the door snapping shut behind me. I take the MUNI, like Tila would have. As I enter the station, in the corner of my vision I see Tila's name and the amount of the fare deducted from her account. It's true. I am officially my sister.

I step on the train and it takes off. I stare at the strangers, lit green by the algae of the tunnels. I feel like people are watching me, but perhaps it is merely because I am showing more leg than I usually do, and humans are biologically programmed to stare at bare flesh.

I'm nervous about meeting the owner, Sal, and Leylani. I fear what they will say, what I might find out. I fear I will disappoint Nazarin and be a poor undercover agent. More than that, I fear I will fail to find out what they need to know to free Tila, and she will go into stasis. Or worse, that I'll find out things about her that I'll never be able to forget or forgive. This is the point of no return. For both of us.

I leave at the correct stop and walk along Montgomery Street, the mica in the sidewalk sparkling.

I feel very alone as I look up at the TransAm Pyramid dwarfing the surrounding buildings. It was rebuilt a century ago, based on the original Transamerica Pyramid but twice the size, all glass and quartz-concrete. Evidently in the foundations, echoing the original, there are thousands of dollars' worth of credit chips instead of coins, thrown in for good luck as the concrete was poured over it. I hope I can take a bit of the luck, though evidently it didn't work for my sister.

I take a deep breath and enter the lobby, nodding at the doormen before making my way to the glass elevator.

I have to let Taema fall away again. I have to become Tila.

I'm alone in the elevator – most of the other hosts and hostesses won't arrive until later. I rise above San Francisco, staring down at the sparkling lights in the growing darkness.

'Hey, Echo,' the hostess at reception greets me. Too brightly. I fight the urge to narrow my eyes. Does she know? Does everyone know what actually happened in the back room three nights ago? Are they all being bribed a king's ransom to keep quiet, or did the SFPD really manage to keep it under the radar?

I nod to her, and the brainload intel tells me her nickname is Pallua. All the hostesses choose nicknames. Psychological distancing, I guess. I was touched when I found out Tila's was

Echo. Now I'm the echo, a thin replica of Tila. Even my serviceable walk in heels is different from her feline prowl.

Through my VeriChip I'm able to bring up Tila's employee file, but Nazarin had the owner expand my access. I bring up internal communications from the club over the last few days into my ocular implant overlay. Since the incident, nobody's used the back room where the crime scene was. Everyone's been told that a high roller's rented it out for a long, exclusive Zeal trip.

I've been staring blankly into the distance for too long. Pallua looks down at her bright red nails. She's a prototypical hostess – perfect features, perfect body, golden-brown skin, her hair a riot of purple, blue, and green. Tattoos of peacock feathers glow around one shoulder, snaking towards her breasts, which are on display in her low-cut gown.

I wave vaguely, and something stills in the other girl's face. A crease appears in the smooth skin of her forehead, tense lines deepening next to painted lips. She swallows and busies herself with the reception desk. I rub my clammy palms discreetly on my dress, avoiding eye contact with the few other hosts and hostesses who are milling around Zenith waiting for their shifts to start.

'Your client's waiting,' Pallua says, her bright smile back in place. 'Cute, too.'

'Thanks.' I smile, hoping it reaches my eyes.

The door to the back room where I'm meant to be seems to stare at me, waiting for me to enter. I pause in front of it, take a deep breath, and the scanner reads my VeriChip, identifying me as Tila.

The door swooshes open. I step through and the dim lights brighten. Detective Nazarin waits for me, perched on a luxury sofa. He must have come in the rear entrance. He looks like a thug in the dark clothing that doesn't quite obscure his shoulder holster.

The room is simple, but everything screams of wealth. I don't look at the round bed in the corner. There's a well-stocked bar, and a wide expanse of polished floorboards and low-pile rugs with abstract designs. Zeal Chairs are parked discreetly in the corner of the room.

Next to him is Sal, the owner of Zenith. He's a tall man, thin and elegant. He wears rings on all his fingers and a dark green suit, the cravat at his neck a vivid blue that matches his eyes. It looks old-fashioned, almost Edwardian, but then Tila said he was like that: picking bits of the past and interweaving them into his look. Sal is one of the few people that Tila genuinely respects. He took a chance on her by taking her on at the club, trained her up, and always treated her well. She spoke of him sometimes, over dinner. He's meant to be fiercely protective of his employees and he prides himself that Zenith has had no scandals, no violence.

Until three days ago. I feel nervous that he knows about the switch between me and my sister. How trustworthy is Sal, really? I asked Nazarin about it earlier, right before I went up to change into Tila's clothes.

'From all we can tell, he's fairly clean,' he reassured me. 'There's nothing connecting him to the Ratel. There's a chance of course that he's covered his tracks well, but it's a risk we have to take. For an exorbitant sum, he's keeping very quiet.'

'Tila told me once that he prides himself on keeping his word,' I responded.

Detective Nazarin nodded. 'We have to hope that's true.'

The door closes behind me. 'We thank you for your assistance with this investigation, Mr Kupka,' Detective Nazarin begins.

He waves his arm. 'Call me Sal, please. And we all know it's in my best interests as well as yours.' He looks me up and down. 'My, but you do look just like Tila. It's nice to meet you, Taema.'

I incline my head. 'It's nice to meet you, too. Tila's spoken well of you.'

I notice he doesn't call my sister Echo. The man before me looks polite, and a small smile rests on his face. I glance around the room, swallowing. There's absolutely no trace of a crime scene, but this is the room where it happened. Did Tila sit on that very sofa on the night that tore both our lives apart?

I lean against one of the pillars of the room. It's rude, but I can't bear the thought of sitting down. Why are we meeting in this room, and not the others? I bring up the logs again. Ah. Because all the other rooms in Zenith are booked, and even if Sal wants to help us, he doesn't want to eat into his profit.

I look towards the floor-to-ceiling windows overlooking downtown San Francisco. The bay is tinged its usual phosphorescent green, the lights of the skyscrapers blue and white. Hovercars wink and blink as they weave their way through them.

'So,' Nazarin begins, and I turn. 'Was Vuk Radke a regular client of Zenith?'

'He'd come maybe once every other month or so,' Sal replies. He seems at ease, relaxed. I find that unnerving. A dead client was found in this very room, my sister covered in his blood, and he doesn't seem to mind at all. I swallow.

'Did he often see Tila or Leylani when he was here?'

'Leylani was his favourite hostess.'

'Did he stay over when he visited?'

'Every other time. So perhaps three times a year.'

'Have you had any dealings with him outside Zenith?'

Sal shrugs a shoulder. 'Here and there. I go to charity events. Sometimes he'd be there. We were on friendly enough terms, I'd say.' A flicker of emotion on his face: regret.

'Why wasn't Leylani here three nights ago?'

Sal takes a cig out of his breast pocket and sucks on it, the end briefly glaring red. He blows out the mist. 'Said she wasn't feeling well and had to cancel her shift.'

'Has she missed any work since?'

'No, she came in yesterday. I haven't told her anything about this.'

'Can you tell us more about what happened three nights ago?'

Why am I here? I want to ask them. I don't want to listen to this. I don't want to hear this slick, shiny-suited man dispassionately explaining the night my sister's life fell apart – and mine, as a side effect. Yet I'm curious, too, and find myself drifting closer. Adrenalin courses through my veins. I force myself to calm down.

'I found her. The room sensed the blood on the floor and it triggered an alarm. My employees are protected – they are never to be harmed. Fantasies like that are reserved for the Zealscape, but even so, we don't allow violent sexual fantasies unless the host or hostess consents to it. Tila was always very clear she was not interested in that, and their engagement that night was not likely to be sexual.'

My shoulder muscles are so tense they feel like they could shatter.

'So I was concerned, obviously, and came in personally. There was Vuk on the floor, with Tila sitting next to him, covered in blood.'

I close my eyes, but the vision is too vivid. I open my eyes to see Sal's blue ones focused on me, curiously watching my reaction. I release the tension in my body, but cross my arms over my chest.

'Did she say anything to you?' Nazarin asks.

'She did.'

I frown, and Nazarin nudges him. 'What was it?'

Sal pauses, as if trying to remember. 'Ah. Yes. It was something like, "He is the red one, the fair one, the handsome one. He came from the Earth and now he returns. The faces keep changing." I had no idea what it meant. And I still don't. I wasn't sure if she actually saw me, or was muttering it to herself. Does it mean anything to you?'

'No. Not yet. Why didn't you tell the police?'

He looks down, slipping the cig into his pocket. 'Slipped my mind.' Clearly, it hadn't. It reminds me uncomfortably of Tila. I wonder why he's giving it to us now.

I can tell Nazarin wants to play the hard cop, but restrains himself – that wouldn't work with Sal. 'What did you do next?'

'Called the police. And it was one of the hardest things I've ever done. I debated letting her go, you know. I don't mind admitting that. Tempted to let her wash herself off and disappear into the night. Dispose of the body. Clean up the blood.' He sighs. 'But I knew I'd never get away with it, and much as I care for Tila, I didn't fancy sacrificing my livelihood for her. So I locked the doors and pinged the police, instructing them to come in the rear entrance and make as little fuss as possible. But then Tila threatened me with the knife, so I let her go. She grabbed Vuk's coat by the door to cover up her blood-soaked dress and escaped out the back. I think Pallua saw something, or realized something was wrong, but she hasn't said anything.'

That explains her nervousness around me, at least.

'Is Leylani here tonight?'

'Her shift should start soon, yes. Will you be telling her what happened?'

Nazarin shakes his head. 'No, I don't think so. No need. But we'll probably observe her and the other clients briefly before we go home.' He nods at me. 'She's going to work a shift like you agreed. Try her hand at being her sister for a few hours. Let the other hosts and hostesses know that she's going away to China with her sister. Then she'll be gone.'

'But Tila's never returning,' Sal says, his voice bland.

'No, I find it unlikely she'd return to your employ, or that you'd let her.'

Sal considers me again. 'Very well. This will be interesting, I suppose.' He tilts his head and points at his eye. 'I'll be watching.'

He smiles, but I'm not reassured.

'It'll be interesting to see how similar you are to your sister,' he continues, standing and making his way to the window as well.

I say nothing. What is there to say?

'We appreciate your cooperation, Sal,' Nazarin says, standing.

Sal looks around at the room and sighs. 'I'll have to redecorate. I got all the blood out, but the memories are still here. All of this will have to go.'

The blood drains from my cheeks. Something terrible happened here last Thursday, but the idea of it all disappearing and being replaced with more bland, expensive furniture is hard to take. The room that changed everything for me will continue to be just another back Zeal lounge in the Zenith nightclub.

'One last thing,' Nazarin says. 'I recommend you check your Zeal supply.' He nods to the Chairs in the corner.

Sal starts. 'Why?'

'I can't give details, but we have reason to believe that someone may be responsible for tampering with Zeal in certain lounges. If you find any anomalies, buy fresh stuff. Check it every time.'

'We've had people plugged in since Friday morning. Why didn't you tell us this?'

'We only just found out about it. And it's unlikely, but I wanted to warn you to take precautions.' I am pretty certain the thought has only just occurred to Nazarin. The lines around his mouth are tight. I wonder if he's thinking about the night he had to provide security to the off-grid lounge. Tila told the SFPD she hadn't been asked to lucid dream within Zenith yet, but it's only a matter of time. Was Vuk sent here to tamper with the supply, and is that why Tila came to blows with him?

'I'll check the Zeal daily myself,' Sal says.

'Good. Please let us know if you find anything unusual and send a sample directly to us for testing. No one else.' His voice sharpens.

'Of course not,' Sal says, all smooth charm.

With a last look out the window at glittering San Francisco sprawling below, the owner of Zenith walks away, and Nazarin and I are left alone.

'Are you OK?' Nazarin asks.

'Yes, I am.' It's not a lie: my fingers shake a little, and I really want to get out of this room, but I'm holding it together. Mana-ma's training is in full effect, and I've dampened my emotions enough to function. I ask if he thinks Vuk has tampered with the Zeal here and mixed or replaced it with Verve.

'I don't know. I don't think so, but I'd rather warn Sal than risk the supply being contaminated.'

'Right. So am I to stay for the whole six hours of Tila's shift?'

'We'll see how you get on. If you like, we can leave early.'

'Are you going to be posing as a client?' I ask.

He pauses and turns to me. 'Yes. I'll be watching along with you. It could be someone here knows more than they let on. Pallua, maybe.'

I nod. 'OK.'

He moves close and slings an arm around me, and I start in surprise.

He leans close enough for me to feel the heat from his skin. 'We have to sell it, don't we?'

I consider, and then nod, pressing my hip against his, resting my hand against the warm dip in his waist. It feels strange, to be touching a near-stranger like this. It happens so rarely for me, these days. It's also a comfort. I want to lean closer to him, breathe in the scent of his skin.

In the Hearth, there was a lot of touching. Not necessarily sexual – people just touched each other more. Greeted each other with hugs, or casually threw an arm around someone else. Here in San Francisco, people are more reserved. Maybe that's why so many feel the need to come to places like Zenith, where they can pretend the barriers between people are thinner.

I shake my head, patting my shorter hair and trying to gain a bit of composure. The door swooshes open. We sidle through, still touching. Nazarin settles into his role with an ease I envy. He laughs, warm and deep in his throat, his hand lingering on my hipbone. I feel the strong ropes of muscle on his back beneath his shirt. I resist the irrational urge to stroke my hand down his spine.

We make our way through the club, which is busier now.

Beautiful men and women with perfect bodies, perfect faces, perfect clothes, laughing their perfect laughs and drinking their perfectly delicious drinks. The minty mist of cigs fills the air, mingling with the flattering blue and purple lighting. There's that *sameness* to so many people in San Francisco and the rest of Pacifica. When anyone can choose to alter their appearance at will, so many tend to go for the same bland, symmetrical features. Now I feel like I'm a little more like them.

I still miss the simplicity of certain aspects of the Hearth. Knowing that if you looked at someone, it was the face and body they were born with, shaped by their experiences. Everyone in San Francisco wears a mask.

Having said that, there's plenty about the Hearth I don't miss one little bit.

We perch at a round table. I access my brainloaded info and lean towards Nazarin to say, 'What'll it be to drink?'

'Gin and tonic,' he replies.

I go to the bar and order two drinks, which will be added to Nazarin's tab. The bartender's name is Ira, and he smiles at me as he gives me the glasses. We chat for a bit, but Tila didn't give much information beyond his name, so I'm glad when other hosts and hostesses come up with their drink orders.

I take my gin and tonics to the table. It's synthetic, like all alcohol in the city. No damage to the liver, non-addictive, no hangovers. I pass Nazarin his, and we clink our glasses together.

I take a cautious sip and fight the urge to make a face. It lacks the peppery, juniper punch of the true stuff. Not that we had that much of it at sixteen in the Hearth. But at the start of each season, anyone could have a glass or two (or ten, in the case of Mardel) of whatever had been brewed for the celebration. The blueberry vodka from the summer we were fourteen was my favourite.

I wonder if Nazarin's ever tried real alcohol. If he was raised in cities, in this supposed perfection, and if he's ever seen through the pretty illusions to the ugliness beneath. He must have, within the Ratel at least. I shudder.

We keep to ourselves as the bar fills with more attractive people. I match the faces and names to the sketches that I gleaned from Tila through the brainload. Eventually, I spy Leylani. She's tall, with razor-straight dark hair to her waist. She has tanned skin, bright green eyes, and wears small shorts and heels so high my ankles hurt just to look at them. She's obviously with a client, an Afghani woman in a hijab, wearing a long, dark blue dress with bell sleeves.

'Invite her over here,' Nazarin mutters under his breath. 'Pretend to be Echo, and then eventually find a way to get her on her own. See what you can learn from her, if anything, and then afterwards, tell me everything.'

I feel a little rush of excitement. After all the fear and uncertainty, the cramming and drilling and brainloading, here I am, about to truly pretend to be my sister to a stranger and start investigating what happened to her. One step closer – hopefully – to setting her free and finding out the truth of what she's done.

I approach Leylani and smile confidently at her. Tila has given me more information about Leylani than any of the other hosts or hostesses – she spoke about her for at least half an hour in the brainloaded conversation, recounting past conversations and what she knew about her. Although Tila was friendly with her co-workers, I don't think she was actually close friends with any of them. I've certainly never met any before. I've never questioned why that was; I assumed she wanted to keep her personal and work life separate. Now I wonder if there was more to it.

It seems like there was always more to it, when it came to my sister.

I smile at Leylani. Below the surface, I'm afraid that she'll immediately realize I'm an imitation of the Echo she knows.

Leylani gives me a hug and a kiss on the cheek. 'Echo!' she exclaims. 'So good to see you. This is Sarah,' she says, introducing her client.

'Won't you join us?' I ask, gesturing to the table where Nazarin lounges. I can see the look of appreciation that Leylani and her client give him. They agree, and follow me to the table. Soon we're joined by others: a host called Boa, and his client, a businessman named Graeme.

At first I'm nervous, but as more time passes and nobody stands up and proclaims me a fake, I gradually relax. I wouldn't say I have fun – drinking SynthGin and chatting with strangers, playing the part of my sister to try and save her life, isn't exactly my idea of a party. However, my confidence that I can pass for Tila is growing, just as Nazarin hoped. When I'm pretending to be my sister, the fear doesn't paralyze me – Tila's confidence seems to seep into me. I sit up straighter, I laugh more, even try my hand at flirting the way I've seen Tila do. While I still feel unsure about my skills at wrapping people around my finger, I can see the effect my new assurance has on others. If Taema was sitting here, awkward and disinterested, it would be a different story – but as Tila, they listen to me, make eye contact, respond and seem to enjoy my company.

When Leylani stands up to go to the ladies' room, I go with her. *Such a cliché,* I think as we totter through the now-crowded club at the top of the TransAm Pyramid, *going to the bathroom to try and bond with another girl.*

Once the door of the employees-only bathroom shuts, Leylani's work smile falls off her face. 'Are you all right?' I ask, reaching out and touching her shoulder.

It undoes her. Her face crumples, and she starts to cry. I stare at her, a little lost. What would Tila do? Tila would be warm, both to offer comfort and to gather the information she wanted. I wrap my arms around the young woman, making soothing noises, stroking her silky dark hair. Leylani sobs against my neck, tears falling on my collarbone to trickle to my scar.

'What's wrong?' I ask, rocking her gently back and forth. It feels strange to comfort a stranger, yet I find it calming too. I haven't hugged or touched anyone since they tore Tila from my arms – unless you count sparring with Nazarin or pretending to be his hostess. It seems that I need the close contact almost as much as Leylani does.

'Sorry,' she mumbles, pulling away. She wipes her hand. 'Sorry, sorry, I'm being so silly.'

I pass her a plush, pink towel from the railing and she daubs her face and hiccups.

'You're not being silly,' I say. 'Not at all. Come on, Ley, tell me what's wrong.'

Leylani collapses on the settee against a wall, and I perch beside her, hoping nobody else will come in to interrupt us.

'A client's missing, I think,' Leylani starts, hesitantly. 'I haven't seen him in a few days.'

If she's speaking about Vuk, I'll have to tread carefully. 'That's not that unusual, right?'

'For most clients, of course not. But . . .'

'He's become more than a client,' I finish, my heart sinking. She must see him outside of Zenith, if he only comes here every other month.

'Yeah.' She sniffs. 'I even went to see him today but no one answered. They say he's gone out of town, but he wouldn't just *leave* without telling me.' She turns, her watery green eyes boring into mine. 'I've been wanting to talk to you tonight anyway. You saw Vuk on Thursday, didn't you?'

My tongue freezes in my mouth. 'Y-yes,' I say. The palms of my hands begin to sweat.

She doesn't look away. 'Did he seem disappointed that I couldn't come? I really wanted to, but I was . . . really unwell.' She looks down and away, and I frown. What is she hiding?

'Yes, he missed you,' I say, hoping that was true. The files the police have on Vuk were relatively light, and Tila refused to speak about him. She pretended she'd never met him before, but I knew that was a lie. *Don't think about Tila just now.* 'Kept asking about you,' I add. 'He didn't seem to be interested in my company at all. He – he left early.'

Each word hurts to say as she looks at me with such hope. I wonder what Vuk was like. He was meant to work for the Ratel, but that didn't mean he was incapable of kindness. Of love. And now he was gone; supposedly killed by my sister.

'What was wrong with you, on Thursday?' I venture.

'I . . .' She hesitates, but she wants so desperately to tell someone that she blurts her secret in a rush. 'I'm pregnant.'

I let out my breath in a *whoosh*. 'Oh. Wow. Congratulations,' I say, my voice flat despite my best efforts, feeling sucker-punched.

'I know you never wanted kids, Echo, but I'm so happy about it. I was going to tell him on Friday, but I haven't been able to find him. I'm so worried. Should I go to the police?'

The police already know where he is, I want to say. 'I don't know, Leylani. Maybe wait a little longer to see if he shows up. Maybe he had to go on an unexpected business trip, and he'll be back any time now.' The lies come surprisingly easy to me, despite my distaste for them. Maybe Tila and I have that in common, after all.

She nods, wiping her eyes. She gives a last sniff and then goes to the mirror to fix her make-up. I sit there silently, waiting for her to finish. When she's done, I give her another hug. She clings close to me.

'It'll be all right,' I say to her.

'You can't promise that,' she whispers, and I stifle a gasp. It's exactly what Tila said to me on Thursday night.

'No,' I say with a sigh, thinking of my sister in jail – with me as her only hope. 'I can't promise that at all.'

•

When Leylani and I return to the tables, our work faces are back in place. Leylani smiles brightly, kissing Sarah on the cheek before going up to get more drinks. I settle next to Nazarin again, brushing my elbow against his.

He leans close, pressing his hand against my cheek. 'Find out anything interesting?' he murmurs in my ear. I smile demurely at him, nodding. He takes another sip of his drink.

We only stay a few more hours, and it exhausts me. I don't know how Tila does it, staying switched 'on' for so long, vigilant for every client's needs. I follow the others, offering cigs and drinks. Later on, we dance, Nazarin holding me close, the bass thumping through my metal ribcage, his hands warm on my waist. I speak to Pallua casually, but if she knows anything about what happened on Thursday, she doesn't let it slip.

I've drunk enough SynthGin that by the end of 'my' shift, the world is fuzzy around the edges. Sal has told everyone this is Echo's last shift, and I bid everyone sloppy farewells, saying I'll send them pings from China and I'll miss them all. I lean on Nazarin as we take our leave. There are a few raised eyebrows at Echo leaving with a client.

'I hope you've enjoyed your time at Zenith,' Pallua says to him as we pass the front counter.

Nazarin reaches into his pocket, grabbing a handful of credits and passing them to her. They disappear into her dress.

'Oh, it's been a cut above,' he says to her, slurring his words very slightly, before we saunter out into the night.

•

We take the MUNI back to the safe house. The green light of the tunnels makes me feel ill and I bury my head in Nazarin's shoulder. Whatever his cologne is, it smells nice. He puts his arm around me. Are we still playing a part, or is he genuinely comforting me? I don't know, and in that moment I don't care.

Nazarin has us get off before the safe house stop and take another train too far before we circle back. I have no patience for the circuitous route, but it makes me nervous just the same. Does he really anticipate people trying to follow us? As we trudge up the steps to the pastel Victorian house, I'm exhausted.

When we're inside and Nazarin is making the strongest coffee he can from the replicator, I tell him about Leylani and Vuk. I kick off my heels, leaving them under the table. He's surprised, and a little sad. I suppose it's reassuring to see that even a hardened undercover cop can still feel for a girl who's lost her lover, the father of her child, and doesn't even know he's dead yet. I doubt he felt very sorry for Vuk, though.

The coffee does nothing to wake me up; my eyelids are drooping as I sit at the table. I trudge to the Chair and climb in. I don't even have the energy to clean my teeth or wash the make-up off my face. Nazarin dutifully plugs me in and draws the blanket up over me, and I'm asleep before he leaves the room, to brainload still more information on the Ratel. Instead of dreams it's endless interrogation scenes, reams of numbers, facts and dates settling deep into the folds of my brain.

Flitting behind all the lessons is my never-ending unease. It's almost like I can sense Tila hiding in my mind, just out of sight and reach.

Do you really think you can find out what happened? Do you really want to know? she seems to taunt.

And my mind can't answer her.

NINE

TILA

That tablet we found didn't last forever, of course. Without charging, something we were unable to do even if we'd known how, the battery only lasted a few months before it died. I felt so sad when the screen went blank for the last time. For a while, I'd had access to a completely different world, and then it was taken away. We were left back in Mana's Hearth, isolated and alone.

Taema even came around. Well, somewhat. She stopped pretending to look away from the tablet, although she never suggested topics to research. We were lucky nobody ever found us with it. We wouldn't have been punished, really, but people would have treated us differently – as if we'd wronged them by showing curiosity about life outside, when life inside was supposed to be so fucking perfect. Disappointment can be worse than anger. They'd also have been wary, wondering what we'd learned. But I knew Mana's Hearth for what it was now, and Taema did too, even if she didn't want to admit it.

It was a prison.

So, you see, this isn't my first time in a cell. I spent the first sixteen years of my life in one, even if it was surrounded by trees and flowers.

I started to notice little things. Then bigger things. How we were kept in the dark about so much. And then there was the Meditation.

I thought it was a normal part of life. That everyone on the outside must do it as well. And some do, but not the way Mana-ma did it. Three times during the week, and then just after Sunday service.

It was always the same. We'd line up, quiet and patient. One by one, we'd each go up to Mana-ma and open our mouths, a little like a Catholic communion. She'd place a small tablet on our tongue. It tasted bitter and earthy. I always wanted to make a face, but forced my features to stay blank like everyone else. The pill dissolved on my tongue, and the world would grow brighter yet hazier at the same time.

We'd lie down in the meadow, or in the church if it was raining. We'd hold hands in one large circle. And we would lucid dream. Mana-ma would guide us through visions so realistic that when I awoke from them, sometimes the real world didn't seem like the true one. The dreams were meant to be calming, with visions of nature.

'A mountain stream,' Mana-ma would say, and all of us world work together to create the perfect one.

'A sunrise,' she would say next, and the sky of our mind's eye would bloom so bright.

The trouble was that collective dreaming hurt. Every nerve ending would feel as though it were on fire. Tears would leak from all our eyes. We'd cry out as each vision shifted. Yet we still did it. Day after day, week after week. I think she did it to bring us closer together, and because she could. Out there, with no Chairs, no needles, we made our own dreamscapes.

We'd do it on our own, too, without whatever drug she pumped us full of (it wasn't Zeal, I know that much), and it meant we never woke up unable to remember our dreams.

It made me and my sister incredible lucid dreamers. I still do it now, especially now that I'm in my cell. I can close my eyes, drift off, and then take off into the sky and fly. It's pretty much the only thing I can ever thank Mana-ma for.

We only had Confession once a week, different days for different people in the Hearth, but it was always just after Meditation. We'd be weak with the comedown and pain and drugs, so we'd tell her everything.

Of course, now the whole ritual seems strange, but at the time it was considered a normal part of our routine. Even with our newly gained knowledge, my sister and I didn't question it too much – until Adam grew sick. Then we couldn't pretend Mana's Hearth was anything other than what it was. What it is.

Adam was born missing the lower half of his left arm, though it never troubled him. I've learned, since escaping the Hearth, that people within are born with a higher chance of disabilities. Like me and Taema. My guess is that it's either because of the bloodline being so intermingled in a small populace, or because the drug Mana-ma gave us for Meditation did something to babies in the womb.

Anyway, Taema and I had both been sweet on Adam. We still hadn't quite figured out how romance would work, with us being conjoined. I guess we thought we'd deal with it when the time came. I think we would have been happy enough sharing Adam, if he liked us.

That might sound odd to some of you, but I don't care. San Francisco has poly relationships aplenty, even if none of them are with conjoined twins. The Hearth would have accepted it just fine.

Adam caught an infection when he was tilling the fields, which most of the men and some of the stronger women took turns with. He cut himself on the plough and didn't wash it properly, or something. It shouldn't have been fatal. If he'd had access to a needle full of magic medicine from the city, he'd have been right as rain in less than an hour. But whatever infection Adam caught was more stubborn than our medicine could handle.

He grew worse, and was moved to the Wellness Cabin. People weren't really allowed to go see him, but Nurse Meadows allowed us to peek in through the window. He was happy to see us. I liked to think he was sweet on us too, but that he liked me best. We brought him some grapes. His leg was all wrapped up and propped up in a sling. He was sweating and pale. I hated to see him like that. But he didn't seem on the brink of death or anything. I figured he'd get better in no time. Just needed some rest.

'How are you feeling?' I remember Taema and I asked at the same time. I hated when we did that. We'd have the exact same tone, timing, everything, as if we were creepy echoes of each other.

Adam smiled weakly at us. 'Been better, T-and-T,' he said, and we both fought down blushes. I'd always liked the joint nickname, understanding we were two, but also one. And he didn't even know we called each other T when we were alone.

We threw him the grapes, and he tried to catch them in his mouth. He missed, or we missed, more often than they landed in his mouth, and soon the floor of the cabin was littered with green grapes. We collapsed into laughter, clutching our sides.

'You cheered me up and no mistake,' he said when we'd run out of grapes. We reached through the window, each of us holding out a hand. He reached out with his one hand and clasped both of ours in it. I remember his skin was so warm. Too warm.

'We'll come visit you every day until you're well,' we promised.

But he was gone the next day.

Considering the rudimentary medicine, there weren't actually that many deaths in Mana's Hearth. His was such a shock for Taema and me. We couldn't cope. He was there, and then he wasn't. We'd never see him again. We lay in bed, arms wrapped around each other's shoulders, foreheads pressed against each other, just sobbing. It wasn't fair.

There wasn't a funeral; we didn't really have them in Mana's Hearth. We didn't gather around a corpse and plant it in the ground, or burn it up. I knew they did something with the body, but not exactly what. People mourned, and people would still talk about Adam and others who died and say they missed them; but there'd be no celebration, or wake, or anything like that.

Seems backwards too, doesn't it? Looking back now, I see that, but the Hearth doesn't celebrate beginnings or endings. We focused on celebrating the day-to-day life that continued. The passing of seasons had a special meaning for us, but other holidays that lingered on from past religions we had nothing to do with. In the Hearth there were no Christmas trees or Hanukah menorahs.

I tried to convince Taema to get a Christmas tree, the first year we were living in San Francisco, but she didn't want one.

'We're never going to believe in it,' she said.

'Does anyone? It's a tree in the living room with pretty lights, and there aren't many Pagans around any more. Santa Claus and a tree have nothing to do with Jesus. And not a lot of people seem to believe in him here, either.'

'Shouldn't we celebrate winter?'

'Why? We don't believe in Mana-ma or her God any more, either.'

She had no answer to that.

Back then, it was almost time to celebrate summer. Taema and I dragged our feet as we made our way to the church, wearing our best dress. It wrapped around our conjoined torso, but we'd taken the time to have it fit around each of our waists. Taema had green ribbon and I had blue. The skirt swished around our legs, edged with hand-stitched lace.

We stood near the back, since the pews were too uncomfortable for us to sit on – the hard wood dug into our sitz bones. We still hadn't gotten over Adam, and we were feeling pretty morose. Nobody even spoke about him – as if he'd shamed us by getting ill enough to die. I looked at the backs of all the heads of the people sitting in the church, and realized a lot of them might not even know that Adam *could* have been saved. And that somehow made his death even sadder.

Adam's death was the first thing that made us really think about leaving. Strange, isn't it? We'd willingly let ourselves be mentally tortured, but that wasn't what made us want to run. It was a boy dying who could have been saved.

Mana-ma was up on the pew at the front of the church. She was the minister, the wife of God, the mayor, everything. She always wore a plain black robe, as if she were mourning all the sin we were surrounded with in the outside world. Everyone in the audience was wearing white with just a little bit of colour. Summer was the season of prosperity and warmth – yes, I know, not that it ever really got that cold in winter, compared to, say, Minnesota – and it was a reason to celebrate. The mushroom crops were growing well in the greenhouse and the fields were lush; aside from the small issue of Adam, health was pretty good. No drama. If there ever was anything, it was swept under the rug to be whispered about after lights out.

So we celebrated summer. We sang the old songs, like 'Let's Live for Today', 'Everlasting Love' and 'Wonderful World, Beautiful People'.

None of you reading this will probably have heard of these songs, but I still love them, despite everything. They remind me of the good parts of the Hearth. The bees buzzing, the scent of flowers in the warm breeze, the feel of the water and sand from the lake between my toes. We had a bunch of vinyl, and a record player that they must have replaced part by part over the years. Taema and I sat in our room and listened to the music a lot. I miss music, here in this cold, dark cell.

When we moved to San Francisco, we tracked down a lot of it with some of our early wages, going pale at how much it cost on the original vinyl. So we bought the songs on the modern players, but they didn't sound the same. We still listen to 'The Sound of Silence' together, remembering all we've lost.

On the day we celebrated summer, we sang loud and clear, our voices lifting to the rafters, and Mana-ma read from the Good Book.

It was a little different, that particular summer celebration. Mana-ma mentioned Adam. She decided she wanted to say something, so she could. That was the hierarchy; if we were sad and wanted to remember him, we couldn't publicly without her say-so. We couldn't change anything in the Hearth, because we didn't hear the voice of God.

'I know that we do not acknowledge endings often,' she said. 'Especially at the beginning of such a warm and prosperous season, but God spoke to me last night. He told me that today, we should have a moment to mourn Adam.'

There were quiet murmurs in the crowd.

'The loss of Adam reminded me of all the other losses we've had through the years. God told me that they are never truly gone. He wanted me to remind you all that those we have loved have returned to the Cycle, to bloom elsewhere in the universe. Remember that in times of sadness, and remember the light. Every time you see the glory of God and nature, remember that those we loved are still a part of it.'

We all bowed our heads for a moment and thought of Adam. Taema and I felt better after that. It was better than pretending it never happened, or never really acknowledging it. Maybe Mana-ma finally realized that.

We went outside and we each rested a hand on the sunflowers now thriving in the summer heat, their yellow faces tilted towards the sky. We thought of Adam.

Afterwards, though, we could not escape the meadow and another Meditation. It was the last thing I wanted to do, but there were no excuses granted unless we were ill. We queued, and took our bitter medicine. We lay on our sides. I looked into Taema's eyes. We both already felt the effects of the drugs, our eyes heavy and lidded. Our whole body tingled.

I'm not sure if Mana-ma realized that this was a side effect, but Taema and I were even closer when we took those drugs. I swear I could read her every thought, her every feeling. We all connected, but no one connected more than me and her. It was as if we did become one person. Even Mana-ma noticed.

I sort of wish I could do that again with Taema. It'd be so much easier to explain everything that way, but I'm too afraid of what she would find.

That Meditation was like all the others. Mana-ma's voice rang out, clear and reverberating. The sun beat down on us. We closed our eyes and held hands, and created worlds with our minds inhabited only by us as our bodies stiffened with pain.

This time, though, the pain was less, which made the dream sweeter.

It ended up being a turning point. We were all becoming better at lucid dreaming. The better we were, the less pain we felt. By the time we left the Hearth, Meditation barely hurt at all.

Afterwards, it wasn't our day for Confession. As we left the meadow, people paired off. For some, the drug made them incredibly horny afterwards. Sex was another way of connecting, a way of expressing God's love, and it was fully supported if all parties were willing. Most marriages were open, though not all. Our parents only had eyes for each other.

Taema and I never did that. We didn't feel ready yet, and no one minded. We wandered through the path into the forest.

The forest was better than any church for me. Nowhere ever felt as holy to me as when Taema and I looked up at those gigantic redwood trees, smelling bark, dirt and leaves, the light filtered through so many shades of green. Mushrooms sprang up beneath the ferns, bright yellow like banana slugs. The sunbeams would catch the swirling motes of dust in the air. Overhead, birds called to each other. I do miss that. In the city there are the skyscrapers of trees, but you know it's manufactured. I miss raw, unfettered nature.

We went to our hollowed-out redwood tree to be surrounded by that perfect smell of charred wood, damp and greenness.

That was when we first felt it.

The irregular jump of our heart in our chests. The painful squeeze. The faintness.

We gasped. We left the tree, and staggered to the forest path. We had to make it back to camp. Our vision blurred and we couldn't breathe. I clutched Taema hard. I was so scared.

'What's wrong?' she wheezed. We could see the roof of the church in the distance. It seemed so far away. 'What's happening?' Her head lolled on my shoulder.

'Don't you dare faint on me, Taema,' I said, pinching her cheeks until she squeaked and her eyes opened wide. 'If you faint, we're a tortoise on its back. Come on, Taema. Come on.'

Somehow, she stayed with me. When we were a little closer to the main town, it felt like we couldn't go any further. We leaned against the fence that lined the path. It was warm, the sun beating down on our hair. I couldn't breathe. Up ahead, we saw a figure. For a second, delirious with pain and lack of oxygen, I thought it was Adam. That he was dead, coming to take us into God's loving arms to begin the Cycle again. But then the figure cleared and I saw that it was Dad. We collapsed, and he started running.

TEN

TAEMA

I have a crick in my neck from sleeping in the damn Chair.

I sit up, managing to unplug myself. Again, it looks as though Nazarin turned it off for me a few hours ago, so I could have at least some proper sleep. It's, as ever, not enough.

It's another day of training. Of fighting Nazarin, a quick pause to eat, and then training some more. My muscle mods have responded well to the extra stimuli, and already I can feel that I'm the fastest and strongest I've ever been. After another shower and a giant meal to replenish my energy reserves, I ask Nazarin what we'll be doing today. I crunched the numbers. Tila was arrested Thursday, I agreed to go undercover on Friday, I told the Ratel I'd be missing two shifts on Saturday and I went to Zenith on Sunday. Tila's shifts are Tuesday and Thursday afternoons for two weeks, and then Mondays and Wednesdays the next two. She went to her last Thursday shift before she went to Zenith and everything went to shit. My next shift is next Monday. One week until I'll have to go in as my sister. It doesn't feel like anywhere near enough time, despite how much information I've had crammed into my brain already.

'Today I'm to show you the crime scene,' Nazarin says.

That brings me up short. 'What?'

'Forensics have finished with it, along with the autopsy. I had them make a recreation holograph here. We can view it upstairs.'

My eyes rise to the ceiling of their own volition. 'Now?'

'Now. If you're ready.'

I feel like he's testing me. 'All right.'

He starts up the stairs and I follow hesitantly. The old wood creaks beneath my feet. At the top, he turns to the right and opens the first door.

'Wait,' I say. I suppose I'm not ready. I need a moment. I'm about to see a recreation of a gruesome crime scene. One that my sister might have created. I've never seen large amounts of blood before. 'Will it look . . . real?'

'At first glance, it'll look exactly like the crime scene, down to every last angle and splash, but remember: it's not. It's only a hologram.'

A flash of Tila gripping my shirt. *Not my blood*. I rub a hand over my new face, composing myself. 'Right. OK.' I push open the door and step inside, Nazarin following me.

A transparent plastic bubble lies over most of the open floor, mirroring the one that would have been put over the real scene as soon as the authorities arrived, and just after Tila had apparently fled the scene. A huge blood stain lies within, wet and glistening, as if it's just been spilled.

I fight down my gag reflex. It is so much blood.

Almost all five litres of it, some of it soaking into the white rug, ruined beyond repair. Just a few days ago, Tila had been in that original room in Zenith, entertaining, joking, flirting, laughing. I can imagine it so clearly now, after being there last night. What happened? What changed?

I want to understand everything – whether she'd known this Vuk she'd attacked, and if so, how, and from where. I move around the bubble, Detective Nazarin watching my every reaction. His brown eyes have flecks of gold in them.

I don't know what he wants me to find – if there is anything to find. There are empty glasses on the replicated coffee table. Most are overturned or shattered, but a wine glass is still upright and unbroken, the imprint of lipstick on its glass. Purple, the same shade I painted my lips last night. I try to remember if it was the same colour Tila was wearing on Thursday night. I only saw her for those few moments before they took her away. The make-up, half-smeared across her face by rain, tears and wiped-away blood. It must have been purple lipstick.

'Have they done the autopsy?' I ask.

'Yes. They sent through the report and a possible recreation. I can show it to you. Are you sure you want to see it?'

I nod, even though watching it is the last thing I want to do.

He takes out his tablet and places it next to him on the sofa. He presses a button and a little holographic display comes up. He could have streamed it right to my implants, but I appreciate him putting it on the tablet instead. It gives me the illusion of distance.

Three-dimensional holograms appear and, unlike the solid-looking crime scene around us, these are as transparent as ghosts.

Vuk is laughing, knocking back champagne. He has a similar look to Nazarin – bulky and muscular, with short-buzzed hair. But where Nazarin's features are strong, Vuk's are almost delicate, the features too small for his face. He sets down the glasses, chatting with his friends. Tila perches next to him, her legs crossed, as she sips from a wine glass. It's a recreation from the infrared sensors at Zenith, so their expressions are only the bare minimum – a huge smile or no emotion at all. One by one, the other people leave, until Vuk and Tila are alone.

The image wavers. Ostensibly this is where Tila and Vuk speak, but the program does not know what was actually said that night. Normally, the cameras in Zenith would, but in the Zeal lounges, clients can pay extra for privacy. When the image clears again, Tila holds a knife. Vuk turns back to her with the drink and she attacks him. He manages to fend her off. She cuts him in a glancing blow to his wrist, which accounts for the blood splatters to the left of the large bloodstain. She manages to stomp on his instep and her knee flies up between his legs. He crumples, and Tila doesn't hesitate. The knife flashes and goes beneath his ribcage and up, right to his heart. She rips the knife down, widening the wound, and Vuk bleeds out on the floor. She has no expression on her face. She bends down to the coffee table in front of her, driving the knife into the wood.

The holographic image goes dark.

I'm shivering, despite the perfect temperature of the room. It can't be true. There must be some mistake. The infrared sensors were tampered with. It wasn't actually my sister. It was someone else. Something. I can't believe that Tila would do that, with no hesitation, with such precision and skill. There has to be more to it. There has to. Because if not, then I have no idea who that woman is I just watched kill someone in cold blood.

'That's only one way it could have happened, right?' There's a note of pleading in my voice, and Nazarin looks at me with a hint of pity. I turn away, not wanting to see it.

'Right. From infrared we know there were two people in the room, but their body movements weren't mapped. This is their best guess as to the sequence of events, judging by the wounds, but the order could be off, and we have no context.'

I ask myself, in reality, how different could it be? Someone stabbed Vuk and ripped him open that night, and no one else was in the room but my sister. He didn't do it to himself. I push the doubt away. It's too much. I've never been more thankful for Mana-ma's training. 'What more can you tell me about Vuk?' I ask. The information I have on him from the police download is scant at best.

'Pretty sure he took out at least one person a week for the Ratel, between his other duties. With all his schmoozing, he could gain access to places many members of the Ratel couldn't. For all that, though they trusted him, I doubt he was in their very inner circle, though he was hoping to be. He'd had a lot of mods and upgrades to his body, according to the autopsy.' He pauses to scroll through the medical chart. 'Muscle implants and nanobots, almost an entirely new face, a prosthetic hand with skin grafts, new teeth. He even changed the shape of his ears. So whoever he was before, he wanted to make sure we'd never know, not even in death.'

I swallow. 'Can I . . . go into the crime scene for a closer look?' I ask, my mouth dry.

'Yes.' His eyes go distant as he accesses the controls with his ocular implant, and the bubble pops. Carefully tiptoeing around the blood, I ignore the body, as that's not what catches my attention. I look closer at the coffee table.

My fingertips hover over the items on the table.

'Can I move things?' I ask.

'Yeah.'

I reach out and move the glass with the lipstick print. I can't feel it. It's like I'm holding air. There's a chip on the rim. It had fallen over, but Tila had put it to rights before she left. Below where the glass was is a hasty carving of five points. Next to it are a few other scratches. The glass falls from my hand and slides back to its original position on the coffee table.

'She didn't stab the coffee table. She carved it,' I whisper.

Nazarin looks over the crime scene notes. 'They noticed those. Five points. That's the symbol for the Hearth, isn't it?'

'Yes.' I haven't seen that simple design in a long time. Why did she leave it here? She hates the Hearth as much as I do.

'We couldn't make any sense of these, though,' Nazarin says, nodding towards the dashes and dots, almost like Morse code. 'No language or code we could figure out.'

I shrug, not wanting to tell him, looking at other things.

'You understand those markings,' he says. 'I can tell.'

I debate lying, and then decide it's pointless. 'It's an alphabet Tila and I made up when we were children, so we could write notes to each other nobody else would understand.'

'She knew you'd see it.' Detective Nazarin scratches the stubble at his chin. The muscles of his bicep flex under his shirt, and I'm reminded of how much larger and stronger than me he is. He's suspicious. And why shouldn't he be?

The fact is, I'm just as flummoxed. Why would Tila leave me a sign? And why *that* as a sign? She had no way to anticipate how all this would play out . . . did she?

I feel sick. I back away from the blood and the scratched coffee table, breathing loudly, and move to the bay window, looking out over the cloudy San Francisco day. The sailboats are coming into port, the hovercars leaving and arriving into the Embarcadero to their sundry destinations. The sun is setting, and everything glows that soft pink and purple of approaching dusk.

Detective Nazarin glides to my side, silent. I press my forehead against the cool glass of the window. Throughout it all, my mechanical heartbeat has barely quickened. Somewhere out there, Tila is in her cell, and her heartbeat is more or less in time with mine.

'What does it say?' Nazarin asks. He's close to me now, but his voice is gentle, and his breath puffs on the back of my neck, smelling of spearmint. But the gentleness is a ruse – underneath he's all steel.

I could lie. Tell him it means something else, and they'd never be able to follow the path any further. Then I could try and do it on my own. But I wouldn't be able to, would I? If Tila is involved with the Ratel, then I don't know the first thing about how to deal with them.

Nazarin does.

'"MIA",' I say, still turned to the window. My breath mists the glass. With a fingertip, I write the letters in our secret alphabet.

'And what's that? Missing in Action?'

'It's not a what. It's a who. Mia. The woman who took us in after we left the Hearth.'

'Why do you think she wrote that name? Where can we find her?'

I shrug, wrapping my arms around myself. I want to go home and close my eyes and wake up and have everything fixed.

'She's an apostate of the Hearth. Like us. She got Tila into hostessing. Used to be one of the best in the city. But now she's a Zealot. We can find her at the Mirage in the Mission district.'

'That's a shithole.'

'Yeah. But the Ratel haven't tampered with the Zeal there and replaced it with Verve?' I ask.

'Not that I know. Fuck.' He rubs his hand over his shaved head. 'If they have, it's dangerous to go there. Someone could be watching.'

I say nothing.

'She'll be there now?'

'She's always there.'

'Then let's go.'

Nazarin accesses his implant, and the crime scene hologram disintegrates into nothing.

•

When people think of Zeal, they don't think of the dark, dingy Zealot lounges. They think of brainloading. They think of the bright, shiny lounges in the nice parts of the city, a place for people to go to let out a little steam and return to the real world, refreshed. They think of the drug that keeps the city largely crime-free, and provides a little fun along the way; all thanks to Sudice, Incorporated. The company I used to work for, along with so many other people in San Francisco. I've never thought before about how many tendrils the company has within the city, and how much the government owes it for its many inventions.

Those dark Zealot lounges, though; those, most of the city tries not to think about, and they do a very good job of forgetting. They don't sit and imagine those who might be the worst criminals, serial killers or rapists or abusers, locked in the Zealscapes, too out of it when they come out to think about anything except plugging in again. The people who go there have dreams so dark they don't dare go to the beautiful lounges. They say the government can't properly eavesdrop on dreams, not in great detail – but not everyone believes that. So they go underground.

Mirage is one of the worst Zealot lounges, and that's where we head in the hope of finding Mia.

Mia. I haven't seen her in a year and a half. She took us in when we left the Hearth. She was like a second mother, or an aunt. We lived with her for years – the only other Hearth apostate, or at least the only one we met. We loved her, and she loved us, but she was always troubled. In and out of the nicer Zealot lounges, but when her Zealscapes became darker, Police showed up at our door. She cleaned up her act until she almost seemed like the Mia we knew when we first came to her.

After the last time she relapsed, and disappeared to an off-grid Zealot lounge, both Tila and I washed our hands of her – at least, I thought we both did. It wasn't easy, but I couldn't watch her self-destruct. She turned down all my efforts of help, of therapy, of rehab. There was no going back for her. Not this time.

I still felt guilty about that, but I couldn't help her if she wasn't willing to help herself.

Nazarin thankfully has the night off with the Ratel, though he'll be there all day tomorrow. There's still a chance we could be recognized if the Ratel have visited Mirage before. We're both wearing masks, like a temporary visit to a flesh parlour. They fit perfectly over our features, light enough not to be noticed but enough to trick the camera drones, and we can peel them off when we wish. There's a small chance the orderlies might notice, if they look too close, but so many there are overworked and underpaid, I think we'll be all right. My mask itches.

We take the MUNI down to the Mission district. By the time we arrive, night has fallen. The streets here are full of wavering holographic ads. They assault the senses as we walk down the street: men and women wearing next to nothing, displaying their wares, licking their lips suggestively and calling out to us what they're offering. Loud, tinny music blares from each of them in a cacophony. If anyone still had epilepsy these days, they'd have to avoid this whole neighbourhood.

I feel the beginnings of a headache flaring at my temples. Shielding my eyes with my hand, I make my way through the glare, Detective Nazarin at my side.

The ads grow darker, more reds and blacks and deep blues. They flicker, leaving the streets in darkness but for the street lights. There's no sense of welcome. The people who come here want only the dreams they're too afraid to dream in a proper Zeal lounge.

Mirage is at the end of the street. An ad of a palm tree in a desert ripples over the front of the building. A stone sphinx wavers in the distance, and as we watch, it opens its mouth and yawns before gazing at us mysteriously. The windows are shuttered. I don't want to enter.

In that building I know there are dozens of people strapped into Chairs, wires poking from their veins, their eyelids twitching as they live out their dreams.

I wonder what causes some people to fancy more violent dreams than others. Some say that people who are predisposed to crime have different brains, like damage to the prefrontal cortex. That means that the two hemispheres of the brain can't communicate properly, and aggressive impulses are in overdrive. Ticking time bombs.

I never bought that, but it's the endless question of nature versus nurture. Free will versus predestination.

Sudice developed Zeal at first as a virtual reality game in which to act out fantasies. They discovered the extra benefit by accident, that if people acted out violent urges, when they came out, vicious tendencies were dampened. The neural pathways are reworked, suppressing the amygdala, or the prehistoric 'lizard' brain we've had since we crawled out of the ocean. It worked on those with so-called 'violent' brains, and those without. Overall, people were calmer, happier. Perfect citizens. Zeal lounges became all the rage.

Sometimes I wondered what Mana-ma would have to say about all that.

The first time doing Zeal is a rite of passage, one me and my sister missed. When we tried it later, it was anti-climactic. All the dreams seemed but pale echoes of what we saw during Meditation back at the Hearth, or when we closed our eyes each night.

'The government and Sudice are both terrified of Verve, aren't they?' I ask.

'Yes.'

'The same drug, but stronger, more powerful, a better high and people wake up not calmer, but angrier. More prone to lash out. San Francisco has peace now, but how peaceful would it be if people weren't kept dampened by Zeal?'

I wonder if I'm pushing too far, saying that. It sounds critical of the government, his employers. Nazarin only smiles sadly. 'I don't want to find out, do you?'

I don't say the other thing I've wondered, from all the information I've brainloaded: what happens if the government gets hold of Verve? Dangerous as it is, it lets people see into other's dreams remotely. And what if there's more it can do?

'How did the Ratel develop Verve?' I ask.

'We think it's Ensi himself who designed it. The genesis is from Zeal. He took it and twisted it somehow. The man is a genius.'

'And where did he come from?'

'That's the question, isn't it?'

'How deep do the Ratel run?' I ask out loud, more to myself than to Nazarin, but he answers.

'Deep. They've got their little tendrils everywhere. Right

now, in a way we're fighting a losing battle. Getting rid of the Ratel completely will likely never happen. What we have to do is have the upper hand, choke off their stronghold before Verve becomes too widespread.'

I understand. 'And the easiest way to do that is to get to Ensi. Cut off the head.'

He gives me a sidelong glance. 'Exactly. This is the best chance we have.'

A sentence from one of the captured men in my brainloads comes back to me: *There are some who don't agree with Ensi. Some who want him dead.* It had seemed obvious to me – of course every organization has those who resent their leaders. The Hearth taught me that. But now I wonder if there's more. 'Unrest?'

'Yeah. That's my primary goal. I'm seeing who might be thinking of causing trouble and gently encouraging them, but in a way they don't suspect me as the cause. Division will make it easier to find a chink in their organization. Not easy, let me tell you.'

I rub my temples, the flashing lights of Mirage getting to me. 'This keeps getting more and more complicated.'

'That's how I've felt ever since I went undercover. The deeper you go, the crazier everything seems to be.'

'But you've still never met Ensi.'

'No. I'm too much of a Knight. There's an upcoming party they've invited me to, though, this weekend. He's meant to be there. After two years, I might finally meet him.'

'I'm not sure how much I'll be able to help with all of this.'

'To be honest, a lot of it depends on how far Tila has delved into the inner circle. The fact she rose to working in the Verve lounge so quickly is impressive, but it's difficult to see the bigger picture. Sometimes she seems to be a relatively little fish, despite being a dreamsifter, but other times I suspect she's almost reached upper management.'

A shiver runs down my spine, and my flesh breaks out into goosebumps. Tila not only involved with the Ratel, but in deep? Without telling me, without asking for my help. Why has she done this in the first place? What does she hope to gain? Money? Tila's never struck me as greedy, not in that way. What, though, do I really know about her? She's been living a whole different life. I bite back a sob.

'Let's go see what this Mia can tell us, if anything,' he says.

'And if she's plugged in, we have to go in? Instead of waiting for her to come out?' That's the part that gives me the biggest pause. I don't want to go into her dreams and see what her deepest, darkest desires are. I had a second-hand view, watching her relapse, and that was awful enough. Zealscapes can be unpredictable – especially, I hear, in these off-grid lounges. For some, they're almost like the real world. For others, they're twisted nightmares. I fear Mia's will be more like the latter.

'Depends on how long she has left. If she has more than twelve hours, we can't wait that long.'

'And if we do go into the Zealscape, you think I'll be able to lucid dream,' I say, looking nervously at the entrance to Mirage. Most of the time, when people plug into other people's dreams, they're carried along helplessly by the other person's fantasy. They can't really change much. It's why most people do it alone. Nazarin hopes if I can lucid dream I might be able to affect things, at least a little. The problem is, lucid dreaming might not always change the reality in a way you'd like.

'Yes. This serves two purposes. Question Mia in the Zealscape, if we must, and see how you fare within the dreams. I'm certain you'll be able to manipulate things, judging by how you've integrated the brainload.'

'Maybe.' I'm noncommittal. And frightened. Years of training at the Hearth – it should be easy. I have flashbacks to those shared dreams. I can almost taste the bitterness of the drug as Mana-ma gently placed it on my outstretched tongue.

'Will it hurt?' I ask. I remember so much pain. And mental pain is so much more painful than the physical.

'It hasn't hurt me.'

'And you haven't become addicted?' That's another fear. I only tried Zeal once or twice, but it's been years ago. What if I've changed since? What if I go into the Zealscape and come out of it to discover my brain is flawed and that I'll want nothing more than to go back in? It's a stupid fear, perhaps. I've seen scans of my own brain. I know all synapses fire normally. That doesn't mean I couldn't still love the violence. That doesn't mean I couldn't grow to need it.

'No,' he says. 'I'm not addicted. But I think about the Zealscape, sometimes. The power. The freedom. I think anyone who's tasted it does, even if their mind isn't hardwired for violence.'

Nazarin's been undercover for a while. I'm sure he's had to commit violence, and not just as a false member of the Ratel. As a detective, he'll have seen things, done things that would be difficult to forget.

'OK,' I say, squaring my shoulders. 'Let's do this.'

My nervousness doesn't fade as we walk towards the door. I've never been in a Zealot lounge, and I've no idea what to expect. I wonder what Mia knows. If anything. I can't help but wonder if Tila wrote Mia's name on the table to send me off the path and keep me out of harm's way. It's the sort of thing she would do.

Nazarin knocks on the door and exchanges words with the guard behind the hatch, a man with a face that's lost a fair number of fistfights in its time. I can't hear what they're saying, but the man looks me up and down, assessing me. Does he think I'm an addicted Zealot? The door opens with a metallic groan.

'Come on,' Nazarin says, holding out his hand. With the barest hesitation, I take it and duck inside.

The Zealot lounge is dark, with red lights leading the path to the back. The front is the waiting room, but dim enough to obscure faces. Zealot lounges do not scan your VeriChip at the door. You pay with actual coins. Anonymity guaranteed.

We wait our turn. Nazarin goes up to the woman behind the bulletproof glass of the counter. She's chewing gum, blowing bubbles and popping them wetly. They murmur through the intercom, too low for me to hear. The addicts near me twitch in the darkness. Their fetid breath floats through the air, their fingers spasm on the fabric of their clothes. A woman leans close to me and smells my neck.

'You're new to this,' she whispers. She's lost most of her teeth. Her glazed eyes stare at me above dark bruises.

'First time,' I manage, fighting the urge to lean away.

'I don't know whether to be envious or sorry for you,' the woman says. She could be my age, but she looks older. Her skin hangs from her wasted muscle. Her hand clutches the coins for her trip.

I lean away from her, wondering what this woman does in her Zeal-fuelled dreams. I'm sure if I knew, it'd make the hair on the back of my neck stand on end.

Nazarin returns. 'Come on,' he says. 'We're up.'

'It's my turn,' the woman says, but weakly, as if all her fight has fled. She stares at the wall. I can feel the other Zealots' eyes on me, even if I can't make out their faces.

'I'll see you in my dreams soon enough,' the woman says, her voice distant.

'I don't doubt it,' I say, shivering.

I stand, and Nazarin takes my elbow, leading me through the dark.

An orderly is there, wearing a reassuringly white lab coat. It's less comforting when I'm close enough to see it's grimy about the cuffs. 'The woman you wish to speak to is in too deep to take her out,' he says.

My muscles stiffen.

'How long until she can come up for air?' Nazarin asks.

The orderly's eyes unfocus as he checks his ocular implant. 'Fourteen hours at the absolute minimum.'

Shit.

'We don't want to wait that long.' A sly passing of credits from Nazarin's hands to the white-gloved orderly's.

'Like I say, I can't take her out without killing her, and I doubt you want that.'

That's an option? Good God.

'But I can put you guys in a shared dream with a small dose, if you want,' the orderly continues. 'You'll have to deal with a lot of crossover, but you should be able to speak to her if you really go for it.'

I knew this was a likely outcome, but I'd been hoping to avoid it, yet it all has a feeling of inevitability. Deep down, I think I knew I'd have to visit Mia's dreams tonight.

Nazarin senses my dismay and leans close. 'The sooner we interrogate her, the sooner we can get to the bottom of this. You can find out what Tila was up to.'

Cheap ploy, Nazarin, but effective. 'Is it dangerous?' I whisper.

'Of course it is. But you'll be fine. You'll be in control.'

'You're lying.' I follow him down the corridor anyway.

•

Within minutes, I'm strapped into the Chair. It's different from a brainloading Chair. Bulkier. More wires. It feels like a cage.

We're in the same room as Mia, in Chairs on either side of her. Nazarin paid extra for privacy, so the fourth Chair is empty. I turn to look at Mia. She looks so small, with so many wires poking out of her arms and neck. People who sign up for long trips have to be catheterized. Her mouth is pulled into a faint grimace, showing yellowing teeth. The wrinkles in her brown skin are deeper, the cheekbones more prominent. She's wasting away, like so many Zealots have before her, and so many others will. She doesn't eat enough, doesn't drink enough, and eventually, her body will give up. The government doesn't step in here, though they're meant to care for each and every citizen. How many people truly realize this is what's happening, right under their noses? Why isn't anything being done?

It's a very small percentage of people who become addicted to Zeal on their first try. Those that do come out and are completely changed by what they've seen. What they've done. They can't wait to plug in again and be who they are in their dreams. Real life can cease to have any meaning. If they have money, they fritter away their savings. If they run out, they receive unemployment, and the amount they receive is just enough to keep them in Zealot lounges. They spend enough time in the real world to eat some NutriPaste, perhaps clean themselves, go to the bathroom, and then they're back to their nearest Zealot lounge, huddled in the darkness, waiting for the cold prick of the syringe to send them back to dreamland.

I still can't help fearing I'll like the dreams so much that I become someone who can commit murder. Someone like Tila could be.

No. Don't think about that. But that recreation of a holographic Tila stabbing Vuk, wrenching the blade up into his heart, haunts me just the same.

The orderly puts on a mask. It's just for show – for all of Zeal's dangers, there's no risk of infection, even in a shithole like Mirage. He plugs us into the slots on the wall, starts up the program.

'Ready?' Nazarin asks. Lying supine, his face doesn't look so harsh. His features look almost tender.

'Ready as I'll ever be,' I say.

The orderly has connected the wires on our Chairs, so that we'll feed into Mia's program when the drug hits us. Couples and such will do it sometimes, so that they can revel in the Zealscape together. The thought makes me sick. 'Sweet dreams,' says the orderly.

I feel the prick of the syringe.

Then we're gone.

ELEVEN

TAEMA

I don't like the inside of Mia's head.

Everything in the dream world has a soft quality of washed-out grey and muted reds, blues and browns. I'm standing outside a building, gazing up at its broken windows. It's a scaled-down version of the tower complexes in San Francisco, all steel, concrete and glass, five stories tall instead of fifty. The sky is dark, the clouds bruised black, blue and purple. Warm wind blows my hair, and the air smells like a storm is about to break. I'm wearing the mini-dress I wore to Zenith, for some reason, and the straps of leather dig into my legs. I can see, hear and feel everything, but it's dampened in the way of dreams.

'Nazarin?' I call out, but there's no answer.

Up above, the angry, frozen sky rumbles. Rain begins to fall, and my dress is soaked, my hair plastered to my head. Like Tila on Thursday night. Shivering and alone, I go into the house. Mia will be inside. Some part of me feels it.

The lobby of the minuscule apartment complex is empty. Crumpled leaves on the ground crunch beneath my feet. I climb the stairs, following the vague prickle of intuition that leads me to the top floor.

I hear the screams first.

The door opens for me into a barren room as long as the building. The concrete floor is cracked, the paint on the walls peeling off in layers. Exposed wires hang from the ceiling, and a flickering overhead light casts a harsh light on the two figures before me.

One is Mia. She's strong here, as she no longer is in real life. Her bare arms ripple with muscle, the fitted jumpsuit hugging her full breasts and thighs. Her hair is long, like it was in Mana's Hearth before she left when Tila and I were eight. But she is a long way away from the gentle woman in soft dresses that I recall. This Mia's face is twisted in rage and bloodlust, and she's wielding a scalpel stained with blood.

I shudder, my hand involuntarily going to the scar beneath my dress. Mia's tool falls, and she bends over. My eyes finally rest on the other figure.

It's Mana-ma.

Our former leader has collapsed to the ground. She's alive, breathing hoarsely. The black robe she wears is heavy with blood. On her back, she gapes at the cracked ceiling, her mouth opening and closing. Mia has cut out her tongue. It lies next to her like a dead fish.

I cry out, stumbling away.

Mia pauses in her terrible work, her eyes meeting mine. Her face goes slack in surprise.

'Taema.'

I'm dressed as Tila. I have her face, and her tattoo snaking down my thigh. Despite this, Mia still recognizes me.

'Why are you here?' she asks. 'You've never been in my dreams before.'

That's a comfort, I guess. She's never wanted to kill me. Mia's covered in blood, and the broken shell of a replica of the woman who leads Mana's Hearth cowers beneath her.

'Mia. Something's happened to Tila. I need your help.'

'You're . . . not part of the dream?' Mia seems confused.

Mana-ma gives a strangled gasp, more of a high wheeze. Without batting an eyelid, Mia brings down the scalpel into Mana-ma's neck. The colours of the warehouse grow brighter, sharper, until they're hypersaturated. I step back, horrified.

Without realizing what I'm doing, I focus on that mental state I found while in Meditation at the Hearth. The clear, calm stillness. 'Stop,' I say. Mia's eyes widen, but her hand jerks back, taking the scalpel with her.

'You don't tell me what to do! Don't make me do what I don't want to!' she shrieks.

Did I make her do that?

Blood spurts out of Mana-ma, and once the blood – the reddest blood I've ever seen – leaves her body, it turns from scarlet to black. The dark oil rises, covering Mana-ma's corpse, and then the figure collapses into a puddle. It reminds me uncomfortably of the spread of blood of the crime scene recreation.

The scalpel is still in Mia's hands. I hold up my own hands, spread wide, to look unthreatening. 'No, I'm not part of the Zeal,' I say. 'They couldn't pull you out, so I took a small dose and came in.'

Mia shakes her head. 'I don't know if I can believe that. They all say they're real when they're not. Either way, you shouldn't have come. You're too innocent for the Zealscape. Especially mine.' Her face creases in a grin, and I take another step away. She is utterly transformed from the woman who took us in just after the surgery, when we were weak as kittens and just as innocent in the ways of the world. I remember the way she pushed my hair back from my face, kissed my forehead goodnight. She took us to museums on weekends, patiently explaining so many things to us that we didn't understand. Mia, my second mother in many ways, is looking at me like she wants nothing more than to stick that scalpel in my eye.

She shakes her head again, mystified. 'Can't believe a girl who escaped the Hearth would ever step foot somewhere where they mess with your brain. Didn't you have enough?'

'Didn't you?' I counter.

That same sly grin. A gesture at where Mana-ma's corpse had been. 'Do you really think I actually escaped the Hearth? It's always here.' She taps her temple, and then considers me. 'Maybe it's still in you, too.'

My breath hitches. I don't want to talk about the Hearth. 'Tila's in prison. She's been accused of murder.'

That penetrates through her Zeal-fog. 'Out there?'

'Yes. Real murder. I'm trying to prove she didn't do it.'

I have to cling to the hope that she didn't do it, even if the crime scene recreation left so little room for doubt.

'So why come here?' Mia asks.

'She . . . wrote your name at the crime scene. She led me straight to you. You tell me why, because I have no idea.'

She shrugs, the scalpel flashing in the light. 'Don't know.'

Even in this twisted dream world, I know she's lying. I can't read her as well as Tila, but we still lived with her for years. I heard her, thrashing in the dark, on the other side of our bedroom wall, unable to forget the Hearth when she closed her eyes. She never told us about her dreams, tried to hide them as long as she could as we adjusted to our new, separate lives. It was because of Mia that Tila and I became halfway productive members of society just before she ceased to be one herself.

'Bullshit,' I say.

She cocks her head, but she's unnerved. Her eyes dart to the side, the tip of her tongue snaking over her dry lips.

'Why did she really send me to you?' I ask. Outside the strange rain grows heavier, thrumming against the window. A flash of green lightning casts Mia in a sickly glow, making her look for a moment like the drug addict she is in the real world.

The black oil bubbles and rises, moulding into a new figure.

It's Tila.

She's wearing her favourite dress, green like the other-worldly lightning outside, or snake scales. She looks at me and holds out her arm.

'T,' she calls. I can feel the steady thump of my mechanical heart beneath my metal breastbone.

'This isn't mine.' Mia's voice is harsh. 'You're affecting my dream world now. With your own memories and fears.'

'How? I don't feel like I'm doing anything.' Shared people aren't meant to be able to change the dreamscape much at all if someone has plugged in first. If it's someone else's dream, Zealscapes are meant to be like reading a script, or watching a film on a wallscreen, except with more sensory detail. I didn't concentrate, like I did to have Mia pull the scalpel away. I've never experienced anything like this.

'Fuck if I know. I never share my dreams. I'm always here on my own.' She's shifty, though, her shoulders hunched. She's keeping something back. Mia holds out the scalpel. 'Take this. Maybe you have to exorcize her.'

I can feel her fear spiralling from her, belying her blasé words. She doesn't like that I've changed her dream, much as she didn't like it when I caused her to pull the scalpel out of the Mana-ma apparition.

My fingers close around the blade, but I don't harm Tila. How could I? How could Mia think that I would, even hopped up full of Zeal?

'Tell me why Tila sent me to you,' I say.

Mia rocks back on her heels, shaking her head. 'Get rid of her first. You're ruining it. This isn't my *dream*!' Her last word rises to a shriek, the whole room tingeing red with her anger.

The anger infects me. It pulses through me, as insistent and inevitable as my mechanical heartbeat. Mia's not giving me what I want. I need answers.

Tila's apparition gazes at me impassively. I ignore it. The irrational anger bursts and I rush Mia instead, knocking her down. She feels almost insubstantial beneath my hands, as if I see her healthy self but feel the wasted version of her that's plugged into the Chair. I hold the cold scalpel to her throat. Mia swallows, and the blade nicks her neck, a small trickle of blood running down the column of her throat to pool at the hollow of her clavicle.

'Tell me, or I'll make both your dreams and your reality a living nightmare. I'm working with people who can make life very difficult for you.' It's a half-bluff, but it's the only card I have.

'You're working with them, too?' she gasps. I press the scalpel slightly harder and she winces. I don't understand how pain translates to her inert body on the gurney, but she's scared, and that's enough.

'Working with who?'

'The Ratel.'

'You're working with *them*?' I ask, incredulous.

'N-no!' Her wide eyes dart to Tila's apparition. '*Her*.'

'You think Tila was working with them? Tell me!' The anger still pulses through me, a roiling, dangerous thing. Have I ever been this furious?

'I didn't mean to tell him,' Mia whispers. 'I didn't want to.'

'Tell who what?'

'About Tila. It's my fault.' She begins to gasp, almost choking in the intensity of her sobs. I feel a twinge of pity for her, for who she used to be, but I squash it down as low as it'll go. I press the scalpel slightly harder.

'Tila found something out, and I got scared and told him. He'd never have known. All for a steady supply of Verve. I fucking hate myself. I can never escape him. Never escape. Never.' After that she can't say anything more, sobbing so much that she hiccups. The drug is also taking a stronger hold, the lucidity fading. Her back arches and her eyes roll up in her head.

'Stay with me, Mia!' I shake her. 'How did they give you Verve?'

Her eyes half-focus, and she laughs maniacally. 'God, you don't get it, do you? This isn't a Zealscape. Why do you think you could infect my dream and change things so easily? This is Verve.'

I rock back. If her Zeal has been spiked by Verve in this lounge, that means the Ratel have been there. Fuck. Fuck. Do they know? Are they coming for us, even now, for mine and Nazarin's bodies, prone and helpless as newborns?

'Why did Tila send me to you, Mia?' I ask again. 'Did Tila tell you anything? I need to know. If you care even a little for us, please, *please* tell me, or we're both good as dead.'

'She found the link,' the figure of Tila says, twisting her torso back and forth, child-like, the green sequins on her dress twinkling. 'The link that no one is to know. He is the red one, the fair one, the handsome one. From Earth, and now he goes back to the Earth. Ashes to ashes. Dust to dust. Changing faces like kaleidoscopes.' My false sister laughs, high and insane. It's almost exactly what Sal said Tila said in Zenith, just after he found her with Vuk's body.

As I recall the crime scene, it starts to blossom around the figure of my sister. Blood seeps up from the floorboards, the coffee table grows like a mushroom, the broken glass scatters. The colours are so bright and saturated, the real world seems a pale echo. Tila reaches her hands up to cover her ears, rocking back and forth, her mouth open in a silent scream.

'This is you, too,' Mia whispers, watching it with awe.

'Go away!' I shout at the blood and glass. It stays, feeding on my anger.

Nothing happens. The anger and fear threaten to choke me.

I have to push them away.

I let out a breath and close my eyes. I try to let go of the urge for violence. I manage to find that small centre for self Mana-ma always pushed us towards. I thrust all emotion away. Slowly, so slowly, the crime scene fades and disappears. I feel the briefest flash of triumph before I turn my attention to Mia. I no longer have the same desire to hurt her. Thank God.

'Tila's words make no sense,' I tell her. False Tila quoted from the Bible, not Mana-ma's Good Book. Once, that would have offended me. Now I grind my teeth in frustration, gripping Mia's shoulder harder, until if this were reality she'd bruise.

'Who's that man you were talking about?'

Mia starts to shudder. She's taken control of her Vervescape again, but she's unstable and it reflects in the world around us. The ground cracks and shudders. Lightning blasts outside the glass window. Thorned trees grow from the cracks in the concrete, slinking along the ground and up towards the ceiling. The trees bear fruit, but in horror, I realize they're small humans, like thorny mandrakes. They reach their barbed hands towards us, dark mouths open in silent screams. Little red lights pulse from the bottoms of their throats, as red as Mia's anger. I try to push them back, but they're too strong.

The scalpel disappears from my hand, and Mia wriggles away from my grasp. False Tila is trapped by looping roots. She twists and turns, trying to free herself.

'Taema!' Her eyes bore right into me, and I can't help but think that she is my actual sister, here somehow in this nightmare.

The demons grasp Tila, their wooden roots digging into her flesh. Black blood seeps from her wounds. Next to me, Mia cackles. She's euphoric, fully caught in the throes of the drug.

I struggle on the floor to free my sister – even though rationally I know she's not real, I can't leave her. My hands are soon slick with dark blood. Mia attacks the mandrake-demons, plunging knives deep into their bellies until the lights in their throats go out.

The faces of the figures are changing and with a sickening drop of my stomach, I realize that many of them are the faces of the men and women from Mana's Hearth. *Changing faces like kaleidoscopes.* Is this what Mia meant? She still hates so many people there, all these years later. She never told us why she left the Hearth, and it was never spoken of while we were growing up in the redwood grove. We'd thought it rude to ask.

I've seen the darkness that threatened to overwhelm Mia, as she tried to escape Zeal only for its tendrils to delve deep into her again. Now Verve had her in its grasp, and it was worse. Would she wake up, angry and enraged, still thirsting for blood?

Clutching the facsimile of my twin, I can't help but fear

that maybe I missed the darkness in her, too. Or in myself, because aren't we the same?

Mia comes back to herself, just a little. 'You should thank your sister.'

'Why?'

'She's protecting you. Or trying to.'

'I don't need protecting.' Even though it's a dream, my body reacts as it would in the real world. My ears feel like I'm going through a tunnel at high speed, and my vision darkens to a little point. I am filled with more rage than I've ever felt. I want to hurt Mia with that same, shocking intensity I felt before. My sister came to her, confided in her, and Mia ratted her out to someone. If it's the Ratel, then my cover is blown before it's even begun. If it's not the Ratel, then we have someone else to worry about. Perhaps it was Vuk, and that's why my sister killed him. To keep him silent.

I know nothing.

Because of this broken woman, my sister might die. Maybe she killed, but would she have been put in that situation if Mia had been stronger?

There's still no proof of my sister's innocence or guilt, I have to remind myself. The forensics report was only one way it could have happened. She might have had to defend herself. I still cling to the hope that there was someone else in that room. Somehow. But if she killed to protect me . . . how would I ever be able to accept that? Especially if I can't save her?

My false sister is dead. The blood flows until she's enveloped in the black, oily muck. The demons with the faces of the people we grew up with open their mouths impossibly wide, the coals in their throats glowing as they devour her. Our parents are among them. I see their twisted faces slurping up the muck in euphoric delight.

Screaming, I launch myself up and leap on Mia again. She has another scalpel in her hand. I manage to dodge it, knocking it to the floor. The demons pull on my ankles but I ignore them. My hands are around her throat and I'm squeezing, squeezing, squeezing. Mia gasps, purpling beneath me. I can't calm down enough to try and affect the dream in any other way.

'Lucid dreaming, my ass,' I gasp.

If this was a straight Zealscape, I know that if I killed her in the dream, she'd wake up, strapped to the Chair, knocked out of her hallucination. That's dangerous enough. But I have no idea what happens in a Vervescape. What if it's more of a shock to her weakened body, and I kill her in the real world?

I should care. But my hands don't slacken.

Strong hands grip my shoulders, yanking me back. 'Let go of her,' Nazarin says. 'Let go. You've learned all you can from her.'

His deep voice snaps me from the iron vice of Verve. My hands jerk from her throat, though a red imprint remains.

'It's the drug,' he says. 'Happens to everyone who takes it. Everyone has a darker side.'

'Zeal or Verve?' I ask.

His brow furrows. 'What?'

'This batch has been contaminated. We're in a Vervescape, not Zeal.'

'Shit,' Nazarin says. 'We need to get out of here.'

'Where have you been?'

'Mia found a way to trap me in a different part of her dream. It disappeared when she was too distracted to control it any more.'

He means when I was half-strangling her. I flush in shame at what I've done.

Mia has already stopped paying attention to us, like I never interrupted her. Mana-ma has returned, whole and shivering in her black robe. Mia is engrossed in a grisly task involving one of Mana-ma's hands, peeling back the skin and picking out the tendons one by one. Simulacra of the hands that once rested on our heads, giving us benedictions, asking us to purge the darkness within.

'Mia,' I say. She looks up, eyes distant.

I gather that stillness within me again. 'You don't need to do this to live. You can be free of it. Try to live your life in the real world again. I loved you so much, and you were so good to us for those years we needed you most. You can be good again.'

Her breath hitches. She gives me a long, unblinking stare, and a flash seems to pass between us, before she turns her head back to Mana-ma, her shoulders heaving with silent sobs.

I turn my back on Mia and her phantom, letting Nazarin's hands remain around my shoulders, reassuring in their realness. It's only as we're leaving I notice that Nazarin is also covered in blood, cuts marring the skin of his arms and his left cheek. He's wearing the same dark clothes from Zenith as well, fitted close to the muscles of his chest and narrow waist. He looks dangerous. What nightmares has he endured, over the past few years?

Or what nightmares has he enacted?

We trudge silently down the abandoned corridors of the apartment complex, the dead leaves whispering underfoot. Outside, we look up at the building again, the rain drenching us through. The sky still boils red, blue, black and purple, an endless, wounded expanse. Even though the bloodlust of Verve still sings through my veins, I am comforted by the fact that I can't imagine how anyone would do this willingly.

Nazarin rests his forehead against mine.

'Wake up.'

TWELVE

TILA

I remember dreaming of trees after we fell.

The redwoods towered above me, the branches criss-crossing like dark lightning against the blue sky. Taema and I were lying on our sides, staring up. There was no birdsong, and barely a rustle of wind. I felt like we were the only two people in the world.

'Are we dead?' I asked my sister.

She leaned close, pressing her forehead against mine. 'Not yet.'

•

It was our heart.

We'd always known it was weak. There'd been a few scares when we were little. Thinking about it, it's pretty crazy that we had as few health problems as we did, without proper medicine and all that. That day, at the age of sixteen, we had a heart attack.

So then it was us resting in the Wellness Cabin, in the same bed where Adam had been when we threw grapes at him. I hated being in the bed where he had died.

I was so scared that we were going to die too. Taema slept a lot. I think she had less oxygen than me, since I was the bigger twin, just barely. The supposedly stronger one.

I kept wondering if this was the beginning of the end.

It was.

•

I had to stop writing for a bit. The lawyer came to visit me. It's not long until the trial.

I don't trust him. His name is Clive Ranganathan, and he's tall, with dark hair slicked back with too much gel. He's supposed to be a pretty good lawyer, but I can tell he doesn't give a crap about me. He thinks I'm guilty, I can see it, so why would he break a sweat really trying to set me free? It'd be bad for his reputation if he did – every guilty fucker out there would beg for him to take their case before they were hanged by the system. Not that there are many, these days, in the Shining Example of San Francisco.

Not yet, at least.

It's more fun to defend the innocents. Mr Ranganathan is already slumming it more than he wants to, having to defend someone who might be wrapped up in the Ratel.

He went through his plan and I sort of half listened to him. He nodded his head as he talked, his big hands flipping over his tablet, showing the evidence against me. There's more than last time.

After a bit, I stopped listening all together. I started humming 'A Hazy Shade of Winter'. He was offended and left. I don't care. He can't do anything for me. The only person who can save me is Taema. And I still don't know if she's trying to, or if I want her to.

I don't want to write any more about the present. It's depressing, though the past is getting depressing too.

Looking back is almost scarier than looking forward.

•

We felt better after a couple of days of rest and we were able to leave the Wellness Cabin and go home. Our parents were really relieved, to say the least. They cooked us our favourite food that first night: amaranth with vegetables and chicken, baked apples for dessert.

Yes, it was real chicken, not the vat-grown stuff everyone eats in the city. We raised them. Killed them. Ate them.

We were all quiet at the dinner table, not wanting to talk about what we all knew: that it was only going to get worse from here.

We'd known since we were pretty little that we might not live that long. But it was sobering to have to actually face that.

I felt so bad for Mom and Dad, though. They were the best parents you could ask for, really. Some of our friends fought with theirs all the time, but we hardly ever fought with ours. They talked to us as if we were equals, asked us our opinions. Even writing about them right now I'm tearing up like crazy. I miss them most out of everything back in the Hearth. I miss all of us sitting by the fire on cold days, me and Taema sewing clothes, or Taema reading and me chattering away to Dad. Dad and I were closer, and Taema and Mom were closer. Which seems sort of funny, now that I think about it, since obviously we spent the same amount of time with both of them.

I wish they'd have come with us.

They were both so worried for us. It hurt to look at them, as they tried to keep the knowledge that they knew we were dying from their faces. They were bad at it.

•

The next day we had to go to Confession for Mana-ma. We'd already missed a week. Neither of us wanted to go, but then we'd never really enjoyed it. Nobody likes to have to list all the ways they're defective.

Mana-ma didn't preach it that way, though. It's supposed to be exposing who you are fully, both the bad and the good, acknowledging it and then letting it go and moving forward. She seemed more concerned with the bad. Like most people.

Before that treat, we had Meditation. It was our first session since the tablet died. I really didn't want to do it, and I could tell Taema didn't either. Even if we said we were still feeling bad, though, they'd wonder why we were missing it. So off we went.

I remember that Meditation so clearly. Lying in the meadow, the day clear and perfect. California weather through and through.

Almost everyone was already gathered there by the time we huffed and puffed our way down to the dandelion-studded meadow. Mana-ma waited by the path. She rubbed the fingers of her left hand against her thumb, something she did when impatient. Another bitter pill to go down our throats. We felt the 'zap' that meant the drug had taken effect. The colours all grew so much brighter.

Dimly, I wondered if we should be taking whatever Mana-ma's drug was, with our heart. Surely our heart could have been an excuse to get out of that day? Then I was so high I didn't care in the least. We stumbled down and joined the ring of people.

Mana-ma stood in the centre of the circle, and we all began humming as the drugs took a stronger hold. We reached out for each other as Mana-ma listed the images for us to create in our minds. A butterfly's wings. The petals of a rose. The sky, dark with clouds, fresh rain falling.

There was a flash, pure and bright, that travelled through

the ring. The pain that had been lessening with each Meditation returned. We writhed and panted, and I wondered if Mana-ma enjoyed it.

'Yes,' I heard Mana-ma say, even though she was speaking so quietly no one should have been able to hear her.

Another flash, and we weren't in the meadow any more. We were standing in a forest. The trees weren't redwoods like the ones in Muir Woods. The bark was all silver, the leaves blue and purple. The sky roiled a deep green. All the members of the Hearth stood in this weird forest, looking about, confused. In the middle was Mana-ma. Triumphant.

'Mardel,' she said. 'Come forward.'

He came forward, blinking, dazed.

'You have often spoken to me in Confession of your struggle with drink,' she said.

Mardel's cheeks, always red from alcohol, flushed deeper. Way to break the sanctity of Confession, Mana-Ma.

'I think together, with me as the conduit for God, we can heal you of that urge, here in the sacred wood. Will you permit us to try?' She held out her hand.

Mardel nodded, visibly shaking.

'My flock,' Mana-ma said. 'God's blessings upon you all. Let us join hands again and think healing thoughts to Mardel. Let him never again crave another drop of drink, so his mind and heart are clear to receive God's love.'

We sent him healing urges, yet with so many people, each had a slightly different emphasis and flavour. Some wanted him to also become kinder, less prone to snap. His wife wished he would smile more. Others simply hoped he'd never again crave drinking to excess. I could feel everyone's thoughts, see into their minds. Except for Mana-ma's. She was closed off, wrapped up like her long, black robes.

Another flash. Another burst of pain.

We were back in the meadow.

'Excellent,' Mana-ma said, bursting with pride. 'I knew it.'

She helped Mardel to his feet. 'How do you feel, my son?' she asked.

'I feel . . . better,' he said, smiling from ear to ear.

'Do you crave vodka?'

'No,' he said, surprised. 'I don't.'

We all cheered.

I hoped that, because of the triumph or whatever the hell we did in the meadow, that we wouldn't have to do Confession that day.

No such luck. 'We'll celebrate after,' she said.

We walked slowly back to the church.

The night before, I had felt our heart flickering, stumbling unevenly as it tried to pump blood to both of us. I wondered how long it'd keep beating. Morbidly, I wondered when it did stop, which of us would die first. Selfishly, I hoped it was me. I didn't want to see Taema without that light in her eyes.

We passed the greenhouses with the mushrooms. We wouldn't be able to help with our chores that afternoon.

We had to wait about half an hour for Confession, slumped against the church wall. There were two people ahead of us. They came out of the Confession room, looking all contemplative. When they saw us, they stopped, rested their hands on our shoulders, and kissed our foreheads. It was meant to be comforting, but I couldn't help but feel they were saying goodbye. *We're not dead yet*, I wanted to yell at them, bashing my fist against their faces to snap them out of it.

Finally, it was our turn. I pressed my forehead against Taema's for a moment.

'T,' she whispered.

'T.'

It gave us strength.

Mana-ma's Confessional was a tent erected within a secluded room of the church. It was made of white silk, and within were only low cushions and a low table, in soft pastel colours. Often there was tea if you wanted it. It was meant to be calming, like a shrine to truth and Purity and release. Really, it was more like a hippie psychologist's room.

Mana-ma was perched on her usual cushion, dressed all in black, a stain on the pale colours of the Confessional. She held a cup of tea in her hands. Her eyes crinkled as she smiled at us. She seemed so damn proud. She was still buzzing from her triumph at the meadow.

Mana-ma looked like a mother – warm and generous, with laugh lines about her eyes. She had skin the same brown as us, eyes so dark they almost looked black, her hair in the same tight corkscrews around her face. No, the Hearth's not inbred, but a lot of us are related distantly to each other, or near enough. It was hard to tell what age Mana-ma was – she always looks the same in my memory. Ageless. I used to think she knew everything. She was a Vessel for God, the embodiment of Love.

That was a lie, too.

I remember wondering what the hell she was up to, in that moment before she spoke to us. What was the point of getting us to connect? What was the drug?

'Sit, my children,' she said, gesturing.

We had to almost lie down on our sides, resting our cheekbones together so we could both look at her. Taema was nervous – even more nervous than me. I fought the urge to stroke her hair. I had to admit to myself that Taema still believed in Mana-ma, or at least she did a heck of a lot more than I did. She felt guilty knowing she might have to lie, whereas I didn't give a fig.

We'd already lied by omission to Mana-ma, and it hadn't sat well with my sister. We never told her about the tablet. How we (OK, mostly I) dreamed of the big, wide world and what we'd do if we could ever get to it. We didn't tell her plenty of things. We skittered around the subject of sex and desire, pretending that we couldn't become aroused when so close to each other. That wasn't true.

'I welcome you into the Enclave of the Self,' Mana-ma intoned, resting her palms on our foreheads. 'Close your eyes and imagine all darkness, all unhappiness, leaving you, leaving only Purity and light.'

We dutifully imagined this, breathing in and out, our chests rising and falling in tandem. I imagined I was covered in mud that dried and cracked and flaked off. The flakes scattered around me, whisking about on the wind like when paper has burned to ash. In my mind's eye, I was just me, Taema nowhere around. When I opened my eyes, feeling her warmth, I felt no better, no lighter. Our heart was still weak. We were still dying.

'The darkness cannot flee until you give voice to it. State the nature of it and it can no longer hold any power over you. Confess, and be free. Let the darkness absorb deep into the Earth, so you may leave lighter than when you entered.'

I wasn't in the mood for this. I'd believed it all, once upon a time, to a point. I don't know why I was never as completely under Mana-ma's spell as the others, what in me refused to give in. After finding the tablet, something irrefutable had changed in me. I knew this place wasn't where I wanted to be. That Mana-ma might not be the real voice of God. It's a scary thing, when all the beliefs you have shift under your feet like that. I didn't know who to trust, how to feel, if my morals were my morals, or just the Hearth's.

Taema spoke first. I listened to the gentle sound of her voice, my eyes half-closed.

'When our heart hurt,' she said, 'I didn't think of the Creator, or light, or goodness, like I should have done.'

'And what did you think of, my child?'

'I knew my soul could leave, and that I should prepare it since I'd have the time, but all I could think of was the pain, and that I didn't want to die. All was dark and cold. I was scared.'

Mana-ma leaned forward. 'Did you have a vision? The Creator will sometimes deign to visit one so close to beginning the Cycle again.'

'N-no . . .' My sister shook her head, shamefaced, hands clenching. I hated to see how easily Mana-ma could influence Taema's emotions. Not that Taema was weak – far from it – but she was sensitive. Mana-ma made her feel like she had been wrong for no reason.

I had an idea, but I decided to wait my turn as I played it over in my mind.

'What other darkness lives in you, child? Speak it and let it free.' I fought the urge to curl my lip and slap her away from us. How had I never seen what a spider she was?

'What else?'

Taema licked her lips. 'The Meditation frightened me.'

Mana-ma nodded. 'I know, my child. God's world is terrifying and vast. But, together, we may access it. This is our purpose. Do not be afraid. This is wondrous. This is transformative. This is divine.'

I noticed she danced around saying what it was for.

'I will try,' Taema whispered.

'Anything else, my child?'

Taema tried to think of something else. Bless her. She had to dig deep to bring up any darkness. It was all too easy for me to think of dark things, but I'd long since stopped telling Mana-ma about them. Partly because I didn't want Taema to hear what went on in my head. Mostly because I hated the way Mana-ma sucked it all up, revelling in the darkness of her flock.

Taema eventually muttered something about how she dreamed of the world outside, and Mana-ma perked up at that, rearranging herself in her seat, like a cat puffed up at a threat.

'Outside is where no one listens to God – to the birds and the trees and the ways of the world. They think all must bend to *their* will. They change the land, their bodies, regardless of how the Creator made them, their very souls. They think they can make themselves perfect, spitting in the Creator's face, for my Husband has already made them perfect. Really, they sully all that they touch, and you must never forget that. Now, let that darkness leave the room, never to return.'

'Yes, Mana-ma.' Taema was all meek, and I wanted to pull my lips back from my teeth and snarl. 'That's all, Mana-ma,' my twin finished.

Mana-ma waved a bit of smoking sage incense around Taema's head, though of course that made me cough, too. She and Taema hummed the One Note, and my face squished up because it was right against my ear.

Then Mana-ma turned her attention to me.

'Tila, my child,' she intoned. 'Envision the darkness flowing from you, pooling on the floor, ready to leave and return to the Earth . . .'

I imagined so much flowing out of me that it flooded the room to the Moroccan lamp hanging from the ceiling, but Tila and I floated on it while Mana-ma squatted at the bottom like a sunken stone. A few bubbles burst from below, then all was still. Then the darkness that had been in me carried us away from Mana's Hearth out to the wide world, to San Francisco, dropping us off in Golden Gate Park. The darkness flowed back into me, and I was just like I'd been before.

'Have you completed the visualization?' Mana-ma asked.

I opened my eyes and smiled. 'Yes.'

'What darkness must you give name to so that it may have no power over you?'

'I thought about dark and pain instead of light and goodness when I thought I would die, too. My soul wouldn't have been Pure.'

Mana-ma's eyes lit up. 'And did you have a vision?'

'I did.'

Taema turned her head. She almost always knew when I was lying. This time she didn't know why.

Mana-ma's eyes shone and she took my hand. Her touch was all cool and clammy. I fought the urge to take my hand and wipe it on my shirt. 'Tell me what you saw, my child.'

She bought it. I think most people in the outside world think the people at the top of Mana's Hearth know it's all a crock of shit – that they've been shrewd enterprisers since the beginning – but I think Mana-ma *believes*. She believes just as much as, or more than, anyone else in the Hearth. That's why what I did next was just so easy.

'I saw a man I'd never seen before and he was yelling at me to turn back, that what lay before me was only wretchedness. That everything I'd been told was a lie. He even told me who he was.'

'Who was he?'

'He called himself the Brother.'

Mana-ma paled, rocking back from us. I think I said this

before, but the mates of the Mana-ma of each generation were called the Brother. Which is kind of weird, now that I think about it. It was just what they were called, and sort of their role in the community. They were meant to support everyone, even Mana-ma. Because Mana-ma could only really be married to the Creator, for she was his voice.

Because of the whole don't-talk-about-the-dead thing, there was no real way for me to recall that name, as far as she knew. The Brother wasn't mentioned in the Good Book, or the sermons, and it was so many years ago now that most people didn't have any reason to mention him, or even think about him much.

Except that little tidbit had slipped into that website about the Hearth, and I overheard our parents once mentioning 'the Brother' in passing. I remember thinking it was weird they were talking about a brother in Obvious Capital Letters. So I asked them about it and they told me and Taema, but told me not to tell anyone else about him. I didn't know why they were so nervous about it at the time.

'You heard from the Brother?' Mana-ma asked. Her voice shook. It was the first time I'd ever seen her scared.

I nodded. 'He was really upset that I was there. Kept yelling at me to turn back, that there was nothing but darkness and pain beyond. He said the forest was poison.'

That was considered bad, if you didn't begin the next Cycle. How else could your soul grow and learn, on our world or another?

'That can't be right,' Mana-ma said. She gripped my shoulder, hard. 'He wouldn't say that. You're lying. You're lying!'

With difficulty, I shrugged that shoulder, the skin of my chest pulling against Taema's. 'I'm just telling you what I saw.'

Mana-ma looked deep into my eyes. Whatever she saw

there, she didn't like it. She backed away from me. 'You're ruining the sanctity of the Confessional by lying within its confines.'

I said nothing.

'You are lying. You must be! He can't contact you. There's no way.'

I shrug a shoulder, my skin pulling against Taema's, all innocent. 'Yesterday we connected with each other. Maybe I can connect with those beyond, too.' I was just throwing things out there and hoping they'd stick, and I'd struck deep.

She grabbed either side of my head, looking deep into my eyes. Whatever she was looking for, she didn't find it. She let me go.

I didn't register that she'd slapped me until I heard the noise and my cheek stung. Taema gasped, but I stayed silent. Taema's hand clenched mine.

'Get out of here. Get out.'

'Don't I have to formally release the darkness?' I asked, still all innocent.

'I don't think the darkness can be released in you,' she spat. 'Get. Out.'

We stood and walked sideways from the room, Mana-ma watching us go.

'What the hell were you doing?' Taema asked as soon as we were out of the church and walking down the dirt road towards home. 'What was the point?'

'She does that to us, wrapping us around her finger. I wanted to see if I could do it, too. And I could.'

It was easy, and sort of fascinating even if I knew, deep down, it was wrong. Like picking legs off of an insect.

It made me wonder what else I was capable of.

THIRTEEN

TAEMA

I wake up completely disoriented.

My mouth feels like cotton wool and my vision is blurry. The room hums with the soft whirr of machinery. I try to move, but there are wires poking from my veins, holding me in place. I panic, not sure where I am. Have I come out of surgery again? My arm tries to move to my scar, but it can't.

'T,' I whisper. Where is she?

'Is she OK?' asks a male voice I think I recognize. 'It doesn't normally take this long to wake up, does it?'

'It's her mechanical heart. Usually when people are . . . excited in the Zealscape, their heart pumps faster – works through the drug quicker.'

I blink, shaking my head. A man leans over me. 'You OK, Tila?'

I start at my sister's name, still trying to figure out where I am. I shake my head, but the man gives me a warning look. I squint. He's a Detective. Detective Nazarin. I remember. I focus on my breathing, everything coming back to me as the last vestiges of Verve leave my system.

The orderly is taking out the needles from my arm. I shudder as I feel them slip out of my skin. Seems strangely barbaric and old-fashioned, but intravenous is still the best way to administer the drug to make the immersion in the Zeal or Verve world complete. *You must know it wasn't a Zealscape,* I want to say. *How much have the Ratel paid you? Have you contacted them?* If he had, wouldn't they already be here? I feel the aftereffects – a buzzing in my veins, a twitching in my muscles. If it was actually Zeal, my urge to kill and maim would be diminished. I'd feel happy and glowing. Because it's Verve, I feel more keyed up than ever. I keep grinding my teeth together in anger, clenching my hands into fists.

Mia's still deeply dreaming, lying flat on the Chair. Time can go a bit funny on these drugs. It felt like I was only there for an hour at most, but it's been three hours out here. According to the clock on the wallscreen above her head, she still has eleven hours of depravity before she has to wake up and remember what she did in the harsh light of day. Perhaps eighteen hours before she's here again, ready for more. How can she bear to do this, day after day?

The orderly finishes and I get off the Chair, unsteady on my feet.

I lean closer to Mia, and then I swallow hard. I'm almost sure I see the barest hint of bruising around her throat, and another thin mark where the scalpel nicked her. But that can't be possible, can it? I clench my hands into fists deep within my pockets.

Nazarin looks a bit better than I feel, though not by much. He's decidedly green around the gills. I want to ask him what he saw. Were his urges to kill just as strong, and if so, who did he hurt in that shared dream world?

Nazarin tips the white-coated orderly extra, and he responds with an obsequious nod. He opens the door for us and smiles, but to me it seems more of a leer. I squeeze past him, as does Nazarin, and the orderly leads us down the hallway, his perfectly coiffed hair solid as a helmet under the dim lighting. He motions towards the discreet side exit.

I brush off my arms after we leave, as if I can shed all the horror of what I've seen. I'm shaking, even though it's a warm San Francisco night. I let out a breath, my ears perked for an alarm, my eyes to the sky for any unmarked hovercars to take us away. I'm grateful we made the effort to wear masks, and can only hope the orderly didn't lean in close enough in the dim light to see the seams. They're not something that works well in the bright light of day, but are usually reserved for costume parties or nights out on the town.

We walk along beside the garish advertisements of the Mission district. All the smiling, bright men and women seem to be cackling at me.

'We need to talk about what happened,' he said. 'But not here.'

'Back to the safe house?' Though I don't feel comfortable there, between the Chair and seeing that spread of false blood in the upstairs room.

'There's another safe house, closer. Just around the corner. We'll regroup there, then head back to the main one.'

He sets off, and I trail him.

•

The extra safe house turns out to be a small apartment, and it's Nazarin's second home. He has one that the Ratel know about, but this is a separate one, not in his name. He'll sometimes meet his superiors here, he explains, since he can never go to the SFPD headquarters. Or he'll come here when he wants privacy, escape. They'll be shutting it down soon, or assigning it to someone else, since he's moved to the new safe house to train me.

Though Nazarin has spent nights here, there's nothing personal about it. It could be a hotel room. It's a studio apartment, though the one room is a decent size. The bed, with cushions against the wall to make it double as a sofa, takes up a corner; a tiny kitchenette takes up a second; a bathroom another (it has a door, at least) and a wardrobe the last corner. A table and chairs are by the window, and he gestures for me to take a seat.

I wonder what his actual apartment looks like, whether there are knick-knacks and photographs that would give a glimpse into his life. Tila and I, when we lived together, had a perfect shelf in my entrance hallway to show people just a little bit about us. Holographic images of the two of us, our arms around each other. My engineering degree, and a little glass award I won for my work on VivaFog. A gorgeous, glazed pot Tila made herself and false sunflowers, some of her smaller pieces of artwork, and a glass sculpture a client at Zenith had given her. All of it rested on top of a scarf we bought when we went on holiday together to United Korea. Now it's only my half, photos and engineering accolades, and it doesn't look right.

Nazarin passes me a glass: more SynthGin and tonic. Better than nothing. I shoot it down my throat, grimacing at the subtly wrong taste. I close my eyes, but I keep seeing the screaming mandrakes with the familiar faces. One had looked like Mardel. My eyes snap open.

'Got any more?' I ask.

He takes my cup the three steps to the kitchenette and dutifully pours me more. I drink it down.

'I don't know what you saw, or what you learned,' he starts. He's barely touched his drink, swirling it around in the glass. He makes a pretty, if somewhat frightening picture. He's taken off his overtop and wears a tank, the muscles on his arms bulging beneath his brown skin. He has more pale scars criss-crossed along his forearms. The light from the ceiling screen casts part of his face in shadow. He's taken off his shoes, and the sight of his socks – the beginnings of a hole in one big toe – makes him look strangely vulnerable.

'What happened to you? What did you see?' I ask. I feel like he has to tell his side before I can tell mine.

I think Nazarin understands this. He finally downs his drink and then goes to the tiny kitchen for more. Begins to pour a drink, thinks better of it, and brings the entire bottle to the chair with him. I approve of that plan.

'Mia doesn't like men much, does she?' he starts.

'No, she doesn't.' More SynthGin splashes into my cup. I think of Mana-ma. 'There's plenty of women she hates too.'

'When I came in, I was in a prison cell,' he says.

I can't help but wonder if it looked anything like the cell my sister is in right now.

'There was no light. I thought maybe the drug hadn't worked and it'd killed me.' He smiles ruefully at this, as if it's funny. 'I didn't realize it was Verve, though I did think something was off. I haven't taken much of either Zeal or Verve.'

Interesting, I think, *considering how many people have it as part of their daily lives.*

'Anyway, I realized where I was pretty fast,' he says, swigging again. 'Found a way out, but then I saw those demon things. They were surrounding the building, like a barricade. Twisted little fuckers.'

'Yeah. A lot of them had faces of the people I grew up with.'

He shudders. 'I fought my way through them but it wasn't pretty. Then the drug hit me pretty hard, and I saw all the people I wouldn't mind dead. That took a while as well.' He drains the drink.

'Wait, so you affected the Vervescape too?'

He stops at that. 'I guess I did.'

'You're a lucid dreamer, then, or you could become one.' I set down my glass with a *clunk*. 'If you can lucid dream, you don't need me.' Can I quit? Can I stop this before it's really begun? The hope is painful.

'I'm untrained, and I can't do what you can. I couldn't get rid of these ones. It seemed like they almost killed me. I ended up having to kill them all. Cut them to pieces.'

I swallow.

'Most of the people I saw deserved it. A few have been put in jail and then quietly locked up in stasis. Doesn't mean I don't sometimes wish I could have had the honour of actually killing them myself.'

'Everyone has a darker side,' I whisper, echoing his earlier words.

'That they do. Still, the shared dream should have worked better, even if it was Verve. I should have appeared right with you. I should have guessed that she'd be so strong. She was raised in the Hearth too.'

'When she was there, the Meditation stuff wasn't as common,' I say, almost distantly.

'Really?' Nazarin leans forward, interested. 'When did it really start?'

I stare off, remembering. 'Maybe a year or two before Mia left, so like . . . fifteen years ago now? Mana-ma became obsessed with the idea that we could all become one, and when we did, that's when God would speak to her even more clearly. So we trained. Before that, it was more Meditation to clear the mind, not to try and impact anything. But maybe that still gave Mia a foundation to start being able to control the Vervescape.'

'And did it work, this Meditation?'

'It did. By the end, we could take a pill and connect into one large shared dream world populated by every member of the Hearth.'

Nazarin's mouth fell open, almost comically. 'What was the drug?'

'I don't know. Mana-ma kept her secrets. Maybe it was God, after all.' My voice drips with sarcasm.

Nazarin's forehead furrows as he turns over this new piece of information. I'm sure he'll follow it up with the SFPD, but I have a question of my own.

'What would have happened, if Mia had killed me in the dream?' I ask him.

'If she was lucid and knew you weren't a part of the dream? She could have found a way to kill you there that would have been . . . permanent.'

'I could have died?' I want to throw my glass at him. 'I didn't sign up for death.'

His eyes spark at that. 'This whole thing started with a death. With your sister killing a Ratel hitman.'

'Accused of killing.'

He makes a noise deep in his throat. 'You still so very sure she didn't do it?'

I say nothing. I'm not sure why I still defend her, when her chances of innocence seem to dwindle the more we follow the clues. If she did kill him, though, I have to cling to the fact that murder and self-defence are two very different things.

'You knew this would be dangerous going in. You knew full well death could always be a possibility, and don't pretend you didn't. You're going into the underworld of San Francisco, Taema, you can't have expected not to get your hands dirty.'

I glare at him, and he glares right back.

'Here's how it'll go,' I say. 'When we do something, you tell me what kind of danger we're facing. Don't just let me barrel into it headfirst without knowing what the hell I'm up against. OK?'

He's the first to look away to take another swig. 'Deal. If it's any comfort, I didn't think today would be dangerous. It wouldn't have been if it was Zeal and not Verve, because Zeal is so much more static when you're in someone else's dream.'

'What a lovely surprise for us.'

'It means we have a problem, though.'

'Don't we already have lots of problems?' The SynthGin has made me irritating, but I can't seem to stop the sarcasm.

'If the Ratel have spiked the Zeal with Verve, they're going to try and eavesdrop on the dreams.'

Oh God. 'And if they have a lucid dreamer see Mia's dreams, then our whole cover is blown.'

'Exactly.'

'We're screwed then.'

'Not necessarily. One: the other Zeal lounge they spiked, the one I was security for? It didn't work. They couldn't get the levels right; no one could mine even a millisecond of a dream. Second: they might not be recording the dreams, but trying to find lucid dreamers based on physiological reactions. That might mean that Mia comes to their attention, but they'll likely discount her because of her ill health.'

I can't banish the mental image of Mia sobbing. 'She's afraid of someone. She told them about Tila. She could be in contact with the Ratel already.'

'Maybe, but if so and if she wanted to sell out your sister, she likely would have already. Third: even if they do manage to record, there will be a backlog of so many dreams. It'll take them time to sift through it all, because they still don't have that many lucid dreamers. That's why Tila was able to rise through the ranks so quickly. So, if the dreams have been recorded, then when you work your first shift at the Verve lounge as Tila, you'll have to erase that one without detection. That won't be easy.'

'Nothing is easy.' I rub my face. I'm so tired.

'What happened in the dream?' he asks.

He's been wanting to know this since we arrived, but he waited (wisely) until I was drunk enough to talk about it without screaming. Though I'm not drunk enough that I don't realize that's what he's aiming for.

I don't answer right away, but stare out of the window. This second safe house is near the Panhandle, on Fell Street. It looks right onto the thin strip of park connected to the Golden Gate Dome. I can just barely see the tips of Grace Cathedral from between two orchard high-rises. It's quite a pretty view – those pure white towers flanked by fruit trees within glass buildings thirty stories high.

I get to my feet and wobble.

Nazarin leans back in his chair. 'You're drunk.'

'Very deductive, detective.'

'Come on. Tell me what happened to you in there.'

I stagger to the little bathroom. 'I'll tell you in a second.'

I pee and then lean over the tiny sink. I press my palms against my eyes, breathing raggedly. It's late and I feel like shit. I've drunk at least a quarter of the bottle of the fake gin. I'm definitely drunk.

When I come back, Nazarin has a huge glass of water and I gulp it down. I've delayed as long as I can. Time to return to the nightmare world, at least for a little while.

So I tell him everything. I don't leave anything out, and I've got a pretty good memory. I tell him about the mandrake demons, false Mana-ma and Tila, Mia's scalpel. 'The drug seemed to pull her in deeper. My sister was there and she started ranting. I guess Mia made that happen? Maybe it's a hint, but mainly she just sounded batshit crazy.'

'What'd she say?'

'Something about finding the link and then: "He is the red one, the fair one, the handsome one. From Earth and now he goes back to the Earth. Ashes to ashes. Dust to dust. Changing faces like kaleidoscopes."'

'Sounds like the garbled scripture that Tila spouted in Zenith, according to Sal.'

'That's what's weird. If Mia was going to give me a hint, shouldn't she have referenced Mana-ma's Good Book? That's what we all have memorized. Mana-ma would show us other holy writ, all sorts of it too: the Torah, the Qur'an, the Book of Mormon, gnostic texts, the works – but out-of-context bits that suited her. Usually she ranted about how they were the warped echoes of the true voice of God, which only she heard. Naturally.'

That familiar guilt twists deep in my stomach. For a long time, I'd believed that Mana-ma did hear the true voice of God. That she was the vessel able to bring us salvation. And I'd been so stubborn, so willingly blind, for so long. After Tila and I had left the Hearth, after the last holds of Mana-ma were finally gone from me, went through a phase of reading all the holy books we could get our hands on. Buddhist texts, ancient Egyptian things (I admit to reading the *Book of the Heavenly*

Cow mainly because it had such a great title), Ellen White's Seventh-Day Adventist texts. A lot of stuff from other cults, especially ones formed after Mana's Hearth. The Contours of God. The Green Cabal, which thought that people who saw aliens were actually seeing fairies, and lived in the woods with toadstools for a few decades.

Everything and anything, wondering if maybe we'd find the truth in one of them.

We didn't, but I remember sitting side by side in our little San Francisco apartment in the Inner Sunset, our legs touching and our cheeks pressed against each other as we read, like when we had been connected. I still feel I think best when I'm sitting like that with Tila, feeling the steady beating of her heart in time with mine, and the gentle sound of her breathing. Maybe that's why I've felt so lost: I can't think properly when she's gone. All the good memories with her hurt.

The silence has gone on too long. I can tell he's been watching me as I stare blankly into space.

'So. Let's start looking at what Mia might have meant. It sounds like religious rhetoric, so I'm thinking the Bible,' Nazarin says. He blinks and his ocular implant activates the wallscreen, bringing up a version of the King James Bible.

Nazarin taps his thumb against his lips. 'Vuk's dead. It could be about him. So I guess that explains the ashes to ashes part. "For dust thou art, and unto dust shalt thou return."'

'Ashes to ashes, funk to funky . . . we know that Mia's a junkie!' I sing. The SynthGin has made me silly.

At Nazarin's confused look, I giggle even more. 'Never mind. Old song by a man called David Bowie. Sorry.' It was from post-1969, so I first listened to it after coming to San Francisco, during mine and my sister's self-taught education on music. I clear my throat, try to calm myself. 'I have no idea what she meant by "the red one, the fair one, the handsome one".'

He searches for quotes relating to *red*. The following appears on the wall:

> Isaiah 1:18: Come now, let us reason together, says the Lord: though your sins are like scarlet, they shall be as white as snow; though they are red like crimson, they shall become like wool.
>
> Exodus 28:15: You shall make a breast piece of judgement, in skilled work. In the style of the ephod you shall make it – of gold, blue and purple and scarlet yarns, and fine twined linen shall you make it.

'Mean anything to you?' he asks.

I shake my head. 'Nope.'

He searches for 'the fair one' and the snippet from the Song of Solomon appears:

> My beloved spake, and said unto me, Rise up, my love, my fair one, and come away.

I still shake my head. Tila is beloved to me, of course, but the quote doesn't jump out to me in any significant way. Does she want me to come away with her?

He frowns. 'I'm sure we'll find out something. There'll be a kink in this trail somewhere.'

He tries a general search, not in the Bible, of 'the red one, the fair one, the handsome one'.

'Got it,' Nazarin whispers.

> The triliteral Semitic root ADM: red, handsome, fair.
>
> And a word from it, 'adamah', meaning 'ground' or 'earth'.

'Adam.' The word rasps from my throat. My head spins

and I lean back on the chair, closing my eyes, hiding my face in my hands.

'The first man? Does that mean anything to you?'

Of course it does. And it has nothing to do with the original Adam from Genesis, the rise of Eve's original sin or the fall of man. It has everything to do with a nice boy with a genuine smile, laughing through the pain as he tried to catch green grapes in his mouth, his left arm a stump on the pillow, his infected foot propped up on the bed. A lifetime ago. A world away across the Bay.

'It does. We knew a boy named Adam. But I don't know how the hell he'd have anything to do with this.'

'Maybe Mia wanted us to speak to him. Where is he?'

Not opening my eyes, I say, 'He's dead. Died ten years ago, in Mana's Hearth. Maybe she meant another Adam. Or she was babbling nonsense hopped up on Zeal or Verve. Fuck, I don't know. I don't know. I can't think about this any more.' I take my hands away and reach for the bottle of SynthGin. It only has enough for half a glass.

'Any more?'

He brings out the bottle of SynthTequila. Holds it out to me like an offering.

'That'll do.'

•

Our empty SynthTequila glasses sit on the table by the window, glowing silver in the moonlight. Nazarin and I are on the bed. The detective is splayed against the wall, his arms crossed behind his head. His eyes are half-lidded, his lips parted. I'm lying on my side, my head resting on my arm. He makes a pretty picture. In this soft light, he does not look so fierce. I can't see his scars.

Nazarin stretches, his shirt lifting just enough to show the muscled planes of his stomach.

'Do you want another drink?' he asks, his voice quiet.

'No,' I say. I sit up, move a little closer. We pause, six inches apart, sizing each other up. We both know what the other wants. What we don't know is if we should cross that line.

The old Taema wouldn't have. The old me would have decided it was too improper, unprofessional. The new me, though? The one who has given up everything, who just nearly killed my foster mother in a dream world? She's a different creature entirely.

Nazarin opens his mouth to say something.

I close the distance between us.

His mouth is warm. His lips part further, his tongue darting against mine, soft and tasting of tequila. His stubble scratches my chin. I pull him against me, and his body is the opposite of his mouth – hard, angular, strong. I roll on top of him, and his lips move from my lips to my neck. I close my eyes, a small smile curling my lips.

I sit up and Nazarin pulls my shirt off of me. His fingers trace their way down my scar before reaching behind me, unclasping my bra. I slide it down my arms, tossing it to the floor before helping him out of his clothes.

We are not slow. We are not gentle. We are not tender. We each take what we want, what we need, yet we do give the other what they desire. It's been almost a year since I broke up with David. It's a long time to be alone. I concentrate entirely on Nazarin and the sensations he gives me, determined to quiet my racing mind.

Afterwards, I lie on top of him, my breasts pressed against his muscled chest. From this close, I can see all his scars, criss-crossed against each other. I trace my fingertips along them as he drifts off to sleep, wondering what story lies behind each one.

His heartbeat is in time with mine.

FOURTEEN

TAEMA

I wake up curled up against Nazarin's side.

In the harsh light of day, sleeping with my undercover partner doesn't seem like the brightest idea I ever had, even if I am delightfully sore and sated. I ease myself away from him, running my tongue over my dry lips. Synth alcohols don't give you a hangover, but your body still understands on some deep level that you've messed with it. I lean on my knees.

I dreamed of Adam. My first crush. How he used to visit us and stay for dinner. He'd flip through the books in our room, and I'd watch his fingers turn the pages. I'd often wondered if he liked either me or my sister, or both of us. He was so tall, and strong from helping plough the fields for grain. I could picture his face so clearly in my mind, as if I'd just seen him the day before.

Nazarin shifts, curling on his side, turned towards me, his face burrowed into his arm so I can only see the tips of his eyebrows and his buzzed hair. He looks cute, something I still find remarkable in such a large, intimidating man. Images of the previous night flash in my mind, and though they are pleasant memories, I'm nervous about how he'll react when he wakes up. I watch him for a minute, willing my body to feel better, even if nothing exactly hurts. Nazarin's breathing hitches, his brows furrowing. I wonder what his dreams are.

I move to leave the bed and Nazarin stiffens, his arm snaking out to grab my wrist. I cry out in surprise. We freeze. Nazarin meets my eyes, the sleep clearing from them as he remembers what we did. His gaze darts down to my naked torso. He lets go of my wrist and I rub it.

'Sorry,' he mumbles. 'Light sleeper.'

It's more than that. He's someone used to sleeping with one eye open and a gun under his pillow.

I stand, feeling his eyes on me as I slip the cotton dress over myself. I go to the bathroom and shut the door. Looking in the mirror is still a shock. My hopes rise for an instant when I think it's my sister, and then crash when I realize it's only me. My imitation-Tila hair is a wreck. I try to pat the blue spikes into some semblance of order, and give up.

When I come out, he's up and dressed in a tank top and sleep shorts, making coffee in the kitchenette. There's a bulge in his shorts. I feel a shot of desire go through me, culminating between my legs. Even in the light of day, knowing it's a bad idea, I'm more than half tempted to go over, push him against the wall and do it all again. I clear my throat, slide my eyes away, and take the cup when he offers it to me, sipping gratefully.

It's real coffee. The caffeine settles into my system. They haven't outlawed that from the city yet, even though it's stupidly expensive to buy with the extra taxes.

'Good God, Taema, you can drink,' Nazarin says, admiringly. 'If that was real alcohol, I wouldn't be able to open my eyes today.'

Are we pretending last night didn't happen? I play along.

It's easier this way. 'So you've had the real stuff?' I ask, taking another sip.

'Of course I have. I haven't always lived in this hippie ecotopia.'

'Where are you from?' I ask.

'I was born in Turkey, but moved to Dakota when I was eight.'

'Ah. Rural boy.' I skirt about asking him why he left Turkey. There was a nasty civil war in that area of the world at that time, though it's stable now. Chemicals, bombs and far too many civilian deaths.

'I grew up on a farm. Might have been a little similar to how you were raised, come to think of it.'

My mouth twists, my hand hovering to the top of my scar. 'Probably not quite like me.'

He raises his coffee cup in acknowledgement. His eyes dart down, but I'm not sure if he's looking at the scar or my breasts. I feel the thrum of desire again. *Get it together*, I admonish myself.

'Definitely not,' he says, as if echoing my thoughts, but he's still talking about his childhood. 'I just have a little more in common with you than someone who grew up surrounded by this.' He gestures out the window at the distant skyscrapers. 'We had plenty of moonshine out there. Real beer. No one out there would touch synthetic alcohol if their lives depended on it. They pride themselves on swilling the real stuff, even if they're left with skull-splitting hangovers.'

He stops and tilts his head, his vision going distant. Seems like we're both plagued with memories this morning. Then I realize he's been pinged. I down the first cup of coffee and pour myself another as he listens to his auditory message.

He shakes his head to clear it and the way he looks at me makes my insides freeze.

'What is it? Is it Tila?'

'No. Not your sister. But Mia is dead.'

•

I can't have my answers right away. Nazarin has been called back to the Ratel, and they're still performing the autopsy report. We've returned to the gingerbread safe house, and I'm alone for most of the day. I work out and practise the fight sequences that I've brainloaded. I order a lonely meal from the replicator, barely tasting it. I take a long shower, turning the water up as hot as I can bear, staring at my toes. First, I try to read, then I try to watch something on the wallscreen, but I take nothing in. I end up wandering the empty rooms, staring blankly into space, numb.

Mia is gone. The woman who took me and my sister in. The woman who helped us navigate our brave new world of San Francisco. She was flawed, she was deeply troubled, but she loved us, and we loved her. Now she's gone. I wonder if they told Tila, and what she's thinking, wherever she is.

When Nazarin returns, late that night, he has the autopsy report. He lays the tablet on the kitchen table and we perch next to each other on stools. We still haven't talked properly about what happened, but I don't want to any more.

'They warned me it's inconclusive,' he tells me. 'They're not going to incinerate her right away.'

I jerk my shoulders up at that. I can't stand the thought of her turned into nothing but ash.

'Sorry. I've been told I can be insensitive in times of loss. When I had a partner, she was usually the one to break any news like this.'

'Yeah, you're not being remotely comforting here. Why don't you have a partner any more?' I can't believe it's never occurred to me to ask. I also don't want to look at the autopsy report just yet, so I'm stalling.

'She died. Not long before I went undercover. Right now, you're the closest to a partner I have.' He looks away from me, but there's a tension in his muscles that wasn't there a moment before.

'I'm sorry.'

'Yeah. Me too.'

'Were you two . . . close?'

He raises an eyebrow. 'We weren't fucking, if that's what you mean.'

I don't react, though of course, his words make me think about him without his clothes. It's a nice mental image.

'She was actually married to Dr Mata,' he continues. 'That's how I met Kim. But yeah, we were close. And she was a damn good detective. We cracked a lot of cases together. Put a lot of bastards away. One got away and killed her.'

'Did you catch him?'

'Nah. Asshole got away with it. I ever find out who did it . . . they won't make it to prison.' He works his jaw, hesitating, as if deciding whether or not to tell me what's on his mind. 'I'm pretty sure it was the Ratel.'

Was that why he went undercover? 'If they hurt your partner, wouldn't they then know who you were?'

'You're not the only one wearing a false face and using a false name,' he says.

I wonder what he used to look like. What his real name is. I'm not sure he'd tell me, so instead I ask: 'What was her name?'

He closes his eyes. 'Juliane. Juliane Amello.'

'Pretty name.' I raise my coffee cup, and he taps his with mine. 'In memory of Juliane.'

He smiles at my sentimentality, and drinks. 'We're toasting with the wrong stuff.'

'Can you stand the thought of more SynthGin or Synth-Tequila?'

He grimaces, and I laugh. I sober when he glances down at the tablet again. I don't want to see a hollow recreation of Mia. I don't want to remember the way she was in the Verve-scape. I don't want to think about how she might have screwed Tila and me over. I want to preserve her in my mind as the woman she was when we were sixteen and scared, and she protected us.

'Did you find out anything about Mirage?' I ask, stalling further.

'Yeah. I think we're OK. Another Knight told me Mirage was a bust for recording dreams, too, and that the King and Queen were annoyed. They've only managed to do it in small batches, with one or two people, and they want to do it with more people at once.'

'How many more?'

Nazarin sighs. 'As many as possible. Get them hooked, get them buying straight from them. Money and information flows towards the Ratel. The Ratel becomes the true power in San Francisco.'

Hence why the government and Sudice have to squash them before they can't any longer. What would San Francisco be like, if we were all under Ratel control? Even less privacy than now, if not even our dreams were our own.

'Still terrifying that the Ratel are using Zealots as experimental subjects. Have any died from Verve?'

'Plenty.'

'Why isn't the government doing more? Surely they could do something to protect them?'

Nazarin's face is impassive. 'In this case, it means the government can watch what they're doing. If the Ratel realizes the government knows, then they'll do something more underground. Maybe take people to experiment on. Zealots are expendable.' His mouth tightens.

Expendable. Like Mia.

'They're both as bad as each other in some ways, aren't they?' I say, my stomach roiling. Am I really on the right side? Is there a right side in all of this?

'Be careful what you say,' Nazarin says, leaning close to me.

I rest my head in my hands. I want to leave all of this. I want to give up. Everything is too muddled, too confusing; but if I give up, then Tila goes into stasis.

'You ready?' he asks.

I nod, and he presses the button and the hologram pops up like a macabre children's picture book.

It's Mia, alone. She's not connected to the machine, but she's just come off it. The medical information scrolls to the right of her, listing all the physical ways the Zeal and Verve have messed her up. Malnutrition. Kidney disease. Skin abscesses near injection sites. Tooth decay. Jaundice. It's reflected in the hologram – Mia is thin and unhealthy, just as she was the last time I saw her, strapped to the Chair, wires emerging from her arms as she dreamed her nightmares in the Zealot lounge of Mirage. But in this her eyes are open, moving from side to side as she staggers back to the hovel where she lives.

Lived.

I swallow, unable to look away. A dark, shadowy figure comes up behind her. A man, most likely, judging from his height. His face is covered in a dark fabric mask. He grabs Mia around the neck and pulls her to him, whispers something in her ear.

I pause it. 'How do they know he whispered to her?' Mia's face is also a lot more detailed and expressive than the recreation of Tila murdering Vuk had been, and everything is shown from the same angle. I can answer my own question.

'It was caught on camera,' Nazarin says.

'Do you think it was the Ratel?'

'I honestly don't know. I hope not. And this isn't their usual MO. If they order a hit, they want you to know it.' His jaw works, and he must be thinking of his partner. He presses play again.

Mia's eyes widen at whatever the masked man whispers. 'Which lost soul are you?' she asks, loud enough to be heard by the camera.

He doesn't respond except to grab her face in his hands.

'I wanted to try and be good again. I suppose it was always too late.' She closes her eyes. 'I forgive you.'

He breaks her neck. She falls to the ground. The man is gone. Mia is also gone, even if her body remains.

The image goes dark and I turn away. A round, heavy weight of dread and grief sits in my stomach. I cross my arms over my torso and hunch forward.

'I don't want to push you, after just seeing that,' Nazarin says, leaning on the counter next to me. He's close, but not too close. Perfectly trained. 'I think there's something in here that can help us. What do you think she meant, when she mentioned "lost souls" just now, and when Tila mentioned changing faces in Mia's dream?'

I lean closer, lowering my voice to a whisper in his ear. I feel him shiver. 'Are you sure the government didn't do this?'

I ask. 'Catch her lucid dreaming because of us, and snuff her before the Ratel found her?' The government being behind this would be marginally better than the Ratel, though still terrifying, but the real question simmers behind those words: is it our fault?

He shakes his head. 'No. I have access to those records. Whoever this was, it wasn't one of us.'

Unless they were off the books and they don't want him to know. That's always a possibility.

I furrow my brow. *Changing faces.* Vuk's autopsy said he'd had lots of plastic surgery. Even changed the shape of his ears. Had she known him, somehow?

Changing faces like kaleidoscopes.

A horrible theory blossoms in my head. 'Fucking hell.'

'What?'

'Turn on the wallscreen.'

The blank wall home screen appears in front of us.

'Bring up the list of Vuk's suspected surgeries.'

He does, and I stare at them. Sure enough . . .

'Bring up his face.'

A photograph of him appears. I look closely, but at first it still seems impossible. The face is totally different.

'Give me the tablet.'

He passes it to me and I take the little stylus from the side and start to sketch. I'm a passable artist at best, but I focus on the shape of the eyes, the nose, the wide mouth. I draw him almost smiling, as if we've just thrown a grape at him and missed. I project the drawing of Adam onto the wallscreen, right next to the picture of Vuk. Maybe, just maybe. The jawline is the same. The eyes are the same colour – that warm hazel I remember. I close my eyes and imagine that face I'd just seen in the dream. I open my eyes and look at Vuk. Yes. Yes.

'The missing link,' I say.

Nazarin catches on right away, which I appreciate. I can't quite articulate my thoughts anyway.

'It'd be difficult, but with enough surgery, Vuk could be this boy, Adam.'

I shake my head. I've made the connection, but it still doesn't seem possible. He'd had his left arm reconstructed. Underneath the synthetic skin, it had been as metal as my mechanical heart. 'The boy I know was a fetal amputee. His arm ended at the elbow. But Adam *died*.'

'Did you ever see the body?'

'N . . . no.' There were no funerals in the Hearth.

What did they do with the bodies?

Adam was in the Wellness Cabin that first day, and he seemed ill, but not on the brink of death. And the next day he was gone. 'Did he escape, like we did?'

'It's possible.' He taps his fingers on the countertop. I think back. Escape for us was hard. Escape for us meant planning. Adam didn't escape. I meet Nazarin's eyes, knowing what he'll say next.

'Or Mana-ma sold him to the Ratel,' Nazarin says.

Which lost soul are you? Mia asked.

Did that mean there's more than one? Who else did we lose in the Hearth? Who else might be here?

'In the year before I left, at least three teenagers died. A cut that went septic. A flu that wouldn't stop. And then they'd be gone. They were all men.' My stomach hurts.

'So you think your Mana-ma might have . . . sold Adam and others to the Ratel?'

'She might. She just might have. It'd mean money to keep us afloat and keep the Hearth solvent. We weren't self-sufficient from trading our makeshift items and selling produce. A lot of us were raised to be pliant, to listen to those in charge. Despite that, though, I can't picture Adam turning into a hitman. And why would she do it? It'd be against the morals she taught us, to sell Hearth folk to the Impure.'

Nazarin exhales. 'Brainwashing can be very persuasive, if it's done over years. The Ratel might have been able to break him, psychologically. And I don't know. Maybe your Mana-ma wasn't as holy as she led you to believe. In any case, this is circumstantial evidence on top of more circumstantial evidence.'

'Stop calling her *my* Mana-ma. She's no such thing.' Not any more. How could I ever have believed in her?

'Sorry. You're right. I'll send the sketch back to the station, see if they can make any matches.'

'My drawing might not be good enough. Unfortunately I don't have any photographs.'

'We'll see what they say in any case. The drawing's good.'

I feel a strange little rush of pleasure at that. 'So, if this is all true, then there could be a link between the Hearth and the Ratel. Maybe Tila found that out. And that's why she went after them.'

I fight down a rush of nausea. Even if this is why she did it, why didn't she tell me? Why didn't she ask me to help? And if Vuk was actually Adam, why the hell would she kill him? She loved him just as much as I did. Wouldn't she try to help him instead?

Tila was stupid, brash, and left me behind. She never used to leave me in the dust . . . but then, she never used to have a choice in the matter.

I look back at the autopsy and the police report to distract myself from the racing, circular thoughts I have no answer to. As I make sense of the words, I gasp. 'Did you see this?' I ask.

Nazarin leans over my shoulder.

It's a report from one of Mia's neighbours, saying she was acting strangely yesterday and this morning.

'Like a totally different person,' the woman said. She didn't give her name to the police. 'She'd been singing really old songs from the 1960s, said she was giving up Zeal, moving away. She seemed happy, but also sort of manic? I thought she might have still been high, her eyes were so glazed.'

'She wanted to quit? This makes things so much sadder,' I say, nearly choking with grief.

Nazarin frowns. 'Something's weird about it, though. We saw her physical stats. She was really far gone, to change so suddenly.'

'Maybe I got through to her.'

'What do you mean?'

'In the dreamscape, just before we left, I told her she could be better if she wanted to be. Remember? I told her to try and be good again.'

Nazarin's face goes still.

'What is it?'

'Nothing.' He gets up and leaves me, confused, at the kitchen table. I can hear him hitting the punching bag in the gym.

About an hour later, he asks if I want to go for a walk, for some fresh air. His eyes dart imperceptibly to the wallscreens.

I agree, put on my coat, and we head out into the night. Nazarin turns on a White Noise, a tiny device the size of a fingernail, which will distort any nearby cameras trying to record our conversation. I wish we could use it in the safe house to speak freely, but the SFPD would wonder at the scrambled readings. We walk along the darkened streets, leaning close. Nazarin has his hand in his pocket, and I know it's curled around a gun.

Whatever he's about to tell me, he doesn't want his employers to know, either.

'I've been developing a theory, over the last few months. I've been trying to find more definitive proof before I go to the SFPD.'

'About what?'

'I think Verve does more than simply giving people access to dreams.'

I focus on him. The light from the streetlamps plays across his face, casting dark shadows.

'I think,' he says, each word heavy and deliberate, 'that some lucid dreamers can influence the Vervescapes and change personalities. I think . . . you might have done that to Mia. And I think the government realized that and they killed her, not the Ratel.'

I take a few steps, trying to process the information. It doesn't want to process. 'Fuck.'

'It makes sense. I've seen other Knights or Pawns in the Ratel suddenly change personality completely. They wouldn't seem to know me, even if we'd spoken the day before. Think how dangerous that makes this drug.'

'Whether it's in the hands of the Ratel or the government.'

'Exactly.'

'So you think . . . the Ratel overwrote Adam's personality, and made him Vuk?'

'Yes. I do.'

'What does this mean for us?'

'It means we stick to our original plan for the SFPD. It's all we can do.'

'If we take the Ratel down, though, then the government will have Verve.'

'Yes.' He doesn't look happy about it.

'There is no good and evil in this scenario, is there? There's only bad and worse.'

We keep walking through the streets for hours. At some point, Nazarin's warm and calloused hand takes my own. I don't pull away.

FIFTEEN

TILA

I feel sorry for those still left in the Hearth.

I've tried to put the Hearth behind me and to forget as much as possible. But I don't think I can ever forget. Not completely. All those people, following Mana-ma's rules set out in the Good Book, listening to her sermons, their voices rising up in song. Did they really think that by following those rules they'd achieve salvation, and have their pick of next lives in the Cycle?

I never knew how many people were actually happy there, and how many people were just pretending. How many knew the truth of Mana-ma?

Mardel discovered it, in the end. True enough, he stopped drinking alcohol. The problem was, he also stopped drinking everything else.

No one noticed right away. I heard my father comment that Mardel looked weak and wasn't able to pull his weight in the fields, but he put it down to alcohol withdrawal. By the third day, Mardel was badly dehydrated. They tried to make him drink water, but he'd start shaking and spit it out. They managed to force some down him. We tried another Meditation, urging him to drink water rather than alcohol. It didn't quite take, not like the first time. Perhaps our fear lowered efficacy. He lingered a few more days. Then he died.

Mana-ma found a way to spin it. God had simply called him home. I saw it for what it was: a failed experiment. Would she try to change us again in Meditation, and if so, who would she choose next? Would it go wrong?

I didn't want to stick around to find out.

My parents were from San Francisco. They'd joined as idealistic teens and I think, somewhere over the next twenty-odd years, they realized they had made a mistake.

Our mom helped run the accounts and our dad was in some ways Mana-ma's muscle, along with Uncle Tau (not our uncle by blood). They didn't often have to be muscle, thankfully, but if people weren't pulling their weight they'd have a quiet word with them. But they weren't Mana-ma's right-hand men; her most trusted advisors were Kieran, Niran and Daniel.

When we were sixteen, Kieran, Niran and Daniel were aged about twenty-seven to thirty. They're probably still her main muscle. She'd groomed them for the role since they were little. Loyal as watchdogs, and just as scary.

After our heart attack, everyone in the Hearth was very nice to us. We didn't have to do our chores (we couldn't really, anyway, we were so weak). Our friends came by the house a lot and we played cards. Taema and I played on the same team because otherwise it'd be too easy to cheat. Our friends were shy around us, not wanting to meet our eyes. They knew we were probably dying, and it embarrassed them. Made me want to force them to look at us, right in the eyes; but if I'd done that, they probably wouldn't have come back and played cards again.

We'd ask mom and dad how much time we had left, but they didn't want to answer. We heard them murmuring at night in the other room, but even though we pressed our ears to the doorjamb, we couldn't hear anything. We knew they were talking about us, though, from the tone. Hushed, worried. Nervous.

We were in bed late one night when I finally asked the question I'd been wondering ever since we had the attack: 'They could fix our heart out there, couldn't they?'

Taema was silent for a moment, and then ran her fingers through my hair. I loved it when she did that. I found the faint tickling so comforting. I ran my hand through hers, offering comfort back.

'They could,' she said. 'But it doesn't matter. Mana-ma won't let us go.' Getting past the swamp was difficult, even with a boat. And Mana-ma had eyes everywhere. My sister didn't say it, but I knew what she was thinking: if we got out, we'd be Impure. Despite everything, she still believed a hell of a lot more than I did. It was so frustrating. Couldn't she see how messed up this place was? It made me angry at her.

'Some have made it out,' I whispered. 'Remember Mia? She left, even though Mana-ma didn't want her to.'

'Nobody knows how, or what happened to her.'

I was quiet for a bit, feeling the coarse, curly threads of Taema's hair. She could annoy me so much sometimes, but obviously I didn't want to lose her. Death did scare me something fierce. Because it'd be the first time I'd be alone.

I also knew that we had to leave the Hearth, or we didn't have a shot. Taema hadn't wanted to research conjoined twins on the tablet. She was afraid of what we might find – though I didn't understand what exactly she thought that might be. So when she fell asleep and the tablet was still on, I'd researched on my own.

I knew that everyone out there could change how they looked, and that most did. There was very little obesity, few eating disorders, unsightly scars or pockmarks or missing limbs. Everyone was whole. Perfect. And I knew that out there, there were no conjoined twins. I couldn't find any, not anywhere. Maybe they were all aborted, never even had a chance to live, or 'fixed' as soon as they were born.

So even if we did get out, how would people react? It explained the way the people in the supply ships acted around us. Even those grunt monkeys supervising the drones were all beautiful. But getting out still seemed better than sitting here, waiting to die. I knew we only had one chance of getting out, although neither of us wanted to put them in such a tight spot.

'Mom and Dad will know.'

SIXTEEN

TAEMA

The next day, I'm alone.

Nazarin's gone to the other safe house to check in with his SFPD superiors. He's going to dig into plastic surgery records at a bunch of flesh parlours, to see if Vuk has any official history there. It's useless – if Vuk was actually Adam, then he won't have an official record of even existing, much less getting plastic surgery.

Tomorrow Nazarin has a busy day with the Ratel, as it's not long until Saturday, the night of the party, and there's lots to do. Saturday is the night when he might finally meet Ensi, face to face.

I can't reconcile the image of Adam, that sweet boy, grown up into a hardened killer. Maybe I'm wrong about it all, but I don't think I am. But then, what do I know about people? My sister could be a murderer too, and I can't forget how I acted in Mia's Vervescape.

I can't stand to think about what happened in that twisted nightmare. Ever since we left the Hearth, I've worked hard to fit in: get a good job, buy an apartment, pay my taxes. I don't stand out, except for my scar. I never wanted to be that strange girl who used to live in a cult. In a world obsessed with perfection, I didn't want to be known only for having spent sixteen years as a conjoined twin. My goal has always been to stay out of trouble.

Now I'm headfirst in it.

Nazarin's been undercover this whole time, balancing training me and his work with the Ratel. I don't have long before I'm to go in.

Being alone is forcing me to consider what's going on. I don't have a job. I quit my last one, and turned down going to China. I want nothing more than to sit with numbers and calculations, or fly out over the bay to visit the machines I helped design, and view the city from the top point of a Viva-Fog. I want to forget about people, and stay with the machines and their cold logic. Maybe after this is all over, I can go back. I hope so.

I have permission to return to my apartment for clothes, so I leave and ping Nazarin with a message of my whereabouts. I take the glowing green MUNI, the ads flashing on the tops of the train. Halfway there, though, I change course; I don't want to go to my place. I get off, take another train, and head for my sister's apartment instead. After all, her clothes fit my cover better than my own.

The door opens at my VivaChip, which makes me realize I would have had to use a key at my own place. Tila's home is a dump, though I'm not sure how much is her usual disarray and how much is from the SFPD searching the place. As I set down my bag, I feel like an intruder, even though I've been here countless times before.

I decide to set things to rights – though it's really an excuse to go through her things, thoroughly and systematically, in case there are any more hints.

Tila stores things in almost the same places I do. Her underwear is in the same drawer, though everything's just thrown in. Her jeans and skirts are likewise crumpled. I take the time to fold them and put them back, arranged by colour. I don't find anything but clothes in the drawers or closet, and I take a few to bring back with me to the safe house. My fingers hover over the green dress she likes, but the memories of Mia's mind are too strong, and I leave it on its hanger.

There's nothing but dust under the bed. No gun beneath the pillow, no grenades in the bedside table. What was I expecting?

I give up and sit on her bed, sighing. I snuggle under the cover, missing Tila so much it's a physical ache. I'm angry at her, I'm terrified for her, and I'm a little terrified of her and what she might have done. But I've never gone so long without speaking to her, or seeing her. The blankets even smell like her perfume – lily of the valley. I press my nose into the pillow.

I allow myself to cry about it all. I've kept most of it bottled up close inside, trying to stay strong, to dampen everything through Mana-ma's training; but I can't do it any more. It hurts too much. It's not pretty tears. I'm keening and sobbing, my nose running almost as much as my eyes. I rock back and forth, clutching the pillow to my chest. I feel like a lost little girl. I don't know how to save Tila. I don't know if I can. I don't know if I will. If I don't figure this out, then my sister will go into stasis. I can't even imagine never seeing her again. I really would be ripped in two.

It takes a long time before I stop crying. I sit up, sniffling, and take a tissue from the box on the bedside table. Beneath the tissue box is Tila's sketchbook. Still sniffling, I take it and rest the book on my knees, flipping through the pages.

She loved to people-watch. She used to say she liked to record the people that surrounded her in her sketchbook. *It's different than a picture. This is more honest,'* she'd say, bending over the paper to shade in an eyebrow. She never used a tablet, always drawing the way she had at the Hearth, with pen and paper. *'So many people. And we don't really know what makes them tick. So few people we really, truly know in this world. With the rest of them we're just pretending. But when I'm drawing them, I feel like I can find something about them that's real. That maybe they didn't want me to see. Sometimes I feel like I'm pretending with everyone except for you, Taema.'*

I turn another page. Here are hosts and hostesses from Zenith – I recognize Pallua, Leylani and a few of the others, either that I saw that night or from the police information brainload. There are a few of her favourite clients – beautiful men and a few women, smiling and holding glasses of champagne. Their names are neatly printed next to them in our alphabet. Nadia. Jeiden. Locke. Men and women with money to burn to stave off their loneliness.

Here are total strangers. People Tila would sketch in cafes and restaurants. I can remember when she drew the old man at the bar down the street – not that he looked that old (hardly anyone in San Francisco does), but you can still tell when someone's over seventy. Something about their eyes.

This man was always there, at the same seat at the bar, with the same glass of SynthScotch, staring into the distance with the withdrawn look that meant he was accessing his ocular implant. We often used to wonder what he was reading or watching, lost in his own little world, not moving except to raise the glass to his lips or lift his finger for a refill. I remember how my twin looked, bent over the sketchbook as she shaded in his features, while I sat across from her sketching out calculations for whatever project I was working on. Companionable silence.

I close my eyes tight, not wanting to cry again. But I don't have any tears left. I make my way through the rest of the house, looking under the sofa cushions, in every kitchen cupboard, all the various nooks and crannies.

In the middle of the kitchen, I stand up, my eyes wide. Why hadn't I remembered?

I *do* know where Tila hides her secrets.

She showed it to me once, not long after she moved in. It was to be her version of the cookie jar, where I could leave her messages if I was passing by. Such a childish game, but I'd appreciated it. Yet in all the months she lived here, I never left her any messages. I kept meaning to, but never did. Hers were always so clever, so thoughtful, and when I tried to think up a return message, they all seemed unbearably dull. She never mentioned the lack of baubles and notes. I never knew if she was hurt by that or not.

I go to her spare bedroom, grunting as I pull back the bed. Another reason I didn't leave messages: it's harder to get to than a cookie jar in the kitchen. Tila was always the more paranoid of us, though, and now I understand why.

I can't see any evidence that the police moved the bed, and the cubbyhole she built behind it seems untouched. I take the key she gave me from my purse and put it into the lock, and the door swings open.

Inside are another sketchbook and a datapod. The pod is only the size of my thumbnail. I want to bring it up on my implants right away, but I'm also afraid of what it may contain.

I open the sketchbook. The first few pages are blank, but near the end, the pages are filled.

The style is looser, more abstract. It's how she draws when she's drawing from memory rather than from a model. These faces, though still beautiful and symmetrical in the way of San Franciscans, are harder. Some have scars or predatory tattoos.

Hissing snakes inked around a neck, the fangs of the open mouth framing a cheekbone, the forked tongue tasting the skin. They look like criminals. Their names are written next to them, too. A fair-haired man named Hatchet. A Japanese woman with long, sleek hair named Haruka.

The next page has a more detailed drawing of a man with the too-smooth skin and haunted eyes that mark him as older. He has a luxurious mane of dark curls around his face, high cheekbones and symmetrical features that are purposefully not perfect. The mouth is wide, the nose long and thin. He has a mole just under his left eye, with a tattoo of a crescent moon around it. Next to the sketch is the name in our secret alphabet: Ensi.

Here he is. The King of the Ratel. I lean close, until my nose almost touches the paper. I memorize every detail about him. This is who Tila was after. Who I am now after.

I turn the page. There is Malka, the Queen of the Ratel, supermodel beautiful, dark hair in long ringlets around her face, a quizzical smile on her face. A few pages later, among other hardened-looking criminals, is an unmistakeable sketch of Nazarin. He looks crueller here, his eyes shadowed by his brow, the scars on his head sharper. His sketch is detailed. She'd drawn this from life. The name next to him is 'Skel'.

Nazarin himself has told me he's met her a time or two before, so it shouldn't surprise me that he's there with the other members of the Ratel, but it's still so strange to see a sketch of him done by my sister. There's a familiarity to the drawing that gives me pause.

I close the sketchbook and go to the kitchen. I log into my messages on the wallscreen. I want to turn something on and zone out and forget about my life, at least for a few moments.

Of course, it's Tila's account on the screen, not mine,

because my VeriChip is under her identity. It makes me wonder: did they change Tila's chip too, and, legally, is it Taema who's in prison and Tila's who's free? Or is she a non-person at the moment?

I shake my head. Curiosity gets the better of me and I delve into her inbox with the same systematic ruthlessness as her apartment. Everything is squeaky clean, nothing stands out. I enable the motion sensors and flick my hands, bringing up her remote storage. I go through each folder, taking my time. I grab a glass of Synthehol white wine, knocking it down far quicker than I should. I stop once I feel a little fuzzy around the edges, numbing the pain.

It takes me a long time to go through my sister's files. I look through all the photos, many of us together, smiling identical smiles. I spend a lot of time looking at the ones from our trip around the world. I got a big return on the initial investment in VivaFog when it was officially bought by the city, and I used some of the money to take three months off work and take Tila with me around the world. We went absolutely everywhere: Jakarta, New Cairo, New Tokyo, Auckland . . . so many places with such vivid memories. No country we were remotely interested in went unvisited. It changed both of us, seeing things so far outside of our limited realm of the Hearth and San Francisco. So many different ways to live.

Nothing suspicious is there. That's because it'll all be in the datapod.

I finally pick it up again. Such a small thing, nestled into the palm of my hand, the swirling designs on the metal like a seashell. I sigh, and put it in my ear.

The datapod connects to my auditory implants and begins to download information directly to my ocular ones. I focus on the white expanse of the table. The information within is for my eyes alone.

A folder called 'Eko' flashes before me, a misspelling of her Zenith name. Within are some files with gibberish titles. I pour another glass of the ersatz wine and drain half of it, and then open the top file.

The first file is an invitation to a party, and my eyebrows rise in surprise. It's the same one Nazarin is going to on Saturday. Did he know Tila had an invitation? It's at the Xanadu. A reclusive millionaire named Alex Kynon is said to own the historic building, rebuilt perfectly after the Great Quake to mirror Frank Lloyd Wright's original design. I've never heard of a party, or anyone going there. I also never realized whoever owned it was tied up with the Ratel, but considering how secretive they are, I suppose that's not too surprising.

I open up the second file. I suck in my breath. I open more, reading through them quickly.

I've struck gold.

It's Tila's notes on the Ratel, all written in our hidden alphabet and scanned, the originals destroyed. Tears prick my eyes as I read them. Yes, it's proof she was working with them, but more than that: it's proof she was really working against them. She'd hidden the notes in a place I knew about – if I'd come to leave a message and found these, would she have told me everything? I hide all the files in an encrypted subfolder, deep within my implants. I thank whatever fate or stars aligned that I found these before I went back in. These notes might just save my life.

I sift through more of Tila's notes in my mind's eye. I come across something that makes me both furious and shamed:

There's a delivery boy/security Knight I'm going to use to get closer to Verve, she wrote, about four months ago. *His name is Skel. There's a party tonight. I'll turn on the charm and get him to take me back to his. After, I'll convince him to introduce me to Malka, and then I can prove I can lucid dream.* I force down a flush.

The doorbell rings. I jerk in surprise. Hurriedly, I finish hiding the files in my implants and take the datapod out of my ear.

'Coming!' I call as I run to the guest room, stash the sketchbook and the pod in the cubby hole, and push the bed back into place. A few days ago, this would have winded me. Thank you, gym practice and muscle mods.

I peer through the peephole. It's Nazarin. I take a breath, composing myself.

I open the door and Nazarin pushes past me, closing the door behind him.

'Why are you here rather than your place, like you said?' he asks.

I look around, shrugging. It's a way to avoid meeting his eyes. 'I realized I hadn't been here since it all went down. And I needed more clothes.'

'Let's head back to the safe house. We have your VeriChip putting a false signal here most of the time, in case the Ratel decide to track you, but you actually being here has messed with it.'

'There's cameras there, right? In the wallscreens?'

'Yeah?' His forehead crinkles in confusion.

'Not here?'

A beat as Nazarin accesses his implants to scan the apartment. 'No.'

'Then we should speak here for a moment.'

Nazarin opens his mouth to ask why, but I hold up my

hand, cutting him off. My anger over what I discovered in the notes crystallizes to a fury just as strong as I felt in Mia's dream world. I lead him to the living room.

'How well do you really know my sister, *Skel*?' I ask. I had hoped I'd somehow been wrong, or read the notes wrong, but his sheepish face shows I'm right. My gut twists. 'Spill, and you better not tell me a word of a lie, or I'm out.' It's an empty threat, but I still cross my arms. 'You haven't just met her once or twice.'

He swallows, looking down and away. 'I have only met her a few times. I just didn't clarify what . . . happened during one of them.' He licks his lips, trying to figure out what to say.

I pour another glass of SynthWine, but don't drink it. I've had enough, but at least it's something to do with my hands. Anger bubbles inside me. No one trusts me to have all the information. The decisions I've made without knowing the full story . . .

'I first met her a few months ago. She was at one of the parties for Knights, Rooks and Pawns. I thought she was a young hopeful, trying to get into the Ratel, get a taste of power by latching onto a powerful member. She had a way of drawing the eye. I guess she would, being a hostess and all.'

He stares into space. He's still standing in the middle of the kitchen. He takes the chair across from me, its legs screeching softly against the linoleum.

I say nothing, letting him find the words. 'Near the end of the party, we were both pretty drunk. Real alcohol at those things, and neither of us were used to it. Whatever she'd been there for, she hadn't found it. But she took a shine to me. I didn't understand why. It's not like I was important. She asked me to go to a hotel with her.'

I feel like I've been punched. I should have seen it, guessed it. I try not to think about his hands on my waist when we danced at Zenith. I try not to think about how he took off my clothes, so expertly. How well he seemed to know my body.

Tila got to him first. She always gets there first. And if he was attracted to me, it wasn't actually for me. It was because I look like her. In a surge of paranoia, I wonder if my sister slept with any of my exes. David? Simone? I shake my head. The constant lies are getting to me, and I'm not even undercover yet.

I pick up my glass, the wine within sloshing. I set it to the side.

It's always weird, when Tila or I meet someone the other has been sleeping with. It's knowing that this other person, this stranger, has a pretty good idea what you look like naked, even if they haven't slept with you. It's the worry that they'll look at one the same way they look at the other.

This is so much worse than any of those other times.

'I didn't go with her,' Nazarin says, calmly. I look up, confused.

'I was tempted, but I went home alone. In the end, I knew that sleeping with her was a bad idea. My orders were clear: not to become involved with anyone in the Ratel. Yet she stuck in my mind.'

'Did she try to get you to do anything?' I ask carefully. I don't want to tip him off that I have her notes. I'm not sure whether or not to believe him. Tila always gets what she wants, when she puts her mind to it. I can't remember a time anyone rebuffed her advances. If people were to choose between us, they'd be almost certain to choose Tila.

'Yeah. Later, she asked me to introduce her to Malka.'

'The Queen.'

He inclines his head. 'At that point, I hadn't met her, or

even seen her, so I couldn't give her what she wanted. She didn't bother with me again after that.'

That sounds like Tila. Slyly, I bring up my notes again. She never definitively said she slept with him. After that one entry, her focus shifted to other topics. She mentioned her frustration, and that she was having difficulties seeing Malka, but 'Skel' wasn't mentioned again. He could be telling the truth. I hope he is.

'When I saw the murder charge, saw her picture, and discovered she had a twin, I realized I could figure out what she was up to. At first it was curiosity. When I learned she was working in the Verve lounge as a lucid dreamer, I figured she's in deep – deep enough that nobody could follow her.'

'Except me.'

'Yes. Except you.'

He's run out of words. I sip the wine. No, I gulp it. 'Why didn't you tell me about this? Especially before you slept with me?' I ask once the glass is empty. I'm trying not to think of them together.

'Nothing happened. She's not the only one in the Ratel who's tried to sleep with me.' He shrugs. 'I don't know your sister. I can't pretend I do. For what it's worth, I don't think she'd have killed without a reason.'

'She didn't kill anyone.'

'As I've said, are you still so sure of that? Or are you saying it out of habit now?'

I glance down at the empty glass. 'You still should have told me.'

'You're right.'

I meet his eyes. 'No fight? No protests?'

'No. You are entirely right. I shouldn't hold anything back, even if it doesn't seem important to me at the time. It might prove to be. I'm sorry.' His body language is open. He seems sincere. I feel like I can't trust my own judgement in anything, any more. Tila's fucked with my head.

'That's twice you've not told me things I needed to know,' I say.

Nazarin stares at me, sombre. 'I wanted to sleep with you. Not your sister.'

My breath catches. He had cut to the heart of what was bothering me. I look away. I see the framed holophoto of me and Tila, arms around each other and smiling. We look so young, so happy. I feel like I've aged about twenty years in less than a week. I thought I knew her better than anyone. 'Still probably not the best idea to sleep with your undercover partner,' I say. 'Did you, uh, mention that to your superior?'

His face goes still. 'No, I didn't. If I did, they might throw me off the case, despite all the inroads I've made. Conflict of interest. They'd put someone else on, and starting all over again means they probably wouldn't be able to help your sister.'

The careful way he chooses his words makes me tired. 'Relax. I'm not going to tell the SFPD.' A horrible thought occurs to me. 'Does the other safe house have cameras?'

'God, no. Don't worry.'

I let out a breath.

'It might not have been the best idea, what we did,' he says gently. 'I don't regret a moment of it, though.' He hesitates, glancing up at me. 'Do you?'

I can't help it – the smallest smile hooks to my cheeks before it disappears. 'No. I don't. But I don't think it should happen again. Not while we're doing this.'

He nods. 'That's fair.'

I stand up, hold out my hand. 'So. You'll tell me everything. I may not be an actual member of the Ratel, but I'm not stupid.

I'm your best chance of figuring out what's really going on in the Ratel. Stop trying to protect me or cover your own ass, or you'll get us both killed.'

He stands and takes my hand in a warm grasp. 'I promise,' he says.

I look at him for a long time. He doesn't look away. He wants to kiss me. I want to kiss him, but only our hands touch.

I'm still confused and a little jealous, but I push it away until I'm calm and steady.

It's a new start. We're partners.

•

I'm getting sick of the safe house. It's not home.

Nazarin tells me about the party, and that he wishes he could somehow add my name to the guest list, as starting there versus at the Verve lounge would be easier. The look on his face when I tell him Tila has an invitation too and I should probably go with him is priceless.

I've hidden all her notes, but I bring up the invitation onto the wallscreen. I tell him I found it in her hard drive. It's a white lie, and pretty rich considering I just made him promise to be honest with me in all things. I can't mention the other files, though. I haven't had a chance to translate them all yet, and there could be something incriminating in them. She's my sister. I get first look. If I find anything useful, I'll tell him.

I give him the sketch of Ensi to take back to headquarters, as well. He shakes his head in amazement. 'This is what he looks like? Do you know how long we've been trying to find this out? This alone will help us so much.'

Good, I think. Maybe that'll make it easier for the government to let my sister go. Regardless of what she might have done.

That night I'm strapped into the Chair yet again, to download more confidential information on the Ratel from the SFPD. Since I've been undercover, I haven't seen another cop except in these scenes. But they're there. They'll be ringed around the Xanadu, hidden, supposedly lending whatever support they can, with another few stationed at the safe house. Though I know as well as Nazarin that if we're truly in trouble at that party, they're unlikely to go in and blow the SFPD's cover. We have until Saturday to prepare me as much as possible.

We'll be on our own.

The next day is Thursday. One week since my life turned upside down. It doesn't seem possible. Nazarin is away for most of the day with more Ratel activities. More security. More drop-offs of Verve, to other Zealot lounges.

I wonder how far he goes when he's undercover. How deeply does he play his role? Does he hurt people? His actions do, at the very least. By delivering a weapon of a vial of Verve, someone will be harmed or killed. Soon, I'll see what he does first-hand.

Soon, I might have to do some of it myself.

Will I be able to? I've prided myself on following the letter of the law since I left the Hearth and arrived in San Francisco. The crimes I may commit while undercover are sanctioned by the government, but I can't help but fear they'll find some legal loophole afterwards. What if they don't honour their side of the arrangement, and keep Tila locked up? Or throw me in with her? I know Verve's secret. Will they want to cover up its true purpose?

I have a little ammunition in that regard that I'm keeping close. A week ago, I never would have considered these mercenary thoughts.

I read through Tila's notes. I sit cross-legged on the floor, tilting my head back, eyes closed. I've read them so many times by now. They have so many things I need, like details of the relationships and hierarchies between the various members of the Ratel. There are smaller things, too, like what people like to drink, or their favourite foods – side effects of her training as a hostess. Tila recounts crimes she's witnessed: people picking up packages full of Verve. Information gleaned from dreams. I know what businesses have Ratel members integrated into every level, gathering insider information to their advantage or bullying the owners to give them protection money. Some of this information is incriminating to the government. I know a few high-ranking officials who have tried Verve. A few members of Sudice as well. This is what I'll keep close, to protect myself and Tila when this is all over.

Tila has written her suppositions about Verve – how if it becomes widespread, the Ratel could essentially create an army to do their bidding. The government, or Sudice, wouldn't stand a chance. She also wonders what would happen if it fell into government hands. *San Francisco sure can look beautiful,* she writes, *but it's corrupt to the core with the Ratel and a government not much better. It's all infested, like termites in rotting wood.*

Her notes also seem to echo what Nazarin said outside Mirage – that there is unrest within the ranks of the Ratel. She mentions a young man who's risen quickly through the ranks but still seems discontented:

Leo. White-blond hair. Black eyes. Has realized how much Ensi keeps at the top end and how little the others are rewarded. Can't be sure if he'll actually do anything about it yet. He's cautious and methodical, but still a bit of an upstart. I figure he's going to get himself killed sooner rather than later, before he can actually make any trouble. One to watch. Could be an ally.

There had been a drawing of him, too, in her sketchbook. Serious, intense.

'Oh, Tila,' I murmur aloud. She is in deep. She's been doing this for months. And she'd come to my apartment, pretending she was only a hostess at Zenith. I should be hurt. I should be angry. It's as if I've moved through that, to the other side. Now I'm only sad, disappointed, and still deeply afraid.

All day I read the notes, until I have everything memorized. I take breaks to practise in the gym using the virtual reality overlay, dodging imaginary foes, aiming imaginary weapons. I brainload as much as I can on hacking into implants and hiding information within them, with the hope that the government will not discover what I have hidden.

Thursday melts to Friday. Nazarin stumbles in close to dawn, and I wake slightly as he turns off my Chair. It's only later that day I manage to build up my courage to tell him something in the notes I have to mention before we go to the party.

'I'm going to be Tested tomorrow at Xanadu,' I tell him over coffee.

He's slept perhaps three hours, and looks drawn and haggard. At my words, he glances up sharply. 'What makes you say something like that?'

'I've, um, found Tila's notes at her place.' I give him handwritten, printed-out translations. I've left out the information about the government and Sudice, for our later protection, and a few other things where I didn't understand what they meant and feared they could be dangerous. Everything else is there, and our handwriting is similar enough he doesn't question it.

Nazarin reads the notes right there. I sip my coffee, watching his bowed head, the way the light through the bay window highlights his cheekbones. When he's finished, he holds his head in his hands. 'Shit. This changes everything.'

We prepare even more intensely. There's a hint of desperation in the detective – he doesn't turn off the brainload to let me have uninterrupted REM. There's no time. Nazarin trains me, and my muscles grow stronger. I can run faster. The SFPD sends still more information to my brain. Out there in the city, my friends are going on with their lives, and so are Tila's.

I meet the team who will be watching us from outside Xanadu. It's only four people, because they're still containing how many within the SFPD know about Tila and me. I recognize the Indian-American officer who helped bring us in that first, awful night. Her name is Officer Jina Shareef. Her handshake is firm. Officer Oloyu is there, though he's only helping part-time. The rest of the time, he's up wherever they're holding my sister. I want to ask him how she's faring, but I'm afraid of the answer. The other two have worked on undercover operations, including with Nazarin, many times. Their names are Detective Lucas and Detective Tan. Both have the large, blocky look of bodyguards, and of men who know how to use a gun. The officers will be watching surveillance, and all four will be posted near the Xanadu, a hovercar at the ready if we need a quick escape.

The morning of the party, I read through the notes one last time. I don't think there's anything more for me to learn from them. The puzzle pieces have fallen into place.

All we know of the Test is it's another lucid dreaming assessment, perhaps to let Tila into the next level of the Verve lounge. No one knows what the Test exactly entails. Not Nazarin. Not the SFPD. Not Tila, though I expect she had some inklings that never made it onto the pages. We've done all we can.

But we won't know if it's enough until I pass or fail.

Tila was after Ensi. The leader of the Ratel. Though I still don't see why, or how she could ever have thought she could take him down. All I can do is get closer to the quarry at the party in Xanadu.

SEVENTEEN

TAEMA

The Xanadu is just off Union Square.

I wonder who the billionaire Alex Kynon really is, for it's a pseudonym wrapped in many layers of bureaucratic red tape and obfuscation.

I've wandered through Union Square so many times, especially around Christmas. Tila and I would always come here to see the lights. The giant Christmas tree in the centre, the man-made ice rink where people zipped to and fro on old-fashioned ice skates. The city tries to trap the past like an insect in amber. It doesn't really succeed in capturing a sense of what it must have felt like – not with those hypermodern fashions the men and women wear as they bustle about, actually shopping in person for the sheer nostalgia of it, droids following behind carrying their wares – but I do appreciate the effort.

Nazarin and I discussed our plan over and over before I left. We'll take different MUNI trains, arriving at Union Square at different times from different directions. We'll enter the party nearly together, though. Tila and Skel have been seen flirting with each other at previous parties, so we can act friendly, but won't linger together too much. Nazarin is hoping to network, and speak to one of the discontented members of the Ratel, try to become closer to him. He tells me the name, keeping his promise not to hold anything back: it's Leo, the man that Tila wrote about in her notes.

My objective is to do the Test, try not to die, and find out what happens at the next level of the Ratel.

No big deal.

Nazarin appears on my right. I'm waiting for him beneath the pillar of the Dewey Memorial. Far above him, the young woman balances on one toe, holding her wreath and trident.

He pauses. 'You look nice.'

'Thanks.' He saw me leave with my coat, but I have it unbuttoned in the warm evening. I must have tried on all the clothes I'd taken from Tila's place three times before I decided on an outfit. In the end I chose a form-fitting silver zip-up catsuit that covers me from neck to wrists to built-in heels. According to Tila's notes, I'm meant to attract attention at these things. Here's hoping no one misses me, looking like a human-shaped disco ball from space.

'Have you ever been here before?' I ask, jerking my head in the direction of the Xanadu.

'No.'

'And you think both the King and Queen will be there?'

'They're meant to be.'

Ensi is the named leader of the Ratel, but if the chess analogy is to be carried on, the Queen is the most important player. She's the one who does the dirty work and takes out the other pieces, if need be. I recall Tila's sketch of her, the beautiful woman with long dark hair, a sardonic smile and a cruel glint to her eye.

'OK,' Nazarin says. 'It's nearly time.'

'Right.'

He reaches out and grips my shoulder. 'We're in this

together. You've prepared for this as much as you can. You can do this.'

'You have more faith in me than I do.'

A short smile. 'I have no doubt you can do this. You're tough as nails.'

His words hearten me, as they are meant to. I watch him walk away, counting in my head.

Then I follow him, my silver heels clicking along the sidewalk.

It doesn't take long to arrive at the gates. The whole block used to be high-end stores, but now it is all a private residence. I didn't know this before the SFPD told me in the brainload. The average civilian wouldn't. Distribution of wealth isn't as uneven as before the Great Upheaval. Most people make enough to live comfortably, poverty is erased in all but the worst of the Zealots, and though citizens can order vast amounts of goods from the replicator, all can be recycled back. There are still obscenely wealthy people in this city but they tend to keep a lower profile than, say, those in Hollywood, where status and ranking have more pull. Having far, far more money than you need is seen as wasteful.

Nazarin walks through the gates. I approach a minute later, projecting Tila's invitation from my ocular implant onto a little wallscreen to the left. The door opens with a *snick*, and I walk in.

In front of us is the large, faux brick building, now made of bomb-proof, acid-proof material. We walk through to the second gate, a replica of the original Art Deco iron arched gate, topped by four rings of brick. Like many buildings, it was destroyed in the Great Quake and rebuilt to be larger than the previous plans. The original building was a store, and now it is a mansion.

Nazarin – no, Skel, he is *Skel* now – lingers enough that we almost walk into the darkened tunnel at the same time. He does not turn back or acknowledge me, but I'm thankful for his nearness.

I take a steadying breath. I am about to enter the same building as the Ratel King and Queen. It's what I've prepared for. I am now, for all intents and purposes, my sister: a lucid dreamer for a Verve lounge for the biggest mob in the city. None of it seems real. I can't really be doing this. Still, I place one foot in front of the other, moving closer to whatever is to come.

The tunnel fills with soft lights of green, blue, and purple, and a light fog drifts at waist height, scented with lilacs.

'In Xanadu did Kubla Khan a stately pleasure-dome decree,' I whisper.

Nazarin stiffens and almost turns back in confusion. I guess he's never read Coleridge.

We enter, still staggered, and the droids take our coats. I shed that outer layer like a carapace, wearing only my silver, shining second skin. Nazarin passes over his gun. No weapons at parties. Nazarin's eyes slide over me, but I ignore him, staring upwards, unable to stop myself from gaping.

The whole ceiling is open, showing the stars and moon above. It's made from the finest bulletproof glass. Despite the seriousness of the situation I can't help but be transported by the beauty of it. The main ballroom has a recreation of the original spiral staircase along its edges but much larger, like the inside of a shell, perfect circles cut out of the sides, like the holes in an abalone. The walls are creamy white, lights tingeing the smooth plaster green and blue. Twining, living vines hang from the ceiling, framing an enormous organic chandelier suspended above the dance floor, twinkling with emeralds and other jewels among the leaves. Elephants drink from a palm-framed water hole, and birds fly overhead. They're all mechanical, their eyes cameras for security posted in the next room, available to come in at a moment's notice if needed.

There aren't as many people here as I would have thought, but everyone looks so sleek and stylish, they nearly put Zenith to shame. Yet they are obviously dangerous too, marked with moving tattoos and wearing their scars proudly. A few dance to music, twining their bodies together, skin pressed against skin. Others huddle together, murmuring amongst themselves, while some wander from group to group, hovering here to say a few words before fluttering onwards, like butterflies sipping nectar from each cluster. Despite their prettiness, I cannot forget the venom they all have the ability to spread. More lines of that poem come to me:

And there were gardens bright with sinuous rills,
Where blossomed many an incense-bearing tree;
And here were forests ancient as the hills,
Enfolding sunny spots of greenery.

I straighten my shoulders and put on Tila's sultry smile. I let her personality settle over mine. I'm Tila. I'm confident and strong. I'm unafraid. A droid leaves the bar nestled at the back and passes by, offering me a glass of champagne. I take a sip and almost choke. It's real champagne – nothing remotely synth about it. The liquid burns slightly, and my taste buds tingle, the bubbles popping against my tongue.

I recognize some of the faces from Tila's sketches. I stay calm – my eyes flicker over them quickly, but I don't see the King and Queen of the Ratel.

Nazarin leaves me, mingling with others before returning. He greets me, giving me one of those small hugs you give people you don't know very well. 'Something's not right,' he whispers in my ear. 'Be careful.'

Before I can ask him more questions, he disappears, and I'm taken aback. I know we can't be seen too much together, but surely if Tila flirted with him at a previous party, we could take up the same cover again. How can he just leave me here on my own, with what I'm about to face?

Some of the familiar faces from Tila's sketchbook come to greet me, and I smile and kiss them on the cheeks, greeting them by name, all too aware that the hands gently resting on my shoulders have killed people. All these polite guests are hardened criminals, many with hits under their belts. It's almost like I can feel the ghosts, a press of the invisible, cold corpses these people are responsible for, crowding the room with the revellers.

I shake my head, which feels fuzzy. I eye the scented fog in suspicion – have they put something in it, like the way they release extra pheromones in the casinos? Was there something in that glass of champagne – real champagne! – I drank far too quickly?

I have to keep my wits about me.

I understand a lot more than I did before, but there are still so many gaps. Tila came into the Ratel from a different direction than Nazarin. She may have run errands briefly, but as soon as she proved that she could lucid dream, she worked her way in deeper without going through the official steps. Until now. She's close enough that they want her to do something more important for them, if she just passes this Test. If I just pass the Test.

I force myself to stay calm, to smile at the guests as if nothing is bothering me.

What did the Ratel think, when Vuk disappeared? Do they

think he went rogue, or do they know that something happened to him? Tila wasn't supposed to be working that night, but surely someone at the club noticed her. Sal saw her. Did he change his colours and decide to turn her in to the Ratel? There is a chance that this is all an elaborate trap. Nazarin said that the hitman, that Adam-turned-Vuk, wasn't after her. I'm not sure if I still believe that.

I look around for Nazarin again, my mouth dry. I drink more champagne to wet it, though the bubbles are going to my head already. It all just seems so very, very stupid. We're here with essentially no back-up because any type of surveillance would be instantly recognized by the scanners we passed at the gate. There's plenty of cops seconds away if we can manage to call them, but the odds of that in here are next to nothing – all signals are blocked.

I'm beginning to panic, sweating beneath the silver fabric. Where is Nazarin? He wouldn't leave me, would he? I keep saying hello to strangers, fudging conversations, my mind working in overtime not to step in the wrong place. Nobody mentions a thing about the Ratel. They comment on the decor, how amazing this building is, the champagne, the salty caviar blintzes. I want to scream.

Be Tila. She'd know how to react. None of this would faze her.

The party wears on. My cheeks ache from the effort of appearing cheerful and flirtatious, uncaring and unaware of the precariousness of my situation. I dance with people. I sip more champagne, nibble at the decadent treats. There's still no Nazarin. I can't help but feel he's thrown me to the wolves. The shiny, silvery distraction.

Nazarin finally returns. He has a pretty man next to him, who's flirting shamelessly, and he's flirting in turn with considerable skill. I feel an unwelcome flare of annoyance at the display. With a start, I recognize the other person: he's Leo, the young man Tila mentioned in her notes. The potential ally. I make my way towards them.

'Good evening. Great party, right?' I sound inane.

Nazarin gestures to me. 'Leo, I believe you've met Tila.'

'How could I ever forget?' he says, taking my hand and kissing the back of it.

I wonder what sort of impression Tila made.

Leo seems composed, but his eyes keep darting about the room. Perhaps he's uncomfortable with eye contact. He moves with the grace of someone who knows how to fight.

He meets my eyes. 'The party's only just getting started, isn't it? Lots more entertainment to come, I'm sure.'

I smile, though something makes me uneasy. Nazarin narrows his eyes at Leo.

'Leo,' Nazarin says. 'You'll have to excuse us, but I want to steal Tila for a dance.'

Leo smiles. 'Of course. I might have to steal her after, if you don't mind that is,' he says to me. Smooth. Very smooth.

'That'd be lovely,' I say, thinking it would be no such thing. 'Excuse me, I'm going to find another drink, first.' Nazarin reaches out to touch my elbow. He wants to tell me something, but there's no way he can. The crowd is thicker than at the start of the evening. Too many ears to overhear a whisper. Ocular and auditory implants have been blocked by tech dampeners.

Nazarin's eyes follow me as I take another flute of champagne I will not drink from a droid servant.

I turn around and a woman stands right before me, flanked by two guards. She looks me up and down, smiling in recognition. She knows me and has seen me before.

And I recognize her, though it takes me a moment to realize who she is, with her hair up.

It's Malka. The Queen of the Ratel.

She has the tightness around her eyes that speaks of face-lifts. Her brows are high and arched, her full lips curl at the edges. She has skin of a deep brown, her hair in a slick updo, with a web of metal and crystals holding the hair in place.

'Tila,' Malka says. She reeks of power. The two bodyguards at her sides are droids, their blank faces twisting from side to side for danger.

I smile blankly in return, my mind running in frantic circles. I glance at Nazarin and his eyes are wide, locked on me.

'The Khan of Xanadu is ready to see you now. It's time to Test your mettle.'

I blink quickly, then put another inane grin on my face. 'Wonderful. I've been looking forward to it.'

She laughs, low and throaty, rubbing the fingers of one hand against the fleshy base of her thumb. 'I wouldn't be, if I were you. Come along, little canary.'

Malka takes my arm and leads me through the crowd. She stops as people greet her, introducing me. I watch other people's reactions, the awe and fear she inspires in them.

People notice me at her side, and wonder why I've been so favoured. Why has she come to get me herself? How well does she know me? Tila's notes didn't tell me much about her. I'm lost.

'Come,' Malka says. 'We musn't be late.'

All my nerve endings seem to freeze. Malka takes my arm, unlocking me, and I follow her towards the spiral ramp. I chance a look over my shoulder and Nazarin's staring at me, barely concealed panic in his eyes. Leo is speaking to him, but he doesn't seem to hear. He wanted to tell me something, but now it's too late. I try to smile at him, but I can't. I turn away and walk up the stairs.

I don't have a choice.

Nobody is up on this level. The clear glass of the ceiling seems almost close enough to touch. Up here, little rooms helix off around the huge circle in the centre, a maze of little hidden nooks and crannies. I peek over the banister down at the revellers below. Nobody looks up except for Nazarin. I nod at him, try to smile.

I feel strangely detached. Deep down, I'm aware I should be more scared about this. But it feels . . . inevitable. I'm following Tila's breadcrumbs, seeing if they lead to the gingerbread house and the hungry witch.

The Queen opens a door. I can't see anything inside but another dark, curving hallway.

'Put these on.' She passes me a small white box. I open it. Inside are small electrodes. She helps me attach them to my temples, the back of my neck, my heart. There's a thin pair of dark glasses. I put them on, feeling silly.

'These will track your physical responses,' she says.

'All right.' I wonder if my mechanical heart will impact anything. They'll know of it, I'm sure. They know everything; except, hopefully, that I have changed my face and taken my sister's place.

'There. Now. Go down to the end of the hallway and turn left.'

I lick my lips. 'Any advice?' I ask, striving for a light tone. Desperate as I am, she's my only point of contact and I'll take any help I can get – even if it's from the devil herself. I sense she appreciates that I've asked her.

She leans close, and she smells of jasmine and expensive

make-up. 'Don't speak unless ordered. Don't lie. Don't look away. Don't let us down.'

She looks into my eyes, deep and searching, as if she knows all my sins. After a moment, she leans back. I don't know what she found. With a twirl of turquoise silk, she is gone.

I've never been more confused. My head hurts, and I'm still dizzy. There must be something in the fog in that room downstairs. I should be tempted to throw myself out that window, climb down, jump the impossibly high fence, and make a break for freedom. How would Tila feel, if it was still her walking down this hallway to this Test? If she'd never come across Vuk, if he'd never ended up dead, then she'd be here, right now, and I'd never know. My head feels unattached to my body, like it's floating down this darkened hallway.

I turn to the left as instructed, and push open the door.

I'm the last person to arrive. In the room are four chairs. The other three are occupied. One is a girl with bright crimson hair down to her waist, dressed in black trousers and a glittering top. A man with a tuft of blond hair and black eyeliner wearing a red suit, with a tattoo of a tarantula on the back of his hand, sits in the middle. The man next to him has dark green hair and is dressed in black leather. It goes without saying that they're all beautiful.

I sit in the last chair, crossing my legs to stop them from shaking.

The room is completely blank. White walls, white chairs, white floors. I open my mouth, but then I remember what Malka said. *Don't speak*. My mouth snaps shut. I grind my teeth together. The drug from downstairs might be wearing off. I'm petrified.

There's a flash in the corner of my vision, a small beep in my ear. I have a message. Judging by the way the others grow still, they've received it, too. The white wall in front of me seems to undulate in waves. I can feel the little electrodes buzzing against my skin.

'You are here because you have done well. You have served and done all I've asked of you.' The voice is disguised – it echoes, distorting strangely in my mind. 'You have made it to a level that few can claim to reach.'

It wasn't me. I did none of it. *How did you get here, Tila?* I want to ask.

'Now, for the moment, do nothing. Just watch. And listen.'

Don't look away.

Images flow onto the blank wall, so quickly I barely register one before the next flicks into my field of vision. A praying mantis. The inside of a cat's mouth. The glowing algae of the Bay. The aftermath of a battle. Blood splattering on white walls. A decomposing corpse. A little girl in pigtails, holding a teddy bear by an arm. Ink blots, like in old psychological tests. Nature. War. Humanity. Over and over again.

Sounds come with them – from soft birdcalls to shrill shrieks and sirens. Smells appear too, and some are nice: cinnamon, the green smell of broken pine needles and the scent of crushed apples. Others are putrid: rotten fish, decomposing flesh, the oniony smell of unwashed bodies.

The man with the blond quiff bends forward and throws up onto the white floor. I glance at him but then fix my eyes to the wall.

Don't look away.

I don't know what this means. What it's meant to test. Am I passing or failing?

The images go on for what feels like a long time. I clutch the sides of the chair. My stomach roils, but I clamp down tight on my tongue. I won't throw up. Soon, someone else pukes, but still I don't look away. I think it might be the red-haired girl.

The images cease. All returns to pure whiteness. I sag against my chair in relief. The room smells of acidic vomit and new sweat tinged with old fear.

'Now,' says the distorted voice in our minds. 'Stand.'

We stand. I allow myself to look at the others. The other girl has vomit smudged in her red hair. The blond man's hair is in disarray. The green-haired man seems relatively unruffled. I wonder what I look like to them.

'Now, face each other. Tila, look at the man with green hair.'

I almost start at being addressed by this stranger. This is the oddest test I've ever taken. I don't understand the rules. I don't know the score. I haven't studied, as Tila's notes stopped right before I needed the cheat sheet most.

The voice changes slightly. Still modulated, but more familiar. 'Study your opponent's face, Tila. Memorize every line.'

I look at him, and he looks at me. I see a man, but only barely. He can't be much older than twenty. I think he's half-Chinese and half-Mexican, or something along those lines. I wonder what awful things he's done to get this far.

'Good. Now look at the man with blond hair.'

I look, and as I turn my head, I see the red woman and the green man have done the same. As soon as we're all looking, the blond man crumples. Blood pours from his nose, his ears, his eyes. He's dead.

'He failed,' the voice whispers in our minds.

Fuck, I think. I should think more. Feel more. I can't – all I can concentrate on is making sure that it's not me next.

'Look forward.'

We stare at the screens again. More images flash, even quicker this time, so that I couldn't explain them even if I wanted to. I hear retching beside me. Why do they affect them more than me? My stomach hurts, my head hurts, and I feel pressure behind my eyes, but I'm still looking.

Don't look away.

The voice starts asking me questions. I'm to blink once for yes and twice for no. The man doesn't ask me about what I – Tila – have done for the Ratel. Instead they're hypothetical questions. Some are difficult: *Would you kill your childhood pet for X sum of money? Would you risk your life to save a drowning child? What about a drowning person who wronged you?* Some are beyond asinine: *If there were ice cream and sprinkles on that white coffee table right now, would you add the sprinkles?*

I answer them all without thinking too hard. There are hidden layers and messages in this, impacting us all in ways we can't anticipate. Feints and jabs before hooks and crosses. I don't even try to outsmart them. There's no way to.

The scarlet-haired girl goes next. Falls right out of her chair. Her red hair perfectly matches the blood.

This is insane, I think distantly. *This is absolutely insane.* I wonder if I'll be the next person to die.

Maybe this is all a trap. These are people hopeful of moving up in the Ratel, and maybe the King already knows that we're not worthy. He's here to catch us in lies, pick us off one by one. Perhaps it's his idea of sport.

Maybe he wants to discover whether we've betrayed him before he kills us.

The green man is nervous, sweat dripping down his temples. I'm surprisingly calm. I must look unafraid to him, and that makes me feel braver. I stand, staring at him. His pupils behind the darkened glasses dilate as he listens to his own instruction. Then he rushes me.

He grabs my arm, hard enough to stop the blood flow. I try

to jerk out of his grip but he only holds on tighter. The man's face is red, twisted with rage.

He means to kill me.

'Kill him,' the voice whispers in my mind. 'Or be killed.'

I stomp on his insole, the way Nazarin taught me. The sharp stiletto of my heel presses on his foot and I'm sure I hear something snap. He cries out and I twist my arm, breaking free.

He rushes me again, but this time I see it coming. Nazarin's training serves me well enough, but I won't be able to avoid him forever. He's much bigger than me, and much, much angrier. I look for a weapon and grab the nearest chair, stepping over the body of the blond man. I bring up the chair and swing it at him, trying to frighten him off, and then I hold it close to me like a lion-tamer against a rabid man with a mane of green hair. The signal to my implants is blocked – the voice and images are silent in my head, including the self-defence programs for the implants. I'm left to fend for myself.

He attacks me and I smash him with the chair, grunting with the effort. He barely staggers, and then reaches out and grabs the chair so hard that I have to release it.

'Stop it!' I bellow at him, even though I'm not supposed to speak. He gives a shout, more of a roar, and hits me hard on my shoulder and I drop. I cry out and roll out of the way just before he brings the chair down again, and it shatters into splinters. I grab a broken leg, sharpened to a point. Snarling, enraged as I was in Mia's Vervescape, I thrust up.

Blood spurts from the wound, drenching my hands. The green-haired man sputters. He no longer looks angry. He looks scared, and hurt.

'Oh God,' I say, over and over again. 'Oh God. Oh God. Oh God.'

He falls right on top of me, driving the splinter of wood deeper into himself. His blood seeps onto me. I push him away. He's so heavy. I crawl away and throw up, retching until there's nothing left. When I'm done I sit back on my heels, wrapping my arms around my knees and shaking. I'm surrounded by three dead bodies, splatters of blood and sick marring the perfect white of the room.

Now, even if Tila hadn't killed Vuk, I've killed someone. I'm no longer the woman I was a week ago. I'm no longer an engineer and someone who follows the rules. I'm a murderer. I say it out loud. 'I'm a murderer.' I almost choke on the words, but I force myself to say it again. 'I'm a murderer.' My throat is raw from vomiting and screaming. I want to curl up and disappear.

I close my eyes tight. My heart is still beating far too calmly. I tear the glasses from my face and throw them across the room, ripping the electrodes from my body by touch.

'Open your eyes,' a man's voice says.

I obey. The room is now completely empty but for the cooling pile of my own vomit beside me. There's no red woman, blond man or green man. It's as if they never existed. They never did.

Instead, in front of me is Ensi.

The leader of the Ratel.

He's tall, leanly muscled, with skin a little darker than mine and close-cropped, curly hair. It had been longer in Tilda's sketch. He wears a collarless blue silk shirt and black trousers, and looks almost like a priest.

He holds out his hand. 'Up you come. Time to talk.'

I take his hand.

EIGHTEEN

TILA

I didn't know how to approach Mom and Dad about escaping the Hearth. Neither did Taema.

Hey, Mom. Hey, Dad. Can you ignore all your beliefs and help us abandon you?

They hadn't been born in the Hearth, though. They knew the world outside – or at least they had known it, thirty or so years ago. They were the only ones who could get us out.

We were going to die soon if we didn't do something. We felt tired all the time, and our ankles had swollen so much we had to wear old shoes of Mom's, and her shoes were ugly. We never wanted to eat. I'd wake up in the night and Taema's breath would be all hitchy. Sometimes she'd even stop breathing and I'd hold my own breath until she started up again.

I could feel our heart thumping beneath our skin all the time, like it was a fish trying to jump from the surface of the lake. Every day, it was getting harder to do basic things. Mom had to help dress us. Dad, embarrassingly, had to help bathe us because Mom wasn't strong enough to haul us up. Now we had even less privacy.

So after dinner one night, we confronted them. They were doing the dishes, Dad washing and Mom drying them and putting them away, humming to themselves. They were still very much in love with each other. Still are, I hope, though I haven't seen them in a decade. Seemed a shame to ruin the nice moment.

We'd agreed that I'd do the talking. We knew some hard things would have to be said, and Taema wasn't up to it. Her fingers were digging into my ribcage and she was shaking. I was nervous too, but in this I was the stronger twin. I wasn't afraid of saying things to our parents that might make them cry, if it meant we'd get what we wanted. Needed. A lifeline.

'We don't want to die,' I started, cutting right to the chase.

Our parents stopped humming.

Dad turned off the water carefully. 'What, Tila?' Even though he'd been facing the other way, he knew it was me. He and Mom came through and sat on the couch across from us. My mom pushed her curly hair back over her shoulder. My dad worried his lower lip with his teeth the way he did when he was nervous. Their faces were tight, trying to keep any emotion from sneaking out.

'We don't want to die,' I repeated. 'And we don't have to, if we can leave the Hearth and get to the city. Can you help us do that?' I kept the emotion out of my own voice.

Mom's face crumpled, and Dad put his arm around her. 'My girls,' he said, his voice breaking. 'I wish we could. But no one leaves the Hearth.'

'Mia did. We remember.'

It'd been hushed up, but even as children we heard the rumours. I'd forgotten about them until we started thinking of leaving. She'd left. On purpose. No one ever found out how she'd escaped.

Our parents looked away.

'Please. You have to help us . . . we're dead if we stay.'

'If you escape . . .' our mother whispered, 'you'd be apostate. You'd be damned. Surrounded by all that technology . . . all the Impure . . .'

Next to me, Taema flinched. 'That's true,' I said. It wasn't worth telling them we – I, at least – didn't believe in the tenets of the faith any more. Damn, they'd been so brainwashed in the last sixteen years, with Mana-ma battering away at their brains like the rest of us. Could I even break through? I pushed on ahead.

'We'd rather be alive and damned than dead and saved. Please. We don't want to die.'

Though for me, it was more that I didn't want Taema to die. I knew more than her. I knew if we did get out and found a doctor to fix our heart, there was a chance we wouldn't both survive. Of course there was. Medicine out there was really advanced, but it wasn't infallible. I just had to hope that if death took one of us, it took me and not her.

Dad pressed his lips together as he thought.

Shit, I miss them so much. They were good parents. They did their best by us. Even then, when they knew that if they helped us they'd never see us again, they still risked their jobs and their faith to help us.

'What about smuggling them out in the supply ships?' Dad asked Mom. 'We could hide them . . .'

She shook her head. 'Mana-ma would find out that way, as so little goes back out.'

'Even if we bribe them?'

'With what? Hand-stitched quilts? Those few credits we have from thirty years ago are worthless now.'

'What goes out to the city? Just blankets and apples and stuff, right?'

Our mother looked uncomfortable. Next to me, Taema rested her head on my shoulder. She was especially tired today.

'Yes,' Mom said. 'Plus several boxes I'm not allowed to open. If they get paid for any of it, I never see the money. Mana-ma packs those boxes herself, so there's no way to sneak you out in those.'

'Doesn't that . . . worry you? That she's sending stuff out and you have no idea what it is?'

'She must be doing God's will in one way or another.' My mother did not sound convinced as she gave us a tremulous smile. Dad looked worried.

'You're both doubting her, aren't you? At least a little bit.'

Taema's head rose from my shoulder as she stared at them.

'We'd never . . .' Mom trailed off, unable to complete the lie.

'The closer we get to the top,' Dad whispered, 'the more we see. The more we aren't able to unsee.'

He wouldn't elaborate more than that. This conversation was going very differently than how I'd thought it would.

'We'd have to go behind Mana-ma,' Dad said. 'It won't be easy.'

'Can you do it?' I asked.

They looked at us as though we were crazy for asking. 'Of course.'

'Will you come with us?'

A pause. My parents exchanged a glance. 'We can't. It'd be too hard to sneak all of us out. We can do more good here.'

I lost it then and started crying. So did Taema. Mom and Dad came and put their arms around us. Nothing would ever be the same as before our heart attack. Or before we found that tablet and realized that there was a whole world out there, and this one was fucked. Maybe, even if our heart hadn't been weak, we would still have tried to escape. I'd like to think we would have. Somehow.

Taema finally spoke up. 'Thank you,' she whispered.

They kept their arms around us, kissing the tops of our heads.

Our heart kept skittering in our ribcage. If they were going to save us, they would have to do it soon. If they were going to be able to do it at all.

•

The worst part was waiting.

I was never very good at waiting. I'd rather barrel in head first and figure it out later.

Our parents were formulating a plan, but didn't tell us the exact details. They said it'd be safer that way. It made Taema and me feel guilty and confused – what would Mana-ma do to them, or us, if she found out we were trying to leave? I imagine she'd been furious when she found out that Mia left. None of us were meant to speak of her, in any case; just like nobody spoke about the Brother.

It was hard going through day-to-day life when we could barely move. We started sleeping more and eating less. We needed canes to support us when we did try to walk.

It was terrible.

When we were feeling stronger we'd walk through the path in the woods until we reached the swamp. The air smelled thick and fetid, cutting through the scent of crushed pine needles. There were no boats on the island, for no one ever needed to leave, at least according to Mana-ma.

We ran our hands along the ferns, their leaves tickling our hands. We wanted to leave the confines of the Hearth more than anything, but we were also so scared.

'What do you think it'll be like?' Taema asked. She always asked that when we were alone. Now that we'd decided, and even though deep down the crisis of faith was getting to her, I could tell she was daydreaming about it all the time so that she didn't have to focus on the here and now. I kept wanting to pretend it was perfect on the other side, that we'd have wonderful new lives. The problem was, I've always been too much of a cynic to believe in happily ever after.

'It'll be the best,' I reassured her. 'We can do anything we want. A whole fresh start. The world is our oyster!'

'What does that even mean?'

'No idea. It was in one of your books I borrowed.'

She laughed weakly. Up overhead, the supply ship flew for its first drop in three months.

Taema shifted uncomfortably next to me, pulling on our shared skin. 'Should we go see it?'

I shook my head. I didn't want to risk anyone seeing us hanging around there this time.

The last time.

NINETEEN

TAEMA

'Tila,' Ensi, the leader of the Ratel, says with a smile. Like so many in San Francisco, he looks hardly older than thirty, but I'm sure he must be at least ten years older or more. Perhaps significantly more.

He's not quite as classically handsome as many men I've seen in the city – most likely intentionally. The crescent moon tattoo by his eye glows slightly green.

I'm still shaking. 'What's going on?'

'I Tested you.'

'The others . . . they weren't real?'

'No. Mere images projected from those electrodes and your ocular implants.'

'I haven't killed anyone,' I whisper. I can't believe how relieved I feel. I'm lightheaded with it.

'Have you not?' He smiles in a way that makes me wonder, with a sickening feeling, if he knows about Tila and Vuk already. If he knows *everything*.

I force myself to appear calm and collected, like I haven't just completely lost it in that white room. But how was that possible? It seemed so real. Not even virtual reality games were that realistic. Only the Zealscape. I shudder. 'Did you drug me?'

'A little.'

'What with?' The thought of being drugged without my permission or knowledge is unnerving, to say the least.

'A Verve derivative.' My breath catches. That derivative doesn't need a Chair. I feel invaded.

He smiles, as if amused by my distress. 'If he had been a real person, you would likely have killed him just the same.'

I feel very cold. 'Did I pass your Test?'

He smiles. 'You did. You didn't hesitate to do what's necessary. Many who move up the ranks traditionally would have come across this situation in different ways. Your situation is . . . unique. After all, we're already well acquainted, aren't we? This was really just a formality.' He moves closer to me and holds out his arms, expecting me to go into them, as I have before. Or so he thinks.

Oh. Shit.

What if this is a trap? If I pretend to recognize that closeness, am I caught, or is it the other way around? The questions whizz through my mind, as quickly as possible. I don't have long, so I choose, praying that I'm right.

I step into his arms. 'Ensi,' I murmur.

The arms wrap around me, strong and muscular. He's a head taller than me, and rests his lips on the top of my head. It's strangely tender. I'm shaking, but hopefully he thinks it's from the aftermath of the Test rather than the fact I'm terrified of him.

I'd thought my sister had met him before, or at least seen him, close enough to sketch him well. Now it seems my sister's done significantly more than that.

Goddammit, Tila. She couldn't just infiltrate the Ratel, she had to go and sleep with the leader of it? There was no mention of it in her notes. This makes everything about ten times harder.

Or it might make things easier, depending how I play it. My mind whirrs, scheming and plotting just like my sister's would have.

'So what now?' I ask, smiling, although I'm hoping that he doesn't expect me to jump into bed with him anytime soon. I may be able to fake Tila, but I'm not sure I'm *that* good an actress.

He smiles, full of secrets. I look at his hands, long and thin. With a twitch of his little finger, he could order my death. He's responsible for so much misery. Yet he's still oozing charisma as he holds my upper shoulder, and I feel caught in his trap and angry that there's no easy way out of this.

Shiny, silvery bait.

He leads me out of the white room into another across the hall. Here, everything is comfortingly modern. The room is warm, decorated in oranges and browns. I perch on a chair, crossing my legs and folding my arms. It's a defensive body posture, but I can't help but try to barricade myself against him.

I have two options: I can plead illness and hope he lets me leave and go home. Or I can be Tila.

She's done this. She's trapped him with all her grace and sex appeal. She's someone who stops at nothing to get what she wants. I could do the same and ride this out and see what happens.

As soon as I make the decision that this is what I'm going to do, I relax.

I slouch back, leaning on an elbow. The man sitting across from me is more powerful than the mayor of San Francisco, and maybe even the president of Pacifica.

Out of the corner of my eye I think I spy a spot of blood on my silver jumpsuit, but it's just a play of the light from the false fireplace. I blink, willing the memory of the bloodbath, the bodies, away, but the smell of my own vomit still lingers. *It wasn't real. It wasn't real.* I really wouldn't mind some mouthwash.

'So, now that I've passed your Test, what happens next?' I ask, my voice teasing. I can't be scared. Tila never seemed scared, no matter how difficult things were. She seemed so calm when we ran away from the Hearth. Her strength was what got us out of there. Without her I wouldn't have made it. Now it's my turn to rescue her.

Ensi pours two glasses of what looks like whisky and passes it to me. I drink it, more to get rid of the lingering taste of vomit in my mouth than anything else. Of course, it's not Synth. I don't know enough about whisky to guess at the type, but I'm sure it's one of the most expensive to be found in San Francisco.

I'm trying my hardest to be Tila. But I'm on such thin ice. I have no idea how well they know each other. If he references anything specific, a past conversation or event, I'm doomed. I'm so very aware that the likelihood of me exposing myself as a fraud rises the longer we speak.

So. I'm going to have to get him to stop talking. The best way to get him to stop talking is probably to sleep with him. I look at him under lowered lashes. Physically, he doesn't repulse me, quite the opposite. From growing up in the Hearth, I've always thought of sex as a conversation or a connection. In this case, it's a tool I can use, and I'm fully aware of that. I can't say that sleeping with the head of the Ratel was how I expected this evening to end.

Goddammit, Tila.

'Now, you're in,' Ensi says. 'You help me, I help you, and all of San Francisco is at your fingertips.'

I force myself to smile, as if that's all I've ever wanted. Really, I'd rather grab a nearby candlestick, bash him over the head and run away. Evidently I'm capable of it. I flinch at the violent urge. Did the Verve or the Test change me? I finish the drink and set the glass on the little table by the sofa.

'You caught my eye when we first met,' he says, standing and drifting closer to one of the paintings on the wall. I join him, my mind still spinning. Where did they meet? When? 'You put yourself to any task I asked of you with a single-mindedness few possess. You've proved yourself at the Verve lounge, these last few weeks. I have no doubt you'll be an asset to us.'

He has a way of speaking that seems familiar. Didactic – that's what it is. Expansive, confident, the way Mana-ma would deliver a sermon. His voice draws me in close. I try to resist his spell. I wonder if there are still remnants of the drug in my system, or if he exudes some sort of pheromone that I can't resist, either manufactured or natural, that makes me want to open to him like a flower. I close my eyes and call on Mana-ma's training, imagining a bright light cleansing my whole body. When I open my eyes, I feel in control of myself, cold and calculating.

'When do we start?' I ask.

'Soon enough. Tonight, though, is a celebration. Don't worry about business for now.' He moves closer, holds out his hand. 'Shall we dance?'

I take his hand, warm and soft. No manual labour for him. 'Shouldn't we go downstairs, where the music is?'

With a flick of his eyes, the same music that plays downstairs flows through unseen speakers. 'Much as I'd like to, I can't go down to join in. Not just yet.' He smiles to himself, as if he's told an amusing joke. I shiver.

His hand moves around my waist, slipping on the silver fabric. It reminds me of when I danced with Nazarin, and I flinch from that memory. I put my arms up around his neck. He's six inches taller than me, even with my heels. We move in time to the music.

'Ah, little Tila,' he says. 'What a relief. After that Test I know all about you.'

His words are ominous rather than reassuring. I look into his eyes as he dances. I can't see any sign that he doesn't think I'm Tila, but I'm still nervous. We're similar, my sister and I, but our personalities are not identical. I'm also sure the Ratel have looked up Tila's file and know she has a twin, and I have to hope they know the twin is meant to have a different face.

We dance to the music, soft and steady. It's almost hypnotic. Ensi knows just where to put his feet, just how to move. Before long, he bends his head down to kiss me, and I open my mouth to his. His mouth is warm and sweet, tasting of spices and whisky. He's surprisingly gentle for the crime lord of the city, yet firm. He wants me. And he expects to get me.

It occurs to me again that I still have time to change my mind. Draw away and shake my head and smile, reach for some whisky. I could say I was unwell or on my period. I don't. I'm choosing to kiss him.

There are several things that keep me kissing him. One: sex is a way to get to understand him better, to see him in a state of vulnerability. Two: these are his personal chambers, or one set of them. I'm pretty sure Alex Kynon is actually one of his (several) aliases. There could be something in here I need. There are wallscreens. I've brainloaded a lot of information on hacking during the last few days. If he trusts me, it will make it all the easier for me to get what I need from him. Three: he's a good kisser and I'm surprisingly into it. Four: it's what Tila would do.

It's risky, though. For all I'm close with my sister, we're not close enough that I know exactly how she has sex. I have to hope we're similar enough. Another thought of Nazarin and Tila together. Such strange, inverted parallels. *Stop. Nothing happened. Let that go. Focus on the here and now.*

His arms move lower, and I can feel the strength in his fingertips. Perhaps I enjoy the danger. Perhaps I'm more like Tila than I thought.

He picks me up, presses me against him. His hair tickles my face. I wrap my arms and legs around him and he carries me to the sofa.

The music trails away, forgotten. He pushes me into the soft velvet. I kiss him fiercely. His fingers run through my short, blue hair. I dance my fingers along the skin of his neck, unbuttoning his shirt. He helps me, shrugging off his coat and pulling his shirt over his head. He has a swimmer's body, with hardly any fat to speak of, his abs a rippled six-pack. I touch his skin, and he shivers.

A little notebook peeks out of his jacket, and attached to it, I see a small datapod. I half-lid my eyes as I study it. I want it. It's important enough he keeps it on him at all times in the inside pocket of his jacket, where no one can get it.

He soon distracts me, at least somewhat, from the thought of the little paper book. His lips move from mine, down to my neck. I arch against him, my nerves on fire. The adrenalin of the recent Test is still pumping through my body. I pull him against me, nipping his neck with my teeth.

Those long, nimble fingers work at the zipper at the hollow of my neck. Within moments, I'm exposed to him from neck to navel. He traces the scar down my sternum with his fingertip. It reminds me uncomfortably of Nazarin.

His fingertip moves from the scar to circle my left breast, teasing the nipple until it stands upright. He bends his head and I stare up at the ceiling, gasping slightly.

Bang.

We both start. His head jerks up, and I squirm to a sitting position.

The sound came from downstairs. It sounded like a gunshot. People scream.

'Was that–' I start, but then my question is answered by an outpouring of screams, more gunshots, and the stampede of fleeing footfalls.

He jumps away, reaching into a cabinet under the alcohol bar and drawing out a weapon and a bulletproof Kalar jumpsuit. I have a feeling they are hidden in every room. What that means cuts through the fear for a moment: this is a man who always expects an attack.

Ensi wriggles from the remainder of his clothes, his lithe body catching the light before he covers it with the black fabric. He hefts the gun, not quite pointing it at me.

'Were you the distraction?' he asks me. There's a tightness to his voice. Is he hurt by the possibility? How close are he and my sister? 'Do you know who's down there?'

'No.' I don't have to feign surprise.

A long pause.

'No,' I repeat, meeting his eyes, willing him to believe it. 'I have no idea what's going on. But I'm scared shitless.' I'm shivering, folding in, covering my naked torso with my arms.

The tension bleeds from his shoulders. 'Stay here.' He

starts to leave, then turns back, grabs another gun and tosses it to me.

I catch it, holding the gun like it's a snake that will bite me. I've had training through brainloads, and done a gun simulation, but I've not touched a real one. I wonder whether Tila is experienced with guns. Two weeks ago I would have sworn to anyone that'd she'd never even touched one. Not now.

Ensi gives me a last look and shakes his head before he pulls the bulletproof hood up, until every part of him is protected and obscured by the Kalar.

I want to ask what's going on, but he's already gone.

I stay there for roughly half a minute, listening to screams and gunshots, before I realize that standing there and doing nothing is not an option. I go to the cabinet, my body confused by the whiplash of fear, arousal, and fear again.

There are another few bulletproof jumpsuits hidden in the cupboard, so I shimmy out of my silver outfit and trade it for a black Kalar, pulling it up over my face. I can see through it just fine, and I feel safer.

Like earlier when I went down the corridor to the Test, I have the sensation that I'm just a floating head attached to my body. That this is not me or my life that I'm living, but someone else's. Not Tila – more like, this is all a dream or a movie, and I'll wake up, or the credits will roll.

But they won't. This is me. I'm dressed in a Kalar suit. I've just kissed the leader of the Ratel. I've committed criminal acts, thinking they were real. It was all me. But I'm also not the same girl that set out curry on the table, waiting for her sister to come home from work so she could tell her about that exciting job in China. I don't know who I am any more.

And I have no time to figure that out.

I grab my gun and turn it over, trying to figure out how it

works. I press the button and it turns on, humming slightly. It's not a laser and has actual bullets, but it's more complicated than the hunting guns we had at Mana's Hearth.

I want to test a shot but the room is too pretty to destroy. I have to hope my virtual training is enough.

Before I leave the room, I remember Ensi's jacket. I duck down and take out the notebook. The Kalar suit will hide my fingerprints. I unzip the suit enough to free my face. Will scanning work? I turn on my ocular implants. As long as I don't try to upload it yet, I can scan the notebook. I turn each page, running my eyes along the text. Each shot downstairs makes me flinch. I want to help, but I have to finish this, first.

The notebook is his personal schedule and diary. It's all in a code of scribbled acronyms, and I can only hope I can find a way to decipher it. When I finish, I pick up the datapod dangling from the bookmark. I set it to my ear, but, of course, it's locked, and I don't have time to even attempt to break the encryption. I set everything back in his pocket and arrange his jacket just as I found it.

I leave the room, peeking out into the darkened hallway. All the sounds of the melee are from the ground floor, the ballroom. I grit my teeth against the screams of pain and fear.

My mind spins. Who can it be? Is it the police? Is this why Nazarin snuck off? *Was* I actually the distraction against Ensi? I swear, if that man has lied to me yet again, I'll harness my new penchant for violence and use this gun to shoot him in the leg. Or between the legs. I'll decide when the time comes.

If he's not responsible for this, then that means Nazarin is in just as much danger as I am. More, if he's still down there in the ballroom.

I reach the top of the staircase. Bits of the banister are riddled with bullets. I peek over the edge. The guests are rounded up in one corner. The grand, green chandelier has been shot down, leaves and emeralds strewn along the floor. There are a few casualties scattered on the floor, sprawled out with legs akimbo, red mixing with the green. I swallow hard, memories of the vision of Ensi's Test fresh in my mind. Of seeing Mia killed in the hologram. The death in Mia's dream world. The crime scene in Zenith. Death and blood is following my every move.

Focus, Taema. Focus or death will catch you, too.

A bullet whizzes by my ear and I duck down. At least the other side doesn't have lasers, or we wouldn't stand a chance. I look over the banister again, taking the safety off the gun. There are about twenty people in dark blue Kalar suits, holding weapons. Enough to overwhelm the guards, though dismantling the security must have been a bitch. I see security people and droids scattered on the floor, the droids spilling wires, the people spilling blood. I try reaching out through my implants to contact the police, but that signal's still blocked. We have two members of our team just outside. Did they hear the shots? If so, is there anything they can actually do?

A suited figure fires another warning shot to gain people's attention. He has a rapt audience.

'The King of the Ratel has lost his power,' the man says. Who is it? For a moment, I fear it's Nazarin; but the detective is at the back of the huddled former revellers. I let out my held breath. He's crouched low, poised to pounce, his eyes not moving from the main man with the gun. Is this what he's been planning? Nazarin said he was trying to sow unrest within the Ratel. From the shocked look on his face, though, I'm not sure he expected rebellion so soon.

'I've taken control of the biggest Verve drop the Ratel has ever done. I've taken control of the biggest arms smuggle. You can see the result right here.' He holds up the bulky gun. His voice radiates with pride. 'Ensi is so used to his routine that he's weak. It'll all crumble, having an old man like him at the helm. He makes too many deals with the other side. Getting soft.'

Where is Ensi? While I was upstairs, has he already been executed? Would I care?

I crouch and move down the ramp. At one of the circular cut-outs, I peer out again. Part of me wants to hide upstairs. The masked leader takes a string of men and women and lines them up against the white, curved wall. Even though most of the partiers are hardened criminals, not all of them are, and I think the masked man chose at least some of the business associates under Ratel control. People unafraid to get their hands dirty in crooked deals, but who've never before had guns pointed at their faces. A man pisses himself, the dark strain spreading down his trousers. Another woman shakes so badly she can barely stand. Malka has also been chosen for the line-up, but she does not look afraid. She stands tall, like the Queen she is.

'Here is the court of the Ratel, gathered for their party,' the masked man says. 'Think of me as your jester for the evening, providing the entertainment to you peons. Do you realize that for every tiny bit of money you get, the King gets over one hundred times more?'

He walks closer to the men and women lined up along the wall. 'But for you, I'm not your jester. I'm your executioner.' He raises his gun and points it at the first woman. As soon as he aims, someone lets out a wail. The man is startled and lets out the shot, and the woman crumples. I shudder, hidden behind the curving white wall of the ramp. I can't tell if she's been hit or not.

Ensi – I'm pretty sure it's Ensi – emerges from the shadows, knocking the gun from the leader's hand. Nazarin, seeing that the situation has changed, jumps over a frightened member of the Ratel and grabs the gun out of another of the masked men's hands. The rest of the Ratel realize the tide has turned and follow suit, wrestling the weapons from the other side's grasp. A few more shots fire, but they all go wide.

A masked man or woman falls to the ground, the gun skittering across the floor, the person grabbling for it. Nobody else has noticed yet. After an agonizing moment of indecision, I dash from my hiding place and jump on top of the figure, holding my gun against the temple, praying I don't have to fire. Nazarin sees me, but masked as I am, he thinks I'm one of the insurgents. I hold up my hand and call out 'wait!' He starts, recognizing my voice, and I pull off my hood, shaking the hair out of my face. Nazarin looks stricken. I nod at him.

It's not over that easily. There's a riot of people fighting, and guns blaring. More people fall. The perfect white walls are singed.

Only a few people in Kalar suits have fallen – bullets have to hit the right area of the body at the perfect angle to do any damage. But even in my Kalar suit, I don't feel safe. A fair number of Ratel revellers have died. Blood smears the white floors. I clutch the gun against his forehead, but I don't fire. I turn off the fear, watching everything with a sort of detached fascination. It's that, or start screaming and never stop.

Ensi wades through it all, the bullets bouncing off his suit, wrestling the ringleader behind it all to the ground and ripping off his hood. It's the young man I met at the beginning of the party: little more than a boy, with white-blond hair and black eyes. Leo.

My eyes dart to Nazarin. His mouth has twisted, and I can't guess his thoughts. I'm still not sure he anticipated the coup.

Leo tries to say something, but Ensi doesn't give him the chance. The King of the Ratel takes the gun, holds it to the younger man's head, and fires. The boy goes limp, his head nothing but a mass of blood, bone and brain tissue. Ensi is splattered with gore. I stare at him, not blinking, until my eyes burn.

Ensi pulls off the hoods of all the other masked men and women who dared to rise up against him. Then he calls out a few other names. The Ratel Pawns and Knights bring the people forward. Nazarin holds one of the named men's arms behind his back.

'You really thought I didn't know exactly what you were trying to do?' Ensi asks.

He shoots the first person.

I flinch.

'You really thought that, in my own house, I wouldn't sniff a rat?'

He shoots the next person.

'This is my house. You are mine.'

Another shot. Another fall.

'You should have learned this long ago. Most of you have.'

Bang.

'You cannot cross me and hope to live.'

Bang.

'Reward me with loyalty, and I will reward you.'

Bang.

'Cross me, and reap the consequences.'

All the men and women are dead, to join the other corpses on the ground.

'It's simple, really.' He smiles at us all.

I look at all the bodies on the floor, numb. It feels like a warning. He'll find out about me. And he'll kill me. He's walking towards me. Is he about to shoot me in the head?

He aims the gun. I squeeze my eyes shut. Better not to see it coming.

The gunshot is so loud my ears ring.

I'm not dead.

I open my eyes. Ensi has shot the man I captured. The blood spreads across the floor, a slow red tide. A woman's crying, screaming, and I wish she'd shut up. More lines from the poem return to me. The paradise of Xanadu is ruined.

Then reached the caverns measureless to man
And sank in tumult to a lifeless ocean.
And 'mid this tumult Kubla heard from far
Ancestral voices prophesying war!

Nazarin has a spray of blood on the left side of his face. He stands straight, at attention, his expression blank as a soldier's.

Ensi stops in front of him. 'Thank you,' he says. 'Skel, isn't it?'

'That's right, sir.'

'You saved a lot of lives tonight. You'll be rewarded. Speak to Malka about it.'

'Thank you, sir.' I almost wonder if Nazarin will salute.

Ensi looks around at the silent party. 'Let this be a lesson to you all.'

Does his gaze flick to me? A shiver runs down my spine. He comes towards me, the gun still in his hand, and I steel myself. He's going to kill me. Shoot me in the head. Even if I wasn't involved with this uprising, if he knew about that, he must know about me.

He looks down at me with something very like tenderness. 'You didn't stay.'

'I couldn't.'

He stares at the man I captured. The man that's now a corpse, though not by my hand. 'Good job.'

'Thank you.'

For a moment, I wonder if he's going to hold out his hand, and lead me back upstairs. The blood has washed the last vestiges of the drug from my system, and I've scanned the notebook. I have no desire to go back up there. Then Ensi turns, his head down.

'Malka,' he says.

She comes forward, to his side. I can't tell if they're romantically linked, but their bond, whatever it is, is deep. The King and the Queen walk away from the ballroom, side by side, leaving the carnage behind them.

TWENTY

TAEMA

I dream that I went with Ensi, and I awaken in a silken bed.

The sun streams through the window. Ensi lies next to me, fast asleep, his arm thrown over his eyes against the light. His face is clean of blood, like the events of the night before never happened. But they did. And this, right here, is the man who did them.

His other arm is around me and, trapped in his embrace, I can't stop thinking about all the dead bodies. The fact that I had taken a gun and gone down there, something I never thought I'd do. I still feel like I'm changing and morphing. I'm becoming more like Tila, but I'm turning into someone else I don't recognize, either, and perhaps someone I don't like.

I turn and watch him, sleeping peacefully. I look at his torso, chiselled by modern medicine. What would he look like now if he couldn't alter himself? Would that taut skin sag against a growing paunch? Would I recognize his face, with its lines that show the type of life he chose to live?

He opens his eyes, and his eyes are black pits. His mouth stretches wide, and deep within his throat is a glowing, pulsing light.

'Are you strong enough to kill me?' he asks, his voice crackling like a flame. 'Do you really have what it takes?'

•

I jerk awake, for real this time.

I'm in the room in the safe house where I store my things, but where I hardly ever sleep. It's my first brainload-free night in over a week.

I ease out of the bed, my sore muscles stretching. I have a bruise on my side, where a bullet grazed the Kalar suit. If I hadn't been wearing it, the bullet would have killed me. I rub my sore muscles and stagger into the shower to wash off the sweat and the imaginary scent of blood that still clings to my nostrils.

After I've scalded myself, I go down to the kitchen, ordering strong, real coffee from the replicator despite its warning that caffeine is bad for me. I load it with cream and sugar, to boot.

Nazarin isn't here. He's gone to report in to the Ratel, receive his reward for helping with the fight. I want to ask him if that was his plan all along. I thought he wanted to foster unrest. So why, when unrest presented itself in a very real way, did he decide to help Ensi instead?

Using every security measure I can think of, I bring Ensi's scanned notebook to my implants.

His handwriting is almost impossible to read, so tall and slanted. Each appointment is only a few letters and a time, perhaps a first name. Last night's entry was only 'XNDU', presumably shorthand for Xanadu. There's nothing over the next few days, but Wednesday has an entry: 'D/O. MM'. I flip through the rest of the pages, wondering who the names are. On the last page of the book are various scribbled notes. Up in a corner, I spy 'MM'. Next to it is a phone number, strange enough in itself, and it brings me up short.

I recognize it.

It's the number for the emergency line at Mana's Hearth.

I looked it up, after we left, after the surgery. When, despite everything, I was homesick. So many times over the years, I had turned on my implants, ready to input the number. I wanted to see if my parents were all right. If the Hearth was all right. I was too afraid, and I never pinged.

My throat tightens with unshed tears. It's not totally unexpected, but it's still a shock. We knew there might be a link between the Ratel and the Hearth when we discovered Vuk was Adam. We still don't know what the connection is, exactly. Is Mana-ma sending people to the Ratel, and if so, why, and to what purpose? Is Mana-ma working with Ensi? That means interacting with someone Impure, and having a connection with the world she always taught us was evil.

I flip back to Wednesday's entry. D/O. Drop off. Sure enough, Wednesday is the 15th – the date Tila and I used to look forward to. The date that the supply ship would come from the far-off shiny city of San Francisco. I guess, even ten years later, it hasn't changed.

MM stands for Mana-ma.

'Fuck,' I whisper, wondering if I'm reading the signs wrong. Maybe I'm just seeing what I want to see. I flip through the calendar. Every two or three months, right on the 15th, there's an entry with 'D/O. MM'.

Why? When I lived there, people didn't die more than once or twice a year. Has Mana-ma started making more disappear? Or is there something else the Hearth has that Ensi and the Ratel want? The hairs on my forearms stand up straight. I'm still missing something.

What?

How long has this been going on, whatever it is? At least ten years. That's when Adam disappeared. I have a feeling it's been longer.

I take a deep breath. Nazarin comes into the kitchen and I send everything away, hiding the scans deep within my implants again.

He nods at me in greeting and grabs the SynthGin. It's early in the day.

'Did it go badly?'

He pours liquid into the glass, bringing over a second one for me. 'No. I've been promoted. He's going to Test me, make sure I'm trustworthy. It'll be different to yours, as he's not using me for lucid dreaming, but I imagine it'll be along the same lines. I guess we're celebrating that somehow things didn't totally go to shit last night.'

'Did you know what was going to happen?' I ask him.

He takes a swig. 'No. I knew Leo was going to try something, but I thought he was months away from actually doing it. I guess he didn't trust me enough to include me in his plans.'

'If he had, would you have sided with him?' If he had, would the end result have been different?

'No. Too dangerous. If there'd been even a hint I was involved, I'd be as dead as the others.'

'Right.' I sip the SynthGin. 'Did you know Tila is sleeping with Ensi?'

'She's his canary?' he asks. 'No. I most definitely did not know that.' His eyes ask the question I don't answer.

I take another gulp. 'What does that mean, to be his canary? Malka called me that, too.'

'Tila is – you are – his newest pet. His newest toy. He'll play with you for a time, like a cat with a canary.'

'Then, what, he'll eat me? Is that what he does with the others?'

'Sometimes. If they displease him. If not, he lets them fly away, and then finds another.'

'Right. He's been with her before. Tila. I got the feeling it'd been more than once. He seemed to . . . care.'

Again, the question with his eyes. I sigh. 'I didn't sleep with him. I almost did but we were . . . interrupted by gunfire.'

'Right.' He takes another sip. 'How did the Test go?'

'It was horrible,' I say. 'If you're going to be Tested, I shouldn't tell you about it.'

If he knew it wasn't real, it'd alter the readings to the electrodes. And, in any case, the Test for him could be completely different to mine.

'And if I fail, I'm stuck as a Knight or a Pawn for good.' Or worse. Nazarin's heard of the odd Pawn or Knight disappearing after their Test.

We're silent. I slosh more drink in the cup. I'm drinking too much. Before all this, I hardly ever touched the stuff. At least my liver will be safe. Whoo.

'So what does the SFPD want our next step to be?'

'I take the Test. We keep playing our roles. Kim's been perfecting something she thinks can help us gather evidence.'

I let out a slow breath. 'How soon do you think she'd be able to do this?'

Nazarin perks up. 'Why?'

'Because there's going to be a drop in a few days.' I project the scanned pages of Ensi's notebook onto the wallscreen. He squints.

'I have no idea what any of this means.'

I walk him through what I found in the planner. He also has no idea what the link between the Hearth and the Ratel could be, beyond inheriting occasional men and women without identities that Ensi can brainwash into working for them.

'We still don't definitively know if that's what they did,' I say, thinking of Adam, the way he'd smile more on one side than the other. The way he loved to play with the younger children, and how he loved to go swimming in the lakes with the others, turning back to wave at us as we watched from the shore, unable to join him. He'd never harm another person.

Everyone has a darker side.

I still think there must be more to it than that. Adam was sixteen when he supposedly died. How could he change that completely? I suppose being torn from everything you've grown up with could do that. I remember how confused Tila and I felt. How it was like we were drifting, unanchored, in this strange new world we knew nothing about. Is that enough?

'Verve,' Nazarin says. 'He's rewriting personalities.'

Rewriting personalities. I still don't know if I believe I changed Mia in any way in the Vervescape. Maybe it was only my words that got through to her, rather than a deeper sort of push. Imagine not remembering who you were. Becoming exactly what Ensi wanted you to be. A weapon. An assassin. A tool.

The only reason he didn't do it to me in the Test is because it doesn't work on lucid dreamers.

'You can't do the Test,' I say.

Nazarin's eyebrows lift. 'You think he'll change me.'

'Of course he will. Your loyalty doesn't matter if it's not completely guaranteed. He can make sure you never dare to cross him.' I think of the Zealot lounges where he experimented. 'I worry he might have found a way to reprogram people on a wider scale via Zealot lounges by now. He'd start with his own people and then cast his net wider, wouldn't he?'

'That's what my superior says. He has other sources in other areas. We are certain he can expect them to amass an attack sooner rather than later.'

'We still haven't been able to get any coverage. All recording devices were dampened in Xanadu, and they're dampened in the Verve lounge. We can't pin anything on him, even though we saw him gun down insurgents and splatter us with the blood.' I look up at the wallscreen. 'Does the notebook help?'

'It's a start, but not enough. They're too carefully intertwined for us to barrel in now. Ensi will disappear, along with the Verve, and it'll still trickle its way to the masses. We need concrete proof we can show the public, to turn everything against him. A few scanned pages with some acronyms won't do that.' Nazarin licked his lips. 'That's where this new tech from Kim comes in. It might record, even if we're somewhere the signal's jammed. It's dangerous, but it might work.'

'I don't understand,' I say. Nazarin is animated, driven. It should scare me, but it doesn't. It's infectious. My fingernails trace across my scar.

If we succeed, we'll take down the biggest mob in the city. The government and Sudice will be in our debt. That's not what I care about; it's a side effect.

I'm going to find out what you were up to, Tila. Once and for all.

TWENTY-ONE

TILA

Do you know why they really built that swamp around the Hearth? I mean, the 'why' is pretty obvious, I suppose – to keep some people on one side of it and everyone else on the other – but there were events that led up to it.

I can't tell you everything about them because I don't know that much. I've managed to gather bits and pieces over the years, but I still don't understand how they all fit together.

I'm going to tell it like a story, try and sensationalize it, fill in some gaps. You know when they have documentaries and then the camera goes all fuzzy and golden-tinged if it's a re-enactment of a good event, and dark and dreary if it's bad? This is the dark and dreary kind, and I guess I'm the dramatic voiceover.

First, here's roughly how Mana-ma tells the story when she's lecturing about the evils of the Impure. I'm sure she's told this story dozens of times in sermon:

Mana-ma's Cautionary Tale

One night around twenty years ago now – let's say it was dark and stormy, because what else could it be? – a man from the Impure outside world snuck into the Hearth. In those days, there was just a fence rather than a swamp. There were signs everywhere saying that the fence was charged, but it was a lie. We didn't want to be surrounded by the new generator that would have been used. Surrounded by an Impure circle, the Hearth would feel just that much more trapped. Makes no sense, if you ask me, since the Hearth was already surrounded by, you know, the entire Impure world.

So this bogeyman came into the Hearth from San Francisco, creeping and sneaking his way closer to the main settlement. Mana-ma took great delight in explaining how horrible he looked, with green hair and metal studs, moving tattoos and Impure clothing, none of it made from good cotton, silk or leather.

Why did he come? Let's see . . . perhaps he ran out of money and thought he'd be able to steal from us. (That would have been a failure – we didn't have anything worth anything, except some vintage stuff in not-too-good condition. Well, at least that's what I thought at the time.) Mana-ma said he thought he'd be able to get away with a crime more easily here. And that was maybe true, but she left out how low crime in the evil, Impure world really was, which would have made a few people wonder if it was really that bad if it was so safe.

This bogeyman came right into the centre of the Hearth and stole a young girl from her own home. He drugged her and dragged her, kicking and screaming (evidently not loud enough to wake anyone up), into the forest. Under the silent redwood trees he had his way with her, holding a knife to her throat and saying if she screamed that he'd give her another smile. So he hurt her and she stayed quiet. Just as she was about to give up and scream so he would kill her (because people would somehow hear that scream), a brave member of the Hearth came to her rescue.

This upstanding member of the Hearth fought off the intruder and the miscreant was slain. Though the girl was obviously traumatized by events, through the help of the Hearth she was able to release the darkness the man had planted within her, at least for a time. Later, the darkness took hold of her again and nothing could be done for her.

'This tragedy is why we must remain separate,' Mana-ma would cry, holding her arm up high at the pulpit. 'This is what we seek to prevent. For the Impure can poison the minds of the Pure, and we must guard that untainted spark within us all.'

It was always that sort of lesson – that the Impure would blemish us all and we were the last true humans, unaltered, unsullied.

The thing is: that's not remotely what happened.

The Real Story

The man who came to the Hearth came to rescue the girl, not hurt her.

A gap in the story is, I have no idea how he knew her. Perhaps they met in the forest: her on one side of the former chain-link fence around the border, and him on the other. I could imagine the romance developing – putting their fingers through the metal wires and touching for the first time.

Eventually, the girl wanted to escape and they came up with a plan. When she didn't stick to it, he grew worried. Thoughts swirled through his head: maybe her parents kept her in, or she even changed her mind at the last minute.

So he came into the Hearth, worried, not wanting to leave without her. She'd told him where she lived, and he peeked in her window.

He was seen.

The Hearth would automatically recognize someone not of their own, especially this boy in his synthetic clothing, bright green hair, moving tattoos on his knuckles.

They grabbed him, dragged him to the main chapel. Mana-ma had been roused from bed. I can imagine her, hair wild around her face, wearing her dark robes like a witch. The boy was nervous, probably a bit sheepish. Thought if he apologized and left, it'd all be OK.

Instead, they didn't let him go.

He was thrown into one of the empty rooms that nobody used. They managed to get out of him who he was and why he was there. Then they went and got the girl.

The girl had planned to go. Her parents had caught her leaving with a small rucksack under her arm and locked her in her room. They were the ones to alert the watch, who had found the boy. The girl was more scared than the boy. She didn't like the blank looks on their faces. They could be thinking anything.

Mana-ma was incensed. This boy had infringed on them, slipped past the toll roads, the infrequent park wardens, the fence, to come into the inner sanctum of the Hearth itself. The whole place would have to be Purified to prevent his presence from poisoning everything. The girl was sobbing, but the boy didn't say anything. He knew crying wouldn't solve anything when they'd already made up their minds.

They were all up all night, or at least all of them except the boy. He died at sunrise.

They didn't kill him quickly. Mana-ma did most of it, with only her three trusted right-hand men. (Importantly, my parents weren't involved. I think they learned about this after, and it was what put the biggest dent in their faith.) One restrained the boy and the other the girl. Throughout it all, Mana-ma lectured about the sins of evil and darkness, all while she tortured a boy to death in front of the girl who loved him. She used a scalpel, and she was delicate and dedicated in her work. The room was soundproof, so nobody else heard the screams.

They took the body of the boy away when the sun had crept over the tops of the redwood trees, but they weren't done with the girl. Mana-ma used every trick in the book to brainwash and manipulate her. Before long, she believed it was her fault, that the boy was evil, that Mana-ma had saved her. Yet she was dead inside, walking around like a zombie, unable to feel happiness or sadness.

The spell didn't last forever. Eventually, Mana-ma stopped paying such close attention to the girl. There were other things on Mana-ma's mind besides a follower she thought had been dealt with. The girl started thinking again. Started waking up. And one night, deep in the dark when the moon was just a little sliver in the sky, she escaped and climbed over the chain-linked fence, making her way to San Francisco, where the Hearth could not catch her.

When Mana-ma realized a member of her flock had fled, she was even angrier. That's when the swamp was created. She said it was to protect us from those outside who would want to hurt us. It's really to keep everyone inside.

•

These were the people Taema and I were raised with.

These were the people we were trying to escape from, naive and unaware of what we were really dealing with.

You must be wondering where I learned this story, if we didn't know it when we left. Or perhaps you've already figured it out.

The girl in the story was Mia, the woman who took us in after we left. The woman who saved us before she damned me.

TWENTY-TWO

TAEMA

We've come to see Kim again.

We haven't gone back to that empty safe house; instead, we're going to her home. She seems nervous as she opens the door and ushers us inside. She's been sworn to secrecy. At the moment, not even Sudice is meant to know what she's about to do to us. If they find out she's lied, even if it's on behalf of the SFPD, she could easily lose her job.

Nazarin knew, without a doubt, that she'd do it. His former partner, Juliane Amello, had been her partner as well. Her wife. She died, and Kim wants answers, too. Or at least retribution.

'Well, no point wasting time in pointless pleasantries or offering you a cup of tea,' she says. 'Might as well come through to the lab.'

We follow. I had forgotten how tiny Kim is. At the safe house, she wore a simple suit, but now she's wearing something made of strips of fabric in all the colours of the rainbow, and it billows behind her as she walks.

Her home is large and sumptuous. As she's one of the most talented biohackers in the world, this doesn't surprise me. What does surprise me is how cluttered it is. On the way here, Nazarin told me that Kim collects old memorabilia, specifically from the twentieth and twenty-first centuries, before the Great Upheaval. I think he told me so I wouldn't be quite so taken aback when I saw it all.

Most of the cheesy knick-knacks from the past have been recycled by now, but Kim hunts down the remaining ones and probably pays a lot of money for the lurid plastic and metal figurines that seem to stare at us as we walk through the lounge. Superheroes and celebrities I don't recognize, cartoon animals with eyes far too large for their faces. It all seems strangely alien to me as someone who grew up in the Hearth. There, nothing was made by robots or replicators and toys were hand-carved and took weeks to make. Here, in San Francisco, so much was ordered and then recycled the next day. Clothes worn once, plates made of compostable material. Cherishing things from the past was rare. I mean, what in the world was Hello Kitty?

'Like 'em?' Kim asks, noticing my stare. 'I got the biggest collection on the West Coast.'

'They're . . . interesting,' I say.

She laughs. 'Yeah, it's tacky as hell, but I don't care. A girl's gotta have a hobby.' She was serious when she let us in, but now she's striving for lightness. It's forced. Underneath she's as scared as we are.

At the end of the hall, Kim presses her fingertip to the sensor and the door slides open. We step through into her lab.

Though the lab is small, it's fitted with the best equipment, stuff I would have killed to have in my lab at Silvercloud Solutions. The chair bolted to the floor in the middle of the room reminds me uncomfortably of the Zealot lounge.

'All right, who's going first?' she asks.

'Me,' Nazarin says, to my relief. He sits in the chair, and Kim straps him in.

'I don't know why I'm doing this,' she mutters to herself.

'Yes, you do.'

'Don't kid yourself, babe,' she says, pinching his cheek. 'You're not my type.'

She winks at me and I smile a little.

'OK, then. You want to prove to yourself you can do it. I've appealed to your professional pride.'

'That's a bit closer, but you forget, I've done this before.'

'I guess that's a comfort,' Nazarin says. 'You won't leave me blind and deaf.'

'Most likely not.'

Neither of them mentions Juliane. I have the feeling they rarely speak about her, even though she's a shared link between them. Too painful for them both. Better to banter and tease, even when they're both terrified.

'Now shut up,' she says, without rancour. 'I have to concentrate.'

He dutifully shuts up as Kim attaches the last of the wires. It is almost exactly the same set-up as at the Zeal lounge, and I say so.

'Where do you think they got the idea for it, buttercup?' she asks. 'Who do you think helped develop Zeal, if not the biohackers? Grade A Sudice merchandise right from the start.'

It's rather obvious now that I think about it, but I know nobody who did Zeal, except Mia. My throat twinges as I think of her. She didn't have a funeral, and even if she had, no one would have come.

Kim turns on the screen on the table next to the chair, her quick fingers dancing as she brings up the various controls. It only strikes me now how dangerous this all is.

Kim is going to hack into Nazarin's brain.

'Does it hurt?' I ask. Switching my identity had been easy

and painless. This isn't a chip in a wrist. Implants are wired right into your brain.

'It won't be pleasant, I'm sorry to say.' She fills a syringe with unidentified liquid. 'Why do you think we don't have our implants set to record as standard? Be able to keep our memories and replay them in their entirety whenever we want?'

'No idea.'

'We're not meant to remember every little thing. If we were, that's what our brains would do. They're not meant to store so much. They can be overwhelmed. Even brainloading is too much for many. Not every brain can do it. But non-stop recording? I am part of a Sudice project that works on it.' She pauses, looking haunted. 'Some subjects end up going crazy, and some brains shut down. Aneurysms. Strokes. Poof. Gone.' She snaps her fingers. 'So it will probably be nixed pretty soon. Most of us involved in the project are glad it hasn't been easy, to tell the truth. You know why?'

I shake my head.

'It makes people vulnerable. People already try to hack into implants all the time – send adverts and things. Imagine hacking into your very being. Your very self.'

I lick my lips. And what would the government do with that power?

'The government are trying,' she says, echoing my thoughts. 'Boy, are they trying. They fund all our research, and it isn't cheap. If brain recording worked better, you can bet your bottom dollar that we'd all be recording, all the time. I mean, surveillance is old as time.'

She drifts off, fiddling with something, and then sets the code to process. 'Anyway, it's been abandoned for widespread use now, until they can figure out how not to fry people. Maybe at some point we'll crack it fully. Until then, I developed a way to turn it on for anyone, at least for a little while. A back door.'

A back door into my brain. 'Do you have to . . . use it often?' Forced brain recording. It sounds barbaric.

'Very rarely.' Her eyes go distant and blank. I swallow. I wonder what she's had to see, had to do, but I don't ask. Easier to think of her as a brilliant, eccentric woman with a penchant for nicknames and bobblehead figurines.

She shakes her head, coming out of it. 'Not many people know about brain recording. You didn't for sure, did you, tulip?' Kim asks Nazarin. He's lying back in the seat, his eyes half-lidded. Whatever Kim gave him, he's relaxed and high.

'Educated guess.'

'Smart boy,' she says fondly. His eyes flutter and he's out cold.

Kim sighs. 'Here we go.'

'Wait,' I say. 'You're really not calming me down here. Are we going to go insane or die?'

She meets my eyes. 'I'm very good at this. Yes, there's still a chance. Nazarin understands the risks, and he wants to do it. Do you? You have a choice.'

'Give . . . give me a minute.'

'Sure. You can see what happens with Nazarin. Then decide.' She looks down at Nazarin, runs her hand over the rough stubble of his head, and then presses a button on the Chair.

Nazarin goes rigid. Sweat beads on his skin almost immediately, leaving tracks down his temples. Kim frowns at one of the wallscreens, her fingers dancing over a projected keyboard as she studies code that means nothing to me, for all my courses in software engineering. With a flick of her wrist, a map of Nazarin's mind appears, floating over her head like a nebula.

Kim zooms in on the occipital lobe and the auditory cortex first. I remember when people first mentioned implants to me, I thought they were just one machine, firmly glued somehow to the brain. Really, there's a main receiver and dozens, hundreds of little implants scattered through the brain. They call it neural dust. Microscopic little computers, no thicker than a human hair, all taking the data from the brain and feeding in data from the outside world.

Nazarin has more implants than me. 'What are those?' I ask, pointing at the various other parts of his brain also speckled with neural dust.

She frowns as she concentrates, changing the view to focus on the tiny machines. 'They put them in when he went undercover. Extra receivers for brainloads. Implants to help memory in the hippocampus, extra occipital lobe implants to help retention and processing. There's more in the brain stem and cerebellum to aid with coordination – you'll notice he's not clumsy, and very fast when he needs to be. So they're there, and they help, but they don't record the way you two need the brain to record. It makes this tricky, though. There's a lot of little bits of metal in his head. Now stop talking.'

I snap my mouth shut. Kim's barely blinking. Her fingers gesture as she imparts code to the tiny metal specks in Nazarin's brain.

Machines beep – Nazarin's heartbeat speeds up, warning alarms ping. Nazarin arches on his Chair, his mouth open in a silent scream. He jerks as if he's having a seizure, spittle flying from his mouth. The veins in his neck stand out.

His heart flatlines.

'Shit, shit, shit!' Kim's fingers fly faster.

'What's happening?' I have my hands over my mouth. I dart forward but Kim snarls at me to stay back. Nazarin is already turning greyish. His eyes are open and bulging, their whites red with burst capillaries.

'Shut up!' Kim takes another syringe and stabs it into his heart. I watch, unable to think, unable to speak.

I don't want him to die.

Nazarin's heart starts again, and he gasps, his breathing hoarse.

'Oh, thank Christ.' Kim slumps against a counter. 'I told them, I fucking told them not to ask me to put in so many!'

Nazarin's eyes are still open and staring. 'Is he OK?' I ask.

The skin around Kim's eyes and mouth is tight. She doesn't answer. My mouth goes dry. I stay quiet, watching her work, clasping my hands together and whispering incoherently. It isn't a prayer, not really, but maybe it's a whisper to the universe, a hope that things will somehow work out all right.

Three minutes pass, but it feels like three hours. Kim nods, and the map of Nazarin's brain disappears. Nazarin slumps against the seat, his eyes closed again, breathing through his mouth. He seems calmer, but he's still dripping with sweat and twitching. Kim injects him with another syringe, this time in the shoulder, and the frantic beating of his heart slows. After another minute, his eyelids flutter.

He sits up slowly. 'I feel like I've been hit by a hovercar.'

'You nearly said hi to Saint Peter. You have too many bugs in your brain. As soon as this op's done, come to me. I'll get them out.'

'I like 'em.'

Her eyes go distant again. 'No. Get them out. I spend my life doing this, but sometimes I wonder if we're doing too much to our brains too fast. The more I find out about the mind, the more I realize I don't know and probably never will.' She presses the bridge of her nose with her fingers. 'That was too close, sweet pea.'

Nazarin reaches out and puts a hand on her shoulder. 'I'm OK, Kim. I'm OK.'

Kim gives him a hug, clutching his broad back. There's something between them. Nothing romantic. It's that sort of friendship where the term 'friend' doesn't seem strong enough.

She pats him on the cheek. Her eyes shine with tears. 'Your vitals are all good. You'll need some eye drops to heal the whites of your eyes – you look a fright.'

She unhooks him from the machine. He stands up, but his knees are shaking. He leans against a metal bench of the lab, looking at me from under shadowed brows.

Kim motions to me. 'It's your turn now, Taema. If you still want to. I can understand if you don't, after all that.'

This is the last thing I want to do. She sees it in my face. I look to Nazarin, but his gaze is inscrutable. He's not weighing in. It's up to me.

It's another risk, but I've taken so many risks. For a moment, I do wonder if this is one risk too many. If this is my limit, and I can't do any more.

I can do more. For Tila. For me.

Can we find what we need? Record proof that Ensi is the head of the Ratel? Find out where he stores Verve and what his plan is, and stop it in time? It feels impossible.

'It'll be OK,' Kim says.

Tila's words come to my lips again. 'You can't promise that.'

'No, I can't. You're right. Your implants are newer than his, and you have far fewer. Your heart functions on its own software so it'll stay steady. I'll have less trouble getting your implants to behave. That I can promise.'

Nazarin's gaze is steady. His breathing returns to normal. He gulps a glass of water. I can tell what he's thinking, it's so clear on his face. *We've come so far . . .*

I close my eyes and clear my mind, a small meditation. I bow my head down to my chest. I block out all sound, all sight. I focus on the soft whisper of my breath. In. Out. In. Out.

I can do this.

I sit in the Chair. Kim straps me in tight, and prepares another syringe.

She gives me a kiss on my cheek. She smells of antiseptic and artificial cherries. 'See you soon, sweetness,' she says, and sticks the syringe in my arm.

TWENTY-THREE

TAEMA

My senses scramble. I float in space, but sight is sound and sound is touch and all is strange and beautiful. I feel butterfly wings on my taste buds and fireworks of feathers explode on the backs of my eyelids. Heartbeats pulse against me, crashing waves sending me bouncing against the soft red walls of my own skull. I feel the flashes as the neural dust within my mind sparkles, changing, merging into what I need it to be.

Memories fire at me, without warning, without prompting. I'm six, eating roasted butternut squash, laughing with Tila as Mom tells us a story over dinner. I'm ten, reading as Tila sleeps beside me. I'm seven, and we've fallen by the lake. I've scraped my hip, the pain blooming as though it's just happened. We're trying to drag ourselves upright but we keep slipping in the mud. Tila's panting next to me, and above the birds call. She looks at me, and her eyes are deep and as familiar as my own.

'It'll be OK,' she says.

'You can't promise that,' I say, and I'm out of the memory, back in the Technicolor of my mind. A weird, fractured bit of a memory floats to me. That first moment I saw Tila after the surgery. Standing, unattached. Her own person. Yet as soon as she could, she'd come back to me. She's threaded through my mind. Everywhere I turn, there she is. Tila. My Tila. I see her and I realize: neither of us is the good twin. Not any more. We never were. Tila is simply my other half. Not my better half. Not my worse half.

Then everything goes dark.

It's quiet, and warm.

I wonder if I'm dead. The same thing, perhaps, has happened to me as happened to Nazarin. Maybe I'm flatlining on that chair in the lab. I can't feel my body.

I float there, not thinking, just existing. It's . . . nice. I don't feel afraid. I don't worry about anyone. Not Nazarin. Not Ensi. Not my sister. Not myself.

Being dead isn't so bad.

During our binge on religious texts once we were free of the Hearth, I remember reading a paper that argued we don't have souls. We're nothing but neural pathways and electric pulses, fatty white and grey matter. Once the organ that houses thought dies, there's nothing left. Nothing drifts up to heaven or down to hell. Floating there, in the dim dark, I'm not sure if the author's right or not.

I felt something similar to this when our heart failed at the Hearth. I remember darkness coming, but I was too afraid to embrace it. I ran away. I never saw that light at the end of the tunnel, like they say. Tila said she saw it, in Confession with Mana-ma. At the time I thought she was lying, but maybe she wasn't as afraid as I was. Maybe she spent some time in this quiet place.

I feel the edges of myself slipping away. I imagine my body disintegrating. My skin sloughs away, my veins lift from my muscles, spiralling out into infinity. My muscles unravel into thin tendrils. Just my bones are left, and even they begin to break down, scattering like snow. I'm now just my mind, my metal sternum, my mechanical heart.

As those start to leave me, light returns. It's as if the stars have turned on again. There's a moment where I hover. The pieces of me are scattered all around. I can bring them to me again, knit it all together and go back.

For a moment, I don't know if I want to. Maybe I should let it all fade away.

I remember Tila. How she looked in that surgery room as she put her arms around me and fell asleep. The fear on her face as she clutched me in our apartment a few days ago, terrified and desperate. If I go into that darkness, I go alone.

I pull myself together and return to the real, cruel, painful world.

•

It's bright.

I should hurt. A migraine aura should warble at the edges of my vision. My skin should be rubbed raw and bloody, my lungs charred, my muscles tender. It's like a Synth non-hangover. Somewhere, down deep, your body knows you did something dangerous.

'It went well,' Kim says.

'It . . . was meant to be like that?' I ask, faint.

'What was it like?' Kim tilts her head in curiosity.

'Memories came out of nowhere and my senses went confused, and then it was all dark and quiet. I thought I'd died.'

Kim's eyebrows rise at that. 'Nope, all vital signs were fine. Your brainwaves did drop off at the end there, but not enough to alarm me.'

'The brain is weird,' I mutter.

Kim laughs. 'You can say that again.'

'So how does it work?' I ask. I don't feel any different. 'Is it recording now?'

'No. It's pretty easy. You can do it now. I've linked it to a certain place on your body. I stimulated a particular nerve cluster in your brain, and the code can read it. You press it three times, once a second or so, and it starts. Another three, and it stops. Makes it harder to accidentally interrupt if you're bumped. Here.' She walks over to Nazarin. 'I was tempted to wire it somewhere a little . . . private . . . to make this moment funnier. I didn't. Aren't you impressed with my restraint, my parakeet?'

'Very,' Nazarin says, deadpan. His skin is still a little grey. Kim takes Nazarin's hand and makes him put his index finger to his throat and has him press once, twice, three times in the hollow between his clavicle. He looks exactly the same to me. No little red recording lights in his eyes or ears, not that I expected it.

'How do you feel?' Kim asks, peering at him, holding a hand to his forehead, checking his pulse.

'A bit weird. I have a headache, feel queasy. Does that pass?'

'Probably not, but if that's all you're feeling that's a good sign. It's taken, and your brain's reacting as well as it can to the extra stimuli. Try not to record for more than five minutes at once. Otherwise side effects might worsen.'

He nods, his brow creasing.

'OK, so I'll jabber a bit so you can see how this works when we play it back. Walk around the room and look at things a little.'

Nazarin does so, peering at the lab instruments. He looks at Kim and she does a little twirl, and then he comes and peers at me. I feel strangely vulnerable, knowing that soon I'll see myself through his eyes.

'So, just do this to stop it?' He presses the hollow of his throat three times again.

'Yep, that's all done.'

The crease between his brows eases. 'I feel better now.'

'Good. Come on, let's get out of the lab. Better wallscreen in the lounge.'

I'm not sad to leave that lab behind. I'm fairly sure it's going to give me nightmares. We settle onto the sofas in the living room. I take my shoes off and tuck my feet up on the sofa, wrapping my arms around my legs. It's a childish sort of body language, but I got into the habit after the surgery and it makes me feel more grounded, feeling something pressed against my chest. I'm so tired. I want to go to sleep for at least twelve hours.

Kim passes us glasses of water and we sip as she brings up her interface.

'It'll still send even if we're somewhere all signals are blocked?' I ask.

'They won't be completely blocked, of course. The Ratel can communicate with each other on their own frequency, but they're well protected against any sort of outside tampering. I can use a subfrequency they won't suspect. There might be a bit of a delay, but it should get through to me soon enough. I've had Sudice send to one of my secure drives just now. Nobody can get into it but me, so whatever you find will be safe.'

Perhaps too safe. I like Kim and I've had no reason to distrust her, but she suddenly has a lot of power over us. She could turn us in, pretend we forced her to neurohack us. She could take whatever we record and hold it to ransom, or delete it.

Nazarin sees my hesitation. He doesn't say anything, but

reaches over and takes my hand and squeezes it. *Don't worry*, he seems to say. I wish I could feel as confident.

Kim must have noticed our exchange, but she chooses to ignore it. She logs into the drive and there it is. A little file of two minutes of Nazarin's life. She opens it.

It's a strange echo. It's the words Kim just said, that I just heard, but from a different viewpoint. It's the lab from the vantage point of Nazarin's extra height. I can hear all the sounds of the lab – the ticking of some of the instruments, Kim's voice, the shuffle of Nazarin's feet as he explores. He looks at the lab equipment, and it's like there's cameras behind both of his eyes. But at the same time, it's different to an image from an actual camera. Like the difference between Zeal and Verve. It seems more familiar. More intimate. Like I have become him.

Kim turns around, and then I see myself. He looks down on me a little. I look up at him. Even though it's meant to be just a straight recording, some feelings and thoughts creep in somehow, and I can feel it. I can't tell what exactly the emotion is . . .

I look away, and the video ends.

'It's weird,' Nazarin says. 'It's in my mind with that same clarity. None of my other memories are like that. I remember everything. And when I remember, I get a little headache again. It's far stronger than the memories assisted with my other implants, and I thought those were good.'

'Yep. That's why you shouldn't do it more than you have to. OK, Taema, your turn. Have to make sure it works for you, too,' Kim says.

I dutifully press the hollow of my throat three times. Nothing really changes, except the slightest sharpening of focus, a pressure at my temples, a clenching of nausea in my stomach. It's not too bad, though. I can ignore it. I circle the room, peering at all of her various collectibles from the previous few centuries. I only recognize a few of them – that one's Superman, resting an arm on Batman, who looks rather grumpy.

Nazarin and Kim murmur to each other behind me. I turn on the ball of my foot, twirling around, wanting to see the same blur on the wallscreen. It's a heady feeling, knowing that everything I'm seeing and hearing is permanent. Even if I forget it in the depths of my brain, though evidently that's unlikely, I could relive it all in perfect detail. Someone else could experience this little slice of my life. Anyone. Even centuries from now, all of this could be gone, but if that file somehow survived, someone could be me for five minutes.

I feel a jolt of weirdness as I recall Nazarin, with his implants, probably remembers every detail of his encounter with me better than I do with him. I try not to think about it. If my emotions right now bleed through my perception, what will they think of a flash of panic? I force myself to calm, tapping the hollow of my throat again to turn it off. That same feeling of focus dissipates. My headache and nausea fades.

They play my video. Nazarin glances at me during that surge of emotion. It feels strange, experiencing that same echo again, almost like I'd gone back in time to a few moments ago. How the hell does all that bleed through? It's disconcerting, for sure.

'Well, it's a job well done for me,' Kim says, eyes narrowed in satisfaction.

'Thanks, Kim,' Nazarin says. 'Really. Thank you.'

She waves a hand. 'For you, anything.' Then she pauses.

'I want to give you one last thing before you go, Taema. For Ensi.'

'What?' Nazarin asks. Kim doesn't answer right away, but takes out a box from her pocket and opens it. Inside is a little white strip.

'This will mould around your tooth and harden. I can link it to your brain through a nerve in your gum. If you think a trigger word, then you can bite down and break it.'

'And why would I break it?' I ask.

'It'll bleed a liquid. It won't affect you – it's exempt to your DNA – but it'll affect Ensi. Kiss him. Dose him. This will do the rest.'

'What is it, Kim?' Nazarin asks, wary.

She doesn't directly answer him. 'You realize what he'll do to either of you if you're captured. How he . . . disposes of those who have particularly displeased him.' Her voice grows thick. 'What he probably did to Juliane.'

Nazarin's lips thin in pain. 'Yes.'

'Promise me you'll do this, Taema.' She looks at me, deep into me. 'You're the only one who can get close enough. Even if you catch him red-handed, he has so many people in his pocket – judges, politicians – that he'll find another way to weasel out, or ways to hand over the Ratel to his successor without a hitch. Or send out Verve to the whole city, let it tear itself apart. I wouldn't put it past him. This. This is the real way to get him once and for all.'

'I don't understand what's going on,' I say. 'I can't promise until I understand what it is you want to put in me.'

Kim explains what it will do, and she also explains, in great detail, how Ensi disposes of those who displease him. I very nearly puke on her expensive shag carpet.

We return to the lab. Memories fire in my brain again.

They all feature Tila. I have to remember I'm doing this, risking myself, for her.

She's going to owe me so much when I save her life. She's going to have to do a lot to make up for all I've gone through. As Kim works her magic, I wonder why I'm not angrier at my sister. For all the lies, for what she's put me through. And though I still don't fully understand why she decided to go into the Ratel in the first place, I have to believe that she did what she thought was best. For both of us. And I have to finish what she started.

Though she will owe me the truth. All of it.

Afterwards, I still feel woozy. My tooth doesn't feel any different. But it's there. Third molar from the back on the left-hand side of my mouth. I keep thinking the trigger word, but Kim's given me some tips to try and push it from my mind unless I need it. She recommends chewing with the other side of my mouth, just in case. And if it breaks by accident, Kim says it won't harm me. I have to go back and get another one. If I can.

By the door, she pauses, and then gives us both kisses on the cheek. 'Safe travels. I'm trusting you two to get the bastard, one way or another. And I know you will.' We walk out of the door. I look at her and Kim smiles, but it doesn't reach her eyes. Those are dark with remembered grief and anger.

'Taema,' she says. 'I still want that drink and chat when this is all over and done with.'

'Yes.' I wonder if I'll bring my sister. If I'll be able to. If I'll want to.

TWENTY-FOUR

TILA

The trial's going to be soon. My lawyer said so today when he came to visit. He didn't give me any false hope, so I guess that's something. It's better than him saying I actually have a chance of staying unfrozen for longer than a week.

I've had this notebook open in my lap for hours, just staring at it. I debated continuing the story, but I figured I should write at least a little about what it feels like to know that I'm about to die.

Well, go into stasis. It's basically the same thing.

I'm not afraid of the actual trial. I just have to stand there and stare straight ahead. I can pretend I'm somewhere else. They're still not letting the media in on it, so I won't be livestreamed into almost every home and head in San Francisco. I guess that's something. I'll still be recorded. At some point, they'll let it out. The whole world will see me, a murderess in a city that prides itself on murder being a thing of the past. Never mind that murder happens in this city all the time, jut quiet and unseen. The Zealots. The Ratel. The Ratel's victims. So many deaths.

I'm not afraid of the trial. I'm afraid of what happens after.

I keep looking at my hands. All the whorls and wrinkles in them. The almost-invisible bump of the VeriChip, just to the right of the vein under the skin of my wrist, like blue lightning. I have a mole in the crook of my elbow. Taema has one there, too. I keep looking at these little details that make me Tila because I realize that soon, they'll all be frozen in time. The blood won't pump through my veins any more – it'll be all congealed and disgusting. My fingers will lie still. My skin will turn grey. And then, if the power of that wing fails and defrosts us – a few days after they freeze me, a few years, it's all the same – they'll burn up the dead corpse into nothing. My bones, my skin, my brain, everything will be gone. I'll just be dust.

Right now there are two of us, but soon there'll only be one. Taema will probably be better off without me, but I can't help thinking she'll also be all alone.

•

The supply ship came for its scheduled drop and we made our way to where it would land. Taema and I watched it fly overhead. It cut through the air so smoothly, a bird diving underwater to catch a fish. We went to watch it all happen, like so many times before.

But this time was different.

Dad oversaw everything, ordering men where to program the droids to put the boxes coming off of the ship. Mom came to sign off on all the shipments and deliveries. And there, just around the side, there was a box or two going on the ship. I'd seen that happen before, but I'd always assumed that it was the blankets and trinkets we made to sell in the city for people who liked that crap. Things that had been made by human hands instead of robot ones or replicators. Now I know that it was a hell of a lot more than that, but back then I had no idea.

The woman Mom was speaking to earnestly shook her

hand. There was something hidden in her palm, which my mom took. After the woman went away, Mom put it in her pocket. She looked guilty, and worried. I knew it had something to do with us.

'What do you think it is?' Taema asked me.

'We'll find out soon enough.'

We did.

That night after dinner, Mom and Dad drew the curtains and asked us to sit at the kitchen table. They wiped off the worn wood with antiseptic. They took out a little package and unwrapped it. Little silver squares fell onto the table, glinting in the buzzing electrical light overhead. I knew they were whatever the woman had given my mom that afternoon.

'What are they?' I asked.

'VeriChips. For identification. Made out to Taema and Tila Collins,' Dad said.

'Our last name is Amner,' Taema said.

Because the VeriChips had our real first names, it meant that Mana-ma would be able to find us more easily, if she really wanted to, after we escaped. After losing everything else, we couldn't stand the thought of having to call each other false names, too. We didn't think there was anything she'd be able to do to us once we escaped. Once we arrived, we kept our past hidden, kept our noses clean. We thought it was enough.

(We were stupid.)

Mom and Dad got out the medical supplies. They were going to put the VeriChips in now, since we'd leave on the next supply ship out. Mom arranged it with that same woman, who was in charge of the ship. I don't know how – we wouldn't have had anything to bribe her with. Maybe she appealed to her conscience or something.

Mom did it. She swabbed our right wrists and numbed the

area with some ice. It didn't do much for the pain, but we didn't cry out as she used a scalpel to cut the skin and slot in the ID chip. She told us everyone in the cities outside had VeriChips. They were important. She closed the wound with a tiny stitch and wrapped it. It was autumn so it was getting a little colder, and she ordered us to wear long sleeves and not show anyone the bandages while we were healing. There might be a small scar, but we could get it erased once we were in San Francisco with a bit of our first pay cheque. I remember wondering what a pay cheque was, and how I would receive one.

Mom and Dad spent several hours that night telling us all the outdated information they knew about San Francisco and the outside world that the Hearth hadn't taught us. Even though Taema and I had already learned some of it from our contraband tablet (still hidden under our mattress), we were both totally overwhelmed. It was so much information that we couldn't take it all in. Mom and Dad were desperate to try and give us as much of a head start as possible, so we didn't say anything and just listened.

That night we lay forehead to forehead on the bed, looking at the bandages on our wrists.

'We're already Impure, I guess,' Taema whispered. She looked so young, so vulnerable, and I hated that I must have looked the same way.

'The Pure and Impure stuff is bullshit, Taema.'

Her mouth twisted. She knew that on some level, but she couldn't help her gut reaction. That the technology she'd been taught was evil her whole life was now implanted under her skin. 'It's really happening, isn't it?'

'Once we're gone, we'll never come back,' I said, and I felt both triumphant and a little sad. For all Mana-ma and the Hearth's philosophy weren't for us any more – especially me

– it was the only place we knew. Our friends were here. Our parents. Our whole way of life. Through that tablet, we'd only had a little peek into the window of the Real World. Everything was going to change.

We fell asleep that night knowing our time in the Hearth was coming to an end.

TWENTY-FIVE

TAEMA

It's time for my shift in the Verve lounge in a warehouse down by the docks. The reminder came through on my implant, on an untraceable line. This week, Tila's shifts are Monday and Wednesday.

Nazarin's on security duty. They're trying to arrange his Test, and he's bending over backwards trying to find excuses for it to be delayed until after the drop.

As I take the MUNI through the glowing green tunnels, I can't stop thinking about the Test. All the images that flashed before my eyes, the smells, the confusion. The simulated murder that had seemed so real. Murder. The word that seemed so ugly when I first heard it, but now I've acted out homicidal violence in two simulations. I'm about to dive back into another Vervescape, and who knows what or who I will find there.

Once I'm at the warehouse, I force myself to push the macabre thoughts from my mind. I have to focus on being Tila again, one of the newest lucid dreamers in the Ratel. A Rook.

The outside of the warehouse is boring, blocky concrete. A faded sign once proclaimed 'Geary Hovered Automobiles', but it's faded and tagged with moving graffiti. A stylized bunny holds knives and does a cartwheel above the old image of a hovercar, over and over again.

Malka opens the door before I can even knock. I can't help it; I start and take a step back in alarm. She narrows her eyes and smiles at me. She's wearing a long dress of artful folds, like a Grecian tunic.

'Hello, canary,' she greets me. 'Come on in.'

I cross the threshold.

Inside, I expect it to be as dilapidated as the outside, but instead it's bright and fresh as a hospital room.

Malka leads me down the long hallway. Her heels click on the tiles, her hips swishing back and forth. She glances over at me. 'I'm glad you're feeling recovered. We've missed you, the past few shifts. Could have used your expertise. Now you're all Tested, though, we can trust you with more than the menial dreams, canary girl.'

Like Kim, she seems to be fond of nicknames, but there the similarity ends. Kim is warm and genuine, and everything about Malka is carefully engineered. She gives a throaty laugh and stops by a door. It opens with a soft exhalation of air. 'In you go. Think of this as part two of your Test. What can you do with a juicier dream?'

I step in, my palms damp with nerves. Inside is a Chair, far smoother and sleeker than the ones in Mirage, or even in the training room at the safe house. A man lies down, strapped in. He doesn't seem to be there against his will. Next to him is a second, empty Chair.

I look closer and jerk with surprise.

'Thought you'd recognize him,' Malka says, smiling. If I'm the canary, she's the cat with the cream.

'This is . . . Mr Mantel.' The owner of Sudice, Inc. One of the most powerful people in the world. He was technically my boss's boss's boss's boss. I've only seen him from afar a handful of times in my years working for Silvercloud. It's so incongruous, seeing him plugged into a Chair in this secret Verve lounge run by the Ratel. Does the government know?

I put my hand up to my necklace, pretending to fiddle with it. While Malka gazes down at the man's supine form, I press the hollow of my throat. One. Two. Three.

I swallow against the nausea and the migraine.

'You see why trust is important to us,' Malka says smoothly. 'No one else may know that he comes here. And no one will learn of it, will they?' The tip of her tongue darts out to wet her red lips.

'Of course not.' My breathing is shallow. I force myself to fill my lungs. It doesn't help. I still feel as though I can't breathe.

Hold it together, Taema. Hold it together.

'Are you all right?' Malka asks with false concern.

'Fine,' I say with a little half-smile. 'Just . . . amazed to meet the man in person. So to speak. I'm to . . . go in?' I eye the second Chair.

'Yes. You observe the dreams, I observe you, and we see how you do. Another Test, as I said, yet this one is not quite so . . . complicated.'

I give a strangled approximation of a laugh. 'Let's hope I do as well.'

'Yes. Let's hope.'

The half-hearted smile slips from my face.

The room is soundproof. Outside in the hallway, dozens of people must walk by, but I can't hear any of them. It's as if this room is all that exists, and the only sounds are the short susurrations of the machine, and the faint sounds of three humans' breaths.

'What do you want me to suggest to him?'

'Nothing this time. Just observe. You don't want him to notice you.'

'All right.' I turn off the brain recording. I'm not sure if it'll work in the Vervescape, and Kim told me not to use it for too long.

She plugs me in, prepping syringes. If they can do it Chairless, like they did with my Test, why go through the steps here? Perhaps it's still in process, or the level Ensi dosed me with was too low. I hadn't even realized I was on it.

'Night, night,' Malka says from above me.

I float away.

•

Mr Mantel's dream is grainy. Small flecks of white float along my vision like static. I focus on making myself invisible as a ghost. *I'm not here*, I try to tell the dream. *Don't notice me. I'm just another speck.*

The static parts, the dream clearing. The colours brighten until it's as vivid as Mia's dreamscape. Mr Mantel has a woman tied up on a bed in a penthouse apartment. It's Sharon Roux. The woman is the mayor of San Francisco.

She's as naked as he is, their clothes scattered around the room. Fresh bruises paint her legs and upper arms. Nowhere they'd show in her suit. I furrow my brow, until I see her smiling. She wants the restraints, and he wants to restrain her.

He crawls on top of her again, beginning anew. He hurts her, she cries out, she smiles, he smiles. It's different to the Zealscape. He's not killing her. There's no blood. No oily muck. No monsters. They're both enjoying themselves with pleasure and pain.

It seems to me like he's reliving a memory. Verve can

enhance memories, so you relive them in glorious hyper-saturated colour. It's a strange sensation, to watch someone having sex, knowing that you're strapped into a Chair and another woman is monitoring your physical sensors. I don't look away, though. I'm doing my duty and observing everything, in the hope I notice what Malka wants me to.

Why has Mr Mantel chosen this memory to relive? What is he enhancing? How will he be when he wakes up? Angrier? Ready to come back again tomorrow? And what will the Ratel suggest to him? There are so many options. To take a deal that will profit the mob? To hold back a patent or push forward another? Or they could overwrite his personality completely, and make him into whatever they want. If they have the main man of the most powerful company in the world as their puppet, think what they could do. Control the top of Sudice through Mr Mantel, and control the bottom by sending violent, hungry Zealots, reprogrammed by Verve, into the fray. Topple the structure and make what they want of it.

After what seems like hours, Mr Mantel and Mayor Roux have finished. Mantel unwraps her restraints and they sprawl across silken sheets.

Pillow talk. Time to focus. I shift closer, keeping to the shadows. Neither of them notices me. Even in the dream world, my temples throb and my stomach feels as though I've swallowed rocks, despite the fact that I turned off the brain recording.

Mantel and Roux lie next to each other, but don't quite touch. I can't tell if they love each other or are using each other. Maybe both.

'It's getting out of hand,' Roux says, staring up at the ceiling. Static dances across her face. Strands of dark hair cling to her glistening forehead.

'What is?' Mantel asks, folding his hands behind his neck.

'The Ratel situation. Do you know how much of my time it's taking up these days?'

'I can only imagine.'

She bares her teeth. 'They have to be stopped, Mantel. It's your pharmaceuticals they've twisted.'

'You think I don't realize that? I don't see how they can be stopped.'

'Yeah, yet it means the criminal bastards are out on the streets. There was a robbery last week. From a civilian. We had to cover it up. But I don't think we'll be able to do that much longer. And what if there's a murder? We'll have riots. This is a delicate balance, and I don't want it to fall in the Ratel's favour.'

'We're trying to find a counter-measure, but it's taking time.'

'We don't have time.' Roux sits up, the bed sheet falling to pool at her waist. Her large breasts defy gravity, thanks to the wonders of flesh parlours. I don't feel Mantel's emotions like I did when Kim played Nazarin's memories, but it seems somehow linked. How else can these drugged dreams be so clear, if they aren't somehow messing with implants?

Everything's connected.

'If you still had Veli, then you'd have a cure by now.' I have no idea who or what Veli is. The name hasn't been mentioned in Tila's notes, or in the SFPD's brainloading.

'You don't know that. And he was an imposter. Some little upstart my father plucked from one of his pet projects.' Mantel's brow draws down. Almost against his will, an image flickers on the wall of a younger man with a strong jaw and angry eyes. It disappears almost immediately, until I'm not sure if I really saw it at all.

'He was a genius and you were a jealous little boy.' She sounds bored, as if she's said this to him many times before. She swings her legs over the bed and begins to pull on her stockings.

'Be careful, Roux.' Mantel's voice simmers in anger.

She looks over her shoulder at him. 'I always am.'

The dream shifts. Another woman enters the room, and I don't recognize her. Mr Mantel looks over his shoulder in my direction, and I worry he sees me as everything fades away. His dream continues, but I leave.

I wake up in the Chair, Malka watching me, unblinking. In the Chair across from me, Mr Mantel has a hard-on. I avert my gaze.

Malka folds her hands over her knees. 'Well, what did you notice?'

I think through it, replaying the conversation over in my mind.

'Be careful, Roux.' Mantel's voice simmers in anger.

She looks over her shoulder at him. 'I always am.'

'Roux knows that Mantel's not to be trusted.'

'What makes you say that?'

'She doesn't give him any specifics. She hints that she's doing things to bring the Ratel down, but that's all. She chides him about letting Veli go . . .' Here I falter. 'Who is he?'

'He's the man who truly invented Zeal. Mantel ousted him from Sudice and put a hit on him, so they say.' She raises an eyebrow. 'Veli hasn't been seen since, in any case. What else did you notice?'

'The government still wants to take us down,' I say, though even pretending to be a part of the Ratel sets my teeth on edge, 'but we already knew that.'

Malka smiles. 'Good girl.'

'I'm right?'

'On the right track, in any case.' She stands, and I mimic the smooth movement. 'We already knew you were a fine dreamsifter. We'll up the stakes a little next time. You'll have grown more used to his dreams by then, and will be able to make one little suggestion.'

'Of what?' I ask, my stomach twisting in dread as I give her a plastic smile.

'Next time is time enough.' She leans back. 'I had my doubts, but I think Ensi was right about you.'

What a backhanded compliment. I stretch my plastic smile. 'Thank you.'

'Don't thank me just yet,' she says. She drifts closer, puts her hand on my face. I force myself not to stiffen. 'I have to show you what happens to little birds who chirp. Just in case.'

She takes my hand and leads me from the room. I take a last look at Mantel before the door closes. He's panting, low, animalistic, rhythmic. Lost in the throes of Verve, where sex is better, and even memories of threats make you smile.

•

Another soundproof room. Outside the door, Malka takes a sword in a sheath from a hook on the wall with a familiarity that terrifies me. I play with my necklace, turning the brain recording on again.

Inside the room is another face I recognize from Tila's sketchbook. A woman named Nuala. She's small, dainty. She has pale skin and her hair is a lilac and gunmetal grey. She looks like a pixie from a fantasy film.

She looks terrified.

'Hello, Nuala,' Malka says, as if they're about to have tea. 'How nice to see you.'

Malka unsheathes the sword. It looks ancient. Nuala squeaks and pushes herself back in the corner, as if that could make any sort of difference. Whatever's about to happen won't be pretty, and I won't be able to do anything to stop it. I clamp down tight on my emotions. The only way to get through this is to be a robot. My knees are still shaking.

'Nuala, this is Tila. Your replacement. Tell her your crime.'

Nuala bows her head. I stare at the straight parting of her hair. Every muscle in my back is so tight I fear if I move, they'll break.

'I squeaked,' she whispers.

'Yes, you did. And who to?'

'The police.' Another whisper.

If anything, my muscles go tighter. She knows. She has to. I'm not a replacement at all. The Queen is going to kill both of us in this soundproof room and nobody will hear our screams. I force myself to stay quiet, my breathing even. My mechanical heartbeat thrums, steady and strong. I still have the headache and the fist of nausea in my stomach. All of this is recording. Even if I die, Kim will get this. Hopefully.

'That you did.'

Malka hefts the sword.

'I prefer to do this the old-fashioned way,' Malka says conversationally. 'This is from the twelfth century. Beautiful, isn't it?'

It is, in a horrific way. The metal blade is scratched with time, but its edges are still sharp. Emeralds embellion the hilt.

Nuala is crying. 'Please,' she says. 'Please.'

It's a useless plea. Malka drifts closer, the light overhead catching on the blade. She's stalking her prey. Nuala pushes back into the wall as hard as she can and starts screaming for help. Nobody can hear her but me, and I clasp my hands over my ears. My resolve breaks and I hear the rough sobs from my throat. I want to shield Nuala with my body, but I know it won't protect her. And I'm too much of a coward. I'm not Tila. Tila would rush Malka and disarm her, consequences be damned.

'Don't you dare close your eyes, Tila,' Malka says, her words almost singsong. 'You need to understand just how imperative it is to keep your goddam little mouth shut.'

I open my eyes wide, afraid to blink. *Don't look away.*

Nuala keeps screaming, a high banshee wail. Malka presses the point of the blade through the hollow of her throat. Nuala's screams cut short.

Blood stains the white uniform, falling in a crimson tide down her front. It was quick, at least. No torture. No scalpels like in Mia's dream.

Malka draws the sword out, wiping the blood off with the end of Nuala's tunic. The girl's eyes stare straight ahead, still shining with tears. Her beautiful hair is matted with blood. Malka looks down, and all the anger has fled from her face. She looks serene, as if she's come out of the dreamscape, wiped clean of her bloodlust, at least for a time.

'Now you see what happens if you cross us.'

'Did I not already see that at Xanadu?' I whisper. I wish this could be a Verve hallucination like the original Test, but it's not.

'Nothing like a repeat lesson to drive it home.' She comes closer to me, until I can smell her perfume under the iron tang of blood. It smells of incense, dark and smoky. She pauses scant inches from me. I can see each perfect pore in her face, the glitter of her eyeshadow.

She's close enough to kiss me. I feel the tip of my tongue touch the false-crowned molar. It's meant for Ensi, but would it harm her, too?

'And I don't know if I trust you,' she murmurs. 'See, I liked Nuala. This, this was the kindest way. If you betray us, you won't be so lucky.

'I'm not sure what he sees in you, or what he wants from you. Whatever it is, he'll get it, little canary,' she whispers to me. 'At the moment you're interesting. He's still figuring out what he really wants from you. And, once he gets it, you'll be obsolete. If I were you, I'd make sure I was useful elsewhere, and prove myself trustworthy. To him. And especially to me. Or else you'll find you'll never flee your cage.'

She stays that way, almost nose to nose, staring into me. I worry that she can see everything – my treachery, my fear.

After a moment, an age, she pulls away, putting the sword back in its sheath, like an avenging Valkyrie. I don't want to be against her, because I fear I'd have no chance.

She smiles at me as if she knows this, and then she leaves. I press the hollow of my throat three times, try not to look at the corpse of Nuala, and trail after her.

•

Back at the safe house, I can't stop shaking.

I don't cry, but I want to. So I sit in the living room, wrapped in a blanket, simply shivering. Nazarin sits next to me. I've told him everything that happened. We've transferred both of our recordings to Kim's server. We told her not to watch them. I didn't want her to see that girl murdered. It might remind her of what happened to her wife, just because she came too close to her quarry on what seemed to be just one more case.

'Do you know who Veli is?' I ask. Something about Malka's body language made me think it was important.

'No. I'll ask my superior, see if he knows anything.'

We trail off again. Nazarin's eyes go distant and he pings his superior. His fingers dance as he types in the air. I lean against him, his arm warm against mine. It helps ground me. My eyes drift closed, and despite everything that's happened, I doze.

A time later, Nazarin gently shakes me awake.

'What is it?' I ask. My brain is fuzzy. Memories of Nuala come back, and I want to vomit.

'My superior looked up the name, but it was classified. Even for him.'

'Shit. Really?'

'Yes. He's gained access now, though, and he can share it with us.'

'All right.'

Nazarin gets up and brings back two glasses of water. I gulp mine down. He takes a breath. 'Veli was once CEO of Sudice, Inc.,' Nazarin says. 'Veli Carrera. Alex Mantel's father, Peter Mantel, and Carrera started Sudice. They created Zeal. After Peter died, Alex ousted Carrera, wanting Sudice to be a family-run affair. Carrera didn't take it well. Alex thought it was dangerous to leave Carrera . . . untethered, and so he tried to kill him, hiring a hitman, probably hired from the Ratel. But Veli Carrera escaped and found his way into the mob. He changed his face so that no one would find him. The SFPD think that he worked his way up from the bottom and became . . . Ensi.'

I let that sink in. 'So Ensi is the man who helped invent Zeal in the first place. It explains why he was able to fabricate Verve. He has the technical foundation. It also explains why he's interested in weakening Zeal's hold on the city and replacing it with Verve. They can break down the city, and hurt Sudice in the process.'

'Exactly.'

'So many layers and secrets.'

'I told you. The further undercover you go, the more there seem to be.'

We lapse into silence.

'I think he might be coming up with a form of Verve that doesn't need a Chair and implants,' I say carefully. 'He dosed me with Verve, I think, before the Test.'

'Easier to dose large numbers of people that way, or in places they don't expect.' Nazarin rubs his face.

'He'll be able to peek into everyone's heads at will. No secrets. Not from him.'

'Exactly.' Nazarin sighs. 'One good thing, I suppose. Ensi's asked me to be his bodyguard. That drop from the Hearth? I'm going to be right there by his side, with a perfect view to record everything.' He taps his temple.

'One good thing, good being relative,' I say. 'After the drop, I think we need to duck out. This is growing too dangerous.'

'I agree completely. If we can find out what the Hearth is delivering, prove Ensi is receiving illicit material, and that Alex Mantel is involved, that's enough that we can bring the force of the law down on the Ratel. We're not needed after that.'

'Just until the drop,' I say, in almost a sigh.

'Just until then.'

Then it's over.

•

Monday ends. Tuesday passes in a blur of last-minute preparation and too little sleep. Then it's Wednesday. The drop will happen at midnight.

Nazarin will be there, guarding the King. I'll be on my own, trying to move close enough to watch and record from another angle. Nazarin said I didn't have to go, that he could do it alone; but I can't back out now, not when we're so very close to the end. If there's anything connected to the Hearth, I'm the best person to figure out what it is and who's behind it on the other side of the Bay.

Yesterday was a long day. I didn't have to go to the Verve lounge, at least, and with luck, I'll never have to set foot there again. It was more training, more last-minute information. I picked through the information on Veli Carrera, or Ensi in a previous life, wondering what he was like back then. Sudice betrayed him, but he didn't have to turn to crime. Yet he did.

Now it's Wednesday. The last night of having to do this.

No more watching people's Verve dreams. No more pretending to be Tila and losing more of the Taema I used to be each day. No more putting myself in danger.

That's the plan.

The King of the Ratel doesn't often get his hands dirty, but it seems he'll attend this drop personally. It's clever that Ensi stays out of things as much as possible. Nazarin has seen so many crimes over the past year in his time with the Ratel; but it's always other people. If they were arrested, nothing would really change. They'd be replaced the next day, and Ratel business would continue as usual. We still only have proof of Malka killing someone. We don't have direct proof of Ensi doing anything illegal. Hopefully, in fifteen minutes, we will.

The pier appears abandoned, but the Ratel own it, and no one trespasses. The cranes, built in water, tower over us like strange mechanical beasts. Dotted around the pier are reinforced docks, stacked with rusting cargo bins. I'm hidden behind one, dressed in a black Kalar suit. I've been here half an hour, waiting and watching; Nazarin gave me a gun, now tucked into the small of my back. The air is cold, and I shiver.

The green glow of the algae in the water lends everything a sickly tinge, but it's enough light for me to see.

They haven't arrived yet. I worry that I've messed up and read the notebook wrong, or that Ensi changed it at the last moment and Nazarin couldn't tell me.

Off to my right is movement. There they are. I push the hollow of my throat three times. The headache returns, worse than it was at the Verve lounge. I nearly throw up the scant meal I had a few hours earlier. I bend over, breathing hard, before I peer out around the crate. It's a man, tall and muscle-bound, patrolling the perimeter. There's Nazarin, standing next to other muscle-bound men. Waiting. The men begin to patrol. I press myself into the shadows.

I can see Ensi's profile, his hair in disarray from the wind. He's standing with just one or two other people. The lights of the ships pulse overhead as they slip into the Ferry Building. Ensi's body language is impatient.

There it is.

A ship that looks almost identical to the supply ships that came once a month to Mana's Hearth drops down, its engines flaring. The light illuminates Ensi's face in the green fog. He's smiling to himself.

I'm so focused on him that I don't notice that a bodyguard by Ensi's side has gone missing.

By the time I feel the prick of the needle in my neck, it's too late.

All grows dark.

TWENTY-SIX

TAEMA

I wake up groggy and hurting. I'm strapped into a Chair, like the ones I've seen in the Ratel warehouse the last few days, unable to move.

Nazarin is in another Chair next to me, but he's still out cold.

Unlike the bulky Chairs of the safe house and Zeal and Verve lounges, these have no wires. There are only little electrodes resting against my skin, like during the Test. The Chair is little more than a prop and a way to restrain me.

Ensi sits across from me, legs crossed, eyes staring into the distance as he reads something on his feed. When he sees me move my head, he gives me his full attention.

His face is smooth as still water, his gaze frigid. As if he's never met me before, never danced with me, never unzipped that catsuit. I'm intensely grateful I didn't end up needing to sleep with him, so there is not that extra layer of guilt and betrayal.

'Good evening,' Ensi says, as if we're sitting across from each other at a dinner party. His mannerisms are similar to Malka's. Unfailingly polite, even as they're about to commit cold-blooded murder.

I say nothing.

'You and your sister are cute, you know that?' he says. 'Thinking you're so clever, sniffing around my business. That I wouldn't know exactly what you're doing at all times. You really think that notebook was left in my pocket by chance? Silly, silly girl.'

I'm an idiot. If he knew about an uprising like he did at Xanadu . . . there, he even let them make their display, sacrificing a few people, his own people, before he crushed it and summarily executed everyone involved. He played with us, him the leonine cat and us the little mice.

'How long have you known?' I manage, my voice hoarse.

'As soon as Tila came snooping a few months ago.' I close my eyes. 'I knew her right away. I even fed her some clues, knowing she wouldn't be able to resist trying to solve the mystery.'

My mouth is so dry. I lick my lips. 'You know who we are.'

'Of course I do. You're the only two to make it out of the Hearth on your own terms in years. I've kept tabs on you. You proved more interesting than I thought.'

'Who the hell are you?' I ask. 'What do you have to do with the Hearth?'

He smiles. 'I don't owe you any explanations. In fact, I quite enjoy the idea of you working so very, very hard to find out the answers and then never getting them.' He sighs. 'I'll humour you. I did find Tila amusing, at first. Trying to find out everything she could. For a long time, she went nowhere, and I enjoyed her struggle. I decided to toy with her more, seducing her even as she thought she was seducing me. Then, to my surprise, she actually found something useful that she could use against me. And I couldn't have that, now, could I?'

'So you sent Vuk after her. Or, should I say, you sent Adam after her.' The words feel acrid on my tongue. I feel my face twist in disgust and horror. Images of the crime scene swim in my vision. So much blood.

'Ah, I see you found that piece of the puzzle. She'd realized who he was, so it seemed fitting he should be her downfall. Of course, the plan did not go perfectly.' His mouth flattens in anger.

My implants are still recording everything we're saying, even if they're not broadcasting to Kim right away. It's been over five minutes, and I have to hope the side effects don't kill me. I've gotten enough to hang him with, and I have a feeling he's only about to give me more.

I concentrate on my mind, trying to focus inwards. I can't tell if it's sending or not. And even if it is, then our location's probably blocked as well. We're trapped.

Stupid. Stupid, stupid.

'You know why your sister did it, don't you?' Ensi asks. 'Tell me you at least figured that out.'

'Did what?' I ask, my mouth dry.

'Killed him. Your sister did do it. Her hand held the knife that went right into his heart.' He pauses, just for a moment, revelling. 'She did it for you.'

I hear a ringing in my ears.

'She realized that if she was found out, then I'd come after you to get her to do what I want. I'm still not entirely sure what happened that night at Zenith. She did something to Vuk before she killed him. His mind went haywire, broke through the Verve programming, which I didn't think was possible.'

I can't breathe. I don't want to believe him, but why lie now, when he's about to kill me?

'What's your link to the Hearth?' I ask again. I want – I need – to know.

He only shakes his head.

I want to snarl at him, but I won't give him the satisfaction. 'What are you planning to do?' My voice is even, cool. I'm proud of that.

'To you?' He picks up a syringe of Verve. 'I'm going to plug you in, but I've programmed this Vervescape a little differently. It's extra potent, and not a mix you'd find in any lounge.' I swallow. He's the man who invented both Zeal and Verve. He can do almost anything he wants, for he knows the code and the pharmacology better than anyone alive.

He considers the syringe. 'Who else but me could reprogram personalities and brain chemistries? Who else could take timid, shy Adam and turn him into Adam, a killer on command?

'I've programmed this particular world here so that instead of you enacting the violence, the violence is enacted against you. Your own personal little hell. It's how I execute those who really disappoint me. And, Taema, for all your cleverness, you've disappointed me.' He gestures to his right and I see a third empty Chair. 'I'll be joining you.'

He's going to torture me. I think of Mia and her scalpel. False Mana-ma's soundless, tongueless, painful scream. It's as if I'm made of stone. I want to scream, cry, piss myself, laugh hysterically, but I can't do a thing.

I turn my head. Nazarin's awake, his open eyes locked on me. I can't contact Nazarin through my implants because of the blocked signal. I try my restraints, but they're stuck fast.

Ensi reaches down and pushes up the sleeve of my Kalar suit, revealing the bare skin. He runs his finger down the exposed flesh. I shiver.

'It's such a shame,' he says. 'If I'd found you both right when you left the Hearth, your lives could have been so very different. You slipped past too quickly, already within the system as soon as you arrived in the city. When I did find you, I let you be. Why? Curiosity, I suppose – what would two girls who escaped the Hearth choose to do with their new lives? You went through engineering school. I was at your graduation ceremony, though you never saw me.' My skin prickles. 'Tila grew into her art, and had that gallery show. I went to that, too. I even bought one of her paintings.'

Were we experiments to him? He watched us, to see what we'd do. The gallery showing was so long ago. Did my sister realize had Ensi bought one of her paintings? Does she feel he has a piece of her? Did she know he's been keeping tabs on us for years?

'Which painting?' I ask, still avoiding looking at Nazarin. I think he's worked his way out of a restraint. But how can he get out of the rest? If he reaches around, Ensi will notice.

Just keep him talking. He wants to talk, even if he says he doesn't. I should be more scared, but I must be in shock, using the Hearth training to drive the fear away, at least a little. I'm grateful for it. It means I can think, I can speak. I can try to survive.

'The quasi-self-portrait.'

I know the one he means. It's a woman who looks nothing like us, but her shadow falls out behind her, separate, but connected. She'd painted it in all the colours of the rainbow, yet for all the crazy hues, it was so realistic. My sister had called it *The Kaleidoscope Woman*. I'd been sad when it sold, but she'd said she couldn't turn down the price. I feel sick that he has it.

I swallow. We're alone, but I have no doubt that dozens of guards are posted outside this room, wherever it is.

Ensi stretches his arms over his head. 'Now, fascinating as this conversation has been, it's time for us to be getting on, isn't it?' He aligns the needle against the crook of my elbow, poised over the vein. The electrodes begin to buzz, tightening against my skin. The fear I'd banished rushes back. I stare at the ceiling, and that white expanse may be the last thing I see. How boring.

Ensi leans closer to me. This is my only chance. I think the trigger word: 'sweetpea'. I bite the seal on the tooth. A liquid spreads into my mouth, and I lock my throat. I'll kiss him if I can, and if I can't, I'll spray it into his face.

'I didn't see you partnering up with a detective. And I didn't peg him until he waltzed into that party with you, so I give him credit for that. A good detective – but not smart enough to quit while he was ahead. I'll tell you one thing before you go, my dear,' he whispers. 'You want to know who I am, but I'm a little disappointed you haven't figured it out.'

He presses his lips to mine. I open my mouth, as if gasping, and he presses his tongue into mine. The tasteless liquid spreads into him. There. It's done. I can only hope it's enough.

He presses the plunger on the syringe and the drug begins to work.

'I'm the Brother,' he whispers as my mind starts to go.

Everything that happens next is a blur. Nazarin bounds up from his chair and knocks Ensi back.

My mind burns. I'm still conscious – barely – because Ensi hasn't started the program. It takes all my strength to raise my head a few inches. Ensi is manipulating the fight with Nazarin so he inches closer to the controls. I try to warn Nazarin, but my mouth won't open. Ensi's hand snakes back and the program begins. Soon, I'll be trapped in a dream.

The King of the Ratel knocks Nazarin against the wall. He slumps over, his battered brain out cold again.

With the last of my consciousness, I see Ensi strap Nazarin

in the Chair and begin the program, then strap himself into another, starting his own sequence.

He's grinning like a hunter going in for the kill.

And then we're gone.

TWENTY-SEVEN

TILA

We really thought we'd succeeded.

The month had passed without any problems. We went to school, we did the chores we could do, we listened to sermons, we did the Meditation and we did our best not to stand out at all. Mom and Dad did their jobs. We tried to act both positive and remorseful at the thought that we would be re-entering the Cycle again soon. Our health continued to worsen, and our main fear was that we'd die before we could escape.

We should have been more afraid of Mana-ma.

The morning the supply ship was due to come, we'd gone into the forest to hide near where it would land. It was slow going – we had trouble walking and had to use canes, stopping to rest every few steps. We left before most of the Hearth was awake and kept under cover of the trees, hoping that nobody would see us. We didn't bring anything with us except a bit of food – no clothes, no trinkets, no journals. I think that hurt Taema more than me. She wanted to bring at least one book. I decided then and there that if we survived and got jobs in San Francisco, I'd buy her all the books I could with my first pay cheque.

We waited there in the shade all morning, eating the snacks

Mom and Dad had packed us. We wouldn't have long once Dad gave the signal.

'Are Mom and Dad going to get into trouble if Mana-ma realizes they helped us?' Taema asked. She hadn't asked the question before, though it must have been on her mind as much as mine.

'Probably, but it shouldn't be too bad. Mana-ma loves them, and maybe she won't find out. Maybe they'll think we went off to die in the woods and then animals ate us.'

'That's gross, Tila.'

'What? I'd rather be eaten by a fox or a bear then buried in the ground and then eaten by worms. You're going to be eaten either way.'

I was trying to distract her, though I wasn't doing a very good job. I thought Mom and Dad would get in big trouble if Mana-ma found out they helped us escape. I didn't think their lives would be in danger or anything, though. I didn't know the full story of Mia and her lost lover back then. If I had, I might have been too scared to risk Mom and Dad by running away.

Even to save our lives.

'Maybe we shouldn't do this,' Taema says. 'I . . . can't help feeling it's wrong. That out there we'll lose ourselves.'

I pressed my cheek against hers, then reached around and stroked her hair. 'If we stay, we die. I don't want you to die.'

Her breath hitched. 'I don't want you to die, either. Maybe it's better to be damned by Impure things than be dead.'

I shook my head, pushing down my anger that, despite everything, she could still believe in the tenets of the Hearth.

The ship came down, all silver and chrome and the blue fire of its engines. It was so different to anything in the Hearth. So smooth and sleek and futuristic. I remember thinking how strange it would be to be surrounded by a world where everything looked so flawless like that.

The hatch opened and the worker drones went about their business like ants, crawling out of the belly of the beast, lugging crates to be set onto the grass. Once the ship left, the people from the Hearth would slink down the hill and take their essential supplies back to the buildings, trying to have as little contact with the Impure as possible.

'So fucking hypocritical,' I said out loud.

'What is?'

'All that bullshit about the Impure. Yet they still take regular orders of things they can't make. Never really thought about it before. The Hearth has plenty of Impure stuff that we all use. Light bulbs. Some of the cleaning stuff. Metalwork. We can't make a lot of that here. It's all over, but we pretend we're all Pure and untouched by the outside world. So stupid.'

A pause, and then: 'Yeah. It is.' It was the first time she had really agreed with me out loud. Usually when I ranted about the evils of the Hearth she stayed pretty quiet, tacitly agreeing but not really saying anything out loud that could be considered anti-Hearth. It had always annoyed me. Now, she sounded so sad that I felt guilty for all my ranting. I also felt justified.

'It's almost time,' I whispered, wrapping my arms about her. She rested her chin on my shoulder.

'Everything will be different now,' she whispered against my neck.

'It'll be better.'

'Maybe.' She pulled away, and I could see the dark circles under her eyes, the yellow undertone to her skin, how thin she'd grown. I looked exactly the same. We felt especially weak that day. The excitement of freedom was overworking our already weakened heart.

'Taema?' I murmured, shaking her shoulder. She slumped, and I fell to the ground with her. I clutched her to me, taking deep breaths, forcing myself to stay calm, because I couldn't stress the heart any further. Her arms were slack against mine. I wrapped my own arms around her and rocked us like we were children, resting my face against her slack skin.

'Stay with me, Taema,' I said over and over, careless of who might hear us above. I could feel her inhaling and exhaling against me and tears ran down my face. If she died, I'd be glad that I'd be following her a few minutes later. It wouldn't be fair if this was the end, just as we were about to escape.

I looked up into Mana-ma's face.

She squatted over us, her dark robes billowing.

'And just where do you think you're going?' she asked.

My mind spun, but there was no good excuse I could give – of course there wasn't. I decided to say nothing, and glared at her.

She looked at us, taking in Taema's head lolling against my shoulder. I could tell what she was thinking: she'd already lost us. She knew that during our last Confession, when I fucked with her and freaked her out.

'You might as well let us go,' I said. 'You can say we died in the forest.'

'But what if I let you go and you find a way to survive?'

'I guess that's a risk you take. We're not doing so hot right now, anyway.' I sucked in a breath. 'Do you want us to die?'

'I want you to follow God's plan. If you weren't meant to die, your heart wouldn't be failing.'

'Maybe God wants us to leave your godforsaken Hearth and go to the city.'

She leaned down, close to me. There was no one around.

Her ageless face gazed down at us. Would she raise her arm in benediction, or would the hand hold a knife?

'It didn't have to be like this,' she said. 'It all could have been different.'

'Well, this is how it is. So what are you going to do?' I glared up at her. 'The power's in your hands, I guess. You going to kill us here? Do nothing for a few minutes? That's all it'll take.' Already my vision was wobbling, going dim. My chest hurt, and my fingers were numb. I wanted her to go away and leave me to die in peace.

'You want to go out into the Impure world?' She sneered down at me. 'Very well. I'll let you go. You can never return. Never contact your parents or your friends. You're cut off from here in every possible way. I know that the big, wide world out there will chew you up and spit you out, until you wish you could come crawling back. But you can't. You're apostate. You're dead to the Hearth.'

'You done?' I asked wearily.

She glared at me for a long time before she finally moved away, her robe whispering against the forest floor. She turned her back on us and made her way through the forest to her Hearth. She'd made her point. We couldn't hide things from her, even if we tried. Our choice was final.

I spat in the direction she had taken.

I looked up towards the spaceship. We heard the low whistle of an owl – Dad's signal. Oh God. If Mana-ma knew about our escape, would she hurt my parents for helping us?

I tried to move, but Taema was so heavy, and I was so weak. We weren't far. I could see the ship through the redwood trees. A little door came down, but as much as I tried to move towards it, I was too weak. Our heart beat so loudly it seemed to be the only sound in the world.

I collapsed against the dirt, defeated. So close and yet so far.

I heard a clicking, whirring sound.

With my fading vision, I looked up into the face of one of the droid supervisors, her machine at her side. 'You're the ones we're meant to pick up?'

I managed to nod.

'Shit,' she muttered, and then she hauled us up by the shoulders and dragged us towards the ship, the droid assisting her. I watched our legs trail through the dirt. She kept under the cover of trees, looking around nervously. I didn't have the breath to tell her that she didn't need to bother, that Mana-ma had already found us and let us go, at least for now.

She put us in the ship and closed the hatch behind us. All sound cut off, and we were in a hallway. Everything was made of metal. I'd never seen that before. Looking up, we could see the metal crosshatches, the boots of people walking past and the wheels of droids.

'I'll get the medic,' our saviour said, and took off at a jog. All fell silent and then I heard the low roar of the engine. I hadn't expected it to echo all around us, from all directions at once. And I could tell when it left the ground.

'We're flying!' I whispered to Taema. But she couldn't respond.

I slumped on the floor, my arms around her, tears running down my face. 'Please,' I kept gasping. 'Please.' I actually prayed. Prayed to a God. Not Mana-ma's. My own idea of a God, one who wasn't a total asshole.

A group of people came running down the metal hallway. About five or six, their footsteps and voices echoing all around me. I was barely conscious. For a moment, when the unfamiliar faces peered down at us, I wondered if they were going to toss us out like so much junk. But my first experience with those from the outside world after we'd actually left the Hearth was kindness.

They'd never seen conjoined twins, and they looked at us with a mixture of awe and fear. They touched us gently, as if afraid they'd break us. I was almost all gone by then, but I still remember those soft fingers laying us down in the sick bay. I could see a grey fog with vague shapes and hear distorted sounds, but that's it.

A mask was put over my face and I could breathe better. My vision cleared, but I still felt so very weak. I wrapped my arms around Taema and closed my eyes, pressing my face against her neck.

The last thought I had before I fell unconscious was that I really, really didn't want us to die. Not when we were so close to that big, wide world out there.

TWENTY-EIGHT

TAEMA

Something is wrong.

Or, at least, it's not what Ensi had planned. I see the tall, towering redwoods of the Hearth. The sky is full of rainclouds, and the luminescent green fog of the Bay floats through the air. I smell sea salt and old smoke. It is more vivid than anything I've ever experienced.

It's almost exactly like that shared dream forest my sister and I visited along with everyone else in the Hearth after we took the little pill from Mana-ma's hand.

I'm not bound. Neither is Nazarin. I don't see Ensi. This isn't where we were meant to end up. This definitely isn't where Ensi would send us to torture us. This is too . . . peaceful.

'Were you able to dose him with what Kim gave you?' Nazarin asks.

I nod.

He looks around, and then glances at his hand. He frowns. I blink, and a gun appears in his hand.

'It worked. That tooth was full of nanites that worked their way deep into his implants and biochemistry.'

I take a shuddering breath. 'How did Kim learn to do this?'

'Sudice's labs and a brilliant brain.'

We start walking through the woods, cautiously. We don't see Ensi, but he'll be here, somewhere.

'How'd you meet Kim?' I ask, keeping my voice low. 'Through Juliane?' We both scout our surroundings, but I want to focus on something other than the fact I could die at any moment.

'I met Kim the first time the SFPD hooked me up with her to put in my memory mods. She met Juliane the same day. Juliane and she hit it off right away, started dating. Then they married, and they were one of those married couples that just worked. You saw them both together and you could only hope to have something like that someday. We both helped each other heal when we lost Juliane. I think if we hadn't had the other person to lean on, we might have both been broken by it.'

We reach a break in the trees and a small clearing. The forest has shifted into an alien landscape. The sky is somehow night and day at the same time; shafts of sunlight-moonlight make the now silver bark of the dream redwoods shine, and the needles are turquoise and vermilion. Even the soil is tinged blue and purple. I listen for birds, but all is silent and still.

'I told the SFPD that they should use Kim to help me in my undercover op,' Nazarin continues. 'She's the reason I haven't been caught and killed before now. She wants Ensi taken down just as much as I do. Maybe more. I loved Juliane, but my love can't compare to Kim's. Not even close.'

We've passed through the other side of the clearing, and the forest towers over us once again. I feel so small, so insignificant. It's as if Nazarin and I are the only people in this Technicolor twilight world.

'Kim knew even if we got proof that it'd never be enough.

She's been developing that false tooth for a long time. Used us, in a way, I guess, though I can't blame her. I would have done the same in a heartbeat.'

Like you used me. The unspoken words hover between us, almost a presence. I can't really blame him, either. It was my choice, too.

My nerves are on edge. I keep waiting for the world to turn dark and ugly. For the mandrake demons to grow from the ground and reach for me, for the sky to burn, for Ensi to appear with a scalpel, pin me down and cut me open.

'So we should be able to manipulate this place? Even you, though you're not a trained lucid dreamer?' I concentrate, and make a knife appear in my hand. It seems solid and I feel better holding it. It was far easier than when I was in Mia's dream world, or even Alex Mantel's.

I remember Kim telling me about the nanites after she'd fixed my tooth: *This will hack into Ensi. Once you dose him, he'll have little control over the dreamscapes he creates. When he goes in to take his pleasure and revenge against someone, he goes in deep, leaves nothing back. If he dies in one of his creations, he'll be brain-dead.*

It was supposed to be a long con. Eventually someone would realize they could affect the dreamscape, fight back and get rid of him for us. I doubt she expected him to go in so soon after he'd dosed, bringing us with him.

'What happens if we kill him while we're still in here?' I ask.

'Kim never said.'

'Well, shit.'

'Yeah. Guess we'll find out.'

I feel like something should have happened by now. The cyber forest is eerie, but not as frightening as Mia's demons with the faces of people I grew up with. It's such a strange echo of Mana's Hearth.

I crane my head and peer through the branches up at the violet sky. Where is Ensi hiding? Does he know we're here?

I start to recognize the tree formations. I grab Nazarin and lead him to the left, to the thin track through the forest that my sister and I have taken so many times. But the redwood forest I grew up with is merged with the dream forest of mercury-dipped trees and their vibrant needles.

I stop. There's the hollowed-out tree that Taema and I used to go to when we wanted to get away from everything. Perfectly rendered in the code of this corrupted dream world. Where we went just after we found the tablet. Where we found out the world outside was vaster than we had ever dreamed.

There is a tiny pinprick of light in the middle of the darkness.

'We have to go inside,' I say, my voice small and far away.

Nazarin doesn't question me. He follows me as I move closer, crouching on my hands and knees and crawling inside. Sure enough, it's like *Alice in Wonderland*.

I take Nazarin's hand and we fall down the rabbit hole together.

•

Ah. Here's the nightmare.

The phosphorescent green fog is here, too, but this is a swamp rather than a forest. It is a recreation of the barrier around the Hearth that no one was meant to cross. It smells of bilge water and sulphur, of decomposing plants and bodies.

In front of us is a boat. We step into it, and it begins to move. Things swim in the deep – creatures with white teeth, scales and long, slithering tails.

'It's like we're crossing the river Styx to the underworld,' I mutter.

'As long as there's not a three-headed dog.' Nazarin is alert, watching for any threat. Unconsciously, I move a bit closer to him.

As the ship takes us through the swamp, large opalescent bubbles shimmer ahead of us, resting on the water. We're heading straight for one, and there's no way to steer. Nazarin wraps his arms around me, as if he could protect me if it was dangerous. I wrap my arms around him, just as tight. We slip through the barrier, and it feels greasy against my skin.

We're in a memory.

Zeal and Verve. Dream worlds and heightened memories.

I'm no longer looking at the scene through my own eyes. Ensi is young, perhaps twelve years old. The memory is from his point of view. Like when we played the recording in Kim's lounge, we can sense some of his experiences and emotions.

He's in the Hearth. I recognize the view of the lake from the cabin window. He's playing with a little girl, and it's Mana-ma. They're playing marbles, and Mana-ma's tongue sticks out of the side of her mouth as she flicks one marble towards another. They hit each other with a click. 'See?' she says. 'You have to have a plan, to figure out the next move.'

Ensi takes his turn, scanning the marbles. Flick. Click.

'Good,' she says, smiling at him, and Ensi beams back.

The boat moves through to the other side of the bubble and we're out, but not for long. We enter another memory. Ensi's older now, perhaps late teens or early twenties. He's standing behind the pulpit as Mana-ma lectures, her face rapturous as she turns it towards the stained glass of the church. The Brother stares ahead, thinking about God, and a higher power. If His will is really what Mana-ma proposed.

The sermon ends, and the Brother follows Mana-ma. They go to the Confession room. Mana-ma sets out a chessboard, and they play as they usually do, but the Brother isn't in the mood for strategy.

'I don't see why I should leave you. Isn't my work for God here?'

Mana-ma rearranges her robes about herself. She's only recently taken up the title from her predecessor. She must be about the same age in this memory as my sister and I are now.

'God spoke to me. This is the way to do His will. You have a brilliant mind. You are interested in the sciences, but you've learned all you can here. You are meant to go on this journey into the unholy land, and bring glory to us. I am not sure exactly how, but He has told me you will find your way. You have my full support, and my faith in you.'

Ensi moves his pawn forward. Mana-ma captures it.

I have a feeling Ensi programmed this world, a personal Vervescape separate from where he torments his victims. A place to categorize his memories, but now they're bleeding into each other, his past and his present colliding.

As Ensi's memories merge, Nazarin and I are thrown into slivers of his life. After coming to San Francisco, he looks into a mirror after shaving. He isn't as beautiful then. His nose is bigger, his hair not as full, his chin a little weaker. He is Veli Carrera, the man I saw projected on the wall in Mantel's Vervescape. He doesn't like this world, how loud and strange and Impure it is. He presses the razor against his wrist. He wants to go back to the redwoods, and back to Mana-ma. At the same time, the lure of knowledge calls him, and he knows he can continue God's work here, and make his Mana-ma proud. Reluctantly, he takes the razor away.

I want to know how he went from under her thumb to being the true, unseen hand that rules San Francisco.

With another shuddering lurch, the boat sails through the next memory.

Mana-ma is in Ensi's apartment. I startle to see her not in the Hearth. They move towards each other, resting foreheads close. Ensi looks as he does now, and Mana-ma looks a little older than I remember. It is a more recent memory.

She has brought him more mushrooms from the Hearth. He takes them, handling the bag as though it's precious.

'We'll need more, if we're to do what we desire,' Ensi says.

'We're growing greenhouses full. You'll have as much as you need.'

'And the government does not suspect?'

'No. They take their regular shipments for Zeal. We are but one of many suppliers. They respect our privacy, finally. They have stopped sending in their observers once a year to make sure we are toeing the line. They do not look too closely.'

'Are you ready?' Ensi asks.

Mana-ma looks up at him, and in that moment, I know their relationship has shifted over the years. Mana-ma was once stronger than him, leading him, but now they are equals in their twisted journey, whatever it may be.

He brings her through to the next room. His apartment is humble, despite the masses of wealth he must hold. Simple wooden furniture, woven rugs that look like the ones we made in the Hearth. No technology, except for two Chairs. One is empty and the other one holds Malka.

'This is her?'

'Yes. It took a lot of doing, but we managed to steal her from stasis. She's not been woken. She is Godless, she has no soul, and thus she can be your avatar.'

'My avatar,' she echoes.

'Yes. Whenever you wish to be by my side, I can bring you forth, in this body, projected through Verve. When we are finished, you will return to your body.'

'And this girl?'

'She remains in stasis, her consciousness never woken.'

She hesitates, her hand rising to her collarbone. I can't remember ever seeing her look uncertain.

'I know it pains you to do this,' Ensi says. 'But it means we can be close together, in a way.'

'You know I never wish to be apart. How did you think of this idea?'

'I dreamed it. Perhaps God chose to whisper to me, just this once.' He smiles, and does not notice the way Mana-ma's eyes flash. 'I believe the initial idea stemmed from the twins, Taema and Tila.'

Mana-ma's mouth curls. 'So they survived? They are in this city?'

'Yes. I lost track of them for a time, but with my resources, I was able to find them again.'

'What will you do with them?'

'Nothing, for now. At the right time, we will know what to do. Come now, my love.'

Mana-ma plugs into the Chair. Ensi runs a program, and connects Mana-ma to Malka. I watch through Ensi's eyes as his fingers tap the code, as he watches their responses, the way their eyes twitch beneath their lids.

Mana-ma's eyes still. Malka's eyes open.

'How do you feel?' Ensi asks.

'Reborn,' Malka says, and her face twists into that chill smile I saw just before she killed a girl with a sword.

They rest foreheads together again.

I come out of the memory like I'm coming up for air. Nazarin and I gape at each other, but there's no time to speak before we collide with other memories. I experience more of the fractured life of Ensi. From the shards, I piece together more of the picture. Ensi is almost sixty, which must be Mana-ma's age as well. She looks younger, but it could be genetics rather than a hypocritical visit to a flesh parlour in the city.

Ensi left the Hearth with Mana-ma's blessing, coming to San Francisco with the plan they had stitched together. He was found on the streets and given a VeriChip and a place in a home for youth, choosing the name Veli Carrera. Seeing his obvious interest in science, the home encouraged him to brainload, and he did so well, he soon had a degree. He researched local scientists and decided Mantel would be his mentor, and he found a way to come to his attention.

He thrived, and Mantel helped him flourish. Mantel had no son, but a few years later, one arrived. The CEO of Sudice still treated 'Veli Carrera' as a son, and when Veli earned it, Mantel passed the company to him rather than to his biological son.

Memories of the lab, of using the mushrooms Mana-ma sent from the Hearth to distill and create Zeal. Brainloading more information than it seems he can bear, shuddering at the feeling of electrodes and wires against his skin, so different from the simple ways of the Hearth. He wouldn't have done it, he couldn't have done it, if he hadn't loved Mana-ma so deeply.

Throughout all the memories is the stink of the swamp, the threat of things swimming beneath the surface.

Ensi, as Carrera, was there through the run-out of Zeal, but as new product after new product was shot down by the government, he grew increasingly annoyed. His and Mana-ma's plan was delayed. Zeal kept the crime low, which kept the city happy enough. Ensi did not share his ideas for another drug, one that could change personalities to make citizens more tractable.

Then Ensi lost it all. Mantel's son ousted him. Ensi was cut loose, and he was making new plans when he discovered that Mantel's son's hatred ran deep enough for murder. I saw fragments of him killing the hitman sent to find him, hiding in the streets, the many surgeries in back-end flesh parlours, and then deciding to enter the very group hired to kill him. He started as the lowest pawn, but strategy had been drilled into him since he was young.

I hate experiencing what he did to become head of the Ratel. He killed so many people through his favourite method: torture by dreams. He experimented on Zeal until it split and became the drug he truly wanted: Verve. I have to live through those pockets of horror and pain: the fate I would be experiencing right now, if not for Kim and her code. A fate I might still face. Where is the real Ensi? I feel him in here, somewhere.

We've reached the end of the memories. We have passed through the swamp, and up ahead is the Hearth. He never left it, not truly. It's always in his head, too. I remember Mia tapping her temple. None of us ever truly left, did we?

Nazarin and I reach the end of the muck, climbing out and setting foot on solid ground.

It's a short walk to the town. It's similar to how I remember it, though there are fewer houses, as the Brother left decades before my sister and I did. It even smells the same, like redwoods, earth, the sulphur of the swamp, the chimney smoke from the houses.

'Where is this?' Nazarin asks.

'Home,' I say, not sure if the answer is truth or a lie.

The green mist thins, wisping around our ankles. I catch

Nazarin's hand. It feels like I'm really touching him, even though in reality he's a few feet away from me, strapped to his Chair. But my brain sends an impulse, and so Nazarin's skin seems warm.

The brain is so very capable of lying to itself.

We walk through the pathways, the sky still the same twilight. Most of the flowers in the gardens are closed, their little heads nodded in sleep.

'It's peaceful,' Nazarin says. 'This is very strange.'

'It's his fortress,' I reply. 'The quietest corner of the mind. He created it in the image of the Hearth. Perhaps he knows something's wrong with the code.'

'So he's come here to hide.'

'I think so.'

'Where?'

I think of the memory where he felt safest. 'The chapel.'

We turn a corner of a path, and there it is. It's an innocuous building, made of wood and painted white. My memories of the place blend with Ensi's. We spent so many hours within its interior growing up. So many hours of Confession, of sermons, singing and whispering and praying. I once loved going into that building. Tila was always more suspicious than me of Mana-ma and the whole Hearth's creed. For most of my young life, though, I was a believer.

The illusion around us is cracking. The acrid smell of the swamp returns despite the fact it's no longer in sight, the green fog thicker. Fractal swirls of black mar the clear blue sky of early morning. The atmosphere is no longer peaceful, but expectant. The Hearth is abandoned, but I swear the place is holding its breath.

A light flickers in the chapel. We walk up the steps, lined with smooth, white stones. To either side of the path, the world continues to crumble, the images glimmering at the corner of my vision. The doors loom before us. Nazarin reaches forward and pulls them open.

Inside, it's dark but for a candle flame. As we enter, it brightens.

Ensi stands at the altar where Mana-ma always preaches. He's looking up at the window. It's almost as if he's waiting for someone.

Water has leaked in. I splash through shallow puddles towards him. I have no idea what to do, what to expect. We have no weapons. Once I stopped concentrating on that knife, it ceased to exist again. I try to imagine it, bring it into being. It starts to appear – it's the same as the murder weapon from the autopsy report at Zenith, the one Tila may have used – but as soon as I almost have a solid grasp on it, it disappears again. The same happens to Nazarin and his gun. The pews shake, as if in an earthquake.

'What have you done?' Ensi asks. He looks almost as he does in the real world, except he's pale and shaking. There are more lines on his face, ghosts of the one he would wear if he hadn't waxworked his features. Still, he moves out from the altar to face us, staggering a little, but standing strong.

'I injected you with a virus. When you kissed me.'

'What does it do?' He sounds calculating, rather than afraid. He's used to being a victor. He won't give up so easily. The ground shakes again, rumbling, and dust falls from the rafters.

'It's eating your world. Gobbling it up byte by byte. When it's all gone, you're finished.' I don't know if that's true, but it sounds good. I guess Kim didn't plan it as a long con, after all. Makes sense. Why take the risk that he'd discover it and destroy the code?

His eyes glint. 'Then I can take you with me.'

Ensi moves towards us, smooth and deadly. A long blade appears in his right hand. He jumps over the shallow steps of the altar, water splashing around his feet. The blade is a replica of the one his Queen – I still can't process that Malka is Mana-ma in another body – used to kill Nuala. The chapel creaks with another violent shudder.

He lunges for me first. I dodge the blade by inches and jump onto the nearest pew to escape. Ensi grabs my ankle and I fall flat, knocking my cheekbone against the wooden pew. Pain flares like a flame, and my breath leaves my lungs in a rush. I taste blood. He drags me towards him and I scrabble away desperately. Far away, my body in the Chair will have begun to bleed as well, I'm sure of it.

I kick back and his grasp weakens. I kick again, pain flaring in my ankle as I hit his torso. Ensi grunts in pain. Gasping, I turn towards him. Nazarin and Ensi roll on the ground, snarling. Nazarin manages to free an arm and punches Ensi, his knuckles glancing along the other man's cheekbones.

I try to stand, but the chapel shudders. The world seems to fill with warm, dark green muck, like in Mia's dream. I don't know if it's Kim's code, my fear, or Ensi's.

The mud laps at my ankles, my knees, my hips. It rises over my head. If I breathe in, the muck will coat my lungs. I can't see Ensi or Nazarin, but I feel them, close, struggling against the collapsing dream.

I close my eyes, think of all my Meditation training. I push and push, and let go.

TWENTY-NINE

TAEMA

The green muck disappears, leaving dregs of dried mud. I fall to the ground, landing on my injured ankle. I hiss in pain, drenched and cold, spots wobbling in my vision.

The dream is still broken. The chapel still shakes and flickers, except where I focus my eyes. Nazarin and Ensi still fight, both of their faces bloody and beginning to bruise. My head pounds.

I hold on to a pew for support and move towards them, biting down on my lip to keep from screaming in pain.

I can't move forward another step. It's as if I've met an invisible barrier I can't cross. Ensi hits Nazarin again, and his head jerks back before he falls to the floor. Ensi's eyes flash to me, the corner of his mouth curling in triumph. Like me, he has found a measure of control in this broken world. He knows I can't come any closer. He moves towards me. I struggle, but I'm stuck fast.

'This is my mind. My dream. Your lucid dreaming may be impressive, but you can never hope to be as strong as me. Whatever you've done to the code, I can fix it. This night may have had an unnerving start, but I can still have fun with you and your pet detective. I can still hear my little canary sing so sweetly.'

The chapel isn't wavering as much. It's almost as if it's repairing itself. Was this all a ploy, somehow? A trap within a trap?

It can't be. Ensi is still nervous, licking his lips, his eyes darting from side to side. He furrows his brow, and the blade that he conjured earlier is back. It's his weapon of choice, like Mia with her scalpel and Malka with her sword. The steel gleams.

Ensi comes closer, until he is scant millimetres from me. He brings up the knife and holds it against my throat. He nicks it, and I wince at the pain. Blood trickles down my neck.

I look to Nazarin, but he can't help me. What does it mean to be unconscious in an unreal world?

Think, think, think. I try to remember all I learned while in Mia's Verve world, and when I experienced Ensi's earlier Test.

If I kill him in here, maybe I can defeat him. If I can kill him.

My first experience in Mia's dream, I managed to make the crime scene go away, even if I couldn't do anything else. And although the Test scared me, I passed.

I can lucid dream, too.

I focus on building my own barrier. I put all my terror into it. The barrier grows over Ensi's, pushing the knife back from my throat. Ensi's face twists into a snarl. What will unnerve him most? What will give me the upper hand?

I focus. I have the barest bones of a plan, but it's my best chance. My only chance. The air around Ensi ripples, like I've thrown a rock in a still pond.

'I know who you are,' I say. 'I know your dreams and desires. I know what you've done.'

I imagine Ensi wearing the face he was born with. I imagine Ensi as a young child. I imagine him as the man who has just joined the Ratel, hungry for revenge and power. The three acts of his life: child, Brother, King.

The true Ensi drops the knife. It disappears before it hits the ground. He feels the dream warping, wrenching away from his control.

The air vibrates with energy and green, crackling lightning flashes overhead. A bolt comes down and hits me, and I scream as it sears my skin. Where it struck my shoulder, fractal burns appear, snaking down my arm like tree branches. The energy travels through me.

Three more bolts of lightning hit the floor of the chapel, creating rents in the fabric of the dream. The sulphur smell of the swamp returns, mingling with the ozone scent of lightning and thunder. The holes in the dream widen.

Child. Brother. King.

I bring forth the three versions of Ensi from the dreams. Ensi, a small boy of eight, his arms spindly. Ensi as the Brother, about to leave the Hearth. Ensi as he looks now, just after he killed a man and left the persona of Veli Carrera behind. None of the three do anything. They stand, waiting for my instruction.

The King of the Ratel looks at his past selves in fear. I take the threads of the dream in my mind. I have no idea what I'm doing. I am only instinct, a result of Mana-ma's training.

The knife appears in my hand again, cold and reassuring, but I no longer need it. I send the three simulacra towards Ensi. He backs away, pressing against the chapel wall. He's gone grey, beads of sweat on his forehead. He glances at me, then away, as if he can't stand to meet my eyes. He's not the leader of the Ratel, the man who's tortured many men and women to death, been responsible for many more. He slides down the wall, landing hard. He's a frightened man, a broken man, huddled with his arms around his knees, completely unable to face himself.

The three versions of him open their mouths wide. Red light pours from their throats, and then the same green muck emerges. Ensi closes his eyes, scrabbling for his own threads of lucid dreaming. Some of the muck pushes away, but I redouble my efforts.

The child, the Brother, and the King wrap their arms around the true Ensi. The green liquid covers them all, until it forms a perfect sphere. Another bubble of memory, sealing the King of the Ratel within.

The chapel ceases shaking. The lightning fades.

I go to Nazarin. He's awoken, and watched the whole thing.

'What do we do now?' I ask. 'How do we leave?'

'You do it,' Nazarin says. He sits up slowly, coughing. One eye has swollen shut.

'Yes.' I gather the remnants of the shattered dream around us. I press my forehead against his. 'Wake up.'

•

I open my eyes, and then close them immediately against the brightness. Everything hurts. My entire body feels as though it's been charred. I wheeze, my tired lungs struggling to take in oxygen.

'Nazarin?' I croak.

'Taema.'

I almost cry in relief.

'Is this real?' I'm so afraid that we haven't escaped. That we've been launched into another memory, another subset of Ensi's mind. I open my eyes again, ignoring the pain of the light.

We're in the room Ensi took us to after he captured us on the pier. I'm strapped into the Chair, the bindings pressed tight against my arms, my torso, my forehead.

I hear rustling and just manage to turn my head. Nazarin pulls himself upright, struggling from his bonds. He rips the electrodes from his skin. The mechanical sound of his heartbeat on the monitor flatlines. Mine still beeps, steady despite the lingering fear.

I turn my head in the other direction. Ensi is strapped into his own Chair. His body is still alive, but the monitor showing his brain function barely moves at all.

I did that.

Nazarin limps over and begins to untie me. His face isn't as swollen as it was in the dream world, but it's livid with bruises. Tracks of blood have dried from his nose, his ears and even the corner of his eyes. The whites of those eyes are red with broken capillaries, but his gaze is clear.

'Nazarin,' I whisper.

He leans close to take the strap off my chest. 'I never told you my real name, did I?'

'No.'

'It's Aziz. Aziz Keskin.'

'Aziz,' I echo, tasting the name on my tongue. He smiles at me. I smile back. After all that has happened, we're able to smile at each other. He helps me sit up. I peel the electrodes off and throw them away, then lean against him, my head spinning. My ankle hurts. He wraps his arms around me, holding me close. I can feel his heartbeat. We both smell of sweat and blood and fear.

'Let's get the fuck out of here,' I say.

'I couldn't agree with you more.'

We stand, leaning on each other. We look down at the fallen King of the Ratel.

'Should we kill him?' I ask. I feel nothing at the prospect of it. I already killed him off, bit by bit. Now, it would be more or less getting rid of the shell.

'I want to. I really want to.' He turns from Ensi. 'Let's not cross that line. I think we've avenged enough today.'

We start to hobble towards the door. Our guns are hidden in a cupboard, and Nazarin passes me one. We keep them in our hands, at the ready. My tongue keeps niggling at the molar, now missing its strip and the virus. My mouth tastes of iron.

Nazarin opens the door, darting his head out and back, gun held up by his ear. 'It's clear.'

We leave that awful room behind, staggering against the walls. We don't seem to have any lasting damage, but my brain still feels . . . confused. Senses still don't seem anchored to this plane of reality. My brain is still recording, but I don't turn it off yet, despite the headache. I guess I can handle it better than Kim's subjects. I swear, the white of the walls tastes like lemons. The squeak of our shoes against the floor feels like fear. I can't trust what I see. Only Nazarin feels real. Aziz.

We're so disoriented, so very focused on getting out into the fresh air, away from this place of terror, that we don't think about alarms. As soon as we open the outer door, high, piercing wails sound. It's too much for my raw, mixed senses. I clap my hands over my ears, screaming, adding to the cacophony. Nazarin cries out too, but recovers before me. He takes my arm. The King of the Ratel had not taken us far. We're still on the pier. I can even see the cranes where Ensi and his men were earlier that night, the storage crate we hid behind.

There are the men that had been with Ensi. Standing guard. With them is Malka. The Queen.

Mana-ma, wearing a poor soul's body.

She wasn't there before we went in. Ensi must have sent notice. Was she on her way? Was she going to join us in the dream world, and visit one of the missing members of her flock? Or did she only come when things went wrong? Is her true body lying supine back in the Hearth?

Malka, or Mana-ma, is the first to see us. She raises her head and meets my eyes, and I can read her expression: *You've failed this Test.* She wishes it was me, her, and her sword in a soundproof room.

She yells a warning, and the men run towards us.

'You've got to be kidding me,' is all I can think to say, staring at them. I'm so tired.

Nazarin takes my hand, pulling me with him behind the nearest crate. He shoots over the top of the crate and ducks down. There's a distant cry of pain. Nazarin shoots again. No cry of pain. I can only seem to stare at the gun in my hand. A bullet ricochets against the metal of the crate with a crack that seems to hover in my vision, a riot of yellow, red and orange. It's beautiful.

My sister's voice is in my head: *Get your gun, T. You have to get your gun.*

I'm imagining it, but it's comforting to hear just the same. The gun still lies in my numb fingers. More shots fire. I can barely see. My head is splitting. There is a ringing in my ears, like tinnitus. Another shot. Where is Nazarin? Is he all right?

I clutch the gun to my chest, and the cold metal grounds me. Nazarin is next to me. A bullet has grazed his forehead; his Kalar suit didn't have a hood. Blood pours down the side of his face, but it hasn't stopped him. He shoots and dodges, shoots and moves. Another bullet hits him, and he falls. I can only hope it's the force of the bullet that felled him, not that it's breached the not-always-infallible Kalar.

Shit, shit, shit, shit. I can't tell if I'm thinking it or saying it out loud. Gunshots still pepper the storage crates. I unlock the safety of the gun and put my finger on the trigger. My hand shakes.

I peek over the crate, and then dart back. There's only one person left: Mana-ma. It's fitting. Her against me.

I gather the last of my strength and bravery and stand up from behind the barrier. I try to gather my senses together to make sense of the world again. I fire off shots, my vision still blurry enough that I'm not sure if I'm aiming at her. The shots focus me.

The first few miss, but then a bullet hits her in the arm. She folds forward. She's wearing a Kalar, but I've still hurt her. I aim again, and hear the crack of her gun. I squeeze the trigger and start to move back behind the crate. Everything slows. Mana-ma crumples, the bullet hole over her third eye beginning to weep.

I watch, almost disinterestedly, as the bullet she fired hits me straight in the chest. It does not puncture the suit, but I feel the impact against my metal sternum. My mechanical heartbeat slows.

Then stops.

THIRTY

TILA

I don't remember actually arriving in San Francisco.

Taema and I were out cold, but we woke up in the ambulance hovercar. The attendants pulled back the window screen, and even though I felt the worst I'd ever felt in my life, I remember how beautiful San Francisco looked the very first time I saw it. The sun was just setting, and it was like seeing a whole new planet, alien and strange. Tall buildings full of people, others full of trees, cars flying through the sky, bridges linking the lands across the water. It was so *big*. I knew billions of people lived out here in the world, but it was still something else, this city where over a million people lived, flying and seeing straight out to the horizon, tiny people walking down below. This new world seemed infinite.

At the hospital, they stabilized us and Taema woke up. I started crying when she did. I was so scared that she wouldn't.

The doctor who spoke to us had the same mild confusion about us as the rest of the people out here. We were so lucky, though. He knew our VeriChips were brand new, and he later quietly found someone who would be able to advise us about claiming sanctuary from Mana's Hearth and make our identities real.

He was one of the most attractive men I'd ever seen. I hadn't grown used to how everyone was perfect in the city yet. I kept doing double takes as we went down the corridors of the hospital on our way here. It almost made me wonder if there were no humans in the city, and everyone was a robot. There were differences in height and some in weight (though nobody was too thin or too overweight), but everyone had unnaturally symmetrical features.

The doctor kept staring at where we were conjoined, but I guess he'd have reason to, considering what he was proposing. Everything we saw was new and strange. So shiny. I didn't know how to describe any of it or what any of it was called. I missed my parents and wished they were here with us. Mana-ma must have realized what they'd done. How would she punish them?

'You have to go into surgery immediately,' the doctor said, cutting right to the heart of it (ha, ha). When he spoke, I kept getting distracted by the pretty curve of his lips, the way the blond stubble was just beginning to come in on his cheeks.

'What will you do?' Taema asked, evidently less blinded by his beauty.

A flash of emotion crossed the doctor's face. Discomfort? It was gone before I could tell.

'How much do you know about life in San Francisco?' he asked.

I remember thinking it was a strange sort of thing to start with. I thought he'd talk about the intricacies of whatever he was going to do to us. Though it's not like I knew what doctors did. I'd never met one before.

'Only a little,' I said.

'Well,' he began. 'I have read up on where you've come from. It must feel almost as if you've travelled into the future.'

It sort of did, though I hadn't really thought of it like that. We hadn't seen enough of this new future yet.

We nodded noncommittally.

'There are no cases like yours any more,' he said, and I could tell he was choosing his words with care. 'The fact that you've survived in relatively good health as thoracopagus twins with rudimentary medical care is extraordinary. You therefore have a choice to make. We can operate and fix you, but the team I'm working with wish to separate you. Two separate hearts. Two separate bodies.'

I felt what little blood there was left in my face rush away. Separated? Of course we'd thought about it, but we'd never considered it a real possibility. My feelings were all tangled.

'The way San Francisco is now, you would perhaps find it very . . . challenging to remain together. People would not be cruel, necessarily, but you'd be stared at wherever you went. It would be difficult. Very difficult. I tried to convince them to let you stay together, if you choose, but they wouldn't agree to it. And I can't do it alone, not even with the help of drones. I'll leave you to discuss, but there isn't much time. We need to operate, and soon.'

He nodded at us and left, closing the door behind him.

'We have to do it,' Taema said.

'I don't think we *have* to do anything.'

'The team won't operate if we opt to stay together. They just won't do it. But they won't let us die, either. That doctor made it seem like a choice, but I don't think it's really a choice at all.' She saw through it all.

'Do you want to separate?' I asked her.

'I don't know. Not really. Or I wish we had more time to decide. We don't. I do know I want us both to live.'

She made it sound so simple. 'OK then.'

'Yeah?' She seemed as scared as I was.

We sat in silence, holding hands, until the doctor returned. We told him our decision. He seemed relieved – he could pretend it was our choice instead of taking it away from us.

The doctor explained what they'd do to us – give us new, mechanical hearts, restructure our sternums and part of our ribs and chest (despite everything, I still remember being excited by the thought of finally having proper boobs), straighten my spine because it was a little crooked. We didn't have time to process it much, because they hauled us into surgery right away, put us under, and then I woke up alone.

I remember that part so clearly. I spoke about it with Taema, sometimes. How very wrong it'd seemed, to wake up and not have anyone else in the room. How alien. I couldn't take the silence, so I'd worked myself out of the foreign machines and found my way to her.

We always find our way to each other. The first thing I did when I woke up from the surgery was find my other half.

This time, Taema will find her way back to me.

THIRTY-ONE

TAEMA

When I wake up, I think I'm in the Chair.

I thrash against the covers, crying out. The machines around me beep. I have the fuzzy, floating feeling associated with pain medicine. I realize that I'm not in a Zeal or brainload Chair, but I still can't place it. Hospital? The last time I was in a hospital was ten years ago, when I woke up alone for the first time in my life.

I'm alone again.

Screens surround the bed, all of them showing different parts of me – my steady heartbeat, my blood pressure, my brain activity. An IV stands sentry beside me, pumping nutrition and fluids into my veins. I can't sit up. I'm too weak. What happened?

I was shot.

My hand rises, hovering over my chest. I have bandages. I remember the bloom of pain, shooting straight through me, more painful than being hit by dream lightning.

I'm alive, though. That's something.

With difficulty, I manage to sit up. Moving triggers an alarm and a nurse droid comes in, topping up my medicine before going away.

I curse the droid as my eyes grow heavy again. I sleep.

•

The next time I wake up, I'm not alone.

Nazarin sleeps in the chair next to me, scrunched up awkwardly. His name is Aziz, but it's hard to break the habit. I feel much better this time. More awake, more alive.

There's a bunch of flowers on the nightstand next to my bed. Little white roses. I take one out of the vase and flick the stem at him. The water droplets splash him and he jolts awake.

'Hi,' I say, managing a weak smile.

'Hey,' he answers. His bruises are almost gone.

I try to sit up. Nazarin helps me and then passes me a cup of water, and I sip gratefully.

'Tila?' I ask.

'She's been given a full pardon. It's all still out of the press. You're not being held for any crimes committed while undercover.'

'She'll be free?' My voice quavers.

'Yes. She'll be transferred and released tomorrow. You did it. You freed her.'

I laugh, though it sounds hollow and weak. 'I did it.' My sister is safe. Safe. I fall back against the pillow. It hurts. 'What's my prognosis?'

'The doctor will fill you in on the jargon and everything, but I can tell you what I know. You were shot in the chest. It didn't penetrate the Kalar suit much, but the impact of the bullet against your metal sternum messed with your heart and broke the skin. They had to repair and restart it. You flatlined. You'll have another scar, unless you want to erase it.'

He snuck it in there, among the other stuff. *You flatlined.* I died. My fingertips graze the bandages. 'Can I unwrap it?' I ask.

He shrugs. 'Probably not yet.'

'When can I go home?' I want to go home and sleep. I want it to be tomorrow, when my sister is free.

'Soon, I expect. Let me call for the doctor.'

'Wait. One thing first.'

'What?'

'Tell them to send down the waxworker. Get them to give me back my face.'

•

We're silent as the hovercar takes us to my apartment. Not the safe house. My real, actual apartment, where I haven't been since they asked me to become my sister. My fingers trace my features. My nose is back to its usual shape, my cheekbones a little lower, my cheeks a little fuller. My hair is still short, but it's curly again and no longer blue. Even my old face in the mirror doesn't look familiar any more.

I look out the window at San Francisco. It's foggy today, making everything look soft and dreamy. The algae tinges the grey with green. It reminds me of the world in Ensi's head, and I look away.

Nazarin helps me up to the flat. He seems to have recovered much quicker than I have, though he wasn't shot in the chest, so I suppose that makes sense.

I collapse on my sofa. It feels like I haven't been here in so long. A different person has come home than the one who left. It's going to take a long time for me to make sense of what happened in my head. I wonder if I'll ever be able to fully trust my own mind again.

'Give me some SynthGin, will you? It's in the cupboard to the left of the fridge.'

He dutifully pours two glasses and comes to sit next to me on the sofa.

'Fill me in,' I say.

Nazarin's voice is soothing. I take a long gulp of gin and

close my eyes, listening. Ensi's body is still alive, but he's brain-dead. The government plans to put his body into stasis all the same. The Ratel has crumbled somewhat at the loss of its King and Queen. The government is breaking up the rest.

'They'll find Verve,' I say.

'Yes, though Sudice is arguing that Veli Carrera began his research in their labs, and is trying to patent it. We've one saving grace, though: they're not exactly sure how to recreate it. It seems only Ensi knew the recipe.'

'How?'

'It's what the drop was. Mana-ma grew a mushroom at the Hearth. I expect it's the same ingredient she used to dose you before Meditation. She processed it as much as she could there, and Ensi personally put the final touches on it once it arrived in the city.'

I sigh. 'It's only a matter of time before they figure out how it works.' I'm not sure if I'm talking about Sudice or the government. Does it make a difference? 'Have we really helped anything?' If Verve goes to market, the violent after-urges removed, it remains a way to make people more tractable.

'It won't be that easy for them. Someone might have leaked a medical report detailing the true effects of Verve to the entire city.'

'Kim?'

He only smiles in response.

So things are not fixed. It is not a happily ever after. We can hope the Ratel stays scattered, and there's a glimmer of hope that Verve won't be released to the city from another's hands. A glimmer of hope. That's all.

'I suppose that's enough for now,' I manage. 'What's next for you, then, now that your undercover op is finished?'

'I've asked for a leave of absence.'

I manage a smile. 'A well-deserved break.'

He sighs. 'I don't know if I want to go back.'

I understand. At the moment, I can't imagine going back to engineering. I feel too shattered to be a functioning cog in society.

I drain my glass and look down at the bandages beneath the collar of my shirt.

'I haven't seen the full extent of the damage yet,' I say.

I begin to unbutton my shirt. Nazarin stands up. 'Do you want me to go?'

'No. Stay.'

I slide the dress off of my shoulders. I suck in a breath, looking at the fractal marks from being struck by phantom lightning in the dream world. The red has already faded to white, stark against the brown of my skin. It shouldn't be there, but it is. My mind thought it was hit by lightning, and the body obliged.

'They can erase it,' Nazarin says.

'I don't want them to.' It's beautiful, in its own way. And it'll always remind me that I was strong when I needed to be.

He stands again, moving closer. He raises a finger, hovers it over my skin. I meet his eyes and his fingers rest, lightly, on the fractal marks. He traces the swirling branches of the scars.

'It's like trees. Or blood vessels. I've never seen anything like it.'

I don't reply. His touch makes me feel grounded and alive. It cuts through the dregs of the pain medicine. My whole body tingles.

I start to unwind the bandages across my chest. I'm afraid to see what's underneath. The last of the bandages fall away. Nazarin and I both look down. Between my bare breasts is a new scar, just to the left of the one that bisects me from collarbone to navel. It's healed cleanly. It looks a little like a star.

Nazarin presses the scar gently with his fingertip. 'Will you keep this, too?'

'Yes.'

I look up at him. His eyes are soft.

I want to ask him, but I'm not sure how. 'Is Tila –?'

'No. Only you.'

We stop speaking after that. I've wanted to have him again since our ill-considered night, and now there are no barriers. He pulls me to him, and my body presses against his. I melt into him, and he melts into me. We kiss, my fingertips running along the short buzz of his hair. He wraps his hands around my waist and lifts me off the ground. I wrap my legs around him.

We fall into the sofa, tasting each other. After we came out of Ensi's mind, my senses were confused, and Nazarin was the only thing that made sense. It's the same again. His skin, warm and firm, giving beneath my touch. The feel of his breath on my neck. The flicker of a tongue along the pulse of my throat.

My fingers unbutton his shirt, sliding it off of him. I run my hands along the firm muscles of his back, over the fading bruises. He's kept all his scars. His skin shows a life lived with danger – a shallow slash along the ribs, little nicks along his arms. I kiss each one.

I nip his skin with my teeth, and he pulls me up and crushes my mouth to his, holding my tongue between his teeth, just hard enough to hurt. I run my fingernails along his upper arms and he gasps against my mouth.

We shed the last of our clothes to mingle on the floor. I still feel weak, but Nazarin holds me. He moves into me, and I draw him closer, as if our flesh could blend. The only sounds are the soft gasps of our breathing, the sound of our skin sliding against the fabric of the sofa. We move together. I roll on top of him. I kiss him as we move, faster and faster. We are the closest two people can be without being conjoined.

I shudder against him, my eyes shut tight, focused on that point deep within. I keep my mouth against his as we finish, loving the sound of his moan of release thrumming through me.

I lie on top of him, our limbs entangled, his heartbeat racing against the skin of my chest. My limbs grow lax and tingling with the ebb of desire. All thought has left me, and for the first time since this all began, I feel at peace.

Later, when we are in bed, I breathe in, long and deep, resting my lips against the top of Nazarin's skull. My fingers toy idly with the sheet. There's something about someone asleep next to you, vulnerable and breathing softly, that's so comforting.

It's not long until dawn. In a few hours, I'll see my sister again. I set out to free her, and I did.

I'm terrified. She's the person I know better than anyone else possibly could. All these people I see every day, they couldn't understand my relationship with Tila. How for so many years we were two people, yet we were the same. We can't hide from each other. All our strengths, all our weaknesses. We knew it all.

She kept all this from me. If she hadn't been caught, if Vuk hadn't attacked her, would she ever have told me?

She would never have been able to keep those secrets from me if we were still connected. Perhaps we should have fought the doctors harder. Claimed religious reasons – they wouldn't have been able to argue with that. But we didn't know that then. We were so young. So very innocent, compared to how we are now.

I want to let go of the anger, but I can't. Tila killed someone. She killed him to protect herself, and to protect me. I can't blame her for that. I don't think I ever did.

It's easy to take a life. We're such delicate creatures. Nazarin slumbers on, and my thoughts continue to circle. Thoughts of death, and blood, and wondering what will happen tomorrow, when I see my sister for the first time since they dragged her away from me.

Part of me wonders if I still want to see her.

THIRTY-TWO

TILA

I've been moved back from the prison in the Sierras (or wherever it was) to a holding cell in San Francisco. The guards told me I'm getting out in a few hours. So this will be the end of my testimony, which is good, I guess, because the notebook is almost full anyway. I still can't believe it, though I should know better than to ever underestimate Taema.

I've tried to tidy myself up a bit, but the girl in the mirror still looks like shit. Circles under my eyes, and my hair frizzy thanks to the cheap prison shampoo. Now I'm sitting here on the uncomfortable bed, alternately writing in here and looking out through that tiny window at the blue sky.

I'm scared to see Taema, after all this. Will she blame me? Will she be hurt at all I kept from her, even if it was to try and protect her? I don't know.

I've decided to spend my last moments in jail writing out what really happened. I'm taking this notebook out with me, and nobody else will read what I write in here now except my sister.

T:

I've made mistakes. I thought I'd be protecting you by not involving you, but now . . . I know that you were shot. You're going to be OK, but still. You were shot because of me. I put you in danger because I didn't want you to realize what I'd be willing to do to find out the truth. If I'd told you from the start, if we'd done this together, it would have worked out so differently.

How are we going to move on from this?

This is what happened. Here are your answers, T.

I first stumbled onto the whole Ratel business by accident. Mia met Adam in a Zealot lounge. He recognized her, but she didn't know who he was. They met up a few times. He tried to get her off the drugs, and they bonded enough that he told her who he really was. She ran, moved house, changed as much as she could, terrified that he was sent from Mana-ma to kill her. Remember when she upped and moved halfway across the city and took a few trips to the flesh parlours? That's when it was. Maybe he really was after her, too. I don't know.

She didn't tell me everything at once. I was curious from the start. Someone from the Hearth who had changed their face? Who? When she told me it was Adam, that he was alive and working for the Ratel, then I knew I couldn't walk away. I tried to, but it burned at me.

It didn't take long for me to figure out that Vuk was a hitman for the Ratel, so that to even look into this meant capital-D Danger. I still couldn't leave it alone, though, especially when he walked into Zenith. I watched him for months, whenever he came in, though I didn't get too close. He didn't recognize me because I'd waxworked myself (that's why I did it, T: for your protection, not because I didn't want us to look the same any more). I had blue hair, and you don't expect to see one half of a pair of conjoined twins from your former cult in an exclusive club in San Francisco.

That's what I thought at first, anyway. Until I realized the

Ratel had changed him. Overwritten his personality with what they wanted. Someone who could kill in cold blood, to order.

He fell in love with Leylani while I watched. When I saw that, I thought: if he can still fall in love, maybe they haven't made him disappear completely. Maybe there's still a little bit of Adam in there. I asked Mia, but all she told me in her Zeal-addled state was, 'He is the red one, the fair one, the handsome one. He came from the Earth and now he returns. The faces keep changing.' She said it over and over, until it freaked me out enough that I left her in her Zealot hovel.

It wouldn't surprise me if she did sell me out in the end for more Verve, but I can't prove it. Never will, now that she's gone.

I knew it was risky to speak to Vuk, so I didn't, at first. I kept my ear to the ground, and I heard that the Ratel were looking for lucid dreamers. It seemed too good to be true. No matter how much I tried, though, I didn't know how to get the Ratel's attention.

So I spoke to Vuk.

I didn't tell him I knew who he was. I told him only that I was the best lucid dreamer in the city, and his boss should speak to me at his earliest convenience. He said nothing and left the club early. I thought maybe he'd come back and kill me, and there would go that plan before it had even begun.

Instead, he came back a few nights later, and told me I had to prove it. We plugged into the Zeal Chairs. He'd swapped the drug with Verve without telling me. I followed all his instructions, moving through the dream world, making it do what I wanted. I liked that feeling of power, but I was also terrified of ending up like Mia.

Vuk was the one who got me into the Ratel. I started working for them, and it didn't take me long to become a dreamsifter in the Verve lounge. I met Ensi. One thing led to another. The closer I kept to him, the sooner I could learn secrets. How had the Ratel found Adam? How was Mana-ma linked to it all?

Eventually, I realized the best way to find out would be to speak to Vuk himself. I was going to get out of the Ratel after I did. Never go back. Go with you to China. Yeah, I knew you had that job before you told me. Saw the letter on the wallscreen at your place while you were in the bathroom. I peeked. Sorry. If I went, I thought I'd change my name, change my face again. I thought it'd be enough. I don't think it would have been, really. I can be so damn dim sometimes.

So I went to Zenith that night as usual. I'd met Leylani for coffee the day before and given her something that would make her a bit sick. Nothing to harm the baby or anything (I figured out she was pregnant, with all the running to the bathroom she did), but enough that she wouldn't be able to come in to work. I cozied up to Sal, saying I'd cover for Leylani that night. And I did. Vuk was in with a group of people. He didn't notice me any more than usual. He knew I worked for the Ratel, but otherwise we didn't interact. He was sad, wishing Leylani was there.

Eventually, most of the other partiers left, going to the main bar, and I managed to catch him.

'Adam.'

He flinched. 'Come again?'

'Adam, it's me. Tila. From the Hearth. I know I look a little different, but it's me.'

He shook his head, as though batting away flies. 'Don't know what you're talking about.'

I moved closer. 'You do. Some part of you remembers. Taema and Tila. T-and-T. We came to visit you. We brought green grapes.'

His face twitched. His body shook. It was like he was having a war with himself. I stayed close, keeping my eyes on him.

He fell down on his knees, his hands rising to his temples. His mouth opened in a horrible, silent scream. I went to him and clasped my hands on his wrists.

'Adam,' I said again.

At that, his entire body went rigid and he started convulsing, like he was having some sort of fit. Then he went completely limp. I thought he was dead. I wondered what would happen if someone opened the door in Zenith right then and saw him dead – they'd blame me.

Funny I worried about that then. Considering.

I pressed my fingers to his throat and he was still alive. I sat with him, holding his hand. It was his metallic one, though it felt just like cooling human flesh. I kept looking down at his face, trying to find the skinny boy I'd had a crush on in that blocky body, those different features. It really drove home how completely someone can change.

After a while he started groaning. I waited for him to wake up, and when he did and saw my face, he started crying. 'Tila,' he said. 'I remember you.'

'Hi, Adam,' I said.

He really looked at me and his eyes popped. 'Where's your sister?'

'They separated us.'

I started to say something else, but his body devolved into spasms again. 'Adam?' I asked, scared.

Spittle began flying from his mouth, and I really thought he was going to die.

When he could speak again, he clasped my hand. 'I'm going to lose it, to go back to who I am now. I'll want to kill you. I'll think you're a threat.' He clutched me closer. 'When I go back, I'll have to tell him everything. About you, about your sister. I won't be able to stop it.' Another shudder. 'It's who he made me to be.'

His eyes rolled up in his head. His eyes focused on me. Sharpened. 'You're a threat.'

I scrambled back, knocking over a bunch of the glasses and breaking them. Adam-turned-Vuk stood up and started coming for me. He took out a knife from his inner jacket pocket. I picked up a broken shard of glass but I knew, I knew it wouldn't do a damn thing.

Adam-turned-Vuk's face was twisted with pain. 'I don't want to do this, Tila. I don't want to. I'm tired. I don't want to go back to the man who made me into this.' Every word was a struggle.

It took me a moment to realize what he was saying.

'Do it,' he said. Every muscle was straining. He held out the knife, and I thought he was going to kill me. But instead he dropped it, and it landed on the floor within reach.

'Don't have . . . long,' he gasped. He juddered again, knocking over more of the furniture.

I hesitated. I didn't want to. But then he said, 'If he finds out about you, he'll find out about your sister. He'll –' another shudder – 'hurt her to get to you.'

That decided it.

Of course that decided it.

It wasn't as easy as that. He didn't lie still and let me kill him. His programming took over. His hunter's instincts. I took a swing and he blocked it, so I only cut his wrist. He grabbed me and I twisted back, stomping on his foot and then kicking up between his legs. He wheezed, dropped to his knees. I knew I couldn't hesitate. If I did, I would die.

I had a lucky strike. It went right into the upper part of his stomach, and I thrust up, and I think I hit him in the heart.

He fell down almost immediately. But he wasn't quite dead. He met my eyes and I didn't look away until he was gone.

I remember the blood was warm and sticky. That everything smelled of red, rusty iron. I felt angry, like I'd been trapped. I slammed the knife into the coffee table and it stood there, quivering.

The puddle of blood got bigger.

The blood must have triggered an alarm or something. Sal came in, and it was the first time I ever saw him shocked by anything.

I knew I should say something to him, but I was really out of it. I ended up parroting Mia's words: 'He is the red one, the fair one, the handsome one. He came from the Earth and now he returns. The faces keep changing.'

That definitely freaked him out. He snapped his fingers in front of my face until I could look up at him. It was hard to focus.

'Why?' he asked me. I blinked like I was waking up from a nightmare.

I told him. Not everything, but a little. That Vuk was a hit-man for the Ratel and he'd asked me to kill him to free him. Sal, bless him, believed me right away. Barely even blinked before he was thinking of a way to fix it. Mostly to help himself, but still, he wasn't a totally selfish bastard, either.

'They'll be sending the Ratel here. The only way you won't die tonight is if you get out of here right now. Go home, get your things, and then go. I'm trusting you. Go straight there.'

So I followed his advice. Before I ran away, I felt like I needed to . . . I don't know. Leave my mark. I scratched the sign of the Hearth, sad because I knew I'd never figure out exactly how everything was connected. Then I wrote Mia's name in our alphabet. She was the only person who knew I was undercover. If the Ratel got me before I made it home, then I knew you could ask her, Taema, and at least have a few answers.

I started going home, but then I changed course and went to you. Sal ended up phoning the police after all, though, and they tracked my VeriChip and came and found me.

I wish I'd done it differently. Ripped the VeriChip out of my wrist, made you do the same, and we could have disappeared before they could find us. I don't know where we would have gone, or what we could have done, but it would have been better than all this mess.

You know everything that happened after that. I think you even know more than me now.

They were supposed to put you into protective custody. That's what they told me they were gonna do, just after they took me, when I said you were in trouble, too. That Mia might have sold me out to the Ratel so my cover was blown. But instead, they made you become me, and you got put in just as much danger.

Bunch of fucking bastards.

I'm sorry, T. I made a huge mess out of everything. And, as usual, you found a way to fix it. But that's not fair. It's not fair on you at all.

I am so nervous. I almost want to stay here, so I don't have to face you. I only scratched at the edges of the Ratel. I'm afraid to learn your full story. It's going to be painful to listen to it. But I will.

The guard just came and told me it's time to go. I asked him for five more minutes. Five more minutes of scribbling crazily, the muscles in my hands cramping, as I try to figure out how to end this.

I guess I'll be trite – it's not like what I've written is good. Maybe I'll get you to help me write it into something properly resembling a story, if you're still speaking to me after all of this.

So this isn't an end but a beginning. This morning, I thought I was going to be frozen solid and put in a freezer with other frozen humans. Now, I find out I have my whole life ahead of me again. You are the one that brought down Mana-Ma and broke up the Ratel. Maybe Adam's story can be told, along with all the other men and women whose memories were stolen. I heard Mia was killed, and I'm sure it was another one of Ensi's poor creations. Changing faces like kaleidoscopes.

Maybe we can see our parents for the first time in a decade. Go back to the Hearth, walk through the forest. Listen to the birds. We could swim in the lake for the first time.

I don't think we'll really change anything in the long run. But I've always been pessimistic. You've been the one with all the hope.

So, this is my new chance. My clean slate. All thanks to you. As soon as I finish this, I'll tuck my notebook into my pocket, give my lipstick a touch-up, walk out of this shithole and look you right in the eye.

THIRTY-THREE

TAEMA

I'm too afraid to go into the building where Tila's being held, so I wait outside. It's quiet, this time of day. People mill to and fro, heading to the MUNI or their offices and homes. They don't spare me a second glance. They don't know what I did and what I helped prevent, or at least delay. I hope they never find out.

The SFPD will send someone to the Hearth, to see how they're faring. They received an emergency phone call from our old cult. Mana-ma was found dead the next morning, tangled in her bed sheets, electrodes attached to her head. I've asked if they can send Nazarin, and if I (and maybe Tila) can go with him. We're not banned from the Hearth any more, and I want to see my parents. I *need* to go back. Both of us do.

It's a cool day, even though it's late spring. It's the famous uncertain San Francisco weather. I'm wearing a scarf and a hat, my hands deep in my pockets. Nazarin isn't here. I came alone.

The door opens, and my breath hitches, but it's not her. A man in a suit walks down the steps and past me, not even glancing in my direction. I rub the palms of my hands against my thighs.

I turn away from the door for a moment, taking in the view

of the gunmetal grey of the water, the graceful arches of the bridges. The islands, half-hidden in the mist. Boats are out on the bay, gliding slowly through the white breaks, occasionally calling out softly to each other. It all seems so peaceful. I turn back.

There she is.

Tila stands on the top step. She's already caught sight of me, and her body is stiffly uncertain. Security drones circle her head like bees before drifting away to continue their perimeter check. She hesitates, and then begins to walk down the stairs.

It's so very strange, watching her come to me. She's no longer my reflection, now that I've changed my hair and my features back, but we're more different to each other now than ever before. I have two scars she doesn't have, and that's only the physical ones.

My sister stops a few paces away. We don't speak. She looks a little thinner. She glances down, takes something from her coat pocket. It's a notebook.

'Here. I wrote this, when I was inside. It was sort of a good-bye to you, I guess. When I thought I was going to freeze.'

I take it from her, not touching her fingers. I swallow. My mouth is so dry.

'It's not very good, but it . . . explains a lot of it,' she says. 'I'll tell you the rest.'

'I know some of the rest,' I say quietly.

'Some of it was curiosity, but in the end it was all to protect you. Even if I did a monumentally bad job at it.' She pauses, ducking her head to the side. 'They told me you were shot. Did it hurt?'

I give her a half-smile. 'Like a bitch. But not as much as getting struck by lightning when I was in Ensi's head.'

'What –?'

'Come on,' I say. 'Let's go home. Figure it all out. And then move on from here. Any more secrets I should know about?' I'm only half jesting.

'I don't think so.' With a strangled sob, she throws herself into my arms. I wrap mine about her, resting my head on her shoulder. We're both shaking. I hold her so tight, like I'll never let her go. We have a lot to work out. To get beyond. To heal from. But we will. We have to.

We stand together, forehead to forehead, chest to chest, our scars aligning, and beneath our bones our mechanical hearts beat, beat, beat.